THE ISLAND

About the author

Maria Ian was a human rights counsellor for over fifteen years before moving from copious late-night legal writing to authoring suspense fiction. She holds three graduate degrees and has also worked in publishing as an editor and in education as an instructor, for national security and foreign relations topics, among others. As a child and young adult, Maria lived in six different countries and had exposure to disparate cultures and languages from a young age. She identifies her heritage as Finnish, British, Ukrainian, Italian, Turkish, central South Asian and Chinese, and ardently pursues the accurate on-the-ground reading of history and politics. In her spare time, Maria studies fitness, eastern medicine, African animism and East Asian Taoism.

Her tetralogy, of which *The Garden* and *The Island* are the first two installments, centers on the incommensurability of values in contemporary society, and on the changes created by the western and eastern attempts at resolution. She is also a wildlife conservation enthusiast.

MARIA IAN

THE ISLAND

Vanguard Press

VANGUARD PAPERBACK

© Copyright 2022
Maria Ian

A CIP catalogue record for this title is
available from the British Library.

ISBN 978 1 80016 314 0

Vanguard Press is an imprint of
Pegasus Elliot MacKenzie Publishers Ltd.
www.pegasuspublishers.com

First Published in 2022

Vanguard Press
Sheraton House Castle Park
Cambridge England

Printed & Bound in Great Britain

Dedication

For NB, The Eternal One

Acknowledgements

The author would like to express her most sincere thanks to the herbalists and especially her parapsychologist for their help in bringing the unseen to light.

I
IN BALANCE

Attorney Craig Malcault stabilized himself precariously on the cold polished pavement one early March morning at 6:50 a.m. His right foot was stuck on the lever behind the driver's seat of his teal Dodge Challenger, The Demon, a recent birthday gift from his partner Juan. Craig strained to raise the seat from its forward-slumping position, while, with tan backpack battle-ready and clutched underneath his arm, he hopped back and forth on his other foot. He was caught up seeking a good connection on an old flip-flop cellphone still registered to a former roommate from law school. The fancy iPhone had been stowed away underneath a pile of sweaters in Juan's and his apartment in the brownstone walk up on East 82nd Street in New York City diagonally behind where the car was parked. Craig was certain its high technology would otherwise today immediately be bugged and tracked. Pablo's panicky crackling tone did nothing to alleviate the leaden tenor of the apparently frozen early morning light. Pablo without the Picasso that is, Craig reminded himself with a chuckle.

"Eh, amigo," he concluded, pirouetting to slam the backpack on top of the car's roof so he could push back the seat with his free hand. "What is the purpose of your early call? Remind me I owe you $2,500, or notify me you screwed up the material evidence in this case?"

"Listen, man, among friends, okay," plaintive Pablo continued in seeming endless litany. "I was born gay, raised gay, lived my entire twenty-one years as a gay man. It is not in me to write up a heterosexual couple having sex. It is not in me, period. I couldn't, basta. I had to go to the bathroom, where I then proceeded to throw up."

Relieved at the still stable connection, Craig jumped into the driver's seat while making sure he didn't crease his favorite light-blue and silver pin-striped designer suit. In the event that today the opposite party actually and finally, managed to kill his client, he would not want to face her corpse in any less an attire than what she was worth.

"I have two minutes," Craig proceeded snidely, mentally churning over the expenses in this case which the client couldn't reimburse as due today if she ended up in hospital, or worse, dead. $3,000 for Pablo's last-minute training in one-on-one combat skills. $5,000 in 'bribes' to a friend to place him as replacement valet in the two marble-cast stories high above Fifth Avenue. $2,500 for Pablo's two-week 'salary' as a newly minted spy, which included a generous tip for his willingness to risk bullets. Another $5,000 to borrow surveillance equipment from the New York Police Department NYPD, and the $200 a day to borrow the Annie's Pretzels truck to serve as undercover hideout from a private eye friend. At least the two officers from an NYPD Special Unit had agreed to volunteer their time, or at least they had been persuaded without ado by Craig's succinct 'attorney's eyes only' top-secret affidavit that a threat to the public did indeed exist. The expenses piled up with no one to reimburse besides the client, and certainly not the federal government, intentionally kept in the dark, who otherwise might have been willing to pitch in for a case with such far-reaching players and consequences.

"Amigo, listen." Pablo fidgeting tried to buy time. "He is weird, they are weird, it was all very weird. I mean, she just sat there staring at him, and he was staring at her, you know, like in old movies. Then they were embracing, as if in a trance, and it was very strange, because they are in the living area, where anyone can see. Then suddenly it appears she loses her mind, and… sorry, Craig, I have to puke."

The retching sound confirmed Craig's belief in a disaster a la carte, or as how they would never teach you in law school. "That was before he hung her by her hair from the chandelier, tied in two big knots around the decorative crystal angels, so as she struggled to free herself, all she could see were these angels, streaked with her blood." Gasping for air, Pablo sounded apologetic at having now gotten these details straight. "And everything else I have sent to you and delivered per istruzione. No apologies from my side, amigo."

Overcome by a razor-thin smile, Craig whisked a blond lock off his forehead, measuring his angular visage in the overhead mirror. The powder along his hairline blended imperceptibly with his sharp jawline, gracefully setting his otherwise curly coiffure slanted to suit his more rebellious side. Craig donned a pair of sleek square sunglasses while jump starting the engine.

"Gotta be more attentive, my dear Pablo," he mused into the phone, maneuvering the car back and forth to squeeze it out of the narrow parking spot. "First you were gushing, *gosh, oh my, everything is just such a lucid white, the entire two floors, it is just so brilliante... white floors gleaming superior to mirrors, you could capture a fingerprint, white marble pillars with matching statutes, billowing marble staircases...* even the tiny little stars engraved into the white oriental furniture you described like Picasso par excellence. Now you have collapsed into Guernica as the soldier trampled underneath the horse... Dimme, Pablo," Craig goaded Pablo's knowledge as an art student, pleased at having rapidly disentangled the voiture. "Which one represents our client: the staggering woman staring into the blazing light bulb, or the grieving woman holding the dead child, a bull watching over her? And where is *he* now?" he exclaimed, abruptly departing from his reverie.

"Who, the bull? Or the horned husband?" Pablo held his ground.

"That we are unable to determine as of yet," Craig interjected chagrined. He alluded to the unspoken secret, buried for eternity at the core of the earth, of his client having married and having remained married to two men, which Pablo suspected but was too scared to ever state out loud. Craig slowed himself into a smooth ride. "The parties do not agree on the definition of the terms."

"The horned husband is doing just fine," Pablo emitted rapidly, lest he loose connection, or maybe any interest in the case at what he perceived as unpleasant heterosexual innuendo. "We calmed him down last night, remember. It is in the highly detailed write up that I sent to you. He is back in his icy mold. And it is also on the tape I miked, which you have. We are expecting the son's fiancé for brunch." Pablo regurgitated the facts presently compelling Craig to the Annie's Pretzel undercover truck where the two NYPD special unit overnight forces were about to be exchanged in two minutes at 7 a.m. "Then he is leaving to the territory, to Ara Pacis..."

The connection miraculously holding, Pablo blundered on without the Picasso, suddenly intent on making a case that Craig appeared to have missed, which Craig ascribed to Pablo's immaturity. "I must say, amigo, listen to me: he is quite impressive, actually, more so than the media makes him out to be. Calm and quiet, really, just changing into a ballerina at times, you know, amigo, and he is quite beautiful too, not at all like his fifty-four years…"

Inwardly, Craig could but snarl at the man in the pictures that had been gracing prominent Washington D.C. publications. Patrick Chataway would never deign to as much as say hello to the gay attorney who had advanced almost $20,000 in expenses on his credit card to save a human life. The small, pointed chin, the large steady blue eyes and poised physique down to the sleeked-back blond hair served as a cherubic cover for about any crime, real or imagined, no matter his real marvels and his label as a "progressive."

"Gotta go." He cut off Pablo like an inexperienced subordinate who has failed in the intricacies of detail. Craig hated anyone who worked for him and did not go any extra way to defend his clients. "Great work otherwise." Apart from his annoying faltering in the face of heterosexual activity, Pablo had done a fine job considering his limited skill sets and last-minute training. Placing him had been a salute to his southern Italian physical attractiveness, which made him a superb fit as a fixture in the glossy sparkling empire, rather than to any talent he had been taught to feign.

***

The expanse of Franklin Delano Roosevelt Drive above the gurgling of the East River streaming underneath opened up without mercy. Craig waited patiently in line before the Demon skipped incognito into the cascade of cars approaching early morning rush hour. Along the river, he would scale the length and depth of the Manhattan peninsula, entering the city at the junction with Brooklyn Bridge. At rush hour, Craig likened that point to God's finger pulling vehicles out of a carambolage. From there it was upwards and onwards onto Bowery, cruising onto Park Avenue at Union Square, then on Madison Avenue until the real point was reached, and he could park and walk the short distance to the Annie Pretzel's truck shaded by trees less than a block from the Metropolitan Museum of Art.

The entire clear-cut excursion serviced to ensure that he was not being followed. In just over an hour, Craig would arrive back in from a grand loop only a few blocks from where he had just left on East End and East 82nd Street. He would be a few minutes late to the 8 a.m. tête-à-tête between the son, his fiancée, and the son's parents.

Taut at the wheel, hawk's eye fixed on the rear mirror, Craig was oblivious of the intrepid rush of traffic that bore him along the river's edge. He was scanning the occupants of vehicles behind and passing, mentally placing big green check marks over their visages perceived as square boxes. An expert at multi-tasking, Craig mentally zeroed in on the most relevant passages produced from Pablo's affidavits he had devoured last night and very early this morning.

"I can't bug the master bedroom, no matter how hard I try, and that is because she is in there all of the time, and boy, can the lady see. She has eyes on the back of her head, and eyes surrounding her head as well. And she is fast, slim, and muscular, and many times she was right next to me without that I heard her approach. Her office is just off the bedroom, like in a large closet attached. If she ever leaves it, she comes back any second, since her whole life appears to be in that closet... She bolts the door shut with a high-security lock. I can't say I like her. She isn't one who likes gay men. She is coquettish and boy is she proper."

"Tuesday, February 27th, is when he clearly loses it. It has been coming for about five days prior. Every time he reads the papers or constantly looks up things on the internet, he grows irate, and he calls her, 'Moura, where are you, you bitch? You foul bitch, you obnoxious bitch.' Every variant of bitch and more. It is clear to him that whatever he is reading is her fault, is led back to something that she caused, and she will be punished. I can't see what he reads because he hides it from everybody. The feeling won't escape me. He tries to hide it even from himself."

"I try hard to stay away from him, so I don't make myself suspicious. He is gorgeous. He wears Valentino mostly, and I think he must have the entire recent collection. He even wears Valentino sweatpants! I walked

in on him in his private gym to remind him of a meeting, and he was doing chin-ups and glides off the rings like an angel through thin air. His feet barely touch the ground when he looks at me or through me, as if I am not there, 'Hey, I am right here!' He turns and walks to the shower. A cross between a strength athlete and a ballerina. Why isn't there any sweat on his body?"

"Tuesday February 27th at 8 a.m., he is in his formal office on the second floor right off that huge staircase that cascades down to the living area (or is it to a ballroom?). That is a good place for me to be, because I can pretend, I am watching the top of the staircase. He has another office down at the end of the hallway where he locks himself up with top secret visitors. Now he is in his formal open office, all fitted out sleek in black including his Valentino dressing grown, and he calls for her again, only now she'd better appear immediately. I hear him printing a paper. She sprints down the hallway in a cute little pantsuit, and I can note she has been up since 5 a.m., in her office. When she sees me, she is not pleased, so I have to step back. But I can hear all. She looks exactly like the woman you showed me in the picture inside the amulet, hasn't changed a bit.[1] There is a joy to her, very strange, it is surreal and uplifting. I would feel she is hurrying to hug me, would I not know that she is not pleased."

"'Sit down,' he hollers, while she retorts that she prefers to stand. 'What is this? Take this paper from me and explain it to me.' He sounds like a snake, and she does not reply. He must be showing her the paper he printed. 'Why was this in my mailbox just now, Sender the secretary of the ape?'

'A printout from the stock exchange, Patrick, perfectly legitimate!'

'Is he insinuating I can't find it myself, that it might be something like your cunt?' No response.

'Hold up this piece of paper I just had to give you, you bitch, since you couldn't take it from me as you are lame in the morning without the darkness and explain to me the graph that is on it. Explain in each and every minute detail.' His tone is toxic. Acid corroding metal. Again, no response.

---

[1] The laughing skull lady in *The Garden*.

16

'Is that flat line what the trading people want to see from my company?' Now he sounds like he is pontificating at a cocktail party. 'You are looking at a long flat line, like your cunt. It just goes on and on forever. God damn it, Moura, people want to see life!" That last line, I think he meant to use it as a gun and shoot her through the head, but she is still alive. '"Action, movement, graphs with lines going up and down, and up and down. Like birds flying. Like something that EXISTS."

'You are not explaining anything to me, Moura. You stand there, and your mouth is opening more and more and more, like a fish on dry land. What is hiding underneath that long pathetic and oh so endless line? A dying person on life support? How many are there now?' I can feel from how he is controlling his being derisive, he can't wait to jump off a cliff.

'How many? Still no response? Then let me suggest an answer: Put your hand on the phone and call the ape and ask him how many there are. Or better, you should put your cunt into contact with him, and you'll see how he will start to form tones. He will start to sing aria after aria, and there will be NO END.'

At this point I have to see what is going on, and I inch closer. She stands with her back to me while he is facing her. The edge of the desk is between them, with a computer right there. He looks chalk white. He is measuring every detail on her face, and there is no motion about him, like a doctor dissecting a patient.

'It is an embarrassment, Moura. We are locked, intertwined, you and me. And I am not making the first move! That is terrible, Moura. Let's get the basics straight. Going back to the basics, that is how it should be, only now, it won't be to your cunt. You have been up since 5 a.m., not only today, but all of the last several days, conferring with George, trying to decide what to do (all of the while of course you have been staring at this flat long line, at your metaphorical cunt). The ape sends in a paper, thinking we are going to tell him what to do...'

'That is a very good thing!' she dares to interrupt, sounding like a bird this time, somewhat breathless.

'No, it is not, not for you right now! In the abstract, of course, it is a good thing, but not for you! You like the darkness. You like going back and forth and counting, counting, counting, how many are there, how many only, and oh, when, when finally... What is the matter, my dear

17

Moura? You don't like the darkness any longer? You want to finally see the light instead?'

Things happen very fast now, and I am going to be as precise as I can, as you instructed. I couldn't measure the speed, and I don't know how anyone could do any such thing as fast, but before I know it, he has grabbed her head and slammed the side of her head into the computer. I think he just missed the sharp edge, because while she falls to the floor and there is blood on the computer, it only lasts for a few seconds, while he walks around and towards her raising his foot to crush her head, her body suddenly lurches towards the door, and she slithers out and up, there is a dark flash right past me. She has locked herself into the adjacent bathroom. I can't describe better. It was too fast.

Inside, she cocks a gun. That sound I clearly recognize. The bathroom is towards the inside of the second floor away from the staircase and I retreat, so they don't see me while I can hear.

He drags his feet past me towards the bathroom as if he is somnambulant or can't believe his own existence.

She starts to cry. 'Don't come any closer, or I will kill you, and maybe that is how it should be. It is all your fault.'

'It is not, it couldn't be.' He is complacent now. I peer around the corner, and he stands leaning with a shoulder against the wall, looking at the bathroom as if he is greeting her coming out. 'I am open, I am willing to talk. Even my office is more open than your cunt, pardon my language, sweetheart.' He whistles. 'I am right here, all of the time, whereas you are not. What is the problem, Moura?'

'You know when it started happening, Patrick, don't you?' She has stopped crying, and now she is emotional, flabbergasted at this continued ignorance of his. 'When you went to redacted individuals, and I was only sixteen and you were almost twenty-six and we had just met, and you thought you could just get their support and have them underwrite your future, just with a snap of your fingers. You dished up these marvels about this new company you had been founding and all these riches you found in a territory that didn't even have a government, and it was all yours to take, and you provided all your details to redacted individuals. It was YOU, Patrick, who was a fish on dry land!' A *pregnant pause ensues, until finally he starts to emit a low humming hmmmmmmmmmm...*

'*I don't have to repeat redacted individuals' response, do I?*' *She's got a hold of herself now and sounds factual.* '*One bright day you found yourself in court, with allegations you had been cooking your books, and of course everyone knew that wasn't true and you were being dragged in on made-up charges, everyone besides the judge and redacted individuals. It wasn't yet clear to you that your grand and lofty plans didn't fit the political agenda of redacted individuals. Since YOU, Patrick, hadn't done your research! You didn't have the wits to hire an attorney, which meant we were kicked out of the UK, you and me. Then you came to this country and started visa applications and investments, only here they didn't like you all that much either. You came across as a snob. What they did like is the money of which redacted individuals have enough, so they have been tolerating your presence here, and so on and so forth. It is still going on at the present time. I have one question, Patrick: How come redacted individuals thought you had imperialist plans, if it wasn't you who looked to them like the complete buffoon?*' *He is raising and lowering his shoulders, clearly at a loss of what to say. Neither does he seem to care.*

'*Yeah, yeah, yeah, that I am projecting is such an old theory of yours...*'

'*Patrick,*' *she reminds him snidely,* '*you have been letting it out on me ever since those very days starting right after we first met!*' *She starts to sob.*

'*The women in your family have had too much compassion. Your father was celebrating Hitler's victory on the front lines when the British took him as POW, for God's sake! What a blessing! He was too mad for them to kill him. Had he stayed on the front lines, he would likely have died there. He had been walking the Welsh countryside for over ten years when your mother finally took him in. Took in a lunatic! The last good memory I have of you is you cutting up your passport at your mother's kitchen table with an old rusted German army knife. Then you had to apply for a new one, since we couldn't immigrate to the United States without a passport. And what did the UK passport office tell you? Why do you need a passport? Do you need one to go to prison? And just ongoing nonsense after that, from any authority. Who are you, why are you here, what are you doing, what the hell? And I stuck with you through all of it. I stuck it out with you.' She is uncontrollable in her grief. 'Women in your family have had too much compassion...'*

'Your historical recounting bears no relation whatsoever to the present time. And about your sticking habit, that isn't how you make it out to be.'

I had some time to collect a sample of blood and body fluids from the computer."

Approaching the hellish intersection of highway, bridges and avenues at City Hall, Craig noticed from the coagulating light that early morning was now over and full daylight was about to break. He careened through the simmering combustion, surprised at his own dexterity, with eyes glued onto every sliding inch of metal he passed. If anyone had been following, this was their time to fall back and break out anew from one of the side streets onto Bowery.

'Thursday, March 1st, towards 12 noon, I hear him shout: 'It is bright noon, babe, the time for truth and justice!' The problem with all the beatings, and there were several between Tuesday, March 27th, and Thursday, March 1st, is they happen so fast, I can't prevent them. He beat her after every new information he claims to find on the internet. He has trained himself like that inside his head, and whatever comes out of his head, he lets out on her.

'Maybe you were right, Moura, and you SHOULD be seeing the light. Look, he emailed more pieces of paper, the ape!' She screamed.

He hung her by her hair from the chandelier where the high vault above the living area (or is it a ballroom?) slopes down, close to the large window panel that shows onto Central Park. The vault further up is clustered with lights too numerous to count. She hangs from her long black hair that he has tied around two crystal angels into knots, and now he stands at the light switch at the far left, stating she will see the blast of a thousand volt.

'Poor Moura, my loving babe, first she was stuck in the depths of darkness, with no way to break free. Now the truth of HER brilliant ideas emblazons her brighter than a thousand stars!'

I conclude he is past the point of sanity, and I have to take him out. He notices as much, from the way he turns to look at me, completely normal and expectant in his own domain.

'Don't feel bad, my friend,' he quips. 'I have long known I can't trust anyone who is inside my house!'

'Sir, step away from that light switch.'

'Isn't that view of Central Park just gorgeous, doll?' He speaks to me because he is trying to figure things out. It is clear he wants her dead and he has no clue how to go about it.

One of the bodyguards arrives, and on his heels the son balancing a ladder.²

'Mr Chataway, you have to sit down and drink a glass of water.'

'I prefer to stand,' he retorts with a smirk. 'Bah.' He mocks the whole world. The son looks weird, like an Indian. I think I see feathers in his hair, however, that is because his hair is very long and moves as he does, and his attire of jeans, a colorful ethnic patchwork shirt, leather loafers and silver cuffs at his wrists. I don't look at him too closely, since I know he has a black belt in karate and I wouldn't want him to feel me scrutinize him.

The son is up on the ladder in a whirlwind of a split second.

'Dad,' he calls from above, cutting through him with razor black eyes. 'You will have to stop this. Or it will be too late.'

"Oh. OR,' Patrick responds, diffident.

'I have to talk to you,' the son responds. The son holds her in his arms now, carrying her down. I can see tufts of hair on the floor and she is bleeding from a gash wound at the back of her head.

'Mommy will need a wig for the NY Times *interview in two hours,' the father informs the son, smoothing his sleeves. 'What a dirty job. Stitch the hole in her head, George, and I will meet you in five. Right here, and right now. I have an entire hour to spend with you before MY call with the DOD (Department of Defense).'*

'She is unwell now, because the bright light of the day shone through her and caused her distress.' His smug grin tells me he is convinced he

---

² The young man who showed himself to Craig at the river and was with her in the vehicle at the entrance to El Lirico in *The Garden*.

is 200% embodiment of truth. Nothing can ever bring him down. 'It has all gone to that brilliant, brilliant genius head. Next time I will have to put a boot in her cunt, since I like to walk.'

'I CAN walk, Patrick,' she speaks loudly and threatening, however, with a slur. She massages her neck and spits blood into her sleeve. She regains her composure very quickly. It is very weird. She takes the son by the hand and leads him up the staircase. I can see from the way she walks she is mounting through darkness. I guess they have a first aid kit somewhere close.

The son shouts from above he needs to make a short call and will be there in a second. I surmise she knows how to stitch the hole in her head by herself, too.

The son has moved one of the thick padded white leather fauteuils around so he can face the glass panel that shows onto Central Park. I can see his leg dangle over an arm rest. I prefer to not see his face. He looks so much like her; I could confound the two. I could see from how he moved that fauteuil he is used to moving heavy things.

The father lingers on the arm rest of the sofa some distance away to the son's right. He adopts a tone of camaraderie.

'What's up, George? Let's talk! We haven't spoken, you and I, for what is, how many hours now?'

'Since this morning, Dad. I have something important to tell you. My fiancée is coming over for breakfast tomorrow at 8 a.m. I want you to behave.'

'I can't do right to all of the people all of the time, George, and you know that.'

'All I said is I want to introduce you to my fiancée.'

'All right, let's talk about your fiancées then.' The father hops up and down on the arm rest in what he attempts to make look like anticipation. Words gush out of him like a waterfall. 'Where are we now, at number four? Let's go through them you and I, one by one. It is only four, George, not counting all the whores, so don't get angry at me. Please!'

'The first one had bells sewed into the hem of a colorful embroidered skirt. It might have been El Salvadoran; however, I don't remember from the chaos of her giggling and you being incomprehensible. I know you

22

meant well, George, however, the insult and allusion were very obvious. But I am a kind and tolerant man, so I forgave you. The second one had a Ph.D. in biochemistry. You had me sit there and read her resume. As Project Director of Research and Development, Miss I-don't-remember-her-name has been overseeing a portfolio of technical initiatives to optimize pharmaceutical products for developing market use...'

'I thought she could help the company!' The son is hurt and misunderstood.

'Until I found out she had worked with the FDA on about every single product competitive to our products for which I had to do extensive research since all you knew was her nickname... But I am a well-intentioned man, and I forgive ignorance. I have been very ignorant in life myself!'

'The third was an idiot. What kind of a person shows up at 8 a.m. in a low-cut dress with a bottle of champagne, confused as to why you wanted to introduce me to her? It lasted until I cut off your company credit card and deducted her fake boobs from your paycheck.' He is jovial and doesn't appear angry at all. He even appears to expect a response. He hollers: 'And who is this one now? What is her name?'

'Jacqueline. She is a model. She was on the cover of Vogue.*'*

'Why are you bringing over this Jacqueline tomorrow?'

'Because we are getting married in three months, and I want you to socialize with her parents after we are back from the territory. Her father is a dentist. She is from Brighton Beach, Brooklyn.'

The father gets a hawkish look on his face and seems weary. Then he forces himself to state, 'I am not getting involved in any modeling business.'

'I asked her to marry me, and she said yes.' The son stares at him askance as if he had expected something entirely different.

'Did you tell her what you do for a living?'

'I said I work in security for my father's company. I am not going to lie!'

'Did you tell her about the territory? About the ongoing operations? About Ara Pacis, or about what the ape named the Altar of Peace?'

'She is my wife, and we have spousal immunity.'

'Has she ever been interrogated by the DOD?' The question rings a bell.

'Look Dad, she knows what she has to know.'

'Such as?'

'Such as that if the media reports that Ara Pacis suddenly has a government, I might be having a problem.'

'I told you, Patrick, that email was very well-meaning!' The mother's infuriated voice rolls in summersaults down the staircase.

I can see from how she stands there, her long hair pulled to a side (thankfully I can't see the other side), massaging her neck to make sure she can still turn her head, her eyes lost in agony, a blood-stained towel wrapped around her shoulders, that she is the focus of the conversation, and they just can't talk about it openly."

Cruising onto Park Avenue through the tunnel that arched through the former PanAm Building, now the MetLife building, Craig felt like he always did at this location: Like royalty. He had once vowed to, once through, never look back at the colossal hexagon. Instead, while taking exhilarated aim at the middle of the broad lane, he fixated his gaze towards the bouncing tops of rolling vehicles. Behind and around him the air was clear, the white morning light of the sun dripping in rivulets steaming ahead mixing with a powdery blue sky.

'The NY Times interview is a disaster, as far as I can tell. I am not an expert in journalism or foreign relations. One expert arrived at 3:30 p.m. sharp with crew to set up, a famous one, I think I saw his name somewhere as a war correspondent. A worker is still fixing the chandelier, and I motion them towards the back, to the right of the bottom of the staircase. They have a problem with that, because the ornate staircase as background makes it look like an entertainment venue. Two crew members push aside the fauteuil in which the son had sat earlier, and they set up in front of the glass panel, with the treetops of Central Park as background.

He arrives five minutes late in a Valentino suit of dark purple sheen, looking so disinterested, not to say bored, it is painful for me to see. I note from how they ignore that, they absolutely need to have the interview done. He slides into a gilded chair and feigns the mien of a befuddled yet focused professor...

'I hope you are not looking at putting pictures of apes in the rainforest in this article, if you decide to publish it.'

'Mr Chataway, what makes your presence in the territory so fascinating is you operate in each of the satellite states.'

'Satellite states is a misnomer, a label of journalistic snobbery. The territory is composed of seven smaller territories which you refer to as satellite states, so there are seven satellite states if you will, two of which are islands, and they make up what you refer to as the territory, which in reality is a landmass harboring a tiny capital located on a cliff at 17,000 feet above sea level referred to as Ara Pacis, or Altar of Piece as named by its indigenous inhabitants. If you had brought a map, I could show you.'

'...you operate in each of the seven satellite states...'

'No, I don't operate on the two islands. There are some minerals in the reefs surrounding the islands, one of which is in territorial waters, and the second one also according to the United Nations Convention on the Law of the Sea is in the economic zone of Ara Pacis. That law took effect in 1982, just about the time when I first arrived in the region as a very young man.'

'The satellite states are not strictly speaking states,' he proceeds into faces first astounded, then increasingly angered. 'First, they are miniscule. Second, they don't have governments. Third, the reason you refer to them as satellites, which we will also get into later, is because you don't understand the entire setup of Ara Pacis. You are looking for something tangible where nothing tangible exists. The purpose of these satellites is strategic. Because they are land masses that can be passed through and walked on and in places even built on, distinguishing them from the surrounding landscapes that are entirely useless in this regard while they do have very considerable natural resources. There is a border around the outer land inward circumference of this entire scenery where adjacent countries begin.'

'I operate in the entirety of the territory governed by Ara Pacis. As you have come to realize by now, the entire scenery, including the seven satellites belong to Ara Pacis, in the sense that the entire scenery is self-governing. Ara Pacis does not have a government, because its autonomy consists in the unity of all its component parts that we have just identified.

Neither are what you refer to as the satellite states autonomous or semi-autonomous in the common sense of the terms. Do you now understand: 1. Ara Pacis is not a seat of government; 2. The satellite states are neither states nor autonomous entities; and 3. Their existence is defined by their role in the totality of the whole?'

Pained silence.

'Mr Chataway, could you please help us through this interview?'

'I am more than willing to be of any help I can, however, we have to get the facts straight and down firmly. The likes of you folks are not always very adept at that.'

'Speaking of the facts, a confidential high level DOD source this morning referred to the government of Ara Pacis. The source said to us in a telephone interview quote, "The government of Ara Pacis will have to show itself more malleable and allow for the investigation of the increasing number of dead bodies found in the satellite states," unquote. What is your comment to that? Your economic interests are directly implicated, Mr Chataway, since you operate in the entire territory, as you state.'

'What a confusion of terms!' he exclaims. 'There are military leases on each of the satellite states, as DOD has solid grounds to know, and you might refer to those as autonomous leases, operating in unity as orders of Ara Pacis, which taken all together is an order of self-government and of security as elucidated previously, certainly not a government in your sense of the term.'

'Your response to the DOD requesting investigation is that the areas for which the investigation is requested are governed by military leases?'

'You are just repeating what I said!'

'What will happen if DOD sends personnel into these... military leases?'

'Obviously, folks, there is a high likelihood there is a declaration of war, an ongoing war, since how long?'

'You are going to assist in the killing of American military personnel?'

'What a presumptuous and pathetic insinuation. First, I asked you since when there has been a war or combat operations, if you will, between Ara Pacis and the US DOD, to which you are not responding.

Second, I never said I declared war, not on anyone, I am the CEO of a private company. Ah, there is my son!' His stony mien becomes animated as he takes a paper from the son. The son is now at work and wearing a suit, like his father.

'Another missive shot to my inbox. This time, the line is curving up a little. Just a little, but it is curving, and from some people one can only expect as much.' He sounds like a minister preaching from the Bible to sinners.

'It just began to curve,' the son interjects, indicating he overheard the discussion on getting the facts straightened out and referring to basic public information.

'As of when, George? What does this say? As of this morning? I could have spared myself the noon scene with the chandelier... Sorry, folks,' he says, addressing the crew nervously shifting in their seats. 'We like to act our factual details out in here sometimes...'

'Let's wrap it up then!' He raises himself energetically, with enthusiasm. 'The allusion that I would be killing American military personnel, which you could print as me declaring war on America, is evil minded, and I won't have any more of it. My bodyguards will show you the way out, so you don't get lost. I have a large place with many, many details.'

'Tell the fucking DOD I am cancelling my meeting with them this afternoon.' He nudges the son under his breath as they walk past me and up the staircase to their respective offices. 'Reschedule for one week from now, when I am in the territory. We don't do fucking Easter in this mess...'

***

Finding a parking spot at rush hour on the Upper East side was the least of Craig's worries. As per his accelerated royalty-inspired dash up Park Avenue, he had actually missed the left turn in the upper 70s. Afloat in traffic, he fished for the flip- phone's messenger with one forefinger. '30 mis. Lte,' to the instantaneous reply, 'thumbs up, all good.' Once again ascertaining that no one had been following, Craig applied himself to careening out of the onward pushing flow no later than 96th Street.

Cognizant of his own personal obligations, he turned around in his mind complex calculations. If the lady client showed up this afternoon alive to reimburse the expenses, he might be able to settle her son's case, and his pending cases next week would still bring in enough revenue to permit the trip to the territory as planned on Monday and sign the down payment for Juan's Italianate townhouse in May.

Instead of creeping bumper to bumper through the maze of side streets off Fifth Avenue in search of the perfect spot, Craig decided to squeeze the vehicle between a tree and a bus stop underneath a sign "NYPD Security Camera." With long steps, he bounced down Fifth the remainder of the distance past the Solomon Guggenheim Museum on the opposite left. Craig worried bullets would ricochet off the cobblestones and leave him riddled on top of his own shadow.

'What kind of day is this?' The judge had not been willing to give him the explosives-sniffing dogs.

'Your honor, I have had many dozens of domestic violence cases, and I have been on the ground in Iraq...'

The man on the upper two floors of the hard humongous building diagonally past the Metropolitan Museum of Art had enough explosives to obliterate the Upper East Side of Manhattan. However, the judge stated, "That doesn't show in your affidavit, Counselor Malcault. It might be your thinking since this case is important to you and you are under stress."

Once Craig hit the broad pavement in front of the Metropolitan Museum of Art, he scanned the vivacious tourist crowd ahead amidst the opulent shadows of the trees. He observed a Mexican-themed five-person music band pressed into the stony elevation that separated the cobblestones from the greenery of the park. The players underneath large sombreros paid no attention to Craig rushing by as he greeted them with a brisk "Saludos, señores." However, his compañeros had moved the Annie's Pretzel van from the agreed-upon location back to the end of the block away from the band now resting instead at the front end of the stone monolith on the opposite side of Fifth Avenue. The slight motion of one band member along the stone elevation accompanying him, lurking to the middle of the block then apologetically turning and moving back, was more indicative of a secret operation than a morning serenade.

***

Knock, knock. Craig's knuckles rapped against the back door of the van as the scraping sound of weapons and gear resonated inside. Now cast in the sparse glow of the surveillance equipment on loan from NYPD, the otherwise dark inside of the van served as operating space for Craig's gay intern Tom Masciotti, a former NYPD officer and currently a 3L student at Fordham Law School. Faced with the prospect of post-graduation homophobia and unemployment, he would rather sit out all-nighters for Craig than deliver pizzas later in his native Brooklyn. Craig had loved this blurb as the heading of his resume. He crept past the silent shadowed officers and tight focused figure clad in a silvery NY Mets jacket and matching hat angled over one ear, giving him the thumbs-up sign over a tense shoulder.

Craig twisted his body onto the lowered plastic padded cushion against the oxidized metal side of the van. He almost fronted the hooded dozing owner of the van slumped behind the wheel, this morning's *NY Times* plopped into his lap. Without any writing comparable to informed erudition in sight on the page titled 'The Americas', Craig rapidly zeroed in on a short column: "Without Functioning Government or Jurisdiction, Ara Pacis Wards Off Rampant Crime, Money Laundering, and Assassinations." The blurb quoted Patrick Chataway, CEO of Resource Global, as praising unspecified armed forces for keeping his operations safe, alerting the reader that he was not available for further comment while alluding cryptically to fortified autonomous regions. The conclusion had it that unstated confidential sources rumored Mr Chataway to be a potential candidate to the U.S. presidency.

The paper landed with another plop on the empty front seat. A little voice equally cryptically quipped inside Craig's head: "George, call the fucking press and tell them I never told anyone that I would ever register for any political party." Which was the truth, as Moura confided at client-intake just last week: The one time they had been prompted with voter registration, she had been extremely busy with accounting and paying bills.

29

A wink from underneath the lowered hood in the driver's seat summoned Craig in a whisper." "We have company. You just missed The Girl from Ipanema."

"The one who keeps on walking by?" Craig retorted, fazed by the insulting paucity of the blurb he had just perused.

The private eye chuckled. "The one who they *wish* had simply walked by. Seriously, they stopped playing a couple of minutes before you arrived. Now look at that one there."

Craig's reflexive turn of the head at the attentive nod to the street corner where the front corner of the colossal monolith stood impaled confirmed the worst. Liquid daylight streamed through the hulking shadow onto a figure targeting the van with a face darkened by a sombrero while the pose hit home with even greater alacrity.[3] For a split second, flexing chest muscles retracted into the threat of direct attack, unmitigated and face on, like a vulture or, as Craig sarcastically tried to convince himself last-second, a very angry but dignified tiger. Straight and still, the apparition dripped contempt from the distance. Craig's gaze ascended to lucent daylight with reverence as if he were in church grateful for being alive, fixated and chilled to the bone, while the figure took Fifth Avenue in stride and returned to his comrades.

'He isn't all that tall,' he ruminated, hoping for a whiff of the Kyrie Eleison from last Sunday's Catholic mass. 'But he has... something... strength.' The Kyrie Eleison not ascending despite his ready heart, Craig waved away the private eye's palm motioning in front of his face.

"Are you okay? Asleep?"

"I need to think." He arduously slumped on the hard plastic seat. The Kyries that puffed by his mind's eye failed to belie even the rightful seeking of pardon for which they had been intended. Conjured in their stead appeared what to Craig looked like the corpses of Native American Indians poisoned in deep winter by artefacts left behind after the original settlers had clubbed any other survivors to death.

"Judgment Day," he stated calmly, sounding grotesque amidst the surveillance equipment. "A terrorist is walking on Fifth Avenue in New York City."

---

[3] The native from *The Garden.*

"That was not in your affidavit." The hooded driver comfied himself for another round of sleep while the armed special unit forces in the dark laughed in *Schadenfreude*.

"Setting up your own homegrown CIA has its challenges, Craig!" His good friends at NYPD weren't in the mood to take anyone on — or out — today.

"Get up." Craig, miffed, punched the driver in the shoulder.

"They are leaving," Tom seconded him. "It is 8:50. Mr Chataway has meetings at nine."

Startled, Craig and the driver huddled to press their noses against the side window of the empty front seat. Thankfully, the front parking spots were now all taken, so the band could not detect the impromptu commotion.

"You didn't miss anything," Tom proceeded. "He was good this morning. He likes her, he likes her a lot. They talked about her modeling career, he wanted to know how she became a model, and she wanted to know why George's mother never modeled."

"What did the mother say to that?" Craig queried.

"Because she had George. She couldn't be away modeling. What if something happened to him, who would be there to help? Patrick laughed at that, can you believe it, him laughing at something about George? George being the Damocles Sword hanging over his head? That's what I meant when I said, he must really like her, the future daughter in law!"

"*Wow, phew,* look there, now that *is* a model! Here they come. She doesn't look dumb to me at all." Whistles and kisses erupted in the leaden interior faintly warmed by the all-night surveillance equipment.

"She is twenty-nine, three years older than him," the private eye commented. "Why, you were expecting a dimwit?"

"Not in particular," Craig retorted, politely. "I am just noting this quality of some models, features that look so fine, like real classy porcelain, pellucid like parchment paper, there one moment and gone the next, I guess it is only the top models who have that quality... And hair like fluid platinum. I wonder who they were looking at to insult The Girl From Ipanema?"

31

"The old man upstairs. We should be about ready to leave now, Craig. I am cold, hungry and haven't slept in days. Pablo will stay on for the rest."

"Without the Picasso, I am sure," Craig mused, chagrined, hopping out of the back door stretching aching limbs. He still hurt at the material evidence gone missing.

***

Strolling back to The Demon, Craig poked at Tom's cute boyish looks, tight black jeans and silvery NY Mets outfit, seeking to lessen oppressive thoughts. "Is it your black on white day today?

"I'd have to turn myself inside out for that. Right now, I'm happy with my night goggles." Then the mandatory statement. "Hold it straight, Craig. We are being followed."

"Did you see that through your night goggles?"

"In the rear mirrors of these fancy mopeds parked here we just passed. I think we are followed by a gay dude."

"Sad," Craig confessed. "Would *you* follow *me*?"

"No. He looked lonely and terribly uptight. Also, weirdly young, like he's got a tight mask on his face."

"I'll drive." Craig looked down, unlocking the car. "We'll drive around a bit. I'll buy you coffee and a bagel, and we'll see."

***

Progressing through the maze of zigzags of side streets, avenues and side streets and avenues again, Craig lamentably concluded they were indeed being followed.

"My sixth sense sees differently from your Made in Brooklyn night goggles. That is the military, right there. Could be from a number of southern countries, including the one I am going to next week. Damn good drivers. He just rolls without a sigh. And he is gay too," he added after a pause.

Dirty water from recent rain splashed from the deli's awning onto the windshield as Craig brought the vehicle to an impatient stop.

"Disgusting," he exclaimed, indicating a soot-smeared descent into a basement, reeking garbage, and a nondescript substance that oozed into the gutter of the pavement mixing with the stench of dirty cleaning liquid. "The Upper East Side of Manhattan, I guess, begins one inch above my head." He referred to his slight five feet two inches stature and hurried into the deli. Afterward, he exited to hand Tom a paper bag containing a bagel and coffee through the open driver's window. As expected, the black compact Mercedes had dutifully parked in visible sight. Craig felt the dark interior behind the tinted windows seethe.

"Look, I brought you a mutant fly, too," he exclaimed loudly, hoping his voice could reach the Mercedes' occupant. Picked from amidst the rivulets streaking the windshield, the drowned insect on Craig's forefinger indeed sported one excessively long hind leg, to which three other ones were glued. The two additional legs were missing, replaced by a wing with a monstrously thick vein.

"We could bring it to a lab and have it analyzed for traces of chemicals, including entire families of carcinogenics, acid rain, and the host of stinking cleansers, household as well as industrial, that created such fantastic growth. My purpose on this planet has been redesigned to inhaling viral loads from breathing clean air."

Craig noted with some relief that his angry deviation from high-level spying to environmentalism had gone unnoticed to Tom, who was absorbed in scrolling through text messages on his iPhone.

"They've gotten into contact, look!"

The message had been forwarded from the Get In Touch With Us Here form on Craig's website that otherwise functioned as a ready outlet for litanies of complaints from irate, cornered and back-stabbed potential clients.

"Amigo, como estas! Soy Arturo, JC's friend, we met at La Parque Central a couple of years ago." Craig knew of no such friend of JC.[4] The allusion to JC who had been shot dead last week defending his favorite boy Burrito, now a young man, struck him as supreme bad taste. "Es un placer! I am in D.C. now, visiting an old dear friend and was wondering, would you like to come to the opening of our art exhibit tomorrow at 6

---

[4] Dr Juan Carlos Delfin from *The Garden*.

p.m.? For good old times sake, el abogado, who knows when — and if — we will ever see each other again." Underneath was a Google Map address of an event space around Dupont Circle and Embassy Row.

"Respond, Yes, hasta pronto. I am at the office, jammed with clients until then."

Craig furrowed his brow at the instant GIF reply blossoming a firework of red roses while out of the corner of his eye he caught the Mercedes backing out against the one-way street and up and gone on 3rd Avenue.

***

Half an hour later, after dropping Tom off at the Metro for a Friday-included weekend, Craig rejoiced at the pastel sparkling of the overhead neon lights in the puddles left by another brief downpour. In the middle of Times Square stood the apple of his eye: his own private law firm squeezed into the south corner of the 30th floor glass encased skyscraper. No matter the hour, the area bustled with throngs of shoppers and tourists flocking around countless well-lit commercial outlets of every hue and color.

II
FROM A DISTANCE

The high, narrow, heavy glass door jolted open, and Craig sailed left past the receptionist desk to the elevator opposite the other main one north on the far right. Dubbed by him The Island to match his solar flare drive, will, dreams and ambitions, Craig was the only tenant on the 30th floor who ever used this elevator. All other attorneys and their clients and guests crowded the main one leading to the gargantuan international trade law firm sprawling the 29th and 30th floors. Enveloped by white casing which some clients had likened to a space capsule, the gleaming white doors of The Island glided open next to the bright pink orchid that Craig regularly replaced.

Craig entered the Island in his habitual laissez-fair state of mind. The lone diaphanous button to the 30th floor flickered under his soft touch, and in several motionless and breathless seconds Craig had whizzed to his all-white office. The small room made up what it lacked in ground space and windows with an inventive architectural layout and height. Five resplendent white steps with clear-cut edges led down to a narrow winding area, then up again, while a gleaming gold balustrade opened up to embrace the room as if in flight. Craig's desk, also in white, rested on the elevation at the top of the second set of stairs. Clients sat in a white backless balloon accent chair on another elevation to the right where the room narrowed and sloped backwards like a snake's tail. The area ended abruptly in the only window, rectangular and tall and resembling a needle. Clients were separated from Craig's desk by the narrow winding area proceeding from the set of steps at the front door. The arrangement had been likened to a dividing reproducing cell by an envious Washington D.C. columnist. "If in doubt, try the balloon chair... The scenery reminds of a splash of sperm." When the office was dark, the diamond-like knobs of bookcases ensconced inside the walls sparkled like stars. The bookcases, otherwise invisible and installed unevenly at all heights, could be reached by means of a ladder, as found in many university libraries.

In the face of this clarity and sense of purpose, the client's slim crouched figure etched onto the balloon accent in acerbic arrowhead shape.

"You fell asleep," she murmured, at the moment unable to associate herself with the harshness of her image.

"Perdóname, señora." Startled, Craig struggled back into office mode. The obtuse twilight broke immediately. Her rabid-focused gaze met his as if she were aiming from the depths of a tank. The edges of her long, elegant eyes trembled like a hellhound in heat.

He swiveled around facing her, reclined in his leather-padded office chair, fingers crossed over his belly.

"Can we call about George?" she asked impromptu. Long black hair glistened damp over her shoulder. "I was working out and hurried. I didn't want to be late."

Craig scrutinized the small delicate face capable of such joyous effusion, intrigued that she had hardly changed over the ten years since he had first encountered her profile inside an amulet. He felt fervent excitement at the prospect that he could finally be of help, ardent desire to exemplify that the truth was a broad well-trodden road, or rather highway. Yet for now there was only a leaden depth.

He moved the office phone to place it on his desk between him and her and put it on speakerphone, speed-dialing his best contact at USCIS (United States Citizenship and Immigration Services) Headquarters in Washington D.C.

"Counselor Malcault here. May I speak to Officer Watts?"

"This is Henry Watts."

"Hello Officer Watts, this is attorney Malcault, Craig Malcault. I am calling on behalf of my client, George Chataway. We just wanted to make sure there is no stop on his record, so that there are no bars on his entries. The charges were dropped."

"Of course, counselor Malcault, let me connect you to the Pentagon."

'What?' A question mark bigger than the lights of Times Square spread on Craig's visage.

"I am afraid there must be some mistake, General Applebee. I was just speaking to Officer Watts over at USCIS about a client and was transferred to you."

"Craig, it is good to hear from you, even though I am dumbfounded as to the meaning of your query."

Craig continued unfazed, guns blazing. "General Applebee, your racist military police officers arrested my client George Chataway early last week for solicitation of prostitution while walking at night on Constitution Avenue alongside the Lincoln Memorial in Washington D.C. even though the woman he was with was his fiancée and there was no prostitution involved. The charges were dropped once the mistake was realized. I was just calling my contact at USCIS to confirm that our racist system did not put a stop on his immigration record, and now I have been transferred to you?"

"Craig Malcault, now isn't that really you! Aren't all of your clients involved in prostitution in one form or another!"

"No, that's not me. You are referring to the clients of the white supremacist attorneys who are suffocating this floor and the one below... General Applebee, you and I were on the ground in Iraq together, therefore I won't call the media to report your inappropriate and unprofessional commentary."

Craig now thought to fathom a screw-up in the mind of his colleague. Watts may have associated George with another case and willy-nilly Craig had now caught the General in the act. *I must be on to something hot,* Craig thought to himself, having happened upon the General somewhat on the defensive.

"You are irate, Craig. How can I help?"

"Allow me to refresh your memory. First, when George was single or more or less so, and he was going around with all these good-for-nothings, and I agree they are good-for-nothings, your colleagues at the equally good-for-nothing DOD invited him to each and every of your waste-of-time meetings, encouraged him to come out of himself and all that bullshit, and he had to go to meetings all over the Hill and federal government agencies. And now when he got engaged and he is doing some other things besides going to all of your good-for-nothing meetings, your racist officers who have been blind and deaf for all this time suddenly happen onto the scene and arrest him for prostitution, which this time around has not occurred!" Out of breath, Craig was grateful for the opportunity to unleash his pent-up resentment and what he considered his unfulfilled sense of rightful revenge at the DOD. '*Self-defense is Catholic*,' he told himself, his conscience bitten by the term 'revenge,' but who but their attorney would defend some of his clients?

"Are you angry at *me*, Craig?"

"I wouldn't know what you had done, for me to be angry at you *personally*?" Craig hung on desperately, hoping in vain that their old friendship, albeit strained by their incompatible definitions of sexuality, could motivate the General to some integrity.

"I am the United States official in charge of operations in the territory of Ara Pacis." Applebee resorted to speaking loudly, clearly, slowly and with emphasis.

"Sure, and that is well taken." His eyes growing big as saucers, Craig was now smooth as a snake. Clearly the General had thought Craig was calling him to sue the DOD about a matter related to Ara Pacis! "I agree, sir, that we should speak about this at a later time, once everyone has calmed down. Pardon the intrusion. Now if you will excuse me, I have clients breaking down my door."

"Hello Officer Watts, this is attorney Malcault again. Thank you so much for your kind referral. The General indeed has confirmed the case. While I have you on the phone, would you kindly check at your end and confirm with me that there is no stop on George's record?"

"I can confirm there is no prostitution charge on George's record, neither in his file nor anywhere else where you would be concerned."

***

"These human rights attorneys can be such a noisy pestering lot."
Applebee addressed George Chataway who stared past him and over the
phone on his desk. Despite bright noon, the room was dark with a single
light burning between them.

"Besides, we don't torture people here. We just don't do that. You
didn't tell him about torture, did you?"

"I have to go now." George's shifting shape, amplified by the shadow, reminded Applebee of a giant insect. "I can go to the airport by myself."

"What do you mean?" The General squinted, feigning it to look like annoyance at the light which he now turned brighter.

"You don't have to bring me to the airport," George clarified.

"Pray, George, by which authority are you leaving?" The General noted the swiftness with which Gerge had deflected the "You have no authority by which to hold me" he had meant to state. This insight caused Applebee's squinting to grow so violent, he had to avert his face.

"Mr. Applebee, I won't sit here waiting for the boogeyman to lower the hood over my face!"

The General preferred the look of the polished wall to the sinewy figure he now likened to an apparition grasping the file off his desk. Caught in a sick game by the force of circumstances, each had to play his part which neither of them enjoyed or found useful.

"For Dad." George grinned, acting as if at this point anything valuable remained in the file.

"Don't you try to bring that thing back in through U.S. Immigration, it will get you arrested!" came the sudden rapid-fire response.

"Ha-ha." George's grin broadened into laughter. A blast of cold air gushed in from the outside as he opened the door, chilling them both to the bone. George closed the door rapidly behind him to cut off the limpid day light.

***

Having regained his composure, Craig reclined anew, welcoming the warmth of the sweater she stripped herself off and flung onto his stomach. Her gesture revealed a gym top and toned arms and midriff to die for. Disheveled, she rubbed her temples and forehead while Craig tried to discern if her reddened eyes were due to pain or exasperation.

"We have something in common, you and I," she finally pitched in, breaking the silence that had been appropriate to the patent catching in the act they had witnessed. "We both love hypocrites, and we are both people of integrity."

With concern, Craig watched her wince when suddenly sensuously and with untoward speed she piled her hair on top of her head and took aim at her surroundings with gaze alert and replete with rejection and censure.

"I couldn't agree more," Craig interjected, pursuing the route of commonality to guide her out of the mess. "Right now, you have a hole in your head, strangulation marks around your neck, and you had internal bleeding."

"Whereas you have an unpaid bill!" She emitted one roaring laugh, apparently pulled between two realities.

To keep her from tragically disintegrating into a flare of passion and hate, Craig hurried down and upstairs to take the check she snapped out of her tiny black purse. He decided to alight on the low parapet to the right of her seat where the wall sloped backwards to the narrow needle like tall window glowing with white light cathedral like. From the look she immediately shot down to him, Craig caught a glimpse of her interior of gaiety and freshness, yet with that intense, focused and hellish glare scalding him.

"I am a soldier," she responded.

"And I am a frigid old friar," Craig smirked, "who is afraid he has come to you to preach. Did you know that before you arrived?"

She underwent a veritable transformation, yet her horrible focus did not lapse. He knew he had hit a nerve as she turned to face him. With a fleeting smile she caressed his words, evanescent, disappearing and reappearing.

"I am ready," she quipped.

"Moura, which side are you on?" Craig queried evidencing befuddlement. "There are two sides. One is the company, the other is the army."

"Counselor, I already explained that to you." She shook her head hard, unfazed by the old truths she was about to state. "I built the company. It is Patrick who just wouldn't listen. I went with him to the territory when I was only sixteen and dropped out of high school to help. He was constantly screaming for help even when he would not speak to me, which was most of the time. I had three miscarriages because he wouldn't stop beating me, and every time something would go wrong

40

with the company, which was very often, he would beat me because that was the expression of how he felt. I was there when he began to disappear into the jungle for days on end and come back confused and hateful, blaming the entire world for his troubles. Something happened to him, Counselor, and I am not sure it was only Redacted Parties. Something broke inside him. You know he had been studying to become a minister, but then he started the company on top of that, and at some point, he decided deep in the jungle that the company was superior to the Kingdom of God. Or *was* the Kingdom of God? That part in his mind I have never been able to figure out. I was not able to enter into his mind to clarify that horrible confusion even though I was entirely devoted to his cause, and that is my fault, Counselor, my one big failure. Anyways, the company and pregnancy wouldn't mix in his mind."

"And that statement of his that he is in the wilderness working for the common good being ambushed by 'Indians' with bows and arrows while the entirety of the UK is comfy on their couches eating potato chips and watching television?" Craig reverted to the facts to dislodge her from her focus on her failures — failures she had committed in great innocence. "That being lawful as he is, he is hitting these 'Indians' with applications for permits, knowing perfectly well there was no government in the territory that could issue any permits, and none were therefore required? Neither were there any 'Indians'? Do these statements already back in the late 1980s speak to you of emotional and mental vileness and instability? Not to speak of his observation that when you finally ran away and collapsed bleeding on a dirt road, he interpreted that as your 'ardent desire for stray street dogs' which lasted until Stefan plucked you from the filth and 'you could finally do as the stray street dogs do?' 'Why wait Moura for any split second that would bring the glimmer of a better idea? Just fuck any dog! Ayyyyy, the lady was oh so panicky that after three tragic losses she could never get pregnant again...' These are his very words! Is that how a good person talks, Moura?" Craig asked in earnest.

"But maybe it was true," she coaxed. Her pupils suddenly widening, she then declared instead, "He couldn't get the company going, that's why I continued to help him."

"So now you are neither with the company, nor with the military. You are with the stray street dogs." Craig sounded disappointed.

"He can't replace me in the company. You know those tiny things on the ground that he is so proud of hitting the media with because that is something they will never have or know about, those tiny, tiny things, ever so secret, that can change yet so much? Those are mine. They belong to me. I was there on the ground while he was inside the company."

"The candor of your statement does nothing to modify the reprehensibility of the situation," Craig proceeded. "And the reality, let's face it, is you can't stay somewhere where one day for certain you will be killed, okay. Where *for certain* you will be killed." Craig smiled at her mischievously, head on and point blank as she had with her inside-the-tank glare.

He could either give free reign to his photographic memory and continue regurgitating each detail he had learned, since, intrigued by the crude leftist language on his website, she had reached out for help with her son's 'arrest' by the racist military police in Washington, D.C. The request had raised a myriad of urgent challenges provoked by the long trail of United States visas held by George, a British citizen, over ten years, culminating in a Green Card sponsored first by Patrick Chataway as United States citizen father, which the sponsor then suddenly withdrew, and subsequently by means of a trail of employment visas sponsored by Resource Global, Inc., which final issuance at just about the time of his 'arrest' had been significantly delayed by George's refusal to provide his birth certificate, which the agency USCIS had perceived as obnoxious and offensive. The document had inexplicably disappeared from his record in the first proceeding, and George asserted he had never provided such a document in the first proceeding in any event. USCIS finally agreed to accept a baptism record and the statement of a significant number of witnesses, all of which were the mother's relatives.

Or Craig could hone in on the essentials. He was in the predicament of risking to place the lady into a drawn-out divorce case, which Craig considered common habit among abogados ricos lechering to get money out of spiteful wealthy clients of whom he knew scores. But goading over her being drawn as a prawn into a monstrous constellation of American foreign policy constituted moral offense *par excellence* and in addition was blatantly un-Christian. Craig opted to hone in on the essentials.

"This isn't the time for you to act Lady McBeth, Moura." He approached her from the different angle of appealing to her appreciation for the tiny, ever-so-secret things. "What will happen to George if you die? Have you ever been in an investigation for a murder? I have many good friends at NYPD, and they have all the access to my work that they could possibly need," he added, hoping that the light blue eyes he fixated her with were sufficiently bright and charming. "To my knowledge, and I have worked on many cases involving domestic issues, murders, extortions, you name it, George's role is an accomplice's. I wouldn't want my worst enemy in such custody, with General Applebee rushing in waving a thick marked-up file exclaiming, 'I told you! See, how many times have I told you?' George will come out of jail old and fat, using his long hair as toilet paper," Craig concluded with a mean chuckle.

"Don't you get it, counselor? I have failed!" She furtively surveyed her surroundings in search for an escape, for something to lean on. Craig surmised quickly that she had placed herself in the habit to never find any such trusted locus, especially not when she needed one.

"The company isn't what I fought for all those years. I wanted to create a safe place for George, a place he could grow up in, and in this I have completely failed, as I also failed in detecting that radical turnabout in Patrick's inclination. I have failed in my life's purpose..."

"I am convinced George will be very proud of you, should you cease to burden him with the obligation of picking his mother's bleeding limbs off furniture and off the floors and ceilings," Craig interrupted her harshly. He would have none of her emotional effluence, no matter how rationally concocted. Craig wanted her decision whether she was with the company or with the military, a decision she craftily knew to evade. "What does the military manual advise in this grand failure of yours?"

"Shoot me," she stated simply.

"Ah, so it is the military manual now that is entirely at fault." Craig played his Ace of Spades, blue eyes flashing. "Why don't we discard it quick and fast that accursed cherished manual of yours, strip you of your uniform and your badges and leave you out on the beach naked, on one of those two islands where good old Patrick doesn't operate, for the alligators to come, who will come quickly, hard and fast and *en masse*."

"You know I have no pity," he added quizzically. "I hoped at least you would still prefer the stray street dogs to the alligators. But you seem intent on pitting the street dogs against the alligators, and it will all end in one of the biggest bloodiest messes of recent history, worse than Iraq, with the street dogs crying and the gorged alligators pulling at more and more street dog limbs. You are a heartless woman, Moura, cruel, barbaric and crude... And the only winners are American generals, from their helicopters snapping pictures of the bloodbath to sell to the *NY Times* and pad their already over-padded retirement wallets..."

Adamantly Craig motioned an impending return to his desk when his gaze alighted on her trembling head grasped between her hands. Tears blocked by the shock of insight squirted onto a visage drained of all life.

"For God's sake, counselor... For God's sake..."

With a thin smile, Craig acquiesced in his just elaborated irony that Moura, who considered herself a savior to her son and to the little, little things on the ground in the end, would eagerly serve to pursue her own self-destruction and in the process exterminate all. Overcome by her crying, which he considered disingenuous, he pressed her head against his chest and placed a kiss on her hair. That open and candid admission of love and care made her finally relent in the pursuit of more hit-and-run antics. She reached anew into her purse and pressed a flash drive into his palm.

"You know I want something very important to come along with this from you," Craig commanded sternly. He would put up with no more pretenses from her today. She raised her face abruptly to scrutinize him. Her tortured eyes widened like crevices in which rain drops swell.

"Next week, I will be in the territory as well, where I have many good old friends. I want you to promise that no matter what else, if in doubt, you will call me." Maybe because of his status as a gay man who had to battle life's harsh uphill battles by himself, dragging Juan along as yet another rock chained to his ankles, Craig trusted none of the coterie she so indulged to luxuriate herself with. He just sincerely hoped that he was wrong.

"Promise?"

She nodded, appearing untrustworthy and deceitful in the colorful smile that rippled over her visage. Craig preferred to not elaborate on the searing combustion of fire and ash setting her aglow.

"Else it will be alligators plus the stray street dogs, Moura!" In an attempt to crack a joke, he donned the wagging finger friar look, which about placed him in the mood for the remainder of the work he still had to do tonight — reviewing the flash drive before he would proceed to indulge luxuriating himself with his own coterie at the opening of the art exhibit at Dupont Circle in Washington D.C. tomorrow night.

"It's not just the alligators plus the stray street dogs," she injected, hesitating and guilty. "I will gladly call you if need be. However, it may never come to that."

III
INFERNO

Dissipating rays of sun light flittered on drying puddles as Craig on the way home capered down East 82nd Street towards East End Avenue. Falling behind, as yet another testimony to his idiosyncrasies, the Dodge lay deserted in an unkind twist between a delivery truck and a Porsche on 3rd Avenue. No matter the convenience and cordiality towards the vehicle, the underground terrain of the garage just opposite the brownstone building with its many twists and turns and winding dark passages remained incompatible with any notion of going, returning or being at work. Plus, Craig didn't mind the public display of The Demon's Hellcat emblem on the hood. The blood-red eyes, hunters' ears pressed against the head and canines exposed in pointed menace bore an uncanny resemblance to his own mien when angry, at least per his partner Juan.

***

Together with Juan, Craig had inhabited the third-floor walkup for four years since they had managed to extricate themselves out of the dingy East Village dive. They had landed into that place of misery following Craig's impromptu eviction from District of Columbia fame and fortune eight years ago upon his return from the political fiasco in the territory. The nightmare of his last week there had remained crisp in his memory, befitting the warning to never try to cajole with the rich at their expense.

"What, you came *back*?" law firm partner and former superior Bubba had hollered upon sighting Craig packing a couple of remaining boxes in what was now his former office. Apparently in the process of being relegated to the floor's janitorial room, filthy rags, greasy cleaning supplies and an array of unclassifiable, essentially unneeded items had now been destined to occupy the space formerly reserved for Craig and his clients.

"*Ouch!*" Craig stumbled over a broom handle, hit by the insight that Bubba's astonishment was at him having returned from Ara Pacis *alive.* "I'll just be back tomorrow for a few more things," he mumbled.

"We'll see ya," Bubba sneered, scowling at Craig as if at a disobedient child.

The next day, Craig was ambushed in the lobby of the building by a small group of liberal female journalists upon exiting loaded with his last box. The truth confronted Craig that General Applebee's landing on the laguna had been a genuine attempt to provide assistance. Without DOD assistance, he would now have lain sprawled on the floor of the janitorial area with a hole in his head.

"Mr Malcault, have you met many prostitutes on your last trip?" one of the eager journalists bantered.

"Male or female? How would you even know the difference?" Craig hissed, for lack of a readier insult to hurl at them.

"What, Mr Malcault?" the choir gasped for air, "we women aren't even good enough to be prostitutes in your eyes? But how very disturbing and revealing, Mr Malcault!" The grossly flat and gutted pronunciation of the term "women," posed with faked salon propriety, revolted Craig's insides to the extent of making him want to puke for several years thereafter.

"Looks like I have been set up by Bubba's whore, the mistress he has hired to replace me," Craig hissed. He hurried out of the lobby to aim bullet-like at the nearest metro in fear the bitter and frustrated products of a sexual harassment culture would mob him if he stopped to hail a cab. "You can find her as the new face on the law firm's partner-cum-pimp webpage," he shouted over his shoulder. Craig vowed to never go back to check that lady's made-up illustrious profile, probably copied and resized from a former State Department Secretary's, or even as much as Google her name. Until they had managed to pack their belongings and move to New York City, Craig, for his own safety, made sure to wear the oversized pink pussyhat then in vogue at all times when showing himself in public, even if only for as much as moving the car from the street into the driveway.

Their miserable lot to survive on Craig's client referrals and Juan's interior design freelancing abated once due time had passed. New clients had been successfully pushed, and in many cases, dragged through landmine contaminated late night hours, courts and administrative bodies. The Pimps & Co. eventually sunk alike to a leaden rock into the bottomless, still and pitch-black waters of what Craig had concluded, despite the hidden treasure accolades bestowed on him, really constituted an unremarkable and exploited past. He swore he wouldn't even recognize The Pimps & Co., were he to pass them on the street in NYC.

By now, Juan's freelance gigs rumbled in heavy flow, yet Craig could not disengage him from the habit, written into stone, to not leave the apartment unless for highly formal ceremonial outings as a couple to prominent landmarks such as Central Park, the ice-skating rink at Rockefeller Center and Brighton Beach in Brooklyn.

"Not after what happened to you in Washington D.C.," Juan had declared once, solemn and with finality. "I, or we, are not going anywhere unless we look ready to defend ourselves, against anyone and anything!"

"But that was many years ago! And New York City is not closeted D.C. prostitution, pardon my language." Juan would have none of Craig's mild-mannered protests, instead remaining drilled into his role as rock and fortress of the home.

"You and your crazy clients! It can happen to anyone, anywhere."

After some quasi-bantering, quasi-venomous back and forth, they reached the compromise that once Craig's private firm had passed the $1,000,000/year benchmark, as it had to in order to remain afloat on top of the island in Times Square, they would invest into a townhouse on East 79th Street towards Fifth. Juan planned to refurbish the small mansion in the idyllic Tuscan and Baroque Style that had been establishing itself as one of his trademarks. The ravishingly unique phantasm would then both attract many more interior design clients as well as provide a welcome three floors of space where Juan could stretch his legs and grow old without having to experiment with the outside world.

"You'll see," Juan had instructed in his curt indigenous style. "We'll go out one New Year's Eve, and neighbors will be dumbfounded. *Who are these people? We have never seen them before!*"

Marveling to himself how far they had gotten in life, Craig had to admit that as recently as several years ago, in that neighborhood, the question would have evidenced a mundane matter, of course.

***

"Hola, bebe," Craig exclaimed. He tore open the bolted thick metal security front door to the greeting of frenetic typing on Juan's desktop computer from behind a tasteful arrangement of three man-high bonsai trees. An array of tall imitation Giacometti statues along the left wall obscured the division of the living room between a settled front area punctuated by three quaint tasseled beanbag seats Craig had acquired on sale at the closing of a modern art exhibit in Berlin, Germany, and Juan's back work desk sanctum.

"Did you see many lunatics today?" Cognizant of the late hour, Juan forced himself to compassionate tone while persisting at banging away on the computer.

"Pablo threw up," Craig retorted. Despite himself, he erupted into chuckles of laughter, which imparted discomfort to his empty stomach and lent the appeal of the braying of an aggravated horse.

"There is Peruvian halibut ceviche for you in the fridge," Juan continued unfazed, relishing in his native cuisine. "And chicha morada. It took me over half an hour to make, which is why I am now late with finishing work. *Povero Pablo.*"

"He couldn't write up a heterosexual couple having sex!" His stomach in knots, Craig reached into his backpack to gingerly pull out notepads and printed drafts with the check reimbursing twenty thousand dollars shoved in between. Making sure Juan was not looking so he wouldn't berate him for arriving home in pursuit of the deposit of money, he slipped the check underneath the right foot of the closest Giacometti figure. From there Juan would recover it together with other checks to deposit next week into their personal account at the bank one short block down First Avenue.

"Which sexual activity, however, is the point forte in the case that includes, just these past days, the client being kicked and stomped on, her head crashed into a computer causing a gash in her head, she being

49

hung by her hair from a chandelier leaving strangulation marks among others, also her having been beaten by the husband for almost thirty years causing three miscarriages now culminating into the many attempts to kill her..."

"Did you call the police?" Juan exclaimed aghast. The typing abruptly stopped; Craig, unflinching, preempted Juan's blue contact-lensed gaze framed by the knotted yet freely cascading Bonsai branches.

"Is a problem, amigo. She thinks in many places that he is right."

"How has she construed that line of thought? Your clients are not only loco, but they are also debilitated cretins!"

"The bastard is the descendant of Nazis," Craig colloquialized. "Of contemporary Nazis to boot."

"How are the 1930s contemporary? You sound as loco as your client."

"The will to power, Juan!" Craig exclaimed exasperated. "Peppered with a dose of at least twenty-eight years' worth of hate and counting buried in the core of the earth to which he is attached by umbilical cord, and starched and ironed glossy for the front covers of magazines... In any event, when there can be a resolution, psychotic breaks step in its place, and the better the outcome looms, the more irate, explosive and uncontrolled the husband gets. That is what my psychiatric manual states, and that is where cumulatively we are now."

"A cracked nut case," Juan concluded empathetically. "Have some Peruvian halibut ceviche, please, you look gaunt. They were having sex, you said?"

"You mean what is really going on, *cher* Juan? His attorney I thought at first counseled him to court, flatter and seduce her, make sure to keep all in the flow of pure and genuine love... But then also upon due investigation, they've been having this thing going for over twenty-eight years where they go off on each other in unadulterated rage, and I don't see how it could stop unless she removes herself entirely from the crime scene which is also her boudoir scene."

"A perverse creep, his attorney, if he has one, and certainly the man."

Craig's heart palpitated in apprehension over his certain knowledge that the horned maniac indeed spent his wasted actor's nights on top of enough explosives to obliterate the entire East Side of Manhattan. Juan anew engrossed himself in his computer, uncomfortable with any additional details of this case. Craig kneaded his shoulders and ruminated over what else he could never confide either in him or in anyone else, including in the spirit of his dead mother. National security as his own inner specter enshrined the oath he had avowed in rebellious averment of truth against the FBI, the CIA, local police and military intelligence agencies, maybe a small number of folks at NYPD excepted.

"NYPD referenced my homegrown CIA in the surveillance truck today," Craig gushed, blushing at the compliment while ashamed he had not slunk his way into the upper floors on Fifth Avenue to catch the lunatic in the act and execute what is commonly referred to as a citizen's arrest, "but the truth is, *cher* Juan, we have created the monster. This country as a dynamic evolving society provides his expression, gives all support, whereas we... we are just hanging in there." Juan galloped on the keyboard. His brave indigenous soul revolted against engaging in intellectual abstractions on the subject. Craig retreated into the bedroom. He prevented himself from voicing the assertion he considered presumptuous, whether what society considered idealistic sideliners like himself and Juan could ever have done as the monster had, or managed to amass a couple of billion dollars, on his own and with his wife, in exotic foreign locations.

Stern and composed, Craig emerged from bedroom and bathroom one hour later. His head wrapped in a towel and laptop clutched underneath his arm, he shouldered a folded satiny Sheraton Hotel comforter a housekeeper *pro bono* client had once removed from the hotel and gifted him *in lieu* of payment for his case.

"Hasta pronto, if not mañana," he notified, prancing past a despondent Juan swaying on his belly on a beanbag seat. Juan's back was turned to the Giacometti figures he at times would consider too ostentatious for his taste. "To the East Riverbank, to work-work-work."

"I'll tape CNN's World Today, coming up at eight p.m." Juan grumbled. He stared at the remote control on the floor away from the pitch-black television adjacent to the array of the statutes. To Craig the aghast dumbfounded imitation figurines screamed in frozen dismay at a great invisible. It took the real artist, rather than the imitation, to portray that perplexed look as instead wise and prescient.

***

In the silent night, Craig proceeded towards his favorite location, the promenade above the East River leading to Carl Schurz Park. In dire need to reflect on his client's continuing refusal to disengage herself from her murderous personal situation, he did not want to bother Juan with the horrors he was about to peruse. Craig yearned to arrive at his usual place, a bench far out at the river's edge shaded by a large clump of trees, where he was in the habit of pondering, usually under cover of the night, the many inconsistencies that plagued his job. He unfolded the comforter to drape it around his shoulders. The towel on his head served to protect his still damp hair. Craig found it inconsiderate to go to sit at this hour with powdered coiffure further back from the river in the public park, lest any late-night passer byes on East End Avenue would mistake him for a prostitute slash con artist.

As was his habit, he slid alongside the balustrade, highly attentive to the thin strip of asphalt ahead separating him from the long row of benches. The rippling of the river drowned out the rumbling of cars directly underfoot, aiding his laser focus. In the darkness he detected miniscule, jagged stones, blades of grass protruding from barely perceptible crevices. Carl Schurz Park had almost emptied at this late hour inching in on nine p.m. Craig perched himself on his usual bench just before the promenade began a slow downwards slope. He paused for a second to listen to the silent wafting of the trees behind him. Mottled with night, the white United Nations building was barely visible river downwards. Craig was preoccupied to remain embalmed. He pulled the oversized comforter over his head. The spreading warmth titillated him in the task of reviewing a history of ghastly crimes.

If Juan would pass by here now, he would take me in as homeless, Craig chuckled to himself before he flipped open his MacBook Air to zero in on the videos identified by relevant dates now spread over the computer screen: *My suicide attempt*; *George in a Body bag*; *With Stefan at Dinner*; and *Parliament (Burrito) Caution: two plus hours long*! But first, he decided on the Crying Rivers Operation, dated two years prior to the doomsday trio and two to three days before his own impromptu meeting with General Applebee on the laguna eleven years ago.[5]

Intrigued by the lady's labeling parts of her life as more ominous than her dismal present, Craig entered a world dim, bloody and barren coming to life amongst the glimmering of the camera.

***

"Mamacita, why is Burrito on the front lines and not me?"

The shrill accusatory tone chilled Craig to the bones as he resigned himself to perusing broken scenes in sorrowful army barracks or in otherwise military themed desolate environs.

The exaggerated 'war painted' visage of George at about sixteen years old. Sulphur yellow and bright red flares cut from his eyes into his cheeks, begging agreement with Stefan's command that all rivers in the territory, of which there were many, would overflow with blood if that pestering American helicopter wouldn't depart beyond the ocean—hence the name of the operation Crying Rivers Operation. George, contorting in agony like one who has to win an athletic contest the next day but just noted insurmountable failings, grimaced, sticking out his tongue at the camera. He sought to express the contempt of one spoiled, of high and noble birth who is inexplicably offended. Behind him were busily shifting military personnel clad entirely in stylish black that Craig had seen nowhere in his own fateful trip to the region.

"I am from Iraq, I can't go back," a male voice shouts to scuffling on the ground as a body is being dragged along. A hand hides the lens of the camera.

Craig recognized him immediately as a former high level military official in the regime of Saddam Hussein, for whom Craig had been unable to obtain asylum in the United States. He had to swallow his indignation at this man's treatment.

---

[5] The Crying Rivers Operation is the background to Craig's experiences in the territory in *The Garden*.

"Should have applied for asylum in America, if you wished to adopt that language."

Craig heard Moura's voice for once sounding calm and discerning.

"Nooooo, it is them who want me dead..."

"We here hire all kinds, call yourself one of a variety of people, and never mention the word 'Iraq' again, or wherever it is that you are from."

"Can you let the man stand so he can present his case?" Craig heard Stefan lucid on tape.

"I have five daughters..."

"For God's sake." The phone's camera went dark in Moura's hand, then flashed again bumping about during a high-speed car ride at dusk with George at the wheel.

"The operation doesn't really have a front line in the sense of the word... Please think before you speak."

"Mamacita, why is Burrito there where I should be?" George wailed fretful. Craig was astounded at her patience, as well as by her precision in the ensuing dialogue, which to him felt strange and unnecessary. The two were alone in the vehicle, where Craig would have expected a cordial tone between mother and son on topics so well-known between them.

"You are talking to your mother, George. Don't call me Mamacita. What are you looking at, your mother? Why are you fixated on Burrito?"

"Because I have trained as hard, and done as well, and I am stuck in the back and my life sucks and I am bored." That explained his reckless driving. She was busy braiding her hair amongst the jerking of the ride at times appearing to oscillate tilted upwards between the left front and left back wheels and the right front and right back wheels.

"What did you do with killing and dismembering the indigena," Moura scolded, "impale her head on an iron stick? What made you side up with MS-13 trying to pass their rites of passage? You are shifting sides like a chameleon, and you expect someone to put you on what you refer to as the front lines of an operation?"

"I am bored, mama," George begged. "There is nothing to do here besides training, training, training, and the territory is so small, we learned it all by heart already yesterday..."

54

"Stop, we are there!" The vehicle came to jolting stop as she leapt from the back to the front seat. "Stefan will be here in a second. Get the dead body ready. Look, that is where the American helicopter will land. And we will be right there. I am not one to lose face."

Since then, Craig had learned through his channels in the labyrinths of federal agencies backrooms that prior to alighting on the laguna to meet him the next morning, General Applebee had been assaulted at nine p.m. by the corpse of a certain high-level member of the Parliament. The dead body had been flung down upon him with brain removed and replaced by blazing flames from the upper regions of a very tall tree underneath which the general had been set to meet with the parties.

"So you just fuckin' god damn leave," as George could be heard screaming plaintively on tape against the Americans who weren't even there, "and I can stop training, stop this fuckin' bitter life, stop getting up at four a.m. in the bitter cold and stop circling this damn' land... Just be fuckin' GONE!"

"You will never stop training, George. And if you don't stop doing drugs and seeing double and triple, we will force you to stop THAT pronto."

Craig could not discern on the crackling tape if the speaker, Moura, was close by, or was her voice carried from a distance by the wind whispering high up in the trees? She moved around, restless and undecided.

"The helicopter was rattling inside my head," George cried apologetically. *"It has been rattling overhead each night for one week already... Nice to make your acquaintance, otherwise,"* he mumbled aside, as if he perceived the General as a cheap flirt.

TWO YEARS PRIOR. MY SUICIDE ATTEMPT.

In his wide-awake and highly animated mind's eye, Craig walked with her as she stumbled, staggered and still somehow managed to continue onwards through a dark area of mud filled wasteland littered with corpses each one of which she seemed to know very well. Among her groaning and wailing, he could not discern if she were kicking at metal gleaming nondescript alongside frail fires or senselessly at the corpses.

"This one should not have been here, this one should have been much further along ahead, and him I just spoke to, he told me he was on one of the islands... Many are missing entirely. Where are you, Stefan?" she screamed blindly into the leaden metal sheet of the night. *"Where??"*

As if propelled by a force, she hit a stone wall and fell onto a steep staircase leading upwards.

"Where am I??" Craig heard him call back from somewhere close, gruesome and lost in complete darkness. *"Where are YOU??"*

Craig stood next to her as the heavy iron door swung shut behind both of them and she ascended sobbing, her tear wet hand slipping off the dingy wet stone wall.

"Open the door Moura!" Stefan shouted from downstairs.

"I am on my way to do precisely that!"

"There is no door there where you are going," he warned from below.

"There is," she retorted, crystal clear. "Behind it is George."

"George is not here!" Stefan sounded alarmed "Where is George, Moura?"

Ice-cold night air incised her collapsing frame. Arrived at the top, the landscape that spread out below glimmered with death.

"They were supposed to head over there."

Craig felt her nudging him as she looked from south to north and ahead and down into the crater of darkness opening beneath her.

Craig considered himself blessed in present time to catch a glimpse of what Stefan looked like before what he feared would be a meeting with him and not with any 'Arturo' tomorrow at Dupont Circle in Washington D.C. Astounded, Craig admitted Stefan looked neither like George nor like Moura, and neither did he look like anything he himself had expected. For a brief second as he removed the phone from her lifeless hand, Craig stared up into a countenance even, balanced, terribly composed, dangerously removed given the gravity of the situation, expressive lips curling into a smile.

He must have hoped he is looking at her corpse, Craig permitted himself a foul joke at that smile. Then he had to admit to himself the reality, which was that Stefan's inexorable mildness, high cheekbones frozen in space as if they were meant to sustain a Roman temple, was evocative of the nude male angels he had relished drawing as a child. That endeavor had caused him beatings at the hands of his father and expulsion from at least one high school math class during which he was caught. *Oh, he smiles because she is still alive…*

"What you don't know can't hurt you," Craig whispered, relieved when the screen immediately went blank. The sudden kiss of sweet dew he had not felt in the decades since he had ceased those high school drawings slid off his heart. *Next video, please.*

A COUPLE OF DAYS LATER. GEORGE IN A BODYBAG. "Give me the phone," she shouts, again despairing in darkness, only now it is next to a body of slushing water, with the faint outlines of a stretcher. "Why are you on the phone Stefan?"

"They won't stop calling. Is he alive?"

Craig immediately concluded the pleasant tone, so dangerously removed again, could only come from the Roman-pillars-themed one.

"My child," she wailed to the sound of a zipper gliding open.

"Are you sure he isn't high on something?" Stefan must be trying to sound consoling, Craig attempted to convince himself. Craig asked himself why Stefan, who liked to keep such polished reputation, would make this quip.

She howled in pain at the analytical probing of the sound, well familiar to Craig, of a body pulled out of a body bag and medical tools rapidly applied. For the life of him, he could not discern if it were her or George laboring, gasping for air.

Blood-soaked clothing was torn off a lifeless pale body emergency mode, with the camera repeatedly darting on and off.

"They tried to cut him into pieces, now they are calling YOU to make sure YOU are here to witness his torture, and you, idiot, attempt to pick up the phone? I should break your jaw, Stefan, and I can't!" Then *something very surprising, ludicrously surprising happened, so bizarre it spoke volumes about the vileness of who was involved.*

Moura grabbed the phone from Stefan standing over her as if dozing in half sleep, and the sound of whoever was on the other end crackled. Apparently not expecting anyone to pick up they had put the phone down and were conversing some distance away, their voices faintly audible:

"His bitch survived, and his son is young enough to recover... Where does that leave us, you dumb ass since you had the idea? Thinking it is the American taxpayer's money that has been wasted..."

A dark shape approached carrying the camera and switched off the phone.

"Rogue elements maybe," a Middle Eastern accent intoned.

"Now that wasn't any rogue element if I were Cerberus with a thousand heads!" she screamed, astounded at so much naïveté. Stefan caressed her hair as the stretcher was lifted and dark shapes huddled around.

"Turn off all lights," she hissed. "Turn it all off, everything. Close it all!"

Regretfully, the quality might not be good enough to obtain a voice print and try to identify the speaker, provided Craig could find anyone of the required confidentiality for the job, which was extremely unlikely.

TWO MONTHS LATER. WITH STEFAN AT DINNER. Craig now found himself in known and trusted surroundings, the location of one of the very few restaurants in the territory, high up on the mountain. From there one of the islands could be seen bracing the vastness of the ocean and rainforest streamed coiling down dark brown cliffs. JC and Burrito had taken him there in summer of last year, during one of the rare periods when the territory was both open and accessible and white boats could be seen adrift about the island. Twelve years ago, the location as yet undeveloped exuded a bare rustic ambience vivified by vines of purple passion fruit flowers. The contrasting dark gold of Moura's dress dazzled against the dark brown cliffs.

"Why is the camera on your phone recording, Moura?"

"So we will know it was us, and that we are still here."

"Personally, I wouldn't know who else I would be besides myself, and neither would I know where else I would be but here."

At Moura's glorious look in the camera, Craig came to understand Jacqueline's suggestion that she should model. The woman had the ravishing look of a glowing twenty-year-old.

"Look, it is all closed now," she said, pointing at the empty ocean. The entire scenic area was engulfed by complete silence.

"Why are you not looking at me?" Stefan interjected.

"I am trying to understand how we can keep it closed. They will keep on calling and trying to schedule meetings. Let's go for a quick walk."

"I came here to eat."

"I want to show you something."

"You want to eat somewhere else?"

"No, Stefan, I know how we can keep it closed, and I want to show you from where!"

Craig emitted a soft cry at the fist that slammed onto the table, sending dishes crashing to the floor and serving personnel screaming into the kitchen. The next scene had her with her back flung against a carved wooden pillar against the idyllic gulf. The distress burning her up from the inside, sparkling as nescience in her wide-open gaze, made Craig bite his tongue. He wished he had been there to counsel her, again and once more. The time was never right to act the likes of Lady McBeth. The characters in the present play were too freewheeling and mercurial for such acting.

"I will just be gone for a couple of months and everything will be all right, you'll see," she stated loudly and irrationally.

Craig perused the two shadows, interlocked, motionless, fused, dazed somewhere beyond space and time. So much passion after almost seventeen years of marriage! Craig was amazed and clueless as to how to untangle the frozen images. Neither was he able to feel for either. He breathed a relieved sigh when she gripped Stefan in a firm hug, tighter and tighter until suddenly she risked to dissolve. That Craig got and could feel for. He had felt much alike when deciding wholeheartedly and from the core of his being that his adoptive dad indeed was just his like own flesh and blood.

Craig had followed with burning investigative passion the subsequent months and year as Resource Global proceeded to open many locations in various unexpected places in the territory (which according to the CEO should not have surprised anyone, since he had always been there and had a right to defend his properties; he simply was just not the extravagant show-off type but a hard-working person) and the Parliament was erected a fortress of steel melted into the cliffs. The incredulity tearing Craig onwards was over how this development was being accomplished on the heaps of corpses, victims of superpower imperialism seeking to hunt for profits in other people's land. The next video, *The Parliament (Burrito) Caution: Two plus hours long,* made his head buzz with details of on-the-ground persons, places and events that coalesced mosaic-like into the many answers he breathed in in half sleep. So much was still to uncover, and none could be gotten at unless he went there again personally to hunt deep into the ground.

Groggy with sleep, Craig resurfaced close to eleven thirty p.m. on the waves of a reality that now exuded the searing life-threatening toxicity from the tapes, bewildered the time had gotten so late so fast. So as to expel the sentiment from his subconscious, he toyed with ideas as with pieces of a puzzle. Craig tried to understand the monster at worst, and the at best too hard to understand Patrick Chataway: How would he himself manage a business that functioned with 24/7 protection by armed forces to prevent constantly threatening losses including thefts by criminal elements hired by greedy, lazy, irresponsible and vile minded arrogant elements of the U.S. of A, some of which Craig had cruelly experienced on his own skin, including vicariously on the skin of George on the tape? The night had descended irredeemably. Craig wrapped himself tightly in the luxurious comforter. With the pondering demeanor of a high priest, he advanced with long steps back up the promenade towards East 82nd Street.

***

In the stillness of the apartment fecund with the fresh dewy smell of the Bonsai trees Juan had watered before going to bed, Craig divested himself of the makeshift robe when a memory struck him with the speed of light. Now that JC was no more, he couldn't forget to give Burrito the ring JC had intended to exemplify their eternal bond! *One* of JC's eternal bonds. Craig giggled at their revealing conversation, eleven years ago and still so culturally distinct and confusing, that the Burrito JC so much cherished had been one of many.

Propelled to the closet next to the open sleeping area caressed by the shadows of the Bonsai trees, Craig located by means of a flashlight the flat rectangular mother-of-pearl box hidden next to the brand-new iPhone underneath the pile of sweaters. Gingerly lifting the cover, he glimpsed the small show-offish gold ring, pinkie small to match JC's significantly larger one he had still been wearing when Craig last saw him alive last summer. The trophy of JC's and Burrito's union was ornately encrusted with diamonds of different irregularly cut sizes conveying aggression and combat. The ring had come into Craig's possession when he had scooped it up together with his toothpaste and toothbrush in JC's bathroom. The closed toilet lid and sink had been awash in Asian Indian scarves that hectic morning of the day that they collided head-on and mercilessly with the Crying Rivers Operation. As far as Craig knew, Burrito as the strategic social climber competed with JC as lover of the extraordinary and extravagant. Craving ever more exhilarating velocity and heights, Burrito strangely had never missed not wearing this ring. Craig yearned to return it to him so as to pacify his conscience before the deceased.

Craig's finger pads glided over the jagged irregular cuts, examining their exquisite sharpness in light of the real danger they would pose in the hands of one dexterous and experienced. Craig mulled over the truism that war is war. Above may be any political powers claiming misunderstanding and miscommunications, unexpected last-minute changes, essential well-meaning and expectation for speedy resolution, the host of excuses, but war remained war and always started with war. Craig often mused over the scenario of soldiers in the field refusing to obey their commanders, instead opting for just going home. To Craig such scenario could and should be reality, but in reality, he knew he would never encounter such drive for peace... Tonight, pondering the majesty of the rugged cut was no different. Aware of his own idealism in particular, given the extensive and thorough brainwashing of most soldiers, Craig yet was sparked to great intrigue, not only by the concept of killing for killing's sake, but one step further the idea of drawing blood as a means of nourishing life, so popular with some soldiers and in particular with the ones he would soon encounter, struck him as helter-skelter since no one wins in a war. For some, war was the supreme existence, as exemplified by this ring. *Maybe my fascination is because I could never feel the same?* Craig queried his conscience carefully returning the ring next to the eleven-year-old tooth-cleaning relics. Craig bristled inwardly as he was not one to hide behind closed lids.

61

The Acela had not yet departed NY Penn Station when Craig donned a pair of Touch Me Not and Don't Sit Next to Me headphones and engrossed himself anew in the videos and pdf files on his laptop. In the window seat, he had draped his velvet Victorian jacket over the empty seat to his right. He hoped to keep away any neighbor. Passengers would notice his freshly powdered curls, dazzling white starched French cuffed shirt and the diamond rosette jewelry sparkling beneath the open collar and mistake him for an unpleasant pretentious artist. He was lucky. As the Acela rumbled out of Penn Station quickly picking up its whizzing speed, not only the seat next to Craig, but the entire compartment remained precariously empty.

"Ho-ho!" he laughed out loud, browsing what he immediately ascertained as the most deplorable CIA file he had ever encountered. The document had been saved there by George just recently in January of this year, with the note scribbled in the margin: *Darn! Already redacted. Where is the original copy?* Of low security, the memo's gusty tone was suitable for a news article.

The subject, a lifelong inhabitant of the territory, first came to the agency's attention when as a sixteen-year-old he repeatedly rebuked attempts by his wealthy Saudi father to make use of him for money laundering purposes. The subject's personal life was one single big mess. Insensitive to cultural differences, his father had impregnated his mother, an illiterate indigenous to the region, in exchange for a large amount of cash, the significance of which the mother had not comprehended. The extraordinary insult and offense had immediately been picked up by local individuals who beat the Saudi to a pulp on his next trip, and he has not been seen in the region since.

The subject grew up in a hut on the land-inward island of the two islands in the territory. His mother, deeply suspicious of him and his motives, avoided him by living some distance away with the cash allegedly buried deep underneath her property. Not much is known about the subject until the money laundering incidents. Apparently, he lived like a vagrant, stealing books from libraries in the surrounding countries which he spent long periods studying.

Redacted sources reported the wealthy Saudi as impressed by his son's erudition. The agency traced laundered funds to an individual by the name of Redacted, an angel investor of sorts, who came to visit the subject. However, the door was shut in his face repeatedly, and no conversation ever took place.

A couple of years later, the subject met a woman he has been identifying as his wife on the street where she had been cast out as a victim of domestic violence. Not much is known about her apart from that she is one year older than him, which was learned when the subject's mother found out from an acquaintance about the liaison and cursed and yelled in public that her son was a disreputable rat going around with older women. The agency tried to trace her many times, to no avail. Redacted sources claim she worked at times as a secretary for the international development company that operates in the region, now identified as Ara Pacis. The agency's attempts to trace her there have been unsuccessful, due to the large number of Hispanic and oriental-looking housekeepers and secretarial workers employed by Resource Global. A large number of such employees are indigenous to the territory, and the CEO cannot be dealt with for redacted reasons.

The subject lived with his wife in the hut for one year, during which she gave birth to a son, which is when the subject's fortunes changed. Redacted angel investor resurfaced, and this time he was let in. Redacted sources reported Redacted angel investor and the wife doing some legwork, during which it was discovered that the subject was much better liked in the territory than he thought he was. The wife became extraordinarily involved and even visited remote hard-to-reach places to convince illiterate inhabitants of the subject's great value and potential to improve their lives. Events became convoluted and hard to follow, however, after another year, it was reported the subject held some kind of public office. The agency had no steady interest in the territory, whose inhabitants are crude and inhospitable, the land being hard to access, surrounded by rainforest and marshes from all sides and almost impossible to travel through. As soon as one has found a road, a deep ditch would follow.

Nothing was known about the subject for the next fourteen years.

"What?" Craig exclaimed. Clearly, he was reading a low classified document.

The agency became again aware of the subject when he had a verbal altercation with the CEO of Resource Global over an allegedly territorial issue. The subject suddenly had a small army at his disposal which he used to cause damage to the operations of Resource Global (See Attachment 1A). This in turn threatened to disrupt the supply and pricing of several pharmaceutical chemicals widely in use in the United States (See Attachment 1B). The agency was able to briefly trace a woman believed to be the subject's wife and his son in the subject's operation, which the agency managed to disrupt.

Events anew became convoluted and hard to follow. The subject and the CEO of Resource Global must have come to an agreement since further attacks ceased. The last that is known about the subject is that he currently trains and sells fighters to Middle Eastern war lords and other rogue forces, and in turn he imports arms and technologies from them for his own fortifications. The agency has no reason to believe that the subject's overall scheme really wants to cause damage to United States interests. REDACTED, revolted Craig's inner eye, OR AT LEAST DEVOID OF ANY IOTA OF CRITICAL REASONING, AND THEY JUST DELETED IN THE ORIGINAL AND REPLACED WITH THIS SECONDHAND COPY. THE AGENCY AFRAID OF ITS OWN REALITY GOES TO GREAT LENGTH TO HIDE ITS INFORMATION. REDACTED AGAIN.

Craig, after a moment's pause, concluded complacent, knowledgeable that at least for him, any darkness had its own light at the end of the tunnel.

"Ha-ha!" he guffawed. He looked up and into a group of Chinese tourists disembarking in Delaware, blurting, "My homemade secret services work much better!" The tourists nodded deferentially, bowing their way out.

***

No sooner had the Acela pulled into Union Station than Craig's good spirits dissipated. Surreptitiously, he twisted himself into the velveteen jacket as the train was coming to a stop, as if his bare presence in the District of Columbia represented a transgression. No matter his recent successes, he could never discard the gnawing rotten sensation that here he had been had, used and discarded like toilet paper. Humiliated, fitting himself into the long line of exiting passengers, he almost puked while trotting through the large entrance hall whose arched dome was plated in gold. 'Gold on the outside, black on the inside,' he muttered, and, 'It is not all gold that glitters.' Finally, outside in line for a taxi, he reeled at the sight of the loitering homeless people, some of which had set up home on the plaza in front complete with tent, sofas and battery-powered kitchen utensils. The heaps of misery went unnoticed by the throngs of people towing baggage and the honking of arriving vehicles at hosts of unlawfully parked cars.

'Visitors to the Hill must find a subject to report on to their members of Congress at least at this point of homelessness,' Craig continued venomously. He recalled with sadness and regret the many nights he had spent as a first-year law firm associate copying and pasting talking points for Congressional letters from news clips and federal court cases.

Finally, next in line for a taxi, he embarked and clutched his jacket shut over his open collar, fumbling to fasten his seatbelt with his free hand. He glowered inside that the gold of the dome being too high up for some, the taxi driver might resort to robbing him of his jewelry.

"To DuPont Circle, please," he voiced nimbly.

"*Du* — what? Pardon me, Madam, me not quite hear."

"*Du* as in the letter D and the German Umlaut U two dots on top, or as the French say *Du* or *of* as in *Du Coup* -I-am-from-the-blows-and-struck, for example, if you please." Craig was acerbic. "Pont as in the Chinese Pong, Ping and Pong. Get it?"

"Pardon me, Sir," the driver proceeded in genuine distress at the honking line forming behind, uninterested in Craig lamenting on his backseat. "You tell me to fuck off, I cannot take you there."

"Listen, man." Craig had a client threatened by the most unjust and distasteful death. In emergency mode, he bent forward to cut off any standard subterfuge, such as that as devout Muslim the driver was still absorbed in only just now completing his afternoon prayer and not fully coherent as of yet. Craig had heard barrages of such senseless litanies in this town where ethnic diversity was customarily intoned as excuse and justification for any detail ever as minute, cumbersome and unnecessary. "Just take me to DU-PONT-CIRCLE."

His white blood-drained fist clutched the black jacket at his throat while the grotesque grimace revealed sharp teeth in a cordial attempt to grin. Instead of evoking a shared humanity, Craig's mien ended up succeeding in a trick of scary Count Dracula gimmick. Before he knew it, they were already cruising up Massachusetts Avenue. The driver was disconcerted by Craig's lack of decorum so important in this town and focused on the road ahead. Craig would have welcomed a detour on Independence Avenue with the Congressional buildings and the Capitol more eloquent and picturesque than the imposing large stone blocks now gliding by on Mass Avenue with the driver incommunicado. The structures contained top secret federal government offices, evoking painful memories of the many years he had lobbied executive agencies for members of Congress, NGOs, and his own private clients. Eventually, much to his continuing chagrin, he had failed in his staunch defense of representative democracy against the military industrial complex. Craig had resigned to colloquialize the irksome bulwark as The People's Republic of The DOD.

**

So as to maintain the confidentiality of his destination, he gesticulated to the driver from whom he then departed with neither a word nor a tip to drop him off at the Starbucks on the corner with Connecticut Avenue. The familiar sighting of the compact checkerboard townhouses, many in dark aged shades of pastel colors, evoked the more pleasant memories of the adjacent multi-cultural Embassy Row. Here Craig had entertained many an international diplomat on his better, civil D.C. days when he hadn't been played as goalkeeper against the foulest bombardments by maniacal and uncontrolled forwards posing as Big Law superiors.

He took the rust-colored steps to the ornate entrance portal in stride when upon entering into the small foyer to the swelling of Beethoven's Ninth Symphony, he was promptly detained by a burly bodyguard type in sunglasses and snazzy purple suit.

"Che pasa amigo," Craig intoned, the famous, much sought-after attorney.

"Craig Malcault, encantado! And you are ten minutes early, which is excelente. His Eminence has been having a very busy day." Commandeering him with pincer-like grip, the individual whom he had never met before feigned familiarity. He directed Craig up another flight of stairs to the right, away from what appeared to be an exhibit room sporting a cathedral-like ceiling sprinkled with dark red tinted glass amongst solid woodwork. Craig averted his face. The few early visitors piqued him as the typical asinine D.C. fave international-leaning crowd moonlighting as art connoisseurs. As Craig remembered only too well from his own jaded work days, the crowd hoped the event would help disentangle the echoing sophistications they picked up during the workday.

Craig caught a glimpse of a very large painting that intimated a popular folksy rendition of the Statute of Liberty, replete with long black eyelashes, bright red lipstick and an exaggerated blond wig accentuating if not erasing the chubby look of stony distance. According to the bodyguard, the original image would have endured in its authentic power had her sculptor but put her in a real dress, "neoclassical French couture maybe?" instead of in that boring toga.

"Let me find out if they are ready to see you." Left in an unheated area draped in white, unadorned except for a banquet table set up in the middle, with an impressive array of wines and liquors adorning the walls, Craig watched the bodyguard vanish through an ochre metal-banded side door only to return seconds later, motioning him to follow.

"His Eminence is about to be ready, which is as ready as he will get. Down this way, then at the bottom straight ahead, last entrance to your left. Did you know you are meeting with a head of state? Please button that shirt. And don't you have a business jacket to change into, instead of that thing with pleats?"

Flustered at this last-minute fuzz over his artsy exterior, Craig queried, "A flak jacket, you mean?"

The bodyguard erupted in roaring you-got-it laughter, deigning a flirtatious thumbs-up but not without raising the shades to cast a stern look at the diamond collier on Craig's nude chest.

***

A flight of stairs down into the basement, a narrow entrance hallway cast in porous ochre stone led to a poorly lit uninviting granite back wall which swung to the left onto an ice cold narrow rectangular space Craig could have seen outfitted as a conference room. Instead, the entirety of the left wall had been broken down, revealing a dust-laden area covered in boulders large enough to sit on. A few naked lightbulbs overhead cast sporadic rays. Craig clearly discerned the figure he had sighted yesterday morning on the corner of Fifth Avenue seated on a boulder. Clad in a leather bomber jacket with fur lining, the individual unmistakably appreciated the cold air that flowed in through slits in the wall. He nimbly terminated a lively conversation with a second figure seated to his left with his back turned to whoever would come in from outside, dressed alike but with a hood pulled over his head and face.

Craig furtively surveyed his environs for any more foreboding appearances. His vision, however, remained riveted on the individual's dark brown eyes whose intent he labored to fathom. Craig was hindered in his discernment by their plated presence receding in a controlled and very focused delirium. He decided the individual had locked derision and other overboiling sentiments into an inner jewelry box, breathing slowly, astutely controlled. He returned Craig's gaze not unlike the stern last look of the bodyguard upstairs.

"Move to your right side a little and take two steps to your front. Remain standing next to that lightbulb that is now above your head, so I can see you."

Craig's insightful state dissipated in a fluff of thin air. What was this mass of a presence, commandeered by the staunch level tone, uncharacteristically orderly and intact as compared to the unsteady dilapidation, Craig queried of himself? Not only the state of this room, but what he knew of the events surrounding the individual's doings in Ara Pacis persisted drowning and engulfed in chaos. Thankfully, sudden memories of his time in Iraq surfaced in Craig's mind, when career on the ground commanders whom no other American set eye on would quietly vanish back into the night after a quick similar examination, concluding that Craig was nothing but a harmless debutante. Yet he was now pained that he had to spend time in the presence of a hovering frozen ball of fire, which made communication not terribly fluid.

"Your Honor," Craig proceeded humbly, summoning all tact addressing the figure with the decorum he bestowed on federal judges, "please forgive me. However, this is not the right way to have this conversation. You can place all trust in me. I am sure you have surveyed me well, during the many trips I have taken to your country. It is you, rather, who I regret, but must say behave somewhat bizarrely. See for example your hiding in disguise on the corner of Fifth Avenue… Why do you hide?" Evading the annoying bright light, Craig decided the best approach to the looming impenetrability might be to speak his mind.

"Take me for example," he rambled on, hoping an assiduous childish approach would serve to mellow the compact bullet type to something more mellifluous, more in line with the knight in shining armor or at least the real crafty politician whom Craig wished to confront himself with. "Like you, I also come from very low beginnings, and like you I am a very smart person. However, I had to go on job interviews and network, because I wanted to be an attorney, and attorneys, as any other politician, don't operate in a void. And like in your case, no one was ever kind to me. The first time I went, the interviewer looked at the topaz stone on my bracelet and told me I am overqualified. And at every interview in the same line of business for two long years, I was told the same. Until a good acquaintance told me they were all whoremongering amongst each other, what with that blue stone, he isn't insinuating he deserves a job by virtue of his pretty blue eyes, is he? The impulse to degradation and degeneration rooted in affluent self-flagellation is a vulgar commonality among the low lives of which this world has plenty. But such perversity doesn't mean I went into hiding! I kept persevering, and today the same rat pack that spent such time wondering about the color of my eyes while I was starving on part-time gigs, and the very same individuals really! do *kiss* at fancy events, *uh! oh!* the ingenious Craig Malcault, can we pose for a picture, an autograph maybe? Out of the goodness of your heart, would you spare a minute to advi-ice on a difficult client? Would you deign to chat while squashed into a crowded elevator, the media on your heels? And the worst, your Honor," imitating a whiney affected tone, "how is dear Juan and his designer work? Doin' just as fa-bu-lous and lovely as ever! The very same people, and while it tears my insides, I put up with it gladly, day in and day out, because I know I have to continue my work to greatly benefit my clients! What about you, your Honor?" Craig queried blandly. "Why didn't you go to any of the international meetings you were invited to? Why did you not befriend any of the people who showed interest in your work? Why did you not accept any invitation that could have helped you? Why have you instead chosen to go about your business as if at night, in hiding and in disguise?"

The hooded figure raised his hands over his head in a T-sign or "STOP IT and stop it immediately." Craig ruefully obeyed.

"You won't get killed at Woodstock, or at Studio 54, Mr Malcault!" The vulnerable infant ruse having worked, Stefan spoke in perfect English even though Craig surmised he forced himself to. "And you know well that, had I made myself public, in the beginning maybe 10,000 people would have died. Today, it is several millions, and the number is increasing by the day…"

"I didn't know that," Craig interjected, angry. "But thank you for telling me."

"Of course, you know! You are an expert at finding out such details. Today you are trying to make polite conversation, because we sort of intimidate you and you are trying to get at what I am here for, which I appreciate. We don't mind your stylish appearance, by the way. Do you want to know my favorite pastime for diversion from this awkward and uncomfortable predicament we both are in? I like to get up at four in the morning and step out into the cold and lift rocks. A steep pit descends from the Parliament into the rainforest where it is always ice cold at night. You have gotten far in this conversation, Mr Malcault. Now you even know where to find me, should you really need me!"

"Then what is the problem with our awkwardness, in your honorable estimation?" Craig demanded to know, since he hadn't come on this trip on a Saturday afternoon for nothing.

"The problem is you may not be able to do what I need you to do for me. And the problem is even greater than that. No one may be able to do what I need to have done, but you are the perfect person to get it done, in the theoretical abstract that is."

Craig furrowed his brow, casting himself into his frigid old friar mode.

"And what would that be, your Honor?"

After a pregnant pause, the hooded figure motioned, *Tell him, just tell him. We are not here to waste time either.*

Approaching the core of the hellish uncertainty, Craig noted he was slowly freezing to the bone and pulled his jacket closely around him, suggestive of suspense.

"You know the Parliament."

"Yes, sir, I do!"

"Parliament is in rags Mr Malcault. It is going down and soon will be no more in my country. For example, a file is floating around in the Pentagon, with identities in it. Some are of members of the Parliament, others of persons they want to be members, others are made up and don't exist. They have ground down Parliament to its bare bones, and now those are going to be soon pulverized."

"Maybe Parliament or some form thereof can be secured besides by focusing on that file? Since you know, Your Honor, the preoccupation with paper is a sign of weakness. Sometimes there is a solution to the problem by going to the source of the problem... What I hear you say is democracy is dead in the territory and the US of A is trying to impose a government which is proving exceedingly difficult, operations in the territory entangled in so many laws and regulations one can't take one step without falling over them." Craig indicated the problem as neither Parliament nor the file.

"I know that," Stefan interrupted briskly, continuing Craig's thought. "I don't have the time to do anything about it myself apart from what I have already been doing for decades which is fight them and fight them to death, because I have a business to run. What we are talking about here will take time, by which I mean a meeting or two, rubbing certain people in certain ways, which I cannot do myself since I am not a public person and said people don't like me necessarily while my business needs me sorely. You understand, Craig," Stefan deliberated, pacified. "I don't want the fighting to death to end with each one fighting himself and the others to death, which is what this country of yours highly regretfully is set on."

"Your Honor wants to hire me for that purpose? I mean to avoid that purpose?" Craig enthused. "If so, then this will seal our deal." He was about to step forward to hand him the flash drive he had pulled from in between the pleats when the hooded one abruptly motioned him to not take one step further. Remembering the custom in some cultures to not approach superiors unless commanded to do so, Craig froze in motion. The pleats whirled about him as if he had landed in flight.

"There is something else," Stefan continued, apparently not having heard him speak at all. "I am the head of a military currently undergoing internal shock and revolution as incited by an individual known as Burrito whom you are well acquainted with. I am not alleging Burrito is derelict in his duties. Quite the contrary. He is a superb soldier, which is why there have been assassination attempts against him, including the last one at which his partner instead was hit. My son is between Burrito and me in the chain of command, and my son also is currently undergoing internal shock and maybe even some form of revolution..." Stefan veered to laughing then changed his mind due to the gravity of what lay ahead. "Since you love the territory, Mr Malcault, have been there so often and are going there again next week: Could you do me the little favor to check in with Burrito? Regarding my son, you have to understand: Burrito is your friend, whereas George is an order. If you want to meet with George like two civilized people and you both agree to that and set a time and place ahead of time, that is fine with me. Apart from that, please neither approach nor speak or interfere with him in any way. If you run into him, don't say, 'Hey George, how are you?' "'Hey George, let's have a chat,'" and things of that nature. If I know you to do that, you will be removed from Ara Pacis. Similarly, and listen closely: Should you attempt to put me into contact with your Department of Defense, or should you attempt to negotiate on my behalf, with them or with anyone else, you will be removed from the territory. I have a meeting scheduled with them tonight, and for your purposes that will be it."

Briefly toying with a balancing act between the harshness of admitting to himself that Stefan refused him as his attorney while brazenly sending him on a fact-finding mission, and the threat of never seeing the territory again, Craig then wasn't fazed but curiously relished the prospect of Icarus immortal, or of flying onto the sun with all wax molten and wings dissolved.

"I wonder how your ice-cold Honor in the draft up there ever learned that hell is hot and so is law, and lawyering is a practice that occurs in hell." Craig attempted to crack a somewhat quizzical joke.

The frozen ball of fire he confronted now elongated. Craig was struck by the fleeting gloomy perception of a snake's head, since the plates in Stefan's eyes hid bullet heads, and he was now scanning to take aim.

"Not in Dante's hell," Stefan opined. "That one is ice cold, and I have been chewing some individuals in there for quite some time."

"Don't add your wife and son to those individuals who you have been chewing!" Not one to fall into depressions or other evil deliriums, Craig beamed a broad grin that Stefan countered with a sharp smile.

"Maybe I don't want to add you, Mr Malcault!"

"Don't worry about me, Your Honor," Craig waved away any concerns, sounding the nonchalant and easygoing type. "I have seen it all, by which I mean my very own small part of all. I know well what it feels like to have individuals demand an accounting of dead bodies while in reality it is the same individuals who are causing the dead bodies and you just — really, you absolutely have to, defend yourself..." Craig waxed on Stefan's behalf with a lawyering veneer.

"Who gave you that?" Stefan interrupted briskly, as if continuing Craig's thought, referring to the flash drive.

"Your wife. She is a lovely person, and I have been having some very good talks with her."

Whether Stefan was now genuinely suspicious of Craig given the inordinate attention he was bestowing on his wife, or whether the long-term chewing was catching fire and Stefan now aimed for him to blaze to the ground and out of his business, Craig regretfully did not have the time to decide.

Excelente, Craig opined to himself scathingly, shielding his eyes from the glare as Stefan had traversed the distance between them in no time and now pulled the lightbulb down closer in apparent derision to examine his twitching face. Craig concluded Stefan raging was *au courant* even though how would remain unclear Moura not being the type to recount to him contents of meetings with attorney. *I will have to become the cavalier to rescue the maiden from the haunted castle!* Craig cheered inwardly, correcting himself, *The castle on Fifth Avenue, even though... and in a way... the one on the cliffs as well.*

"You have been having meetings with my wife? She has been seeing you concerning...?"

From behind his hand Craig grinned up through the bright light, gazing as if in passing on a countenance much similar to the one he had viewed on tape bent over her lifeless body, lips curled into a smile. Only this time, the sense of danger was brought alive not only by the proximity but also because according to Stefan, keeping any distance in reality meant bearing a looming crushing rock.

"Listen hombre." Craig cleared his throat, adamant to get himself out of this renewed impasse. Such impasses would continue, he surmised since Stefan, locked in his domain, deigned to trickle bits and pieces of his own mosaic eschewing to reveal the entirety. The lightbulb showed no inclination of being removed from his face. Craig resorted to sticking out his chest, displaying the glittering rosette diamonds in a perceptive twist much alike to his strut when he had first set his sight on Juan in the Bar in San Diego. Ever the romantic at heart, Stefan's simmering lament and jewelry box full of guilt and regrets compelled Craig to say what may have been his most romantic yet. "Your wife has an excelente case. If you were to force my decision between her and you, then I don't regret to inform you that your territory shall be consumed by my blazing fire."

The light bulb bounced back to its former height. Circles of light first flared, then ascended into hoops growing larger, blazing into a halo, causing the ceiling to momentarily bathe in brightness while in the darkness below Craig dutifully placed the flash drive into the outstretched palm. At this point, he noted he had committed an indecency by risking for Stefan to come this close, as Craig readily surmised from Stefan's plated eyes rebounding from the bouncing light, in surveillance of his own inner vertigo.

"Did you see someone limping outside, when you came in just now?" Stefan asked curtly.

"I didn't look that closely." Craig confessed as if to a sin.

"Someone else was here, just before you. He offered to sell me a nerve agent. I had to kick him out so hard, it may have fractured his tail bone. That is what we were speaking about when you came in. Do I look like someone who would buy a nerve agent?"

"It must be your reputation, Your Honor…"

"My business is with living bodies!" In a matter of seconds, the room had completely returned to its former state of stale twilight with no visible traces of any real marking or staining presence. "My dear Craig, I need life long lasting. I don't want anyone dead. You don't mind a question, do you?" he added to Craig, who shook his head. "When your Defense people scheduled tonight's meeting with me, they wanted to make sure I am not paid or salaried for my presence here. Why is that?" Craig snagged at the insides of his cheeks to prevent a broad grin from being perceived as inappropriate and indecent.

"Oh well, Your Honor, let me put it this way: We here are dealing with high levels of government, whereas they there are dealing with the dregs of society, pardon my English. It has occurred that people who don't have authorization to work or to live in the United States nevertheless have received remuneration for services they render here in this country, which is against the law. And since this country the United States doesn't recognize Ara Pacis and neither does Ara Pacis want to be recognized, you don't have a diplomatic passport."

"That's not what I meant," Stefan interrupted, not unpleasantly. "I don't mean to inquire into the laws and regulations that govern your country here, the United States. Rather and disregarding any diplomatic passport, I am not grasping why a person would receive pay or a salary for a function of his government?"

"I know Your Honor," Craig cried in exasperation, "serving one's country is a function of one's being which obviously couldn't be compensated. Serving one's country is one's mother, so to speak. I know your mores and mentality well. What you're asking, I guess, is why does the government you're meeting with in the US of A not think like that, too? There are two answers: One, is they are assholes with an inferiority complex and they feel the need to insult you. Two, this government as you know is preoccupied with your business and finances, trying as they have for a long time to no avail to find out natures and sources. They make sure to remind you of that, and maybe the person who asked is a low life, as many of them are and thought by threatening he'll put you on the fence and you'd decide to talk…" At this, Stefan turned up his nose since the account did not fit his modus operandi at all. Willy-nilly, he promptly lost all interest and already couldn't wait for the meeting tonight to be done and over with. Stefan now conceptualized the invitation as *him* having to pull *their* teeth as Craig deduced from Stefan turning up his eyes with a sneer.

"I will see you in the territory. Give Burrito my warmest regards if he wants them and listens. You'll get the point."

Craig surmised the meeting was now over and he was commanded to leave. The hooded figure pointed in the direction opposite from where Craig had come in.

"There is another exit just around the corner here," Stefan called him back. "So you don't have to bump into the Washington D.C. crowd that by now is certainly wooing that Statute of Liberty portrait."

Feeling glib over the snide insult that he himself could not have put any better, Craig shoved aside the garbage cans that blocked the back-alley exit. He mentally dissected his plan for the coming week, beginning with the cab drive back to Union Station or through the minefield of aspirational D.C. con artists or blossoming small-town criminals *cum* chauffeurs.

***

So as to avoid any untoward inuendo from the driver, Craig resolved to immediately call Juan from the backseat, cognizant of the fact that to a very many in this town, what he referred to as untoward innuendo constituted polite conversation or small talk, hence the complete waste of time of taking anyone seriously in Washington D.C. Thankfully, Juan both picked up as well as ascertained his availability.

"Bebe, I need you to do me a big favor. Remember the white satin bag I won in the sweepstakes of *Bridal Guides Magazine*? Yes, that one! It is folded underneath my undies in the closet… Exactly right, it looks more like the Sheraton duvet with glitter sprinkled all over… Now if you would go to the big pile of sweaters, underneath which you will find a flat rectangular box. No, not that pile. You are at the wrong end. I know, it is a large closet, and yes, I do understand where exactly you are standing right now..." "Craig took the listener on an impromptu ten-minute tour of silk, satin and lace, including his Balenciaga, Dior and Gucci briefs, the array of ties ranging from pastel to neon pink and deep royal blue for formal fundraisers, his prized Tom Ford and Ermenegildo Zegna suits, all resplendent on display in the closet, until Juan finally located the box.

"In that box, if you would open it slowly and carefully so you don't cut yourself, you will find a rolled-up toothpaste and toothbrush, somewhat aged looking, and a ring. The ring is very bright and has diamonds sufficiently sharp to pierce someone's throat... Voila, you get the point. Now if you will take that ring carefully and place it inside the *Bridal Guides* satin bag. I can't forget to bring it to a friend who last week lost his lover in a shoot-out. The lover died defending him, and the ring was meant to symbolize their eternal union.... That's right, Juan, that's right... You can stop talking now and telling me about it, obviously you get the direction in which the story might be heading... And don't cry, my dear Juan, it happens to the best of us... Are we about to arrive at Union Station?" he hollered rudely at the taxi driver, feigning a harsh abusive tone. As Craig had expected, the driver nodded, dignified. He even considerately pointed his head to the driver's window, so as not to be perceived as inappropriately eavesdropping.

***

Accelerating in the Acela non-stop service D.C. to NY, Craig now lightened of his terrible cargo the flash drive, proceeded block after vanishing city block into the pitch-black night. He experienced a dainty melancholy at having left Stefan with his goon in the cold basement. He deftly tapped the window glass, acknowledging that about as much separated the living from the dead. The smooth panel felt breath-thin to his fingertips. Craig mentally situated himself on the icy precipice of the soaring cliff, dropping sharp and steep into the abyss fragrant with rain forest. He knew the light slender core of the white Queen of the Night flower to blossom at night on shards of hard rock. He vowed he would take aim and dive down deep to pierce the ice.

IV
THE DREAM THAT WON'T SLEEP

"I can't reach anyone there by phone, sorry, Craig. The individual you identify as Burrito is either not here, or his schedule so busy he can't come to the phone. No one is available to come pick anyone up, including you, is what I am to tell you... There are no diplomatic relations with the entity referred to as the Parliament if such entity were to exist. They have neither phone number nor fax nor email or website.... Border control? Yes, I did speak to someone at border control. They didn't understand why a visa or permit would be required to enter the territory, neither were they aware of any such requirement. We chatted for a few minutes, while cars were honking stuck in line to have their entry visas checked... Right now, they are particularly strict, some people were turned back even though their visas were in order... Yes, you are welcome to drop off your American passport, in an envelope addressed to Juan, so we can send it back to him directly in the event you don't return. Just make sure to include sufficient postage so your passport isn't returned to us... The Consular Section is open until five p.m. Wait, you know what, you might as well leave it with the front desk immediately in front of you when you come in. I will notify the receptionist of your arrival."

Hauling a formless leather carry-on suitcase down the creaky airport arrivals gate with cell phone clutched between shoulder and ear, Craig perceived himself aphonic at the stream of veiled admissions of incompetence. All he had sought was confirmation, simple and basic, that he could now go in. He had neither asked the Embassy to find someone to come pick him up, nor had he requested to speak to anyone at the Parliament. The rapid-fire presentation on issues beyond his control in any event struck him as an inopportune introduction to the United States' standing in the region.

The call with Enrique, a former date and now assisting with United States citizens' requests at the U.S. Embassy in the Latin American country adjacent to the territory, ended roguish and stale just like another one-night stand. Craig dutifully proceeded to the Embassy immediately upon landing after a surprisingly smooth flight during which patches of bright sunlight had coagulated through thin white clouds instead of the more likely roaring of tropical thunderstorms on prior occasions.

Lugging his oversized carry-on, he had shoved his foot in between the glass panels of the front entrance of the U.S. Embassy to prevent them from closing in on his person and belongings. Craig had cursed the harsh and unfriendly building exterior of glass, stone and metal together with the equally repelling intricacies and gutless labyrinths of American diplomacy in this region. A spindly youth, no doubt a local hire, waved at him perched atop the glass encased elevation referred to as the front desk.

"Frankly, Mr Malcault, I don't even know why this Embassy is even still open."

"We are in *this* country," Craig explained with a grin. His lungs were revolting at the air-conditioned breeze as they had welcomed the warm spring breaths outside. "The territory, where any diplomatic mission is closed, is adjacent and entirely separate."

"We are responsible for their nationals, though," the youth proceeded, showing off, as if he were providing Craig with top secret information. "Some come here, and we have to process their applications for visas... And let me tell you something else. Why are individuals caught using this country's rainforests to get into the jungle of the territory and then just let go? Wouldn't they have to be arrested for trespassing if they were two entirely separate countries?"

"Amigo!" Attempting to peer at the youth through the glass, Craig on his tiptoes waved the manila envelope over his head so as to cut off both the confused and uninformed ramble concerned with special ops, to which the youth, however, was not privy, as well as his own unpleasant memory of the time when the border control of the territory had to be kept in the dark. George, some years ago before he had met the more clear-headed Jacqueline, had been caught by this country's border patrol. The embarrassed U.S. DOD had dropped him off at the mistaken coordinates. "We can educate ourselves on the details of jurisdictions at another time. For now, if you would kindly call me a taxi or anyone who can drive me for eighty miles, I'd appreciate it."

"Where to, Mr Malcault?" The youth spoke abrasively and sounded rude and lost.

"The Mercado Central."

***

The Mercado's wide entrance of corrugated dark green tin doors angled out of joint in the process of closing as Craig approached in the cab at dusk. He instructed the driver to proceed to the opposite end of the rectangular building, two stories in height and tantamount to the size of a high school soccer field. There the crumbling stone of the back wall gave way to seemingly endless fields, scattered with shrubs of reeds torn by gusts of warm wind. The landscape dissolved in the distance in a mountainous rim. The blood-red sundown dripped low, punctured by ochre clouds that lent the weathered ambience a far-reaching depth.

Accessing the secret staircase broken into the crumbling stone with his secret key, Craig experienced a wave of melancholy. Just last summer he had visited with the deceased in the loft above. For so many years, the loft had served as love nest for the deceased JC and Burrito, where the boy had walked his first runway steps in his Asian Indian costumes. Yet today it seemed that memory was receding at light speed into a distance that was neither the past and certainly not the present or future. Overcome by emotion, Craig forced himself to slowly breathe in the dusty smell that hovered from the space above, now unused and not accessed for nine months. "La Patria," the fatherland, had lodged as the uppermost concern in JC's mind, nagging Craig and pulling at his insides. "Por la patria," JC's last words, when, noting the gunman, he had thrown himself on top of Burrito, resounded within Craig, standing empty handed, struggling to budge the weighty carry-on up the stairs with his left foot. The territory, strictly speaking, had neither past, present, nor future, representing a military installation to be used in self-defense. That had been the ominous first saying of the dictum, then voiced by George in the transcript, that someone will not do too well, maybe even will likely die, should the territory ever decide to have a government.

Switching on the bright neon overhead lights cast inside the high ceiling, the now luminescence-flooded area beamed back at him the poisonous green of the walls. The black lacquered floor and the animal-printed cascading back wall had remained pristine and entirely untouched. Even the incisions left in the walls by Burrito's knife-throwing practices still counted the same number of the stars in the sky. Feeling lost like a temporary visitor, Craig dropped on the cold metal chair at the round mirrored table in the middle of the loft, from where he could survey the meticulously made white bed. The feathered head piece burst like a fountain into a crown of glitter.

'*Why would someone who lives for glam and sparkle suddenly become so obsessed with the fatherland as to have to shout it out loud? Wasn't Burrito as the favorite boy more than enough?*' Craig wondered, as of yet not sufficiently acquainted with the very recent developments alluded to by Enrique and the receptionist at the Embassy. "Granted, Burrito was meant as a line of defense, and he was trained as such and had worked as such since his teens. But to the discerning eye, couldn't JC in the moment of crisis have packaged that a ruse reserved for display in the five-star hotels in capitals world-wide where like-minded others likewise could not differentiate political power from…" Craig hesitated, toying with language not in his native vocabulary, "whatever is represented by that bursting fountain of a feathered head piece," he concluded dryly. "Why only shout la patria?" Refusing to sleep in a dead man's bed made so much the less inviting by the still living lover, Craig proceeded to drag the large mattress on which he usually rested out of the closet just behind the bathroom to his right. *Why now suddenly la patria…?* he repeated with his back turned to the feathered headpiece.

Before drifting into an uneasy foggy sleep, the dimmed light now drizzling grey, Craig called to heart Juan's sobbing at the sight of the gaudy dagger ring in the flat rectangular box. "They all die in the end, don't they, oh why… Is it the nature of the game, Craig, can't that be changed? Can't you make them change, isn't that why you are an attorney?" Craig had already explained it on a prior early occasion in this case, so as to prepare Juan for the eventual truth. "What glitters at night

82

expires at dawn, dear Juan. It has been like that for tens of thousands of years."

***

The morning broke with grinding alacrity while Craig wiped the dust off a battered circa 1970s Ford Ranger pick-up truck the unmemorable color of dirt, left parked askance at the secret entrance last night. Fingertips tingling with anticipation, he had vowed to arrive at headquarters by late morning. Now he hoped the vehicle would carry him the one hundred and fifty miles in between. His Dodge Challenger The Demon would have been the safer, much more appropriate bet. Craig grinned sardonically, shaking the dust off his military fatigues. With a crackling roar, he sped off on the empty morning street. His flak jacket draped over a sturdy cardboard box on the backseat painted over with Ananas and Kiwi and containing his laptop as well as stacks of files. The formless carry-on was stuck between driver's seat and backseat.

By the time he lurched left off the broad white highway, its four lanes splitting off to the opposite right to the capital home of the unprofessional U.S. Embassy, Craig gladly acquiesced in having saved time by not powdering his coiffure this morning. His curls were now instead tastefully covered with a thin layer of dust, as he smiled at himself in the rear window. By contrast, to his right, the expanse of the ocean erupted a boundless flaming shield stretched underneath the pinned ball of the sun.

The road ahead curved along the water's edge, as determined to reach its destination as the highway to the capital, however, in places marred by protruding rocks causing backed up traffic. Covering his mouth and nose with a sunflower-imprinted bandana against the stench of diesel sporadically diluted by warm gusts of wind, Craig scanned the about fifty miles of coastal highway from behind dark lenses. The highway was speckled here and there with vehicles driving at different rates of speed. He determined the aura to befit a chess board, with pieces moving about lost in what Craig, inept at the game, painstakingly called to mind as the Fifth Move Rule Juan had taught him: "Neither you nor I

83

win if there has been no capture and no pawn moved in the last fifty moves. You tell me: Is that somewhere you and I want to be?"

The 1970s Ford Ranger pick-up truck inched dangerously close to the water to allow for passage of a mud-sprayed large old white vehicle misappropriated from the United Nations some years ago. Craig pulled a pair of military binoculars from the glove compartment. Too far ahead for clear visibility, a black smudge mark like a hurried tiny fingerprint representing Parliament rested fused into the jagged cliffs at seventeen thousand feet high. Many miles closer land inwards, desultory columns of smoke fluidified in the sun above the tall tropical vegetation, denoting acts of war. Joining in the honking of the onwards-pressing line, the large white vehicle maneuvered to miraculously steer clear of the steep stone decline into the frothing waves. Craig nimbly measured the distance between Parliament and the columns of smoke. He believed to know the line where the smoke would stop, defining the demarcation line after which Parliament could unleash its own annihilating force. Kevin Applebee would have to sneak in on foot from beyond the cliffs, where the two islands, invisible from Craig's view, afforded a trusted vantage point. Kevin would have to hope his presence, when detected, would be allowed to proceed unharmed. Summoning all good conscience, of which he had plenty, Craig could not look forward to that moment.

Mentally, he convinced himself he was riding his Dodge Challenger The Demon to manage the impatience mounting over the last stretch to the border check point. Destination finally in reach with towering clouds streaming in from the ocean denoting impending tropical rain, Craig pressed his back into his seat to reflect upon the fanciful scene. The incoming lane had sloped land inwards where it now forked into two. A huge dividing sign stood reclined slightly slanted backwards, as if to fend off the elements. Colossal deep black lettering, *Fuerzas Armadas*, was partially masked by a brand-new smaller U.S. DOD sign nailed down firmly: *Restricted Area Warning, Deadly Force Authorized, in accordance with the provisions of the directive issued by the Secretary of Defense...*, completed at the bottom with oversized plywood signage in the form of two arrows, *Visas/Habitantes* (visas/residents) pointing to the right and *militar/milicias* (military/militias) pointing to the left.

84

While not an affront to his conscience, Craig was troubled by the remoteness and indeterminacy of the signage's meaning. Were the native forces, becoming suicidal in the generation-long disarray that governed the territory, betraying allegiances by seeking to overpower the DOD and assume responsibility for an "increasing number of dead bodies"? Had the territory, enshrouded in pitch-black mysticism to in turn achieve mastery over the forces of such 'evil,' opted to add the illusion of safe passage for its impoverished, huddled masses, its more moneyed denizens opting for the *militar/milicias* line? Was the DOD attempting a last-minute moralistic pitch to take it all down by coup de force, in line with pharisaic carpet-bombing strategy 'where some are evil, all are evil'? Before Craig could come to a most likely futile decision, a black armored vehicle cut as if out of nowhere into the smoothly rolling array of camouflaged vehicles in front of him. An exceedingly thin silver plaque with razor sharp edges above its bumper glistened engraved with *Whitewater Security* in 3D lettering, denoting the private security company of Global Resources.

Yes, the scene would have remained more a dreamscape, had Craig not been alerted into the present by the small formation of heavily armed border security personnel that popped out of the ground resembling sentries of a bleak fortress. The silver-plated vehicle accelerated the last hundred yards and whistled past and onwards like an arrow. Now that he had no cover and came into full view of the masked guards, Craig resorted to removing sunglasses and bandana to display a peevish grin meant to convey the hell-bent drive of the Dodge Hell Cat logo. The damp wind gusts presaging tropical rain failed to disturb the tiniest crease on the sentries' black tailored vestments, evocative of haute couture (Armani maybe, Craig pondered). He was rapidly directed to park the cumbersome Ford off the road next to a sleek armored Range Rover. A long-haired youth sporting the same masked uniform as the sentries leaned peacefully against the closed driver's door, arms crossed over his chest.

***

Heavy tropical scents choked the air rumbling with approaching rain. "Amigo," Craig addressed the youth, "if you would open a back door so I can squeeze in my belongings and tell me, is that Armani you are wearing?" The youth, who couldn't be older than seventeen, followed the Pineapple and Kiwi box camouflaged by the flak jacket with eyes betraying a sense of irony much older than his age.

"Burrito ordered them, for all one hundred thousand of us. The name you enunciated, Sir, I do not know."

"Last summer you were all wearing the same also, but not nearly as fancy." Craig preferred to sound congratulatory rather than seething with envy. He ducked into the soft calfskin of the backseat, in humble attire a fugitive from the first big splashes of rain.

The black tinted windows functioned as blinders as the Land Rover raced land inwards over rocky terrain. Drenched forest foliage from time to time swashed against the glass. Craig relished the space capsule feeling, not unlike the elevator to his Times Square office. He spent the one-hour drive sorting the paperwork inside the box, relieved that even with the two-hour delay today due to the prehistoric Ford, he was still on time and would be even ahead or at least simultaneous with Applebee's sneaking overture.

"We are at the opposite end of Parliament and the islands, about four to five hours away," the youth explained, guessing his thoughts. "Anyone can drive you there in no time, no problem. You can lower your windows now if you want. It is an amazing sight."

They were gliding into an enclave deep inside the rainforest. A canopy of tall trees with thick gnarled trunks would have replaced a stately entrance portal, were it not for the swift black figures that Craig glimpsed on patrol. The rain had stopped, and the drops that gleamed off the foliage sparkled halos in rainbow hues. An elegant imposing multi-storied building came into view, the size of a city block carved and columned out of a dark mahogany colored material.

"Like the Eisenhower Office Building in Washington D.C.!" Craig exclaimed, recognizing the French Second Empire Style — sharply articulated granite facades colored mahogany with tiers of porticoes, paired Doric and Ionic colonnades, and dramatic slate-covered mansard roofs and massive skylights.

The youth wagged his forefinger. "Much better!" he opined, leaving entirely open the how. "Construction only began in late August of last year," he added apologetically as explanation why Craig had been bereft of the opportunity to view this marvel on past visits. "It is Burrito's headquarters now. There are too many of us to train at the Parliament, which belongs to his Eminence. He prefers to have us in separate places."

***

The youth's sad tone still resounded with Craig as the heavy dark gold front portal swung open and he instinctively looked around for a No Ladies Here sign, since everyone who frequented this building or was a member of the one hundred thousand force was a gay man aged twelve to twenty-five. In retrospect, Craig should have come directly here instead of spending the exorbitant sum on the taxi drive to the Mercado Central. That would have given him one additional night and entire morning to spend with eyewitnesses to the "internal shock and revolution" of interest to Stefan. But the disturbing histrionics at the Embassy, forcing removal from the reality at hand, had made him want to flee and recover his bearings for the important undertakings ahead in already familiar surroundings. The ambience here, on the other hand, was breathtaking. Craig immediately discovered that the four oval floors stacked on top of each other were perfectly symmetrical and marbled in dusted pink, connected at their far ends by unfurling gold-toned flights of stairs. Winged seraphic gold-colored statutes graced the spaces along the walls, of undeterminable gender and exuding a beatific candor at anything and anyone that passed. But it was the murals resplendent on the domed ceilings that Craig immediately came to revere the most. Vibrant in brilliant hues of the primary colors red, blue and yellow, each floor portended to embrace those below with stylistically distinct oversized depictions of Jesus Christ seated in judgment. The diamond-sharp images veered from classical Roman-inspired Da Vinci model imitations to flaming Aztecs evoking caustic revenge, ensuring respect and awe in spectators. The expressions were adorned in flaming togas and fiery exhorting gazes that eradicated any doubt as to the fierce and relentless trajectory that was being commanded.

With the exception of antique leather sofas along the distant walls of the hall-sized room on an upper floor to which Craig was led by a nymph-like youth, all the chairs and tables had been pushed to the back, and he stood alone next to a plush sequin-adorned settee. His head lowered over an executive desk against a gold-encrusted mirror that occupied the length of the wall. Besides a dainty lamp mosaicked with a butterfly motif casting an elongated glow, the mirror was the only light-reflecting object in the room still darkened by the now passing storm. Departing from the Jesus Christ emphasis on the glory of eternal victory, which was a victory in judgment, the ceiling was, as if burgeoning, coated in dewy spring flowers depicting the delicacies of ethereal new life. The traces of oases intimated freshness and vigor, and exquisite drawings of the sun, moon and stars animated with friendly life-like eyes and pouted affectionate lips. Craig recollected the need for the many whispered tête-à-têtes with the witnesses, then suddenly he lost all sense of time. He plunged deep into the blood-red ocean that inundated as the sun, now blazing from the opposite pole, poured its reflection from the triumphant domed ceiling outside. The waxed wooden floor was redolent of an exceedingly sweet scent of frankincense and myrrh, enveloping Craig's lowering forehead that gradually submerged into an enraptured rest. The frolicking pools appeared to have descended from the ceiling to mix with the blood red and mirror his now dozing features. The scenery slumbered enraptured by the stillness of the beatific splendors devoid of gender gracing the marbled voids outside.

Craig had encountered only a few youths on his way up, all dressed in the same black costume, however without masks. He had conceptualized the enchanted ecstasy on fledgling countenances to be precisely what it in reality truly was — an incisive retaliation for the dreary monotony and arid cruelty of their daily existences. And as with the winged statutes and brilliantly hued murals, it was impossible to attract their attention without expending the same singular focus, which Craig avoided as he had to remain clear-headed and compassionate for the interviews with witnesses in the day ahead.

Retaliation, vindication, all done in beatific candor, Craig had hardly been ecstatic at discovering this eschatological leitmotif reflective of the ethos required to keep Ara Pacis safe. Objectively considered, he had long considered Judgment Day a ruse for gullible and easily swayed persons. Had he spent his life addicted to drugs or to dangerous liaisons, he might have been more susceptible to the thrill of making life-like such surreal theories. But he reckoned the callousness of having to die young and beautiful as sufficient to enforce his in this environment, manifestly otherworldly-appearing quest for social justice and human betterment. He chortled to himself that he might have had greater riches and fame and more fabulous media stints while intoxicated by the slaughter of angels young and innocent than he had working ten hours a day on different continents. Now Craig was alone on this upper floor and grasping the entirely different spell of the lucid spring flowers and fragrant waters cut from completely dissimilar cloth. He admittedly was rapturous at the splendid clarity that now beckoned him with far-reaching visions but appalled by the covert complexities. The characters in the game had not left a stone unturned in outdoing one another with snares. All the while they had fended for their own integrity and purity, as if they were the God responsible for Judgment Day.

***

A deep dive into his subconscious submerged in the immaterial dark matter of the universe, Craig found himself afloat on a thick bed of water lilies in a dark pond flowing as one into a star-studded horizon. The jolt that strung him awake through no space and time alerted him to the complete absence of George Chataway. Craig's own body flagged his attention as non-existent, a dissolved breath, while brilliant clarity flushed his immersion into the eternal. Not one to be fooled by the perfect balance that kept him afloat in the paradisical water lilies, Craig strained into the most miniscule fibers of his core for the sudden screech that pierced him asunder: "Mother, don't leave!" Someone was not satisfied with the nature of the universe. Aghast yet amazed beyond words, Craig's breath expanded in a chest cavity not his own. The wildly palpitating heart he encountered there mollified at Craig's ribs embracing its valves in consolation, with the skeleton of two loving hands. The phalanges and metacarpals fluidly concatenated to form the pulsating bone. In this exchange between poles, dark into the dormant blue light of the periosteum, Craig noted he had become George, but of George, besides his disconsolate vital organ, there was none, just his scream: "Don't leave!" She had left, and Craig *via* George knew she would return sporadically, in the few desolate moments when George begged for acquittal from complete abandonment. George lived his life, or lack thereof, edgier than Craig had eviscerated when he had noted the precariousness in the balance of the universe. But isn't that her hand, caressing his face? Craig *via* George shrieked a shrill exhalation. Am I not resting in her bosom, in her lap? Doesn't she impart life with greater tenderness than any angel in heaven? The universe rejected the insight, evidenced its revolt at the cumbersome, unsolicited scene. Incorporeal he hurled back to clash with her breath, her hands. *Oh yes, this now* is *George, no doubt,* Craig remarked. The birthed creation had relapsed into the invisible raging fire.

In the most abject night, George's identity was clearer than daylight. The black hole into which George's body had collapsed, matured from inside Craig's ribcage and now axiomatic to the death of a star, burgeoned to monstrous dimensions. Zero volume and infinite density expanded, annihilated, and obliterated by the finger-wagging universe presided over by her gaze. In her attentive dissecting eyes George saw himself reflected a piercing spear, advancing elongating, spreading to engulf her and be rid of his pain. *'What one doesn't learn from the science of black holes!'* Craig mused to himself. In this future of all time, no time was left for the singularity that required asphyxiation, its own expungement to create its existence in her sight. Smiling glibly the satiated carnivore who had been esurient for meat, Craig rolled on his back, now supine with his hands folded on his chest. "Talk to me, love," he whispered, craving their words. His mind stitched the observations of eye witnesses into the account of the recent murder and insurrection. Events had occurred a threat greater than any renewed abandonment by her could constitute, obliterating, at least for the doer, the possibility of any such inhumanely cruel dereliction.

The fated day of JC's murder less than a week ago, the first witness was the youth. He conversed with Craig who transcribed from his subconscious, remaining eyes closed in his own domain of deep silent space. About fifteen years of age and companion of Burrito, the youth

90

busted into a small side-office of the Parliament by himself, his physiognomy evincing unadulterated rage. The youth confronted George who was busy making phone calls in front of a narrow paneled frosted window that was both bullet as well as fireproof. The youth was dressed to the nines in a red vinyl suit with heels, his hair was mussed up, his makeup, smudged and fatigue tugging at his eyes. George immediately pressed his forefinger on his lips before the youth could spew his spleen and implored him to proceed to his private quarters to speak freely. "I'll send you my last bill," George directed into the phone before turning to follow the youth, albeit with a mien that evinced neither patience nor respect.

The youth walked feverishly down the granite corridor, built as the window to withstand all elements and stomped up the stone staircase to an upper floor with George in tow. They arrived at George's private quarters where the youth already had his coveted Louis Vuitton valise delivered to but was yet to unpack.

"So que te pasa? What's up with you?" George asked. The youth's eyes were distracted, admiring the décor of the room including its stone walls, faux oriental rugs and furnishings including its carved wooden bed over which hung a gilded framed real painting of Bartome de Las Casas, the acclaimed 16th Century Sevillian missionary, Priest and defender of the oppressed in Latin America.

George shrugged his shoulders in resignation, unwilling to reconcile his own austere mood with the youth unleashing his bill of attainders presumptively against him, with no better target around, or so he braced himself for just another annoyance he had to take in strides. — First, the event had been horrendous since the youth, whose name was Cherido, was stuck to pull Burrito from underneath JC's bullet-riddled bleeding body exhaling last breaths, Burrito in an emotional state so severe he clung to the body like a life raft as if it were him dying instead and to boot, some of the restaurant's patrons who had been frozen to their seats were now collapsing and vomiting into their food. And then, upon arrival of the police, they brought a U.S. special agent with them who threatened to have the youth arrested for meddling in a crime scene — a threat which the whole world could see was not within the agent's powers or jurisdiction to make. The youth ultimately had to resort to insulting the agent to his face to let his prostitution fantasies out on someone else to be able to complete disentangling Burrito from the dead body. And then, during this mayhem someone tried to break into his purse — he picked up the purse from the Vuitton valise and pointed to the large gash, but they thankfully didn't take anything since the purse had been empty. And then, holding Burrito propped on an elbow frozen to a block and dazed, he surmised from the agent's befuddlement a surprise that more shooting had not been occurring. And then, the car that picked him up to drive him from the adjacent country to the border of Ara Pacis was far from the limo promised but a jalopy — a beat-up pick-up truck manned by a total stranger, a male dressed in military-like attire who didn't speak any language, didn't introduce himself, and scratched his crotch with his left hand, gazing at him dreamily in the rear mirror as he drove like a maniac with his right hand. Clearly, there had been no expectation for the youth to survive the event, and this farce was a prop rapidly invented after the fact. And then, Ara Pacis' border guard thankfully had the wits to punch the man in the face at the demand of an exorbitant rate for the 'taxi ride.' And then, he couldn't reach George because his phone constantly was busy, and he immediately had to come all the way here to explain what had occurred precisely six hours ago today at brunch...

"Cherido, voila, an elixir to calm your nerves," George decided he did not regret his recent actions. He assigned his callous indifference to his shock at the *other* recent, and secret, news and resolved to play along, and through, smoothly. George ignored the enraged absence of his heart where he was instead disturbed by a lurid gaping void. He handed Cherido a stiff vodka tonic he had prepared from the mini-bar in the adjacent parlor during his staccato tirade he basically tuned out and started to imbibe an extra mini-bottle of rum from the mini-bar for himself. Obviously, they did not suspect him and were not coming for him, which was grounds for celebration. George was extraordinarily astounded at his present freedom indeed. "I am truly sorry about your trials but welcome back home. You must admit that this place is so spectacular." George, who now had to act the psychoanalyst, hoped to get Cherido to focus his attention elsewhere besides fixating on himself.

"Yeah, I feel like I'm in a nunnery — the wood furniture including bed are far from comfortable." The youth was querulous, evidencing knowledge of George too detailed for his own good.

"It's me who sleeps in that bed. Did you happen to call and speak with Burrito since you left there? We have to talk about important matters…" George remained evasive, not wishing to harm Cherido for whom in his tortured abandoned state he forced himself to feel some affinity. 'Better this one than no one at all,' George sneered at himself, cognizant that at the beginnings of Cherido's red vinyl career, many had pursued that insight.

"I tried right at the border and thereafter without success. I got his stupid voicemail." The youth conceded, much to George's consternation who now remembered his official capacity as head security detail in Ara Pacis of whom formalities were required. George would have lots of explaining to do while the youth clearly wasn't in the necessary phlegmatic disposition to assimilate their reality fearlessly.

"What do we need to talk about? I'm in no mood for any of your drama after my nightmare today," the youth asserted.

"We have all evening… It can wait until you settle down — I mean — settle in and feel comfortable…" George tried to be soothing yet ceremonial, knowing the worst was yet to come and keeping the necessary distance.

"I think I should know what I am in for NOW." Cherido clearly was persistent as if sensing that he had been beguiled by George.

"You might want to take a cold — I mean — hot shower — and nestle yourself in a nice bathrobe first…" George recommended.

"But George," "the youth started to whine when his cell phone propped on top of the valise started to jingle the pre-set ring from the jungle, including roaring lions, havelinas and birds of prey.

"And can't you just please change your ring to something more pleasant- like the surf of the sea?" George interjected, feeling for the phone while keeping a bewildered eye on Cherido.

"Yes, Cherida — He is here now — Come over — Yes, but can't your information wait? — Just the code — Red? — Okay, who? — U…? — JUST GET HERE NOW!"

"The U.S. of A, our American friends, killed several guards at the mines and ambushed a group of specialty workers... stated they were looking for terrorists and this must have been a mistake, HA-HA-HA! How hard it is to distinguish between our workers and terrorists... How? Why?" That was all George wished to decipher from the encrypted S.O.S. but even with the absence of data, Cherido, who mistakenly thought it was his twin brother Cherida who now also had died began to tremble apoplectically, wailing with tears over the imagined death as if he could have been responsible for it.

"What's wrong, Cherido?" George was inquisitive indeed but compassionate. The scene was unfurling, boring to him and as planned, just another declaration of total war gleaned from the textbook. George leaned his back against the wall chin raised to avoid the sight of Cherido's pathetic presence. He yearned for *her* figure instead, slight, kind, and warm, but for now he knew he had slammed into the impenetrable opposite wall, to which he would be metaphorically chained for at least some time.

"I came here to... wait... for... Cherida... to... arrive." Cherido could barely eke out the syllables. "I... need... the... bathroom," Cherido pronounced, the room now spinning in his blurry vision, the walls reeling, moving up and down, down and up, a ship adrift at sea...

"Cherido, Cherido, Cherido!" George scolded as Cherido's body collapsed onto the hardwood floor, fainting from a panic attack, fading into a state of unconsciousness. George resolved that his vision of her compelled him to offer assistance and immediately lifted him up, limp but revived. He helped Cherido prop himself into the bed and, resigned, began to stroke wet towels on Cherido's brow and dazed visage, body clammy with sweat. While doing so, he glanced upward at the painting of De Las Casas but couldn't care less who he was or why he had ever fathomed his significance.

"Are you feeling better now, Cherido?" George soothed.

"What happened — and why am I in your bed?" Cherido was embarrassed and motioned as if to dig himself beneath the sheets.

"You only fainted, Cherido..." George continued, "I was just trying to make you feel better with some towels."

They heard a brusque knock at her door. "Just make sure it's Cherida and only Cherida..." Cherido warned.

"Cherida," he heard. "Cherida" echoed back, leading George, who felt he was living a farce, his motions mechanical, to open the door and lock it immediately.

"What's wrong with you?" was Cherida's first question to which George explained Cherido's spell.

"At least you didn't experience JC's destiny." Cherida shook his head while he crouched down against the floor's wall to maintain gravity as he shared the information in short breaths. As Cherido's twin brother and JC's second companion, he sported the territory's traditional Armani garb while his eyeliner had prevailed sharpening moody eyes, and his long hair was neatly combed in curls. In his official capacity of head security detail, George had to act he was absorbing the reporting tirade of today's events while his insides, slowly returning to normal the impact of the shock waning, coveted forgiveness and her earnest embrace.

"American special forces began murdering in the territory early this morning, when JC was on his way to brunch... People guarding the mines and also specialists and a couple of engineers and also some others researching there with advanced degrees... Statements then being made, they are hunting for terrorists... No money is being made where there are terrorists... Right now, they are moving to sell to the low bidders... Right now, the chase is on to locate their next targets before it is too late... Our land is like a dead body at our own morgue where we have to bribe to get it back... JC was threatened last night to resign from the head of it all... They presume he governs our army given his alliance with Burrito, them not knowing at all of course how anything here really works... And I haven't had the time or heart to tell the others who are in the path of death since we are all at risk now..." Cherida was mortified.

"Cherida, couldn't you have entreated Burrito to arrest the killers who are now in the territory?" George perked up, referencing Cherida's role as security detail while Cherido's was the boudoir's and preferring not to mention his own. The situation was just too trite and had been predictable, and George in safety but rattled to his core behind fire and bullet proof walls considered his military training superior. "Cherida, can you make Cherido a drink?"

"But I don't even understand what the hell is going on here!" Cherido was flabbergasted since he had no bearings on his compass to comprehend this calamity. "Murder? Guards? Mines? Advanced degrees? Assassinations? No money? — What the hell is AMERICAN TERRORISTS—"

"Cherido, it'll become clearer and clearer as we talk tonight… Tonight, Burrito and I have to plot our strategy to catch the killers…"

"Well, I don't know if I want to be left out or included in ANY OF THIS!" Cherido moaned in distress.

"Sorry, Cherido, you're here now, the past half hour was not your call to make," George cut him off abruptly since he was acting as a self-possessed distractor, which did not fit in the military rule book. "Cherida, please just get your brother a drink… Can't you see how out of sorts he is?" Indeed, George had never witnessed Cherido so disturbed as he was now, his eyes slammed shut, his head down by his chest, his limbs, flaccid.

"Fine — coming right up, your Excellency!" Despite his resentment, Cherida still complied with George's directive, tarrying through the mini-bar to mix and match an elixir for Cherido — which was an unwelcome diversion for Cherida himself, who preferred to brood in silence.

"What are you going to do now, George?" Cherida snapped his fingers quietly lest he disturb Cherido, directing him to continue to rest in bed, comforted by a hastily prepared Bloody Mary.

"You are sending Americans a bill; you have a job coming up?" Cherido vented his knowledge from the leaden themed pillows, hardly a welcoming locus to place one's head.

"Had a job, in the past tense. Now I'm just going for a walk around the grounds to think things through by myself," George declared as he stretched and yawned himself back to vitality, having spent the entire day since the morning either on the phone, or in shock whereas now he called to mind that he must act and zero in on his disagreeable environs. "Just leave me the key if you decide to depart and take care of each other in the meantime. And by the way, Cherido, thanks for the cold shower." He threw him a charming grin. "American terrorists… We all need a wake-up call sometimes."

"But George... I still don't understand..."

George placed his fingers on his lips, shushing. "Later, Cherido." Closing the door, he just had to ignore the lament of dire confusion since the truth would throw Cherido off-kilter, better acquainted as he was with the boudoir than with the affairs of the world.

***

Returning an hour later refreshed and more in sync with the great urgency ahead, instead of being warmly embraced as a brother in arms, George rebounded from his bed where Cherido lay on his stomach, his head dangling over the bed's edge, examining his hair while Cherida, propped against the leaden pillow, stared listlessly ahead. George was assaulted by the litany led by Cherido violently twisting his head.

"You weren't walking around the grounds, liar! We checked."

"Where the hell were you?"

"Didn't you know JC would be killed, you double-assed agent? Who do you think you are, Tom Cruise?"

"You never listen to His Eminence's advice!" —

"We should call the police, let alone the hospital or morgue on you!"

"Why didn't you at least call ahead to spare US here the bloody game?"

Brought back to the trenchant reality clarifying why his father, Stefan, had thought it advisable for the one-hundred-thousand-man force to be headquartered somewhere else besides the Parliament, George couldn't even distinguish between the alternating screeching reproaches from a petulant Cherida and vitriolic Cherido. *"So, who do you think you are? Moses parting the Red Sea?"*

"Ya, basta, enough already!" George just had to cover the spree of grin from his mouth with his hand at the Moses metaphor. In silence this past hour he had decided, acquiescing limp in his dangerous, unbound, reckless inner state. He had reeled to find a way out to cure, to now withdraw and simply wait, letting events take their to him, acquainted with the on the ground operations of Atra Pacis since a child, predictable course. "Folks, let's get down to business since I need to be off early at dawn, four a.m. to be precise, and I feel you need to remove yourselves and your personal belongings together with me. Suffice it to say that no, I was not au courant with JC's pending murder, and no, I am not being paid by Americans to betray my country, yes, I was on the grounds making many calls, and no, I don't think everyone here will die... At least not necessarily right now. You should have more intel first thing mañana. You won't sleep with Burrito tonight, Cherido?"

Forebodings assuaged, yet yielding to fresh unease, Cherido imperiously commanded, again evidencing detailed knowledge of George, "Cherida sleeps with me here — you, George, get the Jesuit wooden bench or wooden floor with a pillow and sheet."

"Fine with me, set your alarms for 3:30 a.m., which is three hours after I will have returned from more work still." George added, "Sweet dreams" like a packet of saccharin which elicited Cherido's meritorious curse of "FUCK YOU, GEORGE!" George refused to dignify Cherido's daggered insult with any response — so as to draw the curtain closed by a cane on this histrionic and even vaudevillian scene, their commonplace when they were not chained inside black costumes with fitting masks.

Despite the 3:30 alarm, George lifted himself from the stone-hard floor relieved his sleep had been dreamless and not conducive to the experience of the cold floor as instrument of punishment. He saw that Cherido and Cherida remained on distant parts of the bed, enrapt in their symbiotic snoring, alternating from Cherido's whistling-like snore to Cherida's chainsaw-like snores and vice versa. George let the jungle jingle beat go on, anticipating that it would revive them — to no avail even after he raised the volume by several bars. In light of the tight timetable, he hurled his sheet of a blanket and pillow at them, causing Cherida to moan and Cherido to pop up straight from beneath the sheets. "Where am I now?" Cherido was disoriented, rubbing the blur from his vision with George coming into his sight.

"WHO ARE YOU? ARE YOU ME?" Losing his patience at this renewed screaming, George grafted his past onto Cherido, playing with his mind.

"And you really want to depart the boudoir to go into Security and Law where you will wake up in an ambrosia-induced state of amnesia over just which city- country- hotel- the woman, man, or whatever in hell you had just slept with lying next to you?" to Cherido, nodding dreamily and wisely hugging a pillow. "Darling, just continue enjoying your mystery while you go get yourself gussied up in yet another suit so we can proceed on from here and out! You both got three minutes and counting." Tearing open the Vuitton valise, George dropped a snakeskin suit onto the bed and, pulling Cherido by his arm, escorted him into the bathroom.

"No wonder you like this place, George, given your social and personal inferiority complexes just recounted..." Cherido was cantankerous from behind the closed bathroom door.

"I reckon that your assessment of me was off-kilter while I had to towel-bath your clammy chest, throat and face yesterday afternoon." George jocularly mock-defended his former teenage lifestyle's virility.

"Cherida, it's your turn now to get it together."

George gave him a brawny shove on his back face-down, causing him to whine, "Ay, George, what's with this macho mierda-shit?"

"You have three, two minutes remaining, right?" George demanded his action.

"Whatever..." Cherida intoned, "and without YOUR hell..."

Used to obeying orders even though from the different party of Burrito, Cherido emerged from the bathroom in two minutes flat in the jungle-tinged snakeskin-themed suit, his face scrubbed clean and tinted a pearly rose sheen, curly hair brushed in waves like the sea and black leather stiletto heels, looking the picturesque image of his fifteen-year-old self. "Cherido, you look stupendous, but just unbutton the suit and add your black sequined negligee beneath?" George orchestrated for Cherido, having undertaken his own bait and switch operation to substitute his ridiculous on the floor position for the formal fashion of the Armani-esque black gear since any other clothing would give him away as suspicious in broad day light.

Cherido obediently dodged in and out of the bathroom adding the hussy-rendering effect of the negligee to his apparel.

"You two are too loco — crazy — look at the hour! It's not safe to walk, let alone give me a ride!" Cherido, in his quintessential melodrama, disapproved that George and Cherida were attempting to head out without his controlling protection they had enjoyed in private quarters.

"Cherido, now you too have amnesia? You spent yesterday under surveillance and then in a car probably bugged, remember? We'll ensure to get you back safely to your show at the other and opposite end, don't worry... Just keep yourself beautiful while we get through zillions of calls and trillions of other issues, all extremely severe..." George deprived Cherido of the courtesy of any refutation and instead ushered the siblings downstairs to the still dark sky-lit entrance hall and through a narrow secret side door.

***

Darting through the night in the enclosed capsule of an armored vehicle, George listened to events not novel yet in their sequence unexpected. The rapid motion seduced him with the promise of a way out of his personal mess. George attempted to convince himself that his stiffened emotions could also be due to his bewilderment at the American complete and for them devastating failure to assign the cause of the recent insurrection, in response to which they had been in pursuit of JC as suspect, to him instead. 'I can't be that superb a double agent,' George reflected, apprehensive. His recent acts had had suicide as their unintended side effect, yet he was still alive. Cherido recounted in stream of consciousness to George in the driver's seat his dinner in the capital of the adjacent country the last night JC was alive with him and an American businessman interested in investing in SIDA prevention in the territory. JC suddenly received an unexpected call which Cherido deciphered as untoward bizarre media intrusion pelleting him with questions about his relationship with the government of Ara Pacis about which the 'media' caller appeared to know naught, instead aggravated to not have any direct line either to that 'government,' or to Burrito whom they were evidently seeking, specifically about whether it was this or another government to which he, JC or Burrito, it was not possible to discern, was called to answer for his actions. Then, increasingly breathless, Cherido weaved through what to him had appeared a subsequent series of puzzling treacherous contra-temps at the hotel where they had been staying, from a dark figure he had bumped into, jumping back in fear that JC had not come alone with Burrito but accompanied by such a glittering bird of paradise, to a call on the hotel phone looking for someone with an Arab name — which, coming to think of it, had also happened one week prior in the territory — and at their genuine astonishment, excusing himself with "wrong room" before hanging up at his end with a loud bang and crash, to another call early the next morning by a familiar man, reminding them of someone friendly and familiar whose name however at the present time escaped them, confirming them for brunch at the wrong location and being punctilious at having them confirm their real and actual location, until George, well versed in such antics, exclaimed in ennui, "Cherido, ya basta — that's enough. What questions do you have for ME?" anticipating Cherido's whispered report directly into Burrito's ear later that same day. Branches pelted, breaking off against all sides of the vehicle, as George, driving blindly, pursued his own trajectory he knew with eyes closed. He still had to delve into the formal and official proclamations, to which Cherido and Cherida as high-ranking security details were entitled. George resigned himself to the regurgitation of masticated theories and strategies now to wear out his already tried nerves.

"Many, George. First, can you explain why you think these American assailants would dare to target Burrito knowing he heads an army?"

"Welcome to my stage. Isn't it obvious to you yet, the old disgusting tale? Because he is a puto, whore or prostitute in their distorted minds and ultimately expendable. If it was the U.S. of A government, military intelligence, this was their way to just scare Stefan for not following their warning about associating with individuals who want to make Ara Pacis more wealthy and powerful, serving at the same time to destabilize the region… If it was some international rogue network operating at the behest of certain elements in the U.S. of A., this was their way to keep you all from becoming a soplon — rat — about your responsibility, to take naps from time to time, to look away in your sleep so to speak, so from time to time the little accidents at the mines look like accidents and not like the looting of information, materials, information, so as to sell to allies at very low prices, you name it — Ara Pacis is a wealthy territory, dear! For which looting they could then hold accountable and kill both JC and Burrito…"

"I do believe, by the way, that it is both the U.S. of A government and the rogues acting in cohort together since their interests, while appearing so different — maintaining U.S. security in the region and looting — in reality and truth are really one and the same. I am sure you have noted, Cherido, the reality, easy and straight-forward, of our values sinking when they loot or accuse or associate us with terrorists? One hand steals, the other protects the thieves and voices dissonant accusations while the other sells and sells very low… That same suit you are wearing, dear, is worth one thousand on a whorish companion to a third world SIDA event ending in lurid shoot-out, whereas half a million on a live-in mistress lavished in a mansion…"

"And one billion on a terrorist," Cherida grumbled with many meanings, hitherto quiet and slightly bored, leaving the definition of terrorist open with a meaningful glare at George.

"Then how do you explain the American special agent clearly making himself out as such, with no dual reference to himself that he was sent by both his government and the rogues?" The ardent democrat at heart, Cherido was genuine, ignoring his brother.

"How much do you think it would cost the Americans to bribe our territory's goons or staff to find out if, who and when we are or would be informants or reporting to whom? I'd say a billion dollars, which obviously they can't afford." George was too laissez-faire in his stolid tone. "There is no need for them to hide," he quickly added, to completely and permanently dispel any suspicions by the duo that the special agent may have been looking for him instead.

"Okay, here's another one for you, maestro. Why do you think the Americans cum rogues or terrorists kill everyone who they target at our sites, destroying IDs, telephone numbers, notes and laptops? That does not help them since these actions erase any trace of the crimes, they accuse us of, such as being or working with terrorists…" Cherido was sharp as a tack and clearly imbued from head to toe with Burrito's sense of civilization.

"Do the Americans write down mine or Stefan's time entry for when we leave at four a.m.? No, right? They know we do what we are supposed to do and what, by the way, has been JC's intent all along," he added with graven emphasis, the selection of JC as a target not having been far-fetched at all, "which is defend Ara Pacis with any and all means, including by the means of individuals they therefore label as terrorists, which labeling we frankly don't give a damn about, against whoever comes here to steal our resources, of which thieves there are many. They most likely think they could always deny any knowledge of any crime on their supposed watch to protect themselves: no evidence, therefore no crime, and the rogues who steal are in business for themselves, having already departed at some other time and arriving back when it suits them — remember, illusion is our king here." George had a gift to decipher any scenario.

"But now we could be at risk of the American government's interrogation and torture if they caught us since they know JC formed us and shielded Burrito with his body to the extent of causing his own certain death..." George made a mental note that he'd have to follow up with Burrito on calming Cherido's present hysterical mental state.

"Understood. So why would JC have risked all this for Burrito, and implicitly for Stefan and me?" George wondered, testing them.

"Probably because he is gay and, in his devotion, stellar and singular, he did not want to see you hurt — or else he had been becoming attracted to you and Stefan — which was probably not the case unless you were to pay him."

Cherido's snigger caused George to punch him in the shoulder. "You're thinking awfully high of yourself."

"And George, how do you think they find our locations if they don't have insiders helping them here?"

"Cherido, for God's sake, how easy is it to find the locations of a global resourcing corporation? Just follow the signs, in most cases... However, when it comes to thieving and looting, most people rely on the ground experts, people who have spent their lives in the ditches, muds and ravines... In the trenches, people..." This description caused him manifest pain. "Where was your first date with Burrito anyway?" George put the spotlight back on him to chase away morbid thoughts.

"At the pitch-black chasm of water that separates the territory leading to Parliament from... the corporation, three years ago," Cherido murmured beneath his breath, chagrined by George's naïveté. "But why do you think they don't just bomb our headquarters and declare war on our military directly?" Cherido volleyed what he thought was a challenging question to George hoping that he couldn't respond. He appeared to be playing his todopoderoso — all-powerful self- turning the tables on George yet again as he had done this morning — even after Cherido mistakenly thought he had acquired leverage over him since yesterday.

"Why would they? Since, if they would, they'd pull Resource Global into a war which Resource Global HQs are going to KNOW how to DEFEND, my dear... since if they didn't keep US here entangled in all the war-ish laws, regulations, positions, strategies, you name it, as what they hope are genetically predisposed lunatics, snakes and part-time dilletantes, aka prostitutes, we could then easily grow brains and trace back to them all their crimes and offenses they incur just by being present in this territory where they have not been invited, which would then cause them mas mas more problemas, right?" George asserted. "You know, you should probably get Burrito to clean up when you get home, he has spent all evening and night today in the trenches..." George's proposed exercise of disinfecting bad boys' residual gismo was utterly repellent to Cherido, aspiring to higher venues for his lover.

"So what's your answer to my puzzle?" Cherido was shaking George like a toy plastic Magic 8 Ball to prosper from divine providential interpretation.

"Only that they wanted to scare you and ensure the point is made, to everyone all around here, that it is them who controls the looting, the selling at low prices to their allies, and presumptively, even though this makes the Americans look like secondhand handlers, to control who Stefan deals with, just maybe... Look at you, you're still afraid! Otherwise, they would have waited for you at your hotel room to take real action against you, à la carte and complete with torture, as they are wanting to do when they attempt to bring about real change, long and lasting." George mock-yawned, to prevent Cherida on the backseat from irking with another quip as the prior on the net worth of terrorists. "But the point is, you're fine, Cherido. My only warning for you is to keep Burrito nice and sprightly, since at heart he's an odious assassin." George was perspicacious in his concern which Cherido found jarring since he had sought to prophesize Burrito's redemption.

Shortly thereafter, they stopped, prompted by the shouting of the leader of an American patrol at a black sedan packed with a supply of armed teenagers, some in the customary black garb, others displaying camouflaged pajamas and bloated pimpled faces with bulging angry eyes as if just dragged out of bed. This motley crew could have been the children of the American patrol, were it not for their paraded rebellious, hateful, insubordinate nature.

Stretching his legs in the still dark underneath a canopy of trees, George was taking a break from Cherida's brooding silence on the back seat, which he perceived as immature and accusatory of his real intentions, which George hoped to have presented as at least somewhat helpful. At this point in his career, he was no longer willing to tolerate insinuations that he might be a double agent or, which he considered worse, bent on enriching himself by the means of connections or birth.

"So why the hell do you dare to come to a war zone to investigate the murder of some puto?" The patrol leader grilled the ringleader at the wheel of the sedan in high decibels, adopting their terms and language to facilitate inter-cultural communication. "Since when do you care about the lives or deaths of putos? You know are not to do that as a matter of your code."

The ring-leader's responses were inaudible like white noise, while his completely uninvolved eyes pierced the darkness ahead.

"I don't care who you believe murdered or was an accomplice to the murder of the puto," the leader reproached the ringleader. "You know the war zone is off-limits to any and all of you without *our* Jefe's permission — which I do not have on our roster. And who are the anachronistic pajama-ed folks in your back seat? You are not attempting to use a war zone to recruit disciples, are you?" The perspicacious patrol leader used outdated terminology once employed by the criminal gang MS-13 who used to make inroads and offer their services in the territory, so as to insinuate the antiquated and ineffective *modus operandi* of the motley crew.

"Hell, no. For you? I will not and you really, really don't want me to — make any *especial* call to our Jefe for your business. Our Jefe clearly won't honor or believe your intentions and instead can order immediate and permanent punishment against you, understood?" The leader was increasingly incensed by the ring-leader's unabated persistence. "If you prefer, I will report your unauthorized attempt to our Jefe which you can take back to your own disgusting people."

"As I said, one... two... three... Now turn the car around and drive straight back," the leader issued his Dictate which the ringleader heeded by reversing and accelerated in the dark down a sloping pathway that slithered to lead nowhere and certainly did not represent any driving back.

"Ah, Chataway!" the leader proceeded to turn to George, his face unrecognizable beneath his helmet. But George suddenly perceived himself in a wry and nutty mood, unwilling to engage in small talk or exchange any pleasantries.

"Come on, man, why would they be recruiting in a war zone? Do you even have any explanation for that ill-conceived and tasteless allegation?" his words splatted out as if he were underground inhaling mud.

"But why do you care?" the leader shot right back, hurrying to conclusions without rhyme or reason, evidencing the great stress he was under. "They were government agents looking to kill who they thought assassinated a puto yesterday by the name of — something beginning with J — Juan Carlos Delfin, I recall now." The leader was diffident, fixated instead on scrolling through messages on his hand-held phone.

"And..." George sought to tease out more of the well-known story underlying the motive.

"Apparently they thought it was us, the great evil empire, who committed or was involved in the puto's murder." The leader looked across and through George. "And Chataway, to let you know, we don't care if we did or did not participate in the murder since we green-light putos for sport like hunting for animals. If one of us, did it, congratulations! If we didn't, we had our information wrong — which in this god-forsaken territory can happen all the time... Now to your question on recruiting, I don't have to answer it, apart from reminding you of the well-known sad fact that this god-forsaken territory's disgusting military picks up homeless and drug-addicted male children, and in numerous particularly disgusting and tragic instances the children are neither homeless nor addicts, and hardens them in war zones where they have to prostitute themselves in exchange for food and shelter with older males as payment for what is referred to as their training, the older males also prostituting themselves amongst each other for promotions and positions, and everyone of course serving as prostitutes to the terrorists who we have been combating in this region for about eight years, ongoing and counting…"

"Then why would they be government agents, if they are really homeless and putos?"

"I haven't received orders to the contrary!" The leader, sincerely baffled by this query, whisked George aside. "Now if you will excuse me, you hardly made my day, and I have to proceed to guard this war zone from terrorists, whores, bandits, the whole damn' lot that makes up this territory's government…"

***

Left back alone with the night dew and rain dampness from the overhanging foliage dripping on his skin, George confronted his own mortality at the sight of a spectral dawn creeping a dazed pallid light among knotted trunks and roots bulging grotesquely like huge tortoise eyes above ground. Massaging his temples, he decided he had given too much thought to the matter that crawled onwards, inexorable at its own pace to mix with the light and the impending whirls of smoke and ashes of the battle soon to hit ahead, waves of an ocean entirely unlike the vast expanse of the islands behind the Parliament controlled by the sun.

Warned by the familiar hissing sound, George pirouetted and swiftly kicked the snake's head, expertly severed at its trachea by his promptly descending boot, onto wet clumps of earth. Rugged clay swept miraculously past the rigid eye, leaving intact the oddity of a double iris. As the forest was now coming to light, a rapid gust of damp wind wiped the animal's tail remains onto the creviced black stone precipice behind him.

Despondent by the memory of the many nights he had spent in these environs with these animals as friendly companions, George knelt to tenderly touch the somber amber eye with his forefinger. Feeling rejected by not being able to close the non-existing eyelid, he had to resort to caress the scales of the severed head as parting gesture.

"I am sorry," he whispered, directing his focus on the islands in unstated blind hope. The effervescence of holy terrains beckoned in the distance with calm peace uncanny in these coarse subterranean regions.

"I am not sorry, George, and I don't really want any of this news right now," Cherido, having guessed his mind, quipped above his head where he was now commandeering a pose with stiletto heels crushing firmly into the ground, combing his hair with a coquettish bright metallic pink brush. "Plus, I am not impressed by your tactic today to check along these coordinates and ensure no one penetrates the boundary line set by Ara Pacis. There are faster and better ways, such as aerial surveillance by drones already being conducted from Parliament. Chauffeur. You should put yourself into some real motion and drive us the five hours to Headquarters, pay me for the inconvenience incurred by you not picking up your phone and me having to drive all the way to Parliament, including me now refreshing myself in a ditch without a mirror, and then get moving to your own targets later on in the day." Cherido kissed the air with puckered butterfly lips, pouting bright red lipstick — he had used the car's rear mirror, George surmised — and was about to stalk back to the waiting vehicle. Evidently the sights, smells and sounds of the jungle in tune with his boudoir preferences had hastened Cherido's recovery, stymied by the sterility and asceticism of George's present modus vivendi.

"Wait — this news is a secret present only for you." George, again sickened by his malaise festering, suppurating inside his chest, unmanly, unbecoming of a soldier, reaming him, grabbed Cherido's right forearm. George deceived Cherido with the polished demeanor of Cherido's much higher up superior, forcefully reeling him back. "I want to clarify and let you into this game that regretfully is entangled with your fate and destiny."

Luscious blasé visage lifted to catch the swirls of blanched morning light with the look of a snob basking in a sun bath, Cherido rebounded, mocking the scene, including George's own present tortures, with repentant eyes seething skywards, "Oh dios, please let this chalice pass by me…"

"Okay, George? Shoot, since *that* wasn't to be," Cherido continued, miffed by being detained by George as well as distracted by the continued bubbles of rage from his own heart, since he had gotten himself into this mess by his own hysteria.

"Stefan — finito, hm? Does that ring your bell my dear? The climax of your one-hundred-thousand-man-strong one generation without heir or real fortune?" George's tone was cheerful as he pantomimed swinging a machete at Cherido. He hissed, resentment boiling over: "But no, Stefan - finito, that would be too cheap, low life, vulgar psychoanalysis, in the 2000s thankfully passé! We've got more heroic things by far on our great minds…"

"Thanks, George, felicades — congratulations, no? Game is over, truth told. Let's go." Cherido was amiable as possible while feigning repulsion at his own triumphalism over what he couldn't control, and in particular not now having made himself out so wonderfully for Burrito this morning who instead — cold slap in his devout face — had just turned out to be many miles away. In secret and in the grips of dangerous delusion he preferred to interpret for himself as blinded by real burning passion, Cherido wondered when Burrito would add a new victory since, from the demise of what Cherido wrongly imagined as Burrito's rival in power JC through the immediate future, he now racked up real impending war, bloodbaths, hopefully a holocaust of the entire territory as trophy corpses.

"No, Cherido, I need to tell you how," George whispered continuing the charade in the form of an alternative and necessary political elucidation. He looped the love crazed Cherido flapping in his grip into the real occurrences of the last few days. "Once Burrito learned from the first call about the Arab name on his cell then panicked, disconnected and defunct, which most likely is the real reason why you couldn't reach him, and came running to me instead, having dialed an old number, that he had to be green-lighted for 'political reasons', he became crazy loco, running away from Headquarters like an animal. I mobilized my people to find him — and you know where they found him?" He asked wryly. The day of burning, exploding, distorting passions had not belonged only to Burrito, and George was no longer shaking frail.

"Let me guess — the pitch-black still abyss of water?" Cherido stated flatly.

"Homie, how'd you know what separates you from Stefan? You're too astuto, so callate — shut up — and let me finish." George gripped his wrist as if in arrest, pounding Cherido swaying like a reed in heat mercilessly with his words. "We grabbed him when he embarked to cross the divide and took him up to Parliament ourselves to confess," George clarified.

"And what did he tell you?" Cherido feigned perturbation but intrigued while whining "ouch…" at imaginary blows.

"First he acted like sordo mudo — deaf mute — in fear so we had to rough him up with some punches. Then he told us he had been on his way to hang out in Parliament in wait for the right time and place to arrest His Eminence and label him the terrorist par excellence cajoling with each and every enemy of the Americans while pocketing all of the money — then he'd lie to the Americans, saying His Eminence lied to them about his, Burrito's, alleged brothel initiative which, by the way, as an aside, already is one hundred thousand men strong and invincible for that and other reasons — but with His Eminence so elusive and difficult to catch by anyone including the head of his own army, Burrito would also implement Plan B, consisting in copying from the Parliament's computers and files the identities of all business partners, to show that he Burrito hated all putos whether real, actual, or still to be produced and trained and would place himself in a spree to assassinate all putos whether in the territory or abroad — and then he would call the American government both to denounce everyone in the territory besides himself and for his own protection." George ended with eyes zigzagging up and down, chaining guffawing laughter to his insides to prevent eruption. Wisely, he restrained himself from querying Cherido what he thought would happen once the Americans arrived expecting denunciation.

"And you believe his story, George?" Cherido posed this question somewhat incredulously, now fashioning himself to have been the victim of a random homophobic crime at brunch rather than set up by the U.S. of A and this other one (George? Stefan?) to be the fall guy for his lover's now apparent planned rampages and murders. "Because why would the Americans believe Burrito's story over yours when you're Stefan's number two and the one to whom Burrito reports and from which he draws his information? You are making yourself look rather weak, dear George!"

"Listen, Burrito would have made it look believable when he would have called in the Americans with me as a witness to denounce even you — since you're fair game as you're a minor in their eyes and would not be allowed to bear arms or defend yourself. Now, why would he go as far as denouncing even a child, unless what he said was true?" George asserted as what rang to Cherido as only a semi-plausible explanation given his lack of familiarity with the meaning of the terms "minor" and "child" as used by George.

"Well, George, how do you explain then that the American agent did not proceed to arrest me in truth and fact, when he had me in front of him and on the floor? Isn't that what he would have done? Would there have been any fertile ground for the proposed allegations by Burrito which, not even made, you have spent time adjacent to a war zone to elucidate? Instead, he addressed me just like any low life puto and then just dropped the case... How do you explain that I found you chatting so amicably with the Americans on the phone, if Burrito would have been in any position to trump your relations?" Sobered by the exotifying first rays of the sun, Cherido gleamed ethereal against the still wet bark clutching his arms behind his back as if he admitted to arrest. The transformation from howling hustler to exquisite icon of truth was stupendous indeed.

"Easy." George hit the bark above Cherido's head with his fist and dust, particles and small spiders and ants drizzled instead of a bridal veil onto Cherido's expectant visage. "First, you are a one generation operation. After you, there won't be anyone, not even a Jesus Christ, which for me personally is hard to believe, and that might serve as consolation in your predicament... Second, you know the antics that consume your existences when not in frigid black uniform on order and command, even though what you do when locked in those cages is all good and illustrious, I must admit. All the whirlwinds and incendiaries of your passions, I am sorry, I must say, Cherido, ravage and devour your presences and survivals in this world, and Burrito's most recent escapade, sad but true, is another incident of the same exuberance, uncontrolled and completely deviant, besides that..." For a split-second

George hesitated, the same demonic glare zigzagging his sight while he whisked dust, particles and insects off his shirt with his free hand, then he proceeded, deviating. In essence he had acted not unlike Burrito, even though unlike Burrito in complete secret. "Where were you for the time immediately preceding his archetypal outburst? Getting your hair and nails done, luxuriating somewhere in the capital of the adjacent country. Where was he? With someone else or maybe with two or three..." George proffered as clear and logical explanation. "How do you get a fire to burn down? By letting it burn out... What were the other doubts and queries you have?" he asked.

"3:30 a.m. and you're up and about? Why aren't *you* tending to *your* hair and nails too, and why are the Americans on a killing spree destroying all the evidence?" Cherido reiterated with a sigh.

"Listen, hombre," George veered back to the safety of political explanation, "the Americans on a certain level behave very differently even though, the same as your beloved Burrito, they love green-lighting individuals connected to yet other individuals, whether directly or by the means of intermediaries, who in any way can be interpreted as causing damage to their financial economic interests, carving TERRORIST on their chests, making them fall into the rivers of universal conscience, drowning and floating away with the currents — and then they go to their separate locations — I had to come back to Parliament to make sure none of Burrito's tipos would still look for Stefan, but evidently he had been calmed by the blood rage of having embraced a corpse." George was definitely very convinced.

"And why wouldn't the Americans gather the evidence against me and why would they destroy the alleged evidence against us by killing everyone?" Cherido pressed as a compound question, primarily to buy time, since, despite his illusory angelic-satanic somersaults, he knew well where all was heading, better racing without brakes.

"Because the Americans already have the evidence, photographed it, memorized it, don't want to touch it without latex gloves. The evidence is in the files of Resource Global, my dear, who operates and staffs those sites."

Cherido now remained quiet and willfully dubious at such cold logic assault which George sought to dispel. "Well, I exaggerated a little, to make the point. Let me say the Americans could have all the evidence, would they set their minds to it or really want the actual evidence and facts. Let me show you the earnings of Resource Global." George was about to pull up entire sheets loaded with numbers on his iPhone when he decided to the contrary, apprehensive of the added confusion such visuals would cause to Cherido's child-like inflamed and scorching mind. "It is actually quite simple. When the Americans suspect Stefan's business somehow and however convoluted may cause damage to their financial economic reason, they attack the sites to kill the terrorists they claim Stefan has been hiring to produce wealth for the territory. And of course, by labeling them terrorists, gay, putos, you name it, they exacerbate their opposition and propel them further into the arms of whoever has been radicalizing them in rightful defense of this territory... Then the Americans leave, turn a blind eye or fall asleep, it doesn't matter, and their good friends the rogue goons come in to loot, loiter and steal and sell to the lowest bidder suiting their allies, which Resource Global doesn't know in each and every instance. They do know when they find themselves trading in the basement instead of on the stock exchange... What happens next? It is an old game, my dear, and I am getting sick and tired of explaining it to myself, since you at present are dozing and dreaming and not listening at all... And maybe I do the same. In the reality which isn't ours, either Stefan or Resource Global has to make a move soon to exterminate the pest left and created by the terrorist-hunting Americans. Stefan because he tends to know better the vermin's locations, Resource Global because it is his resources and he prides himself to have expended the finances to build a private security corporation for that purpose, which he might as well use." George ended staring over Cherido's head, bland eyed and exasperated into the low blazing morning sun, shrugging his shoulders at the cookie-cutter checkerboard, now the territory, carved into a high-precision war zone. He could not believe that after all these years, the parties still spun the same tale, pacifying himself with the knowledge it had all become aggravated to the hilt by the many statuses of forces agreements, laws and regulations piling up over the years to make the conundrum not only unmanageable but also a tinder box ready to explode.

"So, they are all putos of sorts selling themselves to the highest bidder, the Americans, Stefan and Mr Chataway?" Cherido again tried to trump George. "The more important question is how did you know that line about the Americans already having all the evidence?" Cherido was sly.

"Because in my past life they took me out one night — thankfully without managing to also execute this order to kill me — took me out one night as part of my mission here, at the time, to learn from *this* life." George disguised his bona fide ongoing attempt of rescuing Cherido from what lay immediately ahead as also covering his own past hideous foray into the strategies of survival as a child or young teenager threatened by the care of a raging mad alternative father and fatherland figure. Cherido must stay here in the territory, no matter the success or failure of any pending holocaust constellations.

"Not much to learn from those also drug-addicted American putos, right? They are often late to arrive at those sites in any event, causing all those last-minute desperate flares and smoke of their hit, miss, and runs." Cherido was indignant. "But if he were a puto, why would Burrito still connect with me after three long years..." Cherido waxed dreamily again, which made George laugh loudly.

"Because I was after him, remember, just recently, and he escaped or plopped back into his senses, whichever feels more appropriate to your romantic sensibilities, and mentally he is convinced he needs whatever help he can get... Come on, my dear, his army, which is your army, is a well-oiled machine, which frees up his time to luxuriate in his own shortcomings, and how he could possibly resolve his many problems..." George hoped the brazen truth would goad and not crush Cherido in his ardent hopes for an amorous future.

"It's believable." Cherido maintained his doubts. "But George, how do I not know you are the mastermind of the conspiracy to protect yourself and your high and noble position in Ara Pacis while putting me at risk?" He spun this last audacious question.

"My dear Cherido, I implied clearly if I have not told you forthright, you give me RESPETO, I return your RESPETO. You don't probe into my past life or lives and into people who don't concern you, I won't judgmentally implicate your dalliances for anything which they might

114

not be... I have nothing to lose or gain in any conspiracy — you can ask Stefan, who will just be confused and hand the question back to you..." He provided a post-hoc rationalization as if Cherido really was in the position to confer with Stefan over any of this. "For you, the best is that you may get what you appear to be asking for: A safe place in this haven, where you can live and maybe even prosper, right? We can bring justice to the many murders of whichever style. Punto final — final point."

George started walking to return to the vehicle and out of the now dribbling sun rays with Cherido intentionally trailing behind, contemplating childishly and with information far from complete. How this story left more questions than answers, such as why would his dear Burrito paint himself as the accomplice and also the vanquisher? Why would Burrito have been under the impression the Americans would care about any of the mayhem he planned, since for them, wasn't it all just about killing whom they already and in advance according to their own *a priori* theories had decided they will kill? And how macabre were the mechanics of justice as purported by George, this last question he posed himself, maybe an accurate one?

***

Cherida's strong slender figure glided spider-like from the upper region of the tall tree overhead, along the bark of the tree keeping itself in darkness. Without a sound, he adroitly landed on the hood of the vehicle, intercepting George about to board.

"The borderline is clear," he reported. "No one is there, just the American patrol and other of their patrols further down, all at measured distances and on their side, the war zone's side, only."

"Why are the Americans patrolling *our* border?" Cherido cried from the front seat. The answer, which contained among others, the definitions of the term "children," abstruse to Cherido, was not imparted to him as George and Cherida simultaneously boarded the vehicle and proceeded to speed land inwards along the boundary line. "So, neither your tactics are candid today, nor your mouth work particularly adept, since you are silent..." Cherido proceeded unflinching.

"You shut up," George teased, "we are driving to the island. You deserve a vacation, after the horrors I just put you through." Imprinting the air in front of his face with an orchestra of tiny gossamer kisses at a loss of how else to spend his time and in order to test the water- and kiss-proofness of his lip gloss, Cherido kept himself away from George while Cherida resorted to brooding on the back seat. "Just remember: Keep Burrito nice and sprightly and yourself far from the glories of death..." At this Cherido interrupted his kissing escapade as if puzzled by a paradox, exclaiming:

"Then why the island? And which one?"

"I was born there," George proffered, "the one towards the ocean."

"What made you want to be born on that island?" Cherido queried fastidiously, intoning he might be on to something, then backsliding since what he had learned about his own destiny these past twenty-four hours tingled him as even more monstrous still. "There is only foliage, earth, trees and water... Better to be born in Paris, like me."

"Picking up my mother," George explained, passing the second American patrol that ignored the vehicle and stared rigidly ahead, six feet of the demarcation line along the coordinates in even discipline between them.

"You were born in the gutter, which is the ghetto, or the other way around, however you prefer," Cherida opined from the backseat.

"Well, it isn't all gold that glitters..." Cherido was evasive, determined to not deign a glance at the other two for the remainder of the ride. Cherido was ostensibly really convinced by the truth of his own high and distinguished birthplace.

After two hours of speeding, with American patrols passing at the same distance of six feet camouflaged as brown ochre smudges, the thick foliage gradually lifted to reveal the expanse of the ocean. The vehicle sailed further and further from the border line, towards the water blazing with morning sun.

"Here there are no more patrols," Cherida articulated as if commanded to say so, twirling his gun around his forefinger.

"Hell no," Cherido admonished. "Here is paradise. I am going to go for a swim."

"Wait with disrobing yourself until I have parked the car," George warned, unwilling to drive a nude male model through any black-clad sentries they might still encounter. "We are not there yet."

The broad pathway covered in white rock baked from garlands of sun light was otherwise eerily empty. The small island came into view. The entanglement of burgeoning foliage deftly adrift on alabaster sand slithered languorously into azure waters, giving the entire scenery a breathtaking and hallucinogenic appeal.

"Are you sure you don't want me to come along?" Cherido meddled in George's thoughts, evidently taken in by the beauty of the day.

"Dear, I think we can handle this part solo. Just don't deposit your clothes in my lap, and you'll see you will live to see a better day…" *Than head whore of one of the meanest men alive*, George kept this truth known to him to himself.

The perfect person for his job, he was appalled, if not revolted by the sight of nude young men of whom at times he would see plenty. He parked underneath overhanging foliage a few feet from the worn primitive looking wooden bridge leading the three hundred feet to the island and folded Cherido's snakeskin uniform before depositing it onto the backseat. Diaphanous rose-shimmering fingernails pinched his forearm, Cherido whispering into his ear conspiratorially, "You are not dreaming," breezing a soft wet kiss before he slid out of the vehicle, a wisp of a wind, adding curtly, "You *were* born here, in truth and fact!" From the look of his burnished dark mahogany skin, Cherido spent more hours buffing and depilating himself than mere mortals were able to imagine could be spent on such activities.

The delicate ballerina figure carried itself with the prowess of a lion towards and into the undisturbed glittering water. Thick black hair swayed mightily before he disappeared immediately and at great speed. Had he not known better, George would have feared that even a glimpse of the individual with his mother on the island would adversely impact the trust of a luminous being such as Cherido in him and any subsequent cooperation. But today as he crossed the bridge with Cherida in tow, he fought to convince himself that it would not now soon be the other way around, his stomach in knots.

A clear dark brown eye winked through the peep hole covered with iron bars as his knock on the pinewood door was greeted by a loud, lively female voice. "Hello." The main area of the house was petit, log cabin style. It could have been a *Little House on the Prairie* set except for the fact that its wooden beams were decayed by termites and its square glass windows decorated by flower-motif curtains were counterbalanced by the many iron bars clad to the outside. On his eighteenth birthday nine years ago, his mother had told him this area of the house had been left unchanged since about the time he was born. Puzzled as to why he needed to reach the age of eighteen for this knowledge to be imparted to him, George remembered having spent the day attempting to read one of his father's books on the ancient Spartans. He had hardly made any progress, sweating in the scorching heat of the day, imperiled by the fact that at that time, safety on this island signified no corpses fraying the crystalline waters with blood as well as silence undisturbed by the screeching of birds fleeing bullets. Since then, a larger add-on had been constructed in L-shape to the left, leaving an opening for a glass door, at the present time open ajar and welcoming a fragrant warm breeze. George felt her hair tingle his chin while she clasped his hand.

"Your Eminence, sorry we are late, there was a situation with a hysterical nutcase that had to be resolved," Cherida bantered, even though while at the border line he had been unable to decipher the precise nature of the interaction between George and his brother. He gave a stealthy glance outside, catching a glimpse of the unperturbed silence now burning brightly with sunlight and ushered George and his mother several feet inside locking the door shut where he then remained to guard.

After shaking her head presumably over Cherida's mistaken upbeat tone, Moura smiled widely and grasped George around the waist firmly and repeatedly. "Bienvenido a nuestra casa — welcome to your home, I should say!" At several instances they flickered fused together as they meandered through the shadows cast by the iron bars protecting the windows and the beams holding the ceilings, until they unlocked and disengaged, melting into the sun at the glass door. "Let me take you to meet the new Burrito." Her words fell on him heavily, as if on deaf ears, and he wished she had said something else. Despite the log-cabin feel, the house had a second floor with two rooms to accommodate the numerous surveillance and other secret activities conducted there by the territory's armed forces. Moura had the privilege of having her own small third room where sometimes she slept when the hours between the end of mission and four a.m. the next morning were too few to warrant return to Parliament. George had been able to survey that very small room and had been pleased by its complete seclusion from the remainder of the set-up. Even its window looked straight out onto the open ocean, unlike most of the other windows that focused land inwards, and its door could be safely locked, as occurred when Stefan switched places with her and sealed himself in solitude for many hours on end. But now that she was not there in seclusion, couldn't she have said, maybe… George clenched his jaw shut to swallow burning tears. The large room around the bent of the L shape on the ground floor had no adornments and was new. The smell of lacquer as if fluoresced from the dark impenetrable sheen of the walls. The white beach extended clearly visible through the rugged foliage that covered a large window. George looked away constraining himself from lapsing into a dream.

"Meet Marco, the new Burrito," she exclaimed gayly, introducing yet another shadow figure. Dressed in the same black Armani, Moura donned the appearance of swooshing and sparkling brand new through her surroundings as if she had been recently purchased or bartered at a luxury department store such as Saks Fifth Avenue where, however, she would never set foot notwithstanding her wealth. She had the flair of a polished storefront mannequin; no one would care what couture she wore since her countenance was as lively and engaging as an incandescent starlit sky with sparkling eyes that could raise the dead from their graves. 'Little does she care about shadow figures,' George admitted to himself. She commented to the stony hushed youth seated on the windowsill, leg winkled to demonstrate readiness yet a certain sense of noninvolvement denoting accomplishment and status. "Look at Marco — he is dressed like I years ago working in the forest and countryside among the graves, even though with noted improvement in make and provenance!"

"I know that Your Eminence, I am dressed that way to show you respect for your dignified and honorable work in the countryside. Clearly no one has forced me to dress that way." Marco readily consumed Moura's pretext with a sudden smile of pride, revealing gold-capped teeth. Moura's pretext was genuine to the extent that she held those who labored in the forest and countryside in profound respect given the accomplishments over the past two and a half decades, as well as disingenuous since she never intended to be dressed in such garb for a meeting with her son.

"Ah Marco!" George, adopting her same put-on gaiety, examined the muscular yet subtle figure with crests of wavy curls of black hair, Siamese cat-like marbled colored eyes and dark skin. At twenty-five, Marco was older than the one hundred thousand whose ages tended to peak in their early twenties. At present he had retired from the dreamy obtuse squinting at daylight since he had spent the past few years navigating and familiarizing himself with the territory in deep night. He was dressed in the same black while notably he distinguished himself from mother and son by wearing expertly applied makeup rivaling Cherido, including a deeper darker brown shade of lipstick, mascara and sparkly black eyeshadow. He sported tattoos on his fingers and arms which appeared as Chinese since they were deviations or alterations of gang characters.

"Marco, the star of a future movie? Mucho gusto — pleasure to meet you," George's biting sarcasm caused Marco to glow at the attention bestowed on him and make the effort to get up and greet George with a hearty hug — which George deflected with a handshake to thwart any possible transference given his recent horrendous accomplishment of having completed his brutal merciless training twenty-four hours a day, three hundred sixty-five days a year. Moura tittered discreetly, poking George in his ribs over her Marco, more a firefly at night, being analogized to a film star. George was beleaguered by Marco's fluid yet precocious mien, especially the dark sharp makeup lending a dart like effect. Marco appeared a well-oiled machine in comparison with Burrito's crude battle-hardened self-made image, including his thin preoccupied smile, whether he was genuine in his smile or beguiling himself.

George, playing the role of the patriarch in the room, commenced to engage in small talk since the essence of their communications could only occur in code or secret language, such as "You are happy that your worst is over, now that hell will start?" "Couldn't you have waited outside, since I have to tell something to my mother?" "And your predecessor or-soon-to-be, did you know that one can get him out of jail?" to which Marco responded succinctly and as positively as possible. The last bit veered from the code language requirement in its almost clarifying allusion to one soon to be defunct. The most notable presence for George was Moura who, in her starry radiance, epitomized a simultaneous deafness, muteness, insensibility to reality and in this sense clung to George in a sudden frightful premonition of imminent departure. Even while George stroked her shoulder, bit the inside of his lips bloody to prevent himself from whispering into her ear, it was clear that the looming absence and separation imprinted in her subconscious was a source of stress for her. Stoically and displaying a healthy survival dose of ignorance, George in his decision to play his secret part in recent events had convinced himself that nothing but the daylight schism between her and him could cause her any distress, even of the most severe kind. To keep up the necessity of a united front, George had playfully taught her such sentiments to be symptomatic of her having spent much time with the likes of Marco and the process they epitomized of being broken into pieces and pounded into the ground to then be built up in the image of defense of Ara Pacis, the result of which she had been gazing upon all day. Fear of separation was her reflection of the division between hell and heaven she had witnessed Marco and his likes to scale, so George desired her to think.

The time-consuming enterprise of coming back down to earth and not liking it reminded George that they had to leave — lest Cherido, having raided what could be had of the expanse of the ocean, came back to his senses and to real calamity.

When George announced that they had to leave for the Parliament now, Moura appeared surprised by the brevity of the announcement. Pulling him into the tiny adjoining kitchen, she pleaded for George since, standing adjacent to him, mimicking lovingly spoiled demeanor, she had prepared a special breakfast of fried bull's testicles for all of them, including Cherido and Cherida. George examined them in a frying pan, their spicy condiments wafting divinely.

He characteristically did not want to be insensitive or in a hurry for a mission that, worst come to worst, he suddenly again in her loving presence feared, panicked, could be his last. But he was apprehensive of missing Burrito's appointment with Stefan today and preventing what now could degenerate into the greatest of evils. Moura's presence beside him compelled him rapidly to that leap of faith. He recollected that when in Washington D.C. after meeting his fiancée the email queries from his contacts at the DOD had been sufficiently frantic in demands for meetings once in Ara Pacis that cutting off all contact and sending a final bill represented the most feasible resolution. Luckily, here he had the legitimate pretext of the time pressure placed upon them by Cherido lurking outside which prevented him from indulging in the special breakfast. Moura then insisted that they leave the breakfast for the rainforest animals outside and placed them in a plastic container to deposit in the foliage behind the waiting vehicle. "Many thanks," George commended her to which she responded with a bashful yet proud smile.

"When this is over, which will be within this week, I guarantee there will be more time to share together and opportunity for many, many more fried bull's testicles — right now unfortunately we really have to depart to Parliament, she — I mean he — is waiting for us outside… Please understand and forgive me." George's apology together with a tender kiss on the top of her head in anticipatory gratitude since she would be here in this kitchen preparing the many more fried bull's testicle was met with sighs and shy sadness interrupted stealthily by Marco rapping his knuckles on the door frame. "Why is he 'outside waiting for us'?" he asked, obviously worried about Cherido's involvement in the last days that were now to come.

"Just as escort — you know we couldn't get to and around Burrito much without him." George tried to reassure him.

"Ay, I know. He is why I hate living in this town- you know… When I started out, he used every occasion to ignore me, prancing around with his entourage of twelve- to fifteen-year-olds…" George gently cut him off from narrating his life monologue, replete as it was with ignorance at machismo overtures given the many years spent as watch dog in the woods, offering instead, "Marco, with your permission, why don't we wait to talk about such matters, hombre-a-hombre, man-to-man, in private at Parliament at a later time? Are you all ready, or do you want to spend some more time circling or patrolling this same island?"

"Yes, I am all done." Marco pointed at his military-style duffle bag adjacent to the blue sofa — covered in plastic swaths which provoked George's curiosity since plastic-covering furniture was more of a middle-class than campesino interior decorating style in this territory.

"Just one question, Marco, would you know why she covered this sofa in plastic? My mother doesn't really like to make such things so... elegante," George posed as Marco lugged his duffle bag towards the front door. Moura had snuck out with the plastic container, her departure noticed by the breath of fresh but empty, unoccupied air left behind in the dim ante chamber.

"She said she gave birth to you on that sofa," Marco clarified. "Don't you notice its age from its discolored wooden edges?" He equivocated from within a world in which twenty-six meant grand old age. "I am pleased that you like it."

***

The blazing sun pelted on the vehicle and the scene unfolding around it. Cherido had pulled it outside of the shadow of the foliage so he could sun himself nude on its hood. From within yet another world in which age raced backwards as it sped onwards, Cherido had circled the island with the celerity of wind, landing on his back on hot metal, the scorching sensation of which he visibly enjoyed, wet hair splattered all around him smelting and gnawing into ore. Moura fidgeting around facilitated his descent from the hood where self-possessed self-loving Cherido was enthroned with hugs, beaming smiles, phrases of reassurance like, "Look at the gorgeous you, soon you'll be black like molten metal and clinging and embracing the sun... What is up with you, Cherido, isn't being one of the angels enough, now you want to outshine heaven itself, and like what, a shooting star that will emblazon paradise itself with... ever more heat... This heat that you are looking for, Cherido my dear... is what robs many of their minds..." and her haunting wail as she flung his clothes at him from the driver's seat in a seeming effort to restrain him from charring to ashes.

Cherido, dressed in a flash, in turn embraced her, and cradling her and lifting her in his arms, rocked her like a baby, even caressing her enthralled features until they both gurgled some indecipherable gibberish, leavening Moura's wail into pearly laughter and finger-pointing at Cherido. "I always knew it will be you, you maverick and king of tricks, you... and you... I am not braced for any surprise at all!" which Cherido did not know how to respond to, given the shockingly confidential nature of her insinuations. George had barely dared to breathe during her scenic projection of him on Cherido. Now he cautiously approached and whispered a magic trick for Cherido, directly into his ear and at rapid speed "History is interpreted by those who vanquish." Cherido cried out, grimacing stealthy as if pulling back a pack of galloping horses. He dropped Moura against the volcano-hot side door which quelled her finger-pointing and had a calming effect. She smiled blissfully as if falling into a trance of slumber and was now oblivious to her surroundings.

"It's not goodbye but until we meet as soon as possible," George chimed to Cherido, intimating the dear's regret at having dropped his mother. He shook his head. "Friend, learning who is your friend and who your enemy is one of the greatest feats in life." He picked up the plastic container she had dropped next to the vehicle and proceeded to empty its contents into the foliage. He turned back rapidly so any caution he would express at the hissing of snakes would not disturb the reverence in which he held them. The sun inched briskly towards its zenith, and Cherida and Marco were standing impatiently by a second armored Land Rover Marco had pulled from underneath the grove.

Before they could scathingly remind him of their tardiness, George instructed them to take the Land Rover, whereas Moura, awakening, apologized for their delay, addressing Cherido. "Hola dear."

Cherido returned her gaze, his eyes hued orange. "Back in this world, my dear, hm? What have you gotten yourself into now?" She apparently had a knowing recognition of Cherido beyond Cherido's own comprehension.

As crabby Cherido didn't deign to look back at, let alone respond to Moura, overcoming the awkward moment George motioned her to follow him and return onto the onerous bridge towards the middle from where they could view a slab of undisturbed white sand. Moura heaved a deep breath and rolled her eyes and George dropped his jaw, stunned at her profound foreknowledge and alertness which cued him to clarify. He plucked her sunglasses from the front pocket of her black Armani to place them discreetly on her nose. "That is where Kevin soon will land, as you so well know, and to appease that Cherido like the heat you're presently emitting blinding me as well, please put these on and don't let me see you without them…"

She opted to press her head into his shoulder as if dissolving in ennui. "So what, if that is where Kevin will land? He'll proceed to Parliament, is that what you mean, dear? Just now you seemed afraid of snakes, and now you're trying to speak to me in tongues… They will arrive at Parliament sneaking through the underwood, with our Cheridos and Cheridas sneaking right along them and about them… Face to face, each side will pretend to not see the other. Arriving, they will find everything closed and empty, barren hard rock, even the Cheridas and Cheridos will have disappeared or be in the process to… Well, I should leave the bathrooms open, since the ocean will be far…" "

George acquiesced that this arrangement was fine with him — he'd bring Cherido, his newfound friend, along for the fun "for his added protection" he added as a sleight of hand, shooting a glare at Cherido some distance away as if alerting that he had not found safety yet. Moura avoided reacting to this except like Mona Lisa. Her eyes were cast down, her smile disingenuous. George considered that since his mother, like Cherido, could have multi-hued eye color at her caprice, she presently could also smile genuinely or disingenuously like Mona Lisa depending on the spectator — not that George could fully discern at all times from her smile when she was being truthful. She outshone him in expediency by far.

***

After both Cherida and Marco successfully turned behind them in their vehicle into the rainforest and along the border line, Cherido pondered on the back seat. "George, where are the youths among the American patrol six feet to our right? I only see old men!" referring to males mostly in their thirties.

"Because people your age are not in the work force or professionals there as they are in this territory. These adults that you see are actually quite young. The older ones advance up the ladder to desk work or else they are in trouble, until they become like grandparents taking care of what you see to your right, which are the children." George surprisingly had a fluid description of demography.

"It's sad for the children here to grow up without their parents, of course, but that's where the army comes in, we become their family — right, Cherido?" Moura winked at him, her eyes hueing green. As George before had motioned on the bridge concerning his safety, Cherido did not respond to her glance but looked down at his gold-ringed fingers, still marooned nonplussed by the lack of complete information. Jealous, George made a mental note to file his mother's attempt to bait Cherido as if they had a past or present pact.

"That's the way life is, Your Eminence." Cherido perked up. "When we were younger and poor, we suffered because there was no work. Now that we are older, we get by on my labor, my fixing the problems of who has such a hard time remaining as perky and cheerful as he was when my age, and by living at Headquarters where we only pay by the means of our labor but the building is ours." He sighed, omitting the other source of revenue Moura absent-mindedly alluded to earlier in reference to the army that raises its children: that is, the ill-gotten proceeds of dying at one generation young at the bare sight or smell of an order or command.

The rainforest scenery was as familiar to George as a ride through a dreamscape, not requiring awakening. Deep purple shadows of high trees and foliage burgeoned at known intervals, outdoing the American patrol in their weathered precision. Even the scatters of moist black rock overgrown in places with scrubs of thick moss and the swampy rivulets coiling arduously amidst gnarled roots clawing into the innards of the earth mystified with a beckoning presence brighter than the light of day. As George kept on accelerating, the Land Rover behind them bounded up and down in harmony and all became animated with the promise of the goal gradually closing in ahead.

Cherido, the sole one feeling some malaise, silently popped two large fluorescent-colored chunks of herbal preparations without water from his black purse, which snapped open and closed by the means of a silver skull applique, as if in the attempt to hush away both life and death simultaneously. He pulled from the array he carried around of an herbal candy story for him and others on anti-anxiety medicine, anti-depressants or other narcotics. Burrito told him he'd absorb them much faster without water by letting them dissolve in his mouth like a holy Eucharist, with no sacrilege of the metaphor intended. He wanted to fall into profound slumber until Parliament — especially given the perilous spinning ride meant to keep everyone's spirits high and ready and the lack of any real inner friend, let alone his own facsimile. Plus, at present he'd rather die from the toxicity of herbal intake than be alive and undergo the aftermath of returning yet again to this earth.

Thankfully, Cherido's dream consisted of playing flight attendant — which was his career objective as a seven-year-old since people would need and revere him — on a sleek Lear jet like that of Burrito's multi-millionaire acquaintances — flying along the Equator around the globe. But there were too many flight attendants per passenger so each vied to maintain their status and rank within the dream jet, leaving Cherido at a loss over how to help his colleagues. He relegated himself to a servile, supine position, picking up used trays, garbage and newspapers of passengers to be helpful as even his airborne cohorts were as competitive in fulfilling their job duties as his colleagues at Headquarters lest they be laid off and replaced by the revolving door of the ever young and more beautiful. As he awoke approaching Parliament, he thought to himself, instead of reminiscing over any contemplated suicide, that he had done well to displace the First Purser to command the rank and title commensurate with his charm to please others, and when, where and if he had not yet so done, he should promptly and immediately.

***

"You slept a lot, Cherido," George commented as they entered the maze of the security zone's congested arteries of winding rock and trees. "A

127

donde vamos, papa? Where are we going, papa?" Cherido, without batting an eyelid, seemed hardly pleased.

"The Parliament — a secret between us." George yawned sarcastically since at this point what fatalistic difference would it make if Cherido was found out and by whom — he believed in the American justice precept of "innocent until proven guilty" and that he would have to help him out if in the future threatened with prosecution for Burrito's murder under trumped-up, false pretenses.

"I know its location, George." Cherido strived to please.

"Bueno, good, Cherido, adelante," George exhorted. "How is everyone else?"

"What do you think? I took a deep swim in the ocean!" Cherido piped up, incensed to say the least. "I was like a mummy from the dirt and desert storms! Why you ask, what did you think my life is like?" Cherido's hair and visage indeed were scrubbed clean and portended the captivating allure of a fifteen-year-old. "And look at your poor mother Moura? She bantered with me to the extent of being thrown against the hot metal of an armed vehicle?"

"Cherido, just pretend this was your anniversary outing with Burrito to an island more exotic and picturesque," George teased him in vain since he found no humor in this proposed adventure.

George couldn't countenance the sad sight of Cherido primitively scrubbed clean and sullied by foresight to his innermost in his Sunday best which had become his Sunday worst. "I am very sorry for all the dirtiness but we're almost there," he apologized to him in the back seat.

"At least if there were always water to clean oneself, look at me so ugly from this trip called life." Cherido, annoyed, asserted the self-consciousness if not self-possession of your average image-conscious teenager — which he clearly was not — while shaking out his almost dry locks now entangling to assemble into a jagged halo around his head.

"And you know you haven't been the only one and the worst off in this state, dear Cherido," George added gently but authoritatively to reinforce his awareness of others' dilemmas similarly situated to him. "I myself didn't have a moment's peace, much less what you call cleanliness at the time that I decided to stick on and stick on through, even though I did get my share of burning metal... right, Mom?" George elicited confirmation if not jocular sarcasm from Moura, who once had been equally obsessed as Cherido with her own distorted damaged appearance, the concern having vanished into thin air with her own dives into the deep, deep ocean...

"Besides burning metal, I'd add all nine circles of Dante's hell including lust, gluttony, greed, wrath, heresy, violence, fraud, and finally treachery, which you walked through willingly and now truthfully state you got your share," Moura pushed back.

"Do *you* want to shoot missiles in a closed office off your bedroom, Cherie? Were you always such a smart-assed propriety-obsessed credulous naïve?" George returned her insult that he thought exceeded the parameters of civility, to which Moura stuck out the tip of her tongue. "You'd know a mother's concern if you had any life experience, dear..."

"Did you teach me any?" George snapped back, the stress of the coming days now looming over him incited by the mention of burning metal, together with the insight that no, he might not have sufficient experience for what lay ahead. "Or did you get me and Dad all messed up and confused and hence left me dangling over... how would I describe it, a dark area?"

"You see, Cherido — we are all stuck in this together — and it will be over soon." George hoped to divert his mother by the means of calling out to the back seat. Then Moura suddenly descended a heavy fist on his shoulder on which she rested her chin to pierce him with steely cold eyes as the vehicle came to a screeching stop.

"Why not get out and walk the last few steps on foot, so the wild animals can find you, and let me drive? You are good for the wolves, not the dogs, right now!"

"There's our destination — Parliament, around the corner!" Cherido exclaimed, elated, craning his neck to see.

George transformed his alarmed posture, pushed against the door robot-like at first and aghast, then turning human at the sight of her cat-like eyes until by coincidental subterfuge he breathed in at the same time as she breathed out and he became contrite and rueful at her sharp smile that made her features bask rosily.

"I too know it is not all gold that glitters," he remarked, emphasizing the trite, however fitting, commonplace, correcting himself, "or all metal

129

that burns," evincing politeness and consideration with his indication of some awareness of her passions even though he was far too young to comprehend. "You can stop pushing with your fist, or else you'll pierce that spot at the clavicle where one can put a dagger through my heart."

Her hand retreated slowly as she pushed her back into the seat. He could have fainted at the sight of her heart palpitating in her swelling bosom, grasping her indication of maybe, if the heavens only had mercy, *"yes, George, I know, there are ways around..."* she would not have cared. Her delicate breathing pretended contentment and appeasement at his reaching over to pat, caress the back of her hand with his forefinger. "What's with the conciliatory gesture?" she sighted, ignoring George's frightened tremor in response, steeped in raging regret for which he lacked a target. She was satisfied and not preoccupied by her own self at all. George turned off the terrain of winding arteries, followed by Cherida and Marco, onto a steep incline glistening black along the sky-rising edifice of Stefan's architectural prowess melting smoothly into the cliff. Looming like a forest of glass and mirrored edifices of foreign capitalism, George would have conjectured as any ignorant first-time visitor the stark building was used for off-shore corporate money-laundering since the territory did not have a formal economy to use them for licit purposes. Wouldn't its sky-piercing upper spire to which the edifice circumvoluted to rise assure him otherwise?

"This Tenth Circle of hell, as you call it, is for los ricos and safe," Cherido assured the two on the front seats, fumbling for greater doses of herbals in his purse. "Just look at the armed guards that are now beginning to line up and all the policing security because of that." He displayed disdain while the vehicle turned onto a large round plaza beyond which the ocean and sky melded into a fire-balling line in the distance. "That's where this territory's leadership lives and works — that is, if you really think how hard His Eminence works for our people," Cherido ended, visibly perplexed by the contradiction between the ricos and hard self-sacrificial work.

Once the two armored vehicles had pulled up to the vast portal, beckoning more like a cathedral entrance by means of its light-catching incandescence if not by the more somber aspect of its being closed at all times unless someone had to pass through, a cadre of three armed guards rushed to open the two front doors.

"What brings them here?" The guards scrutinized Marco and Cherido, appalled by the distinctive differences between the battle-hardened and boudoir-bred appearances.

George and Moura took the lead and explained. "He has just emerged from many years spent at night in the marshes below and is greeting daylight for the first time today." Pointing at Marco, George said, "Whereas he, on the other hand, has had all IDs verified and stamped by about any source imaginable, so he doesn't really have to see the light of day even today as he wafts about here in front of you..." Primed to remind him that there were high-level meetings ahead, Moura then told George to calm down and hold his leverage and wits in reserve for when needed. "Also, George, you did add me to your reservations, right, me shooting missiles in the closed office off my bedroom?" Moura dissembled, making George act all the more incensed.

"Love, why were you meant to be my mother only — nothing more, nothing less? I am not the International Red Cross or Doctors Without Borders, you know!"

They stood still for a moment in the middle of the plaza, visibly enjoying the heat of the sun after the closeted consternations during the ride. "The sun is too hot for you," Moura stated calmly. A tint of sadness paled the heated glow that quivered on her demure visage. "Look at Cherido. For him, the sun is just about right, no matter where it is placed. Cherido will not have regrets." Stung by the truth, George glanced down at her. His eyes vanished into liquid slits as he did not know whether he should laugh or cry. Spiked by distress at what he suddenly perceived as his own irresponsibility, he was immobile to respond to her hand clasping and holding his, as the murdered snake had remained impervious to his touch early this morning. Two of the guards rode the cars off to park while the third stayed within hearing range. Cherido circled around the plaza slowly in concentric circles, lost in thoughts, ignoring his brother, sporting the demeanor of sparking his spirits for an athletic competition.

"Don't you remember that I told you last night I was accosted by an American special agent at what should have been Burrito's murder scene? You said that you would take care of me forever — especially

131

after all the information I have been providing you with?" Cherido inquisitorially opened his eyes, now a purple sheen, before, elf-like, they vanished behind closing lids.

"No, no, no, Cherido," George struck back. "I don't recall ever informing you that I will take care of you. Please return with Burrito back to Headquarters after we are finished tonight since it is for your business, not MINE," George demanded.

"But this is the Tenth Circle — the safest zone in the territory — and my and your business may be very much linked in extraordinary and spectacular ways as you will live to see. I would like to Meet You in Las Vegas, even though a pun at the movie with the same name is not strictly intended, not intended by order or command at all…" Cherido, cocksure of himself, swayed gently to an inner rhythm, his hair now dry and combed cascading over his shoulder, inviting the others in his magical trance.

"And what about the expectant army, my love? You'd like to put them in rapture too or render them comatose?"

Cherido suddenly wanted to be someplace else, on his own island in the heat of the sun, as he did not thrive at all on sayings of truth specifically and on being found out more generally. A model at his own fashion show, he whisked towards the edge of the plaza, beseeching the forces of nature to blend him into the lush green panorama underneath the sparkling blue sky.

"The army?" he called back, feigning misunderstanding. "They should just go back to their work of guarding the territory. We will have no need for them here… now…" His tone faded in the distance as he had wished himself to become one and vanish into the embracing, stifling, annihilating rainforest. Looking back over his shoulder, the wind caressed his cheek, his eye visible through interweaving strands of hair shooting a fierce flare in order to lull tearful pain.

"Oh." George had an insight. "So you won't need *us* any longer?" Snuggled against each other hugging, he and Moura posed the portrait of perfect family bliss, beaming smug assured smiles.

"I might fit in better here than with the other putos at Headquarters." Cherido weighted his options, remaining nonchalant and aloof. "They are not nearly as pretty as me and by far not as tolerant as your family relations are concerned…"

Thankfully, they were interrupted by one of the guards dashing through a narrowly opening portal.

"Yes, His Eminence is available to see you," he explained, pointing at Moura and George, "whereas you…" he indicated Cherido and Cherida, "will need to do something about your weirdly clashing demeanors… And you…" to Marco's demeanor, emerging from the night and marshes, he was at a loss of what to say.

"There must be a misunderstanding since they live here and I come and go as I please, right, George?" Cherido snapped in anger, expecting red carpet treatment.

"Well, I can let in the mother and the son right away — but not the other three since they appear not to be on His Eminence's list, at least not necessarily." The guard was disdainful, wary that Cherido and Cherida were devious troublemakers.

"I need to show Marco the place since he will be appointed soon and we don't want him standing around staring holes in the air," George sternly commanded the guard. "The other two, unfortunately it is true, they come and go as they please…"

Seeking approval, he looked down at Moura hugged in his arms while the guard essayed to negotiate with Cherida and with Cherido from a distance as to why they had to do something about their appearances since it was clear they were twins but struck anyone as so bizarrely unlike it risked to threaten the common person's perception of whether the earth moved around the sun. Jacket flung over his shoulder as if he had no care in the world, Cherido suddenly strutted close, sporting a pair of racy sunglasses vying with his sequined negligee in forging a seamless mirage. "Of course, I myself wouldn't mind for the sun to move around me, in love as I am with all things hot. I could imagine others preferring the shadows and safer places."

While Cherido had no qualms to thrust out his hip and motion to the guard to feast his eyes on the lustrous tip of the knife sheath protruding from his waist band, George, who hated to delegate any authority forewarned him, yelling, "Get ready, dear, to obey some orders!"

"But George, it was entirely your fault we had that problema with dear Burrito burning himself out since you as his immediate superior weren't able to follow anyone's lead and guidance." Cherido knew the truth and thought he had the upper hand. "And you have enough problems already — do you really want to play with me about your mistakes? I just want to have some fun!" Cherido thought he had one-upped George to force his hand and look the other way while he enamored and seduced the similarly inclined guard in front of whose visage he now hovered with quivering breath. Cherido was beseeching an icon for love and wealth, which he clearly hoped would end promptly with a rendezvous in the bushes beyond and below the plaza.

Moura, resigned and flustered by the exchange, stated she needed the cool of the interior where she then also immediately proceeded. The vastness of the portal crashed shut behind her like a high wave bracing the stormy sea. George cum interlocutor tried to get Cherido to calm his senses so they could proceed with their real business but pleas and patience to him proved unavailing.

"Come on, George, if it is not all gold, it is certainly all hot that glitters…"

"Cherido, you witch, for once I will cover your expenses so you can stop wasting everyone's time, including the time of nature and of the sun you are so successfully forcing to revolve around the moon and the stars!" George, fuming over being treated rudely and with ingratitude after offering not only to save Cherido's life but also to provide him with a better future, pulled out a wad of bills to compensate Cherido for his services instead of him milking and bilking the poor guard out of his last cent, a scene the likes of which George had witnessed innumerable times in this territory's stronghold, the army.

"George, I just cannot." Indignant, Cherido flew off the handle, turning the tables as he zeroed in on the money instead of the guard as dragnet. "I need to use MY limited money for my high maintenance among other important things here — but since YOU are now begging ME, I vow to pay you back as soon as I can — that is, with the governmental bribery money that will soon come flowing once you will know the extent of my truth. So it all stays in the family, no worries, dear!" Cherido was firm in his entreaty, weaving his arm over George's shoulders with a slight massage of his taut shoulder blades, aiming to leave George resigned to sign off on this dubious arrangement with a sigh of frustration. Instead, he was met with a slap in the face so hard and severe he stumbled back while he made sure he showed no emotion.

Cherido perfunctorily recovered to snatch the wad of bills and at once threw it back at George and to the ground, causing the guard to scramble to collect bill after loose bill as if a poor, desperate beggar Cherido couldn't identify or empathize with. "You have paid us generously already, George. I don't want to take your money any more and can use the plenty I will make for my protection and to repair the damage the likes of you will continue to inflict on my demeanor which will remain spotless and blameless." Cherido expressed his gratitude and independence — and flashed a glare at George, his eyes hueing steel like his switch blade. "You can give George the money NOW you just collected back — it's not YOURS," he demanded of the guard and would have brandished his knife at this creature he deemed as untrustworthy as a snitch.

The guard, alarmed by Cherido's dangerous glare, hastened to turn over the swath of dollars to George, but evidently the guard preferred to keep the cash as he whispered to ensnare George. "Why did you insinuate at first you were not interested in him, one of the nobles at *our* court, and then suddenly had the money acting as if his Highness was trying to borrow it from you? But you left the poor lady dissatisfied, here in the sun. That was a lie in violation of our code."

"Cherido dear, as if you haven't lied your whole life and are a living lie. At present I don't care, and maybe that's the problem. I am numbed. I am glad I kept some dollars in reserve in my wallet in case of an unexpected emergency," George asserted, ignoring the guard. "I am sorry I had to offend you here, but it really isn't in me to cover your costs."

"Don't worry, George, I know how to find you tonight to do some shots together hombre to hombre — man to man." Cherido anxiously enticed George to a mysterious alternative in which he would reveal even more behind his mask. "We have one another's cell numbers to meet up."

"Yes, Cherido, let me see first what's on my agenda." George rattled off the refrain well known and familiar to Cherido in such a situation.

"I'll know sooner rather than later." Cherido flashed a saddened downward look in response to this potential if not probable brush-off by George — when in reality Cherido hoped to soon opt for shots with Marco over what he predicted would be Marco's redundant foray into the gay scene in the capital of the adjoining country which he doubted would distinguish itself much from the rainforest and the Headquarters — except for the presence of closeted, elite high-level government and international business officials and ricos — which would be Marco's only impetus to participate in such an outing. George concluded with him, "Muchas gracias. We'll talk," as he rotated into and through the vast portal swiveling close behind him with Marco in tow. Marco exchanged a parting glance devoid of empathy at Cherido, who observed their exit, his eyes hueing steel at them.

***

Despite its impressive name, the Parliament bore no resemblance to an actual seat of government, let alone to a seat of deliberation. Rather, the high-rise building was a maze of corridors winding on sloping floors spanning the many levels, all built from the same fire — and bullet proof polished stone. The only novelty were the varying shades and colors of the light seeping through the tall narrow windows. Grey on the lower floors ripened into ocher, orange, gold, blazing red, even a colorless crystal clarity transforming with the four corners of the compass and the timing of night or day. Radiating the light that shone in from all three sides, the fourth side dove deep into the cliff from which the edifice was as if smelted. The Parliament lived testament to its creator's free and mighty hand. To George, despite his familiarity with it, the building continued to feel like a challenge to disentangle, a complex labyrinth, or else one would wander through its meandering localities lost and at one's own risk and peril, which meant straight into oblivion.

But besides this architecture marvel, leave it to DOD Kevin Applebee to select the "best" accommodations on their government rate in the adjacent country. George sighed. He resolved to not engage with them at all about their coming secret trip to this house of wonders. The entrance space in which he stood, the portal having swung shut behind

136

him, was reminiscent to George of the cold monkish flagstones of a cathedral. Grey silent light drizzled through the high skylight above. This was the brave courageous space where the few landed who had agreed to risk their lives for the freedom and valor the territory stood for, only to tremble in fear while being escorted by black masked guards through the snare of serpentine corridors above. Once inside the Parliament, one was admittedly safe from the war zones, assassination attempts and death threats that characterized the outside. But one could not achieve safety and peace unless the meandering snakes were vanquished and the secret meeting rooms covering the floors were closed and bolted. The upper regions were resplendent in airy outlay with the working and living quarters of the rulership where Cherido from time to time bolted to vent frustrations, hysteria, anger and hate.

The cathedral-like entrance space, lit sporadically from a concave area high above, incidentally was where George's gaze now met his mother's. She was standing sentry with arms crossed over her chest and back turned to the elevator behind her.

"Such a sweet man and obnoxious whore in one!" She punctured the air with gasps, staring back at him, porcelain features bathed as if by moonlight at bright noon. "And you really want to get him out of this mess?"

Both entered the dim humming of the elevator, George strangely perceiving himself in the presence of a fragrant blossoming flower, which loosened and beckoned his uptight senses. The ambience bristled less distant and cold.

"Sadly, he will get himself out of it by himself, and you and I will only play second fiddle, if we will be playing at all, which I strongly doubt. Get ready for the spectacle, is all I can say at present."

"I won't be watching." She was still disturbed and severely let down by his crying snake's eyes out on the plaza.

"Mom, you really want to leave me out there by myself?" George protested in jest. Exiting the elevator, he followed her steps, attempting to catch a moment when she wouldn't notice, and he could lift her up and carry her for a few feet. Alas, that moment did not come, since she perused the movements on his face with as much alacrity and foresight.

"You shouldn't be around those people any more, George," she lamented. "They rub off on you and inspire you to lie. Agreed, how else would you live an enemy in a sea of 99,999, with no relations between these 99,999 besides cold exchanges of cash…"

"They have all the money in the world." George adopted a gossiping tone, having veered too close to appeal to justifications if not subterfuges. His heart pounded proudly in his chest. At least, he had not and would not betray her this time. Her sauntering alongside with the cogent liquidity of one of the deep ruminating streams in the rainforest appeased any doubts remaining in their intimacy that he tended to perceive like warm drops of tropical rain. George decided that Stefan should pay for a mass wedding of all 99,999 of them, so they could enforce their rights to each other and vent their abuses of one another in the courts, creating a new, busy and clogged judiciary branch in the territory.

***

Walking into the glossy white antechamber of the uppermost floor, Moura having silently disappeared down the opposite corridor, George spotted overly concerned and animatedly eager American Secret Service agents with crew-cuts seated on a leather sofa donning spiffy off-the-rack suits perusing different sections of two separate copies of yesterday's edition of *USA Today*.

George approached the guard who was standing outside of earshot. "Do you happen to know if Burrito was here?" he queried the guard, who responded with a wave of his hand denoting 'he was here and he left,' his shaking masked head denoting disapproval.

"Roger, Chataway, I'm W and this is M." The Secret Service agents introduced themselves in code. "His Eminence must have been waiting for you in there for HOURS! We haven't seen him at all. And I'm sorry, man, you don't at all resemble your pretty security boy image in the Fifth Avenue mansion, rather a weathered replica," M chimed into W's chuckle, thereby confirming to George they had searched virtually the entire public record through any Google internet search where he associated with so many of Resource Global's activities. "What the hell happened to you — the question is why do you look so forlorn and

138

confused? Don't tell us you are here to throw in the towel." M became concerned, scanning the antechamber with his big brown eyes.

"Don't worry, I am only just now checking in… Hell is the best way to describe this territory. And just out of curiosity, why aren't you officially part of the mission or at least accompanying me for security? This is not a cake-walk but a perilous drive," George whispered to the duo, standing up as tall as he could in front of them on the sofa, perplexed over whether they wanted to keep their cover here in these top-secret surroundings or not.

W and M looked at one another squeamishly, waiting for the other to provide George with the explanation. Their extended moment of silence tried George's patience. "Come on, confide in me," George asserted, shaking out his long hair intentionally to give him the gloss of a prima donna. Any dust that had accumulated on the beach trip since four a.m. this morning would fall near their airport-shined shoes as a souvenir from hell.

"Whoa, Chataway, be careful around us. We dressed up for this occasion since we will be meeting with the United States Ambassador later today." M's admonishment quickly was transformed into a joke, "And if you can spruce yourself up and get back into your pretty boy security costume, we'll take you with us."

"You still haven't answered my question!" George's jowls rose and descended in put-on rage, warning they shouldn't play him. "Are you officially part of the mission or not?"

"What if we said that the reason is classified?" W proposed to which M intuitively nodded.

"Classified — that's B.S.!" George called their bluff.

"Okay, okay, calm down, Chataway…" M looked at W for guidance who assented, "Let's just tell him."

"Fine. The answer to your first question, which is if we are carrying weapons, is no, we are not officially part of the mission and therefore don't carry weapons at present," M elucidated. "The answer to your second question as to why we are here is on Embassy diplomacy, to convey our sadness and apprehension at a certain attorney having been hired for dealings affecting your family, more we unfortunately cannot say." M dished the dollop of their self-serving rationale with only a hint of remorse in his eyes. "The kind of attorney who is bumbling and stumbling in developing rapport, and in a war zone we regret to say that kind of... well... behavior bears strange fruit sometimes, which is why it makes sense for this attorney to go it alone here soon... We just want to make sure that His Honor is aware."

"But we both have Black Belts in Karate and can protect you here!" W strived to assuage George's rage, which was so palpable that his pursed lips were turning pale.

"The attorney then is meant as sacrificial lamb of this mission if it went awry? Well, thanks to USG's cowardice, personally I doubt His Honor is willing to meet with you, in particular as you are still here waiting without a sound and haven't proceeded through the proper diplomatic channels, which is why I asked if you are officially a part of the mission, not to find out if you are carrying weapons!" George's disclosure magnetized their sudden attention. "There is a war going on here, gentlemen!"

"Damn it, Chataway, what channels? Diplomatic ones? How? The United States does not recognize this territory, and the mention of diplomacy itself could have jeopardize our mission on the attorney. Why didn't you call and notify the secret service or the DOD that an attorney is pestering your family?" M waxed rancorous to mask his trepidation, the truth of them having already been waiting for too long slowly making inroads — all he wanted was to get out of this building unmaimed and alive. "We would have called the mission off had you been more attentive, and we wouldn't have wasted our time bumping from patrol to patrol in this hellish expansion, territory, you name it!"

George bent over at the waist to gaze straight at them, from one perplexed and unwilling mien to the other.

"And what if I were to tell you that no attorney has been pestering my family? And that you have come here to embroil the leadership of Ara Pacis in some conspiracy theory which they are not going to be listening to, not to one tiny snippet of it?"

"The Ambassador gave instructions to inform His Honor that a weird... attorney type... human rights type... may show up here seeking to foment unrest by the means of some... investigations he would be conducting on behalf of members of the Chataway family which may cause… confusions and…interference with ongoing operations in the theater of war." M gruffly assembled the complete message, filling in the blanks with ehhhmmms for lack of better words.

"No, not the kids with AK-47s but the attorney type… eehhhhmm… human rights himself is what we have been shooting at. It is the… weird type who has been pursuing us in armed vehicles behind dark plated windows." George's mocking intentionally did not reveal the layers of foibles on all sides preceding their attempt at diplomacy as they potentially implicated the top levels at the DOD for lack of judgment. "And even if I were to be pestered by any attorney, I don't have the time to call the Secret Service or Department of Defense since there are too many sides in the theater of war I have to worry about at present — children, terrorists, engineers, Ph.Ds. in biochemistry, special ops. soldiers, military intelligence, some media, you name it." George counted on the fingers of both hands. "And finally, my father's need to maintain security and keep our company Resource Global above water in *your* godforsaken mess — I couldn't call while surveilling the sites since it is too dangerous to talk on the phone from there. If you want to go into the theater and view all these parties to see for yourselves," George offered to help them see their absurdity, "let's go amigos, you have my vehicle at your disposal!"

"Why don't we let the Ambassador decide how to handle this — he is supposed to work this country, we do not." W was diffident, seeking to deflect responsibility.

"Do you think we should notify Chataway the elder now instead?" M blundered, wondering out loud.

"It's really none of our business, since he is a private party, whereas His Honor here is the other side in this war and theoretically we must maintain some form of agreements or communications. I think it is in a law somewhere. Bingo, that is why the Ambassador must have sent us! We're not far now from completing the mission anyways, even Kevin is expected here soon," W reasoned. "Let's leave it up to the Ambassador."

"Finally, gentlemen Black Belts or Karate kids, what have you, are you one-hundred-percent certain that this place is not being bugged and monitored, including the sofa underneath you? We are dealing with

141

potentially important stuff," George rotated his wrists, waving his fingers on his hands to spook them.

The door at the other end of the chamber opened to let out a burly pony-tailed bodyguard who announced with a broad grin, having been prompted by overhearing the part on being bugged and monitored.

"His Eminence sends his sincere apologies, however due to an emergency he has to cancel all meetings for the day."

"I guess this is clean and safe according to our intelligence," M volleyed back at George.

"After your hallucinatory references to the attorney paired with what must have been a dream-scaped drive through this perilous no-man's land, I'd double-check your intel since this will impact on how and where we de-brief," George recommended.

"Definitely roger that," W concurred.

"Now kindly follow the signs, I mean the guard, to the exit and drive yourselves back safely. Remember to not use any lanes for civilians, since that will get you stuck in traffic until after midnight. Let's connect after this week is over — why don't you two just go to the gym and pool in the meantime for some R&R." George left W and M dumbfounded on extended vacation as clueless USG keystone-esque cops.

***

George moseyed through the same door the bodyguard had opened. On the wall opposite the burly figure in the surveillance booth, he locked everything on him besides his clothes into a locker, then he proceeded into the adjoining bathroom where he was greeted by the jittery tense odor of a disinfectant exuding an unexpectedly opalescent miasma. On past occasions he had joked this ambiance mimicked gas chambers during the World War II Holocaust in Germany, even once suggesting to the bodyguard to add a plaque above the entrance displaying Auschwitz in bold lettering. Today the alienating intrusion of W and M had left him too miffed and irritated to convolute himself with survival of the fittest theories.

Sculpted by decades of daylight partitioned into one half of nighttime, cutting the daylight in half, Stefan had developed intolerance to any color except shades of black and white. Additional peculiarity was evinced by Stefan's concomitant aversion to any odors denoting "the outside", excepting the deep jungle smells which denoted "the inside", unlike to be carried by visitors looking for official profitable business. Advisably, visitors should not carry any smell at all, neither should their clothing evidence anything but unobtrusive black devoid of any military inclination, lest the wearer be rightfully rebuked and asked to leave for being so reckless as to hang with such dregs of society.

Metamorphosed into an unobtrusive, sprightly yet subserviently officiating hemp-clad twenty-six-year-old, George deposited his daytime clothes into the locker and rushed down the gleaming white corridor. The elongated rectangular doors alongside were fused shut, concealing the surveillance apparatus of Ara Pacis of air, ground and ocean. The luminescence cloaking the clean atmosphere like the inside of an eggshell burgeoned a short distance to the left into the large oval room on the uppermost floor at seventeen thousand feet above sea level. Exposed to the elements of the ocean from behind its glass enclosure, its back melted irreversibly into the dark cliff.

"'Call Stefan for a wake-up call. George, unfortunately you can't attend — it will break the attorney-client privilege,' is what Malcault would have instructed me now." George sighed, near exasperation, dropping into one of the oversized leather seats.

"We are wide awake," Stefan responded in a hollow tone, standing sentry in the expanse of translucence and sky behind a long conference table covered in collated paperwork. A fax machine buzzed unperturbed. George raised his eyebrows in placid agreement from behind his forearm, which covered half his face in protection from the extraordinary brightness of the ambience. His query into the attorney's role and level of involvement in the internal affairs of Ara Pacis was to go unrequited for the time being. George immediately noted as much from Stefan's gruff distant professional military leadership demeanor, today polished fluid and pleading jubilant at the war that had just been declared. Stefan knew, as did his son, that the current declaration spelled the end of the decades long covert operations.

"Here is something *YOU* would like to do!" Stefan's cell phone whirred through the air landing in George's lap. "Next time Applebee calls again, which will be any second," he notified, pointing at the fax machine spitting out another paper, "pick up, wait two or three seconds, then hang up."

Scrolling through the pictures on the phone George strained to find the one of him scooting out the far side of the beach where the anticipated caller had sent drones to capture feasibility as landing space. Instead, he was bombarded by an entire photo shoot of Moura in bronze evening dress with diamond applique at a dinner event in an underground location. Two shots of him risking dangerous proximity to the drones finally slid in at the end, his heroism apparently having failed to secure him a place at the top of the line.

"I thought you'd force-feed me some bull's testicles. I haven't had breakfast yet," George grumbled in explanation of his reticent silence a couple of minutes to twelve noon as the phone beeped curtly and acutely. *Beep-beep*. As if anything could be kept a secret from Stefan!

"I am confirming receipt..." The command was cut off by George promptly pushing the end call button. George scrutinized a photo of Moura glancing over her shoulder hurrying off somewhere. Her stare declared she had meant to shoot off a bullet, the razor-sharp intent instead having deviated and dropped inside her now rebounding at dizzying speed flabbergasting and greatly pleasing her. *Beep-beep*.

"You can't declare war on me..."

"Yes! And my wife makes them to die for!" Stefan responded, referring to the bull's balls. "But she handed them to the reptiles..."

"'*I* don't really like them,'" George whimpered, chuckling, "is what she has been insinuating." The image of his mother snickering steaming wet with tropical rain intermingled with the remains of leaves and flowers, the diamonds gleaming on the brocade bronze dress clinging to her as if delineating a snakeskin pattern, saturated his chest with eerie warmth in particular at the sight of Stefan hauling her in from the pitch-dark outside. *Beep-beep*.

"The crazy attorney cannot do anything..."

"Dad, has anyone ever told you that you might be colorblind?" George exclaimed, still blinded by the bright light augmented by the sensation of no ceiling.

"How about if I give you something else that *you* would like to do?" George would have thought Stefan would guffaw were it not for the forced consternation with which he pointed at the collated paperwork.

"Papers? But that's not food to eat? I *want my* bull's testicles!" Giggling, George appeared disheartened. "I know I should stop it..." Hopping to seat himself cross-legged on top of the conference table for better concentration, George, aghast and dismayed immediately, complained loudly about the disarray and lack of any particular order in which names and identities, members of the illustrious military of Ara Pacis, were displayed.

"What? These are *who* they want? I thought they wanted me... Let's see... We've got some who one could say could be dangerous, others are just soldiers, a very few really are wanted... Am I meant to discern a pattern here?" he concluded, his voice ebbing.

"Were you to do that," Stefan responded at the snap of a finger, "you'd find some details of interest. In broad outline, this layout corresponds to who they are looking for in different areas of the world which they see as compressed in our military, the minutiae remaining in flux. However, no one is going to use this territory as a battleground for interests half a globe away. Or for *any* personal interests."

"We can continue to feed the bull's testicles to the snakes to whom they will taste spicier and there will be more of a coiling stampede, I guess..." George offered as an alternative, suddenly displaying a wisdom far beyond his years. Stefan weighted in through a frank whisper.

"The attorney in your place will have to blur professional boundaries, since he isn't the bull's testicles type. Is that what you want, more chaos of the same but worse, now bombastic kind? Better to take the bull by the horns yourself!"

Their giggles no longer containable as they were well acquainted with and relished Stefan's speeches in riddles and codes, Moura and Marco emerged in tandem from behind the curved wall that concealed the door opening. The stinging black and brown makeup zigzagged in a caustic geometry of crocodile and Inca warrior on Marco's visage like a sphynx of aspirations.

"The attorney is more likely to develop transference to me as a female than to both of you as men, especially once I tell him the bull's testicles are a recipe from grandma," Moura commented, adding, oblivious of George's passion for snakes, "Doesn't it always fall on me woman. Why didn't you ask me to keep them for you, we could have had them here, you should have told me that you like my cooking, George… And what is that there?" She hushed and pointed at an orderly pile of papers on a far edge of the conference table.

"Look at you!" Stefan exclaimed. "You have been showing Marco around on your feet for half of the morning, while we were sitting here discussing your bull's testicles!"

"That's right — Rome's burning while you are discussing bull's testicles. No wonder this country can't be found on anyone's map. Holy cow, who produced this?" Moura gushed, leafing through the pile on the far edge of the table. Papers scattered as she pulled out some, discarded others, her astonishment unmistakable on her features, as if she was locating a gold mine.

"Burrito," Stefan responded, taken aback by her unwillingness to banter with him about her cooking.

"Wait, you said Burrito was here?" she exclaimed.

"That is not only what I said. He really was here in truth and in fact, early this morning."

"To give a presentation on our military?"

"You don't have to repeat to me what is in that pile. I had to listen to him for one hour."

"Stefan dear, I am not repeating to you what is in this pile," she retorted, befuddled by his immature behavior. "I am expressing some surprise that he returned here, so soon after what he did here just recently, which is pushing the envelope."

"I actually meant you shouldn't waste yourself on interpreting that paperwork." He turned azoic in his stoic self. "Burrito wanted to make sure I know that he knows precisely what is inside my head, and that what is inside my head is the exact same as what is in his head."

"And again, you said Burrito — you mean he will get to keep a name of some sort? You aren't contemplating a change of plans, are you?" she pressed on feigning anger, indicating she might be gravely disappointed.

"I am not sure he will." Flustered Moura had once again guessed his thoughts, which she had a garrulous habit of doing, Stefan assured her,

"My private life is private, worry not." Not to expect he would give in to genuine sentiment noble and just, issue formal pardons and lock Burrito up in the lunatic asylum instead. "Could I have my phone back?" He gestured to George who, scratching his head, was unable to unlock any passwords to the files saved on the device.

Not having grasped the nuances of the intervening conversation, Marco had come to life at mention of the attorney and bull's testicles and now interjected, "And who is this attorney everyone keeps on mentioning? What is his name? I apologize but I wasn't briefed. You can see I am the new head of security by my file. It doesn't strike me as wise that Burrito at this point would give a detailed presentation on the army, which I personally, forgive me if I am mistaken, take to mean weakness on his part, as if he were expecting losses... And an attorney isn't someone who is going to kill the enemy. What country is he from anyway? The United States? And why would he come here now? Public or private business — or just pleasure?" Marco tempered his seemingly benign interrogatories. "We do have a lot of nice places for tourists to visit like the rainforest, the islands, the mountains."

"Marco, I'd advise you to just get all data on the attorney from his files we have here and not suggest anyone go on vacation in a war zone. Craig Malcault is an old acquaintance and well familiar with the territory, including its many intricacies. As to Burrito, unfortunately I don't necessarily agree with your assessment, and he still is one level above you. As of now, you have to cease inquiring into anything concerning Burrito. I agree it is sad and disturbing that after building our military from the ground up and assisting me personally with many favors for over ten years, he should end with a matter of... excessive love. Burrito does not exist for you, period." Stefan confronted Marco, who looked startled by this spurious suspicion.

"Wanting to argue with Burrito? Me? I am innocent and you have my word and honor I am just an employee of Ara Pacis." Marco was unflinching.

"I'd like to trust and believe you — but the age of innocence never existed and will not ever exist here — or in most parts of the world for that matter..." Stefan's prosaic philosophical rumination thankfully exceeded Marco's 'comprehension. "Now Marco, how is the office right next to George's for two weeks? And your promise that you won't leave this place until you know it as inside out as the theater outside," Stefan offered as a conclusion.

"Thank you, Your Honor — I won't provide anyone's name or identity. I took an oath on living in a world without faces."

Marco, while inwardly chiding Burrito for his complete lack of wisdom, readily accepted the order to depart with George to the office right next to his and left the room, shaking his twenty-something head, confounded, contemplating whether he could somehow independently investigate Burrito but decided that whether here in Parliament, at Headquarters or in the territory in between, he could not, else he invited his own certain merciless demise.

***

Moura's hands caressed anew through the pile, halting distracted on some pages, earmarking items here and there. This had Stefan, embarrassed at his own inactivity, resorting to filing them away, never to lay eyes on the litanies of orders to hand over certain men again, the fax machine finally silent. He made mental note of her being stunned and intrigued at the accuracy and detail lightening the burden of his decision to let Burrito be for a little while longer until it floated like a cloud. But was the tingling he experienced really a lightening? He wondered, amused, glancing at her out of a corner of his eye. And did she have the same thought just now? Do two people who are essentially one person tend to see the same path through what in reality otherwise is a labyrinth?

"So, what are we going to do with those who are fomenting wars against us in our leaseholds?" she asked slowly, adumbrating a calamity while anticipating a limpid state free and liberated of 'them' in which 'they' were no more.

"It is not only what they are doing in our leaseholds." He turned to look at her, pleasantly surprised and absorbed each time by the calm within her whirlwind which could make her breeze past him, failing to notice his presence. "It is also their rude domineering manner of speech and their very strange inability to pinpoint things exactly on the ground. If you were to ask my opinion, I'd tell you they know nothing really about what is on the ground, only abstract theories in their heads, and when those don't match what is at hand, they resort to violence. Now they seem to believe I will do the mixing and matching for them so they can fill in the blanks, or so they think, for them to be able to figure out who is who exactly and where, how and why... But I will see none of that stuff no more."

He took a quick tour of the oval room, surveying from seventeen thousand feet the surroundings of billowing lustrous light lost in the distance in the effervescent ocean. As George had, Moura spryly hopped onto and off the table to reach his side, noting to herself the glaring absence of a Plan B as her heart pounded in her chest. In secret, she glorified the carnage of the enemy. Her nostrils trembled, envisioning herself consumed by the smell of the enemy's blood invading her arteries. Fragrant skin freshly torn from flesh gifted her brand-new life. "Will you be there for me?" she queried, clasping Stefan in her arms in a tighter and tighter grip until her rib cage threatened to burst and she saw fog, veering close to lose sense of herself.

"I will be there, and I have a very strong and convincing feeling you will wish I weren't!" Tearing himself free, he cupped her face in his hands, forcing himself to look into her seamless polished murderous face begging for mercy. The anchored white of her eyes shimmered fearless and susceptible to a host of afflictions. All the while, Stefan craved and hoped, since she already was in revolt at daylight, her animus would pierce into the night, as that was the only place, he felt he could call home.

V
BREAKING POINT

Several days into the war with the end already looming in sight, Craig awoke from his trance. His cells, washed immaterial by the universe's flow, had spread, disembodied through the perceptive communications of eye witnesses. Craig had transcribed their created environments to adjust his sentient insides to the witnesses' perceptions. The truth this clearly actualized, Craig now opened his eyes. The crimson ceiling of the large bedroom on the upper floor at Headquarters dripped blood-like in the dim golden jeweled light, stellar and provocative yet strangely devoid of any majestic depiction of the Jesus figures which graced the vaults outside. Instead, the steely mien of Burrito leathered with an inner ardent glow earnestly foreshadowed by delicate wrinkles around silver hued eyes and sculpted lips bent over Craig Malcault with momentary tenderness so big and at the same time furtive. Burrito's readiness poked inhuman and harsh. Lying supine underneath a heavy golden blanket, Craig, batting his eye lashes to ensure he was awake and not dreaming, felt depleted and clueless as to how he had landed on this bed.

Entirely in his domain, Burrito lowered himself, evidencing mathematical precision in well-rehearsed motion. "You interviewed too many witnesses, or the same witnesses too many times, and you won't remember everyone you spoke to since you are neither of my flesh nor of my blood. Only those that are me or like me to the dot receive the whole of the truth." His velveteen tone, highly civilized and at odds with his banzai exterior, Burrito's easy fingertips and perfumed long hair caressed Craig's features who was barely breathing in mounting apprehension. *The reality of this material world is so much less interesting than what I in my professional endeavors am used to,'* Craig, still groggy and incoherent but eminently rational, tried to console himself. Burrito expressed thorough discerning sincerity that he knew fully well Craig was here on Stefan's business. However, with his charismatic fugitivity, he did not seem to take personal offense. Craig thought it wise to not speak or ask how he had gotten into this position. "This environment isn't for everyone, my friend, but you we have befriended or forgiven, if you will, since you gave me this." The small ring with jagged diamonds swooshed before Craig's eyes puncturing the air with the flare of tiny comets. Burrito graciously slunk his upper body aside to reveal at the end of the bed clad in a crimson robe matching the ceiling the blissfully smiling ballerina figure of Cherido. Scrubbed clean of any makeup with hair meticulously combed, he exuded the pleasures of paradise. The terms of their trade in this place appeared so lucrative, Craig pondered, considering the all-out assault of the US DOD on their territory contained by means of their hard work. No wonder the visages of the battle-ready youths he had encountered betrayed that open candor amidst the allure of revenge!

Intrigued, Craig raised himself on an elbow for a clearer view of the gold encrusted furnishings but could not lift his eyes from the angelic mirage that now spoke to him, equally entranced. "You have brought His Honor Burrito so much joy. I am grateful to you eternally…" For a split second, the memory cut like a dagger deep into Craig's innards, causing much pain. He envisioned himself, at that time standing there so aloof and yet so intimately acquainted with the fiery resolute figure of Burrito, when at about the same age he had first encountered him at JC's loft above the Mercado Central. The memory interrupted by Burrito's implacable leap off the bed, Craig was assuaged by his suspicions now confirmed as Burrito captured Cherido in iron grip, grabbed him by the hair at the back of his head and pushed him down into his knees, at which Cherido looked up at him, complacent and grateful in agreement with this brutality.

"There is only one Honor in this territory, dear," Burrito grumbled before he let him go, hurling him several feet aside. "Which you would know, had you your wits about you. But you've spent so much time divulging to our friend Malcault these past twenty-four hours…"

Feigning continued disorientation, Craig seated and stretched himself, rotating his neck, surprised he had remained of one piece while he measured every muscle on Burrito's nude upper body in the love seat where he reclined. Burrito's knightly demeanor, lamenting unperturbed, fully aware of his position on silk and fur while at close distance scores fed the pipeline into hell, Craig concluded the immaculate image depicted the most perfect appealing male physique so entirely unlike his own lean haggard appearance which colleagues at times would compare to a famished hyena... The picturesque vision was rapidly interrupted as Cherido, having resituated himself, scurried with an air of intrepid despair to place his head in Burrito's lap where he drifted peacefully into Neverland.

Humbled, Craig resolved to raise himself and splash some water on his visage in the adjoining bathroom lit like a starry night by miniscule lights. He marveled at his body, intact and without any bruises, still dressed in the same beige and dark blue office attire he had arrived in.

Returning energized to seat himself across Burrito on a heap of sequined pillows, he was greeted with a brisk "The year is the present and the date and time March sixth at nine p.m. You were asleep for exactly five hours."

"Two less than what I need for a decent night of sleep," Craig, emboldened, finished the sentence as Cherido lazily lifted his head to warn him from behind lids languorously closing that he wasn't the one to lead the conversation. "And me getting enough sleep is not that important, that is not what I meant," Craig continued, heartened by Burrito's full attention as evidenced by the appreciative smile that flourished on features initially resolved to caressing Cherido. "I want to talk notwithstanding any animosities or other untoward sentiments that might arise in times such as these."

"Regretfully His Honor misunderstood me," Burrito stated immediately before Craig could take another breath, "or who informed his Honor, which must have been George and his mother."

"Someone showing up unannounced raging like a madman that he will arrest the leadership can be hard to misunderstand," Craig interjected. Pursing his lips, Burrito laid back his head to inspect the gothic marble-beamed ceiling curling Cherido's locks around his finger while dozing into distant contemplation.

"What's up there, Craig?"

"The heaven and the angels."

"Would I lie to you in their presence with him by my side?" Cherido flushed rosy at the attention while Craig cocked his ears at Burrito's patient attentive account displaying the rare quality of amicable cordiality in the face of calamity. "George was tortured by the... I won't say their name, they are below me. You have heard his father refer to him as an order? Part of that is because George sometimes perceives only one half of the situation. He latches on to it in emergency mode, panicking that if he won't, he'll lose. Some neurological pathways in his brain are worn out, that's why. You'd say that makes him not a good choice to operate in emergency situations, right? Well, that's why they trained him worse than me, and I caught you looking at me in great details just now... And they will keep on training him until it breaks him, and they'll promote him to a highly remunerated desk job... You can't compete in the Olympics after a certain age, is what I mean... I wouldn't say their training is abusive or doesn't work," he added after a pregnant pause. "I have seen him do some amazing things with my own eyes, even though there could be more. And apart from squabbling, we are good friends."

Taking Burrito up on his avowal of the angels, Craig begged him to say more. "Then what about that rampage of yours, amigo — come on!" Burrito, critical and irritated, threatened to push away Cherido, who was purring, over-relishing in the attention bestowed on him.

"Amigo look at me." Craig, his shoulder pinched by Burrito demanding he listen and not deviate to Cherido's lascivious obfuscations, understood that even with his vast experiences, including in the upper echelons of the US government, which he thought had taught him the complexities of human nature, some passions nevertheless had eluded him as too rarefied. Could a magician ever really catch a hummingbird or a butterfly, he wondered, in particular those he is lost in mocking up?

"You saw me build this military from the ground with your own eyes. To cut out MS-13 and the likes of them was my idea since they were too embroiled and at times embedded with the... Again, I won't say their name. You were there and you know." Craig stuck his head close to Burrito's to listen closely. "What fighter of any dignity would allow their troops to embed with the likes of MS-13 in any event, Craig, doesn't take a genius to figure out... What are you sniffing, you aren't my dog?

I sleep outside on the terrace amidst the foliage and trees. That bed is for him here... And my eyes can see in the dark, don't forget. Also, I can sense many things from a distance much, much greater than where you are now..."

Craig nodded gravely, swallowing his retort of *Well, it is not every day that I am in the presence of greatness* while noting the arrays of lotions and cosmetics piled along a mirror next to the bed.

"I did it for His Eminence. The sight of him inspired me a thunderbolt from the clear sky: This man does not benefit from the presence of the likes of MS-13 and their allies whether direct or indirect. Craig, let me ask you," clear and refined in his celestial ruminations, he had forgotten even Cherido romancing him, "have you ever wanted to die for someone out of love?" Concluding after a lark thought that the answer might be too personal, Craig still dared, "For Juan *maybe...*" unable to suppress the iconic "How many has it been in your case?"

Burrito pinched Cherido's nose who giggled at his momentary non-responsiveness. "He asked *you,* dear," then turned back to Craig. "You are asking me seriously? I am ready to die for His Eminence, not for him personally by no means, but for what he stands for. Craig, I have to tell you and want this to remain engraved in your mind: I have never seen anyone believe as ardently in freedom. His Eminence is a bulwark of freedom. And now to answer your question which is what the rampage was all about. How long have they or the Americans — since sometimes I have to state their name — and their cohorts been in the territory? And what have they accomplished thus far?"

Craig focused himself as if he had swallowed an iron rod lest he risked to gasp, dizzy and fearful not only at the sudden biting mention of *the Americans* hitherto knowingly avoided, but more importantly because his professionally bred attorney self, had deference for some confidences as more infallible than the Pope in Rome, and he had promised Stefan not to meddle in his business. Now Craig feared the conversation would collapse since Burrito, while not an attorney himself, had received a similar initiation.

"Well, for over a decade, and they are just using it to hunt characters whether real or made up to serve their purposes... and to banter some crucial resources at below market prices..." Craig responded in truth and fact, sad and automaton like, since the US of A still was the country that had issued his passport and he enjoyed unparalleled comforts on the Upper East Side in Manhattan New York City together with his partner, Juan.

"My final question to which I don't expect an answer from you is," Burrito gracefully took the coup de grace, "do you really believe that a very high-level military expert wouldn't know how to get rid of these... Americans? All they've been doing, dear Craig, is entangling us in a quagmire of laws, regulations and their corresponding positions while the end is clearer than the blackness of the abyss that separates the corporation from the area of the inner sanctum. For how long can one grind and wear down everything and anyone that is about? Until one's own country catches on and goes down amidst the diseases, violence that have been projected? What goes around comes around. Tell me, Craig." Absorbed in contentment, Burrito clasped Cherido's hand on his crimson-robed chest. His deep gray patina gaze, absorbed in his lover, molded his countenance into agility and pride belonging to their own physical kind of war in which victory meant abeyance and maybe the only true kind of triumph.

"I'm sorry, I must go," Craig whispered inaudibly and ashamed of himself, since without his presence Cherido would now be frolicking without hindrance of the crimson bathrobe.

"Of course, I forgot to ask you the real question dear Craig, which is why in real death, there is neither suffering nor fear? Because in dying we suffer and fear to not be able to accomplish what we set ourselves to, whereas if we perish at the accomplishment of our deepest desire, then we are not in death..." "Ever the prankster and rascal, Burrito, like a good old neighbor, turned to Craig the Catholic in vain expecting complete agreement.

"Don't Catholics also believe in the immortality of the soul?" Burrito snapped.

"Yeah... but that is our God-granted gift, not something we command by the power of the will..." Craig commented sheepishly, his voice trailing as if he were being dragged to the henchman. "And in any event, now that you have bared your soul, allow me to bare mine also, please and in peace..."

155

Startled by Cherido's sudden outburst of pearly laughter, Craig with bleeding heart had to witness the convivial scene of Burrito clasping his hand over Cherido's mouth, warning, "We are in a meeting, dear!" until Cherido bit him so hard he recoiled. The outrageous heathen ambience was further distilled outrageously by a stupefied Cherido sweetly gasping for air while licking blood off his lips.

"Counselor, what should I do with someone who wants my last drop of blood?" Burrito queried coolly.

"Two as *one* in *your* paradise, I guess…" For one of the very few times in his life, Craig was at a loss what else to say and besides was itching to make a confession of his own, barely enduring the minutes to pass.

"Right, and here is something else for you, Craig. Don't think badly of George please. He is just trying in his own way to defend this territory, this earth, this blood that gave birth to both of us. The problem is his mother, rather, have you noticed?" Burrito spewed quizzical, as if this thought had just occurred to him. "She wants his father as this superb, secluded deity, the philosopher king, if you don't mind use of the term, which I don't disagree with necessarily, what I don't agree with is her means."

"She… wants… to die… for love…" Craig enunciated numbly, stringing the words along his bleak thoughts.

"Right again, this is where I have to turn the other cheek, if I understand you Christians correctly," Burrito interrupted Craig who raised an eyebrow with a nod of his head at an interpretation of Christianity superior to what he had in mind. At this insight, being the lady's attorney, Craig had to strain to gather his wits about him.

"Killing an American general who is opposing her husband… come on now, Craig!" Now it was up to Craig to laugh giddily like Cherido.

"They moved one of the generals rotating for a long time in Iraq to this territory now." He giggled, reddening. "Phew man, try to envision the massive amount of knowledge he has as the mother of all bombs, plus he is the personal acquaintance of my dad and fancies he's got me on the leash!"

Burrito shrugged his shoulders as if all problems had been resolved. "I am too old for this; I am twenty-seven now."

156

"Okay now, please let me bare *my* soul." Craig proceeded rapid fire, exceedingly uncomfortable at their triage governing these regions that only the male body from the age of twelve to sixteen was worth living for. That granted at least four years as ample time to die, elucidating why Cherido now at fifteen was burgeoning and shedding petals at dizzying and ever-increasing speeds. The time chained to this earth thereafter denoted a majestic slow but inexorable demise, and the faster the better. Biting his tongue, Craig would have bet to himself that every single soldier dispatched to the theater was seventeen and older.

"And what is *your* problem?" Burrito queried absent minded. Craig acknowledged he had awoken at the most inopportune time, Burrito and Cherido shackled together by a bond as unsolvable as it was impenetrable and impossible to tear apart. He was yet to successfully converse with Burrito who, ignoring him, was in his own separate world where he cradled his lover with the care and tenderness usually bestowed on a child enamored by suckling his fingers.

"First," Craig said poignantly so as to reposition his thoughts. "What is your opinion on their relationship, Moura and Stefan?"

"That's easy, they are compatible like him and me." Cherido had tempered his breathing. His whimpering in half sleep to mask his searing passion convinced Craig he had practiced enough of the grammar in this town and risked to promptly proceed to string together more literary tunes.

"Meaning?"

"Meaning why is *he* here now while the hallways are full of..." Burrito eschewed vulgar language which would have been inexcusable in the presence of his treasure, "and many just come and go? It is the same with them! Why would a woman leave a wealthy, popular, handsome husband to live underneath the sun's sparse rays in these despicable marshes strewn with dead bodies? Because she is compatible with one and not with the other! There you've even got an example of your old Catholic saying that what God has placed together man cannot take apart."

"All right Burrito, on to my secret then, the core and essence of which consists in me having to, and I will say it bluntly, make a mistake." At Burrito's nonplussed but animated look, Craig motioned him to inch as close as he could and courageously whispered several long-detailed lines into his ear which Cherido, fireworks exploding behind closed eyes, thankfully was not privy to. Having completed this duty, Craig sat up straight, placing his palms flat on his knees as he instructed his clients to during court dates and depositions. Craig breathed heavily at the monstrosity of the tasks impending for the coming days. Recollecting the remainder of the plan, he then proceeded to whisper some more until noting Burrito staring at him, nodding his assent with some admiration, however out of a universe alien, pristine and untouchable, the tie of trust nevertheless unbroken compelled Craig to add, "The story of what a friar once told me. In a nutshell, if we don't notice what we have accomplished, we don't know what we are doing or we are in complete ignorance, it means we are innocent. We are not in sin."

Craig would, for a long time, weight the extent to which Burrito cared about or had listened to this far-reaching pronouncement since he now rested across his lover with his head on Cherido's chest, demonstrating abeyance of time and space. Burrito coyly played with the golden rings on Cherido's fingers glimmering like tiny daggers in a pool of blood.

"We seem to agree you and I," Burrito called after Craig gathered himself to leave. Shame had risen inside Craig that his presence forced Cherido to mummify inside a crimson bathrobe, alongside pangs of guilt that he had not yet oiled the cogs of his war machine in each and every minute detail as the plan required. "We are falling angels not completing their fall. Whether it is because we are unwilling to or because God granted us a smoother ride therefore suspended into eternity... You can use the room next door. It is exactly like this one, only the vault is royal blue to aid with your thinking and planning."

"Right." Craig sniffed defiantly, averting his face so Burrito would not see the tear rolling down his cheek at the remembrance of JC similarly having granted him a plush and comfy mattress alike to the one he and Burrito at the time slept on, so there would be no competition or sense of inequality or foul play between the two friends.

***

The adjacent room still indulged him with a modicum of serenity despite its proximity to the cauldron and — to the uninitiated — to the possibility of its unpredictable eruption. Craig first adjusted his sight to the dim royal blue that galvanized his senses like a steaming effluvium, pressing his jaws together until they hurt to prevent himself from crying. He strategically seated himself on the far end of the foot of the bed, rubbing his forehead and forcing himself to breathe through his diaphragm. The insight coalesced in his mind that he would soon face the snake in what he had made and constructed of the quicksand of the marshes, alone and without weapons or ID. Alone, that is, squeezing his brow fiercely at the two next door, and entirely alone.

Raising himself to look through the window, he was met by the lushest of foliage, breathing soundly in the strong night wind. Nonetheless, the cascading black felt to him more uplifting and dignified than the thoughts he had left behind on the bed's edge, and that wasn't because of any foulness or defect in his intentions. Rather his present morbidity was due to his having to face death in the absence of any good friend and, he feared, with a hellhound breathing down his neck. The only light came from the faint sheen of a narrow cobblestone path immediately below the window, the foliage blocking any starlight. Even the faint sheen fought against the night, evaporating in spots as its light source moved or was covered by shifting images some distance away to the left. Craig opened the window wide to purify himself of the noxious thoughts. He inhaled the healthy earthy smell of trees and vibrant moisture of living brooks. A group of invisible reptiles was crawling about in audible whirls, content and entertained by the nightscape.

Craig neatly folded his work attire to hang against the door in the pitch-black bathroom where he proceeded to shower in the faint light dispersing from the cobblestones outside. He then dried himself with a towel that struck him more like a small plush carpet before donning his sky-blue flannel PJs to protect himself against the cold tropical night. Deciding against his own best advice to sleep with the window open, he snuggled into bed, seduced to slumber by the tumbles, hisses and twists of the reptiles metamorphosing into hypnotic trance tunes.

Burrito was his own very special character, Craig mused in reverie, scenes drifting faintly through his mind from when as a teenager Burrito disappeared for weeks on end into the drab and hateful night to haunt and kill MS-13 and 'their likes' as today he still put it, including any American presence in the territory. All the while Burrito single-mindedly pursued his own goal of establishing a stellar force capable of defending the invisible and elusive power at present living in the Parliament. Now grinning perceptively against the engulfing reptile trance, Craig acquiesced that Burrito had Cherido's tears flushing from his eyes onto his Armani costumes. Burrito never doubted his lover even then when Cherido was hardly cognizant of the origins and authenticity of his own tears, chalking them up to be welcome and ardently desired duplicitous ploys to mine and deplete ore from Burrito's fundamental core instead — be it Burrito's care, affection, compassion, empathy or adulation, sex, money, gifts or... Whether consciously or subconsciously, Cherido was blinded by his and Burrito's passion — reciprocating like two stars, their intertwined paths constantly circled from the core of one to the core of the other.

***

Retaining the image of two lovers, each one reckless in his own world and brilliant together as one very integral force, Craig's reverie abruptly terminated at the plaintive screams and breaking glass piercing the night. At one a.m., Craig rolled onto his back and soaked in the rolling waves of wistful pleadings followed by more breaking glass and Cherido's high pitched accusations. In the ensuing silence, the impenetrable night pressed onto his chest, making him apprehensive he would be bitten to death by the reptiles.

Finally, half an hour later, at the sound of naked feet slapping rapidly on stones accompanied by gasping breaths as if fleeing an inferno, Craig, at peace again with the world, decided to investigate and slipped barefoot over the window sill onto the cobblestones. The reptiles had departed or more likely been chased away. Shining from behind a bend leading to the terrace in front of Cherido's and Burrito's room, the glacial blue light of the moon embalmed their nude bodies frozen by the starlight emanating from within their flesh. Bent over Cherido, Burrito with assiduous resolve cradled the face of his lover whom he had chased to

160

land on a rock blooming with night flowers. Cherido's body, wet with tears and from the nocturnal streams in the forest trembled pale and aghast as he clung to Burrito like one drowning. Craig would have acquired both figures on the spot to place into a museum, would it not have been that their otherworldly surreal beauty in the reality of the present made their embrace too apocalyptically lifelike and too frightening. Craig was astounded at Burrito's desolate squeeze resuscitating Cherido, his body coming to life. Cherido's gaze braced the night with nimble fervor as he cuddled his cheek deep into the muscular shoulder. In guileless observance, Cherido gladly entertained the poisoned arrow that fastened him in intimacy without rupture from the past, present or future.

VI
BENEATH THE ICE

Having risen at 6:30 sharp ready for the action-laden day ahead, Craig came to realize that at a certain level life, at Headquarters could be one endless trail of intrigues at times veering into murder. After shaving and dressing in fresh work attire consisting of a light blue pinstriped cotton summer suit imprinted with tiny orange daisies, he was greeted next door by a knife's blade stuck into the door frame next to a youth who, like him, had just arrived. The knife had no doubt been aimed at the youth by Cherido, who was reclining dexterously in bed in a lilac gown his hair adorned with pink lilies. The blade had been diverted last second by the youth bumping sideways into Craig.

"Meet Mauricio," Burrito called out, emerging briskly from the shower still streaming wet and hurrying to explain. "He will drive you to Resource Global this morning, and he will be your guide for the drive to Parliament. Mauricio is a very good friend of mine, as is he there," Burrito added, pointing hard at Cherido. With that, Burrito darted onto the bed and, extracting two more knifes from underneath the pillow on which Cherido reclined, he slapped Cherido across the face so hard Craig jumped back, fearing Cherido would plummet to his feet. It was not in him to help Cherido to his feet in the present circumstances or to make him feel inferior and dependent on him for help.

"You will excuse me, Craig, but where you are standing now there was a pool of blood once when my dear almost succeeded at decapitating another soldier he considered his rival, as there was next to the bathroom. That one from a more benign blow to the head... Both boys died, you will understand, and he was prohibited from continuing such behavior." Craig cast Cherido, who was recovering, snorting self-effacingly, a stern glare.

162

"He should really have more self-confidence and not be as influenced by the presence of others," Burrito added with a well-meaning slap on Cherido's behind.

Mauricio harkened back in Craig's mind to the danger of Rico, Craig's' ex- from when he had lived in Peru decades ago. Of Italian descent, Rico was well-built with curly locks and distinctive amber eyes. When Craig connected with Rico in one of the then few clandestine gay bars in Lima, Rico had just completed his service in the Peruvian military's special operations unit fighting Sendero Luminoso — Shining Path — guerrillas and their actual and suspected supporters. At age twenty-three, Rico consequently contended with severe post-traumatic stress disorder — then unbeknownst to both Rico and Craig. Craig put his integrity, sanity and life on the line with Rico. After being followed to Rico's home by an anonymous car with tinted glass, Rico confided through tears that he was a high-profile enemy of Sendero given his successful slate of assassinations including against "cholos" — Peruvian indigenous campesinos — which made Craig morally conflicted since his innocent cholo victims were analogous to the Quechua Indians Craig worked with. He displayed to Craig his treasured weaponry, including an AK-47 for his protection he had stockpiled and hid in his house. Rico also had a special landline to call the military secret service when in danger. Rico, per military orders, had to disguise his identity through different attire when in public.

While gentle towards Craig and desperate for his affection, Rico displayed a deep-seated proclivity towards unadulterated violence by picking fights and mercilessly beating random people who annoyed him, including beggars — which terrified Craig. When Craig' instinct for self-preservation led him to break off the relationship, Rico attempted suicide unsuccessfully. He rebounded, Craig later learned from his friend Eduardo by moving to La Selva — The Jungle department of Peru — although to work with Colombian drug-traffickers. Craig subsequently learned from Eduardo that Rico drowned to death one Sunday, torn asunder by the current in the Amazon River. His body had been chewed at by piranhas. As his family was too poor to have any of his remains transported back to Lima, Rico was buried with a simple cross in the Selva. Craig and Eduardo deemed his death a suicide, the culmination of his death wish, since Rico knew how to protect himself from others when he wanted or needed to. He just couldn't love himself and save himself from himself.

Returning ready to depart carrying the Pineapple and Kiwi box with his files and pushing the formless valise with one foot, Craig encountered the trio, entirely transformed, lounging on the bed almost as if nothing had happened. Cherido amorously cleaned Burrito's toenails, applying drops of an aromatic oil that made Craig regret he had not come here on vacation, wiping off the residue with the ends of his long hair.

"Your coiffure may have no split ends, dear, yet the means of your maintenance would surpass most people as too refined and self-effacing for their more vulgar common tastes," Craig teased, balancing the box on a raised knee. Cherido returned the banter, numb and level-stared, while exuding the innocence and freshness of a twelve-year-old girl.

"A matter of course for someone you love… and cherish… and hold dear above all." Had he accompanied that statement with a smile, it would have put Craig at ease to leave him for the coming few days without trepidation. As the ballerina figure instead endured adroit as if unbreakable and cast of metal, Craig resorted to a smirk. It struck him as peculiar that any casual observer would deem Burrito, reposing draped in a lilac gown like Cherido, as insolent.

Delving into Mauricio's visage resting on his chest with the exactitude of a mortician dissecting a cadaver, Burrito voiced loudly to Craig, "I would love each and every one of them, were they not so breathtakingly beautiful. They are untouchable like angels, Craig, don't you agree?"

"Glad to know you face the unknown with buoyant spirit, Burrito, Sir!" During his remunerations last night, Craig had resigned himself that no matter how hard he tried and how noble his intent, he could not change what had already been determined, set and sealed, in a world fantastic and extraordinary that he himself had not possessed the ability or opportunity to shape. He resorted to addressing Burrito as the head of the military to prevent himself from incurring hurt and pain from transference. Guessing his thoughts, Burrito lifted Mauricio's head like a treasure at which Cherido mutated, his breath flaring, his silk gown transformed into liquid fire at the sudden rapid grasp with which he pulled Burrito close. Craig decided that after what he had witnessed last night, at present he lacked the nerve to watch the two lovers embracing, applying their voracious mouths and tongues to each other, their lips inhaling, exhaling each other's inner cries and whispers. Their genuine fervor animated their countenances in bliss too perfect, pure and hallowed for this world, tantalizing him like hot knives twisting in his insides so that he opted to have a choice and not to carry this burden. Craig preferred to dissect his cadavers in the sterilized white of his office, whether on Times Square or inside his own mind he could carry with him wherever he pleased.

***

Mauricio marched ahead carrying the Pineapple and Kiwi box, Craig lugging the valise as the layers of Jesus frescoes receded behind them in their lucid heavens. The day outside was pregnant with sun light speckled with high puffs of white cloud. Once Craig's belongings stowed onto the backseat, they were off at lightning speed, plowing through little known pathways which splattered the tinted windows of the Land Rover with mud.

"Better to avoid anyone coming from or going to this war, which is almost everyone else," Mauricio explained, apparently an expert at navigating amongst brooks, clumps of trees and through very deep foliage. "See, that was a jaguar. And over there another one. Animals flee the war zone, which brings them closer to us humans, or so I like to joke... If we were slower, you'd see entire groups huddled together, including fish, turtles, entire arrays of reptiles of which we have so many. To some people that gives the illusion that increases in dead bodies must be mysteriously accompanied by burgeoning life!"

"Your eyesight is infinitely better than mine." Craig grinned at the allusion that reptiles could denote life. "I can only see shadows."

"Yeah, we have to see in the darkness, otherwise we are fired... There is another jaguar to your right, he just looked over your shoulder! The war has been swelling these past few days, this place is bursting with animals."

"Dimme amigo, speaking of war..."

"How do you know I am Italian?" Mauricio zeroed in on him through his dark shades, poking him with his elbow.

"Oh, that dimme? That just came out of me, it just came flowing out," Craig remained evasive. He would not draw Mauricio into personal reminiscences even though otherwise he trusted his taciturn nature that on this ride he so affably knew how to breach. Even the curls matted by recent experimentation with dreadlocks called to mind Rico's at times brash and unpredictable nature. "You *are* Italian?"

"Yes, amigo, from Calabria, and I've been here since the age of ten, for almost ten years."

"Ten years? Wow, amigo," Craig gushed fascination, "how has the recruiting in this place been sitting with you?"

"Since some of us are dying in this war, you mean? Wait until we reach the highway up the coast, the way to Resource Global is straight and wide, that makes it easy to talk. Here I don't want to hit any of the animals and have to concentrate."

Craig surmised from Mauricio's amicable grin that he welcomed the question while the juxtaposition of reptiles and life conjuring last night's dreamscape of Burrito's and Cherido's great love for each other continued to make him queasy. So did the proximity of nature's four-legged and creeping friends to Stefan's troops.

The coastal highway was soon reached with Mauricio's masterly shortcuts. Craig was informed that now it would be just another three hours, the cumbersome traditional vehicles they whizzed by claiming at least five. 'On the Acela to Parliament,' Craig remarked to himself. The recent visit to Stefan in Washington D.C. appeared as ages ago. On numerous trips to Latin America, Craig often had become submerged in local tastes and cultures, rendering his life in the United States, whether California, Washington D.C. or New York City, a flurry of kaleidoscopic imagery failing to hold his attention. Memories of his American life instead tended to match the short periods he had spent embedded with the US DOD on the front lines in Iraq. Due to the clandestine nature of their meeting, Craig had hoped this time with Stefan to be different. And yes, remembrance of the light-bulbed altercation in the basement was a wooing of the storm. Craig's eminent desire to pierce its eye and gut the chimera emboldened him in his cultural finesse and savoir vivre.

166

"What's up here, my friend, with the social statuses and the recruiting?" Their present racing made the best environment for an intimate exchange since, due to the speed and the black-tinted glass, any interest in the marvels of sky and ocean receded into nondescript grey.

"How I got here from Calabria, you mean?" Mauricio suggested politely.

"And why you stayed here," Craig added.

"As you can surmise yourself," Mauricio began slowly, evading Craig's blunt tone, "they came to pick me up. At the time I was neither gay nor non-gay, I was nothing at all, just an image. They fell in love with me. At first, they thought I was a girl, note I have put on muscle since then, but back then I looked like an elf and my hair was long. I didn't grow it on purpose. No one cared if my cappelli were short or long, hence they grew long. I don't really know what exactly they saw in me, and if I really was that gorgeous, I have no clue. I only remember distinctively they fell in love with me, the one who was oldest, nineteen maybe. He pulled me close and stared at me, piercing, very scary and too insistent, in despair as if he had just been kicked off a lifeboat to drown and at the same time so vulnerable it broke my heart really, I thought I would die. He said, 'Would I still look like you today, I would be promoted even if I had never fired a gun... Whereas now I will be too old soon.' That's why I went with them. I thought that would help him, because the not being promoted tore such a big chunk from his aura of passion and care, and that fear... I never wanted to experience such fear. I wanted to help. In Calabria, the seventh or eighth of many children, and no one even cared if my hair grew to my knees... who knows what could have happened to me... Why have I stayed? There is no reason to leave really!"

Craig mulled over the reason, popular with the US DOD, of their highly particular social structure, according to which as propounded by the DOD the very young recruits have to prostitute themselves for food and shelter with the older ones to pay for their training period and once they were old enough or too old to serve as the prostitutes that were being desired, which usually they are at seventeen, they are sent out into the field to guard the territory or on Stefan's many international missions. From these missions, unless they are killed, they always return, more faithful than dogs and more innocent than angels, to their particular lifestyle unmatched by anything else they could find on planet earth.

"When did you know that you were gay?" Craig queried, grateful they were in a fast-moving vehicle which detracted from any overt intrusiveness the question may possess. Not wanting to shed any doubt on the credibility of the territory's security apparatus, he deliberately did not probe into the very young pre-pubescent ages of the recruits.

"I don't know," Mauricio responded, fazed and genuinely baffled. "I couldn't tell you if I were to stop this car and think about it for a long time. Why do you even ask? I am not looking to be your asylum client!" Knowingly, Craig grinned back.

"That's not why I asked. For most people, their first falling in love is a memorable event!" Mauricio fell into genuine consternation, furrowing his brow as he now had to do some impromptu hard thinking.

"It's not that I saw angels fall, like Burrito, which by the way, he still sees... There was someone, but I don't really remember him. So many times, all of us here just look the same! And then of course there was Burrito."

"Gracias amigo, I really appreciate that." Craig breathed an inner sigh of relief. He really hadn't looked forward to any confidential disclosures of fist and knife fights over financials, physical prowess and military positions disguised as limpid personal acrimonies between lovers. Personally, and despite the lack of logic or coherence in instances, the fairytale of Stefan the rescuer who provided safe haven to the world's discarded, impoverished, talented young men greatly appealed to him, so much the more so as he knew the boundless rage in which upper-level DOD became convulsed at the bare mention of the tale.

"Likewise, I also appreciate you not drawing me into your inner conundrum over another Mauricio or the love I remind you of," Mauricio countered.

"Come on, man!" Craig cried. "Is that really so obvious?"

"Obvious to me! For over ten years I have been working with one hundred thousand gay men, each one of which has stories, the number of sands on the beach and stars in the sky and more recently I have been a supervisor." Craig in silence admired Mauricio's self-effacing characterization as a supervisor.

"Even though I wouldn't take that with the supervisor too far," Mauricio chuckled, guessing Craig's thoughts anew. "Cherido can tell you volumes about that. There is a binder behind the mirror they broke last night, in which he records each and every one of Burrito's lovers. He should write a novel instead, in my opinion. If you can, catch a glimpse of him writing! His procedure is very ceremonious. He seats himself like a princess at the makeup table next to the bathroom, underneath pink golden light amongst glittering powders and shadows, and next to him he has a Tiffany table lamp. Then he opens his binder and writes ardently as if he were composing a symphony, names, ID numbers, dates and places... Why do you think he does that?"

"Amigo, believe me, I have no clue and don't want to know." Craig blushed at the idea of Cherido the grand angelic composer.

"I'll tell you why. Because he loves Burrito so completely, he is so madly in love with him, he is convinced if he writes down each and every one of his lovers, that means he is with him at all times and always..." He sighed. "What an approach to life!"

"A way of looking at it, I guess..." Craig's voice was lost in the distance. His ruminations and troubled yet animated gaze merged into the pearly gray of the asphalt shooting like an arrow straight at a star retreating at lightspeed.

"Let me tell you something else that you didn't know." Mauricio, amused at Craig's mystified state, felt like pulling his leg but then decided differently. "Or let me rephrase it as a word of caution. You know who the worst is among us, or maybe you don't?"

"Friend, if only I knew..." Craig shared in Mauricio's amusement, the corners of his lips trembling as he suppressed a broader grin, risking misinterpretation since the overall situation was grave.

"It's her up there." Mauricio sweetly pointed to the Parliament incised like a bullet high atop in the cliff gradually coming into view.

"Come on, that's not fair!" Dismayed at the mention of his secret client, Craig emitted disapproving short bursts of air. "You were speaking in admiration of Cherido's approach to life, now you just disapprove of someone else's."

"She plots, my dear friend." Mauricio raised his left eyebrow from behind his shades as if querying 'What else do you want to know?' "We

169

don't plot, we follow Stefan's orders, and those are meant to keep us all safe, healthy and free. But her, she plots."

"You mean you don't really know what she does at all times and places," Craig interjected, indicating he considered that the conclusion for now.

"Yeah… sort of. I'll show you tonight what I mean, as long as you promise you won't use your phones or laptop to notify anyone of what we are doing, or for certain it will cost me my job, if not my life."

"You have my word," Craig promised. "On my mother's grave."

"Then let's do it, you and I." Mauricio took a deep breath, arriving at his own conclusion having carefully probed his way. "Tonight, after the SIDA show, since once you have spent the day in an ice cube with the white man, you deserve to see some fun. Or what can appear as fun." Craig laughed hushed, throwing back his head to gaze at the sun blazing behind the tinted glass. *Life is a marvel*, he mused. Now he would be using his time in this god-forsaken land to spy on his client to whom he had pledged all honesty and integrity.

At the sight of Mauricio's ID, the black-clad guard waved them past the checkpoint pursuant to the mutual agreement between Ara Pacis and Resource Global. "Disable any transmissions from your phones and laptop," Mauricio had forewarned Craig. "For one mile we are on their' radar, both His Eminence's and Resource Global's, and they can be mean if they have to."

"They, he or she," Craig injected, reminding him of his own asseveration.

"They," Mauricio rebutted. "Even though in theory, the territory of Resource Global is on His Eminence's radar also, while Parliament is not on Resource Global's, neither does Resource Global want Parliament on its radar. Which amazed me at first, and you need a lot of experience to understand such arrangement. On Resource Global's territory on the other hand, Parliament's radar doesn't work as well, with all of the massive amounts of electronic equipment needed for their operations and their own massive radar forces. Hold on to your seat, brother, you may not be able to believe your eyes."

***

The vehicle curved for one mile through what looked like a glossy white computed tomography tube slit open on the side to allow for the glimpse of delicate silvery waters. His conscience as clear and open as the ocean, Craig did not mind being scanned at all.

"Here your real fun now begins," Mauricio informed him as if he regretted having mentioned the SIDA show earlier. He braked smoothly at the second check point to demonstrate superiority to the Whitewater Security guard who approached stamping armed to the teeth.

"All right folks, how can I assist you?" Mauricio waved his ID at the bald head who, through the lowered window stated a loud and obtrusive, "'I beg your pardon?" at the powder blue suit imprinted with orange daisies.

"This is my good old friend Angelo. He was here even before all of this was built, before the time he already was a good friend of my family. Now I want to show him around, so he can see for himself all of the changes I have been telling him about." The gruff guard, bound by the agreement between Ara Pacis and Resource Global, struggled with himself to believe the story, then gave up since obviously the powdery blue gold-locked one could not pose a threat to the theater of war which strictly speaking was the only concern. The guard simply backed off and stood glaring at the vehicle, hands on his hips, until Mauricio nodded feigning understanding and raised the window.

They crawled onto a vast and wide overhead bridge, the layered granulated look of the sedimented inside of a humongous, extraterrestrial shell. At the top before the downwards slope, Mauricio stopped to let Craig take in the view, squeezed dangerously close to the rim several hundred feet above clashing foaming waves. Craig had expected the beaming white of the small town, bursting with tubes, electrical machinery, tunnels, bridges, the you name it of chemical production equipment. Yet despite trying to convince himself it must be the crystalline of the heavens that served as magnifying glass, casting the atmosphere into an ever-aggrandizing luminous bubble, the stupefying immensity of the panorama still continued to evade his imagination. The entirety must have been coalesced and gathered together by a protecting hand, since miraculously Craig did not feel stultified in his five feet two tall stature, only pressured to take his eyes off the blinding grandeur. His sight wandered ponderously to his right off the shell where the land plunged into an abyss of water pitch-black even in broad daylight. '*That must be due to its equally humongous depth,*' Craig thought to himself. Further to his right alongside the gulf, the rainforest rose again, impenetrable and foreboding. Craig felt too focused on the task at hand to meander further afield. About six miles to his right, in pristine jungle the cliffs tore into the ocean ruthless like primordial reptile claws, then soared into the sky, their upper regions at seventeen thousand feet cleaving the clouds.

"Where is the way in?" Craig, sunglasses raised on top of his head for better sight, called out to Mauricio, who was making calls on his cell phone and stretching his legs outside.

He promptly returned to the driver's seat, warning him, "Psst. This entire place is under surveillance, and if they hear you shout about the way in, they might misunderstand you to intend to force yourself on them, and boy, would they take that badly. They are highly particular with dissecting words." He added, pacifying, "That's why I was on the phone, amigo. Arrangements have been made, not to worry, even though not directly with the big boss who tends to live in the clouds like the other one... You didn't think I would leave you dangling off the bridge, did you? Ara Pacis has agreements with this place."

"I feel as if I have been dangling over this abyss myself," Craig mumbled. "Let's go and see the big boss."

Up close, the machinery dazzled, cut refined in breathtaking detail. The vehicle inched past at five miles an hour until they dove into a canyon dark and desolate like an underground airport terminal. The weapons of the few guards they rolled past gleamed without betraying any interest. Mauricio stopped in front of a large rectangular opening hung over with hard sheets of plastic loose enough to let a single-aisle Boeing breeze through. "You're going up the first staircase to your left, a little long and steep for you, but better than getting stuck with characters in the elevator. Then at the top, once there are no more stairs, take the big broad corridor straight to your right and proceed to the very end. Don't mind that to the left below you'll see an extraction site. He is in the large glass-encased office to the left just where the corridor slopes out further to the right. All is laid out straightforward and simpler than the ABCs, which confidentially between us, is how Chataway the elder likes to describe his own brain."

"Aye, Sir." Craig nodded, pulled his laptop and a file out of the vehicle and proceeded nimbly into the colossal upright standing crater. Grateful that he hadn't encountered a soul, he paused to catch his breath at the top of the steep and long staircase, as per Mauricio's description, of burnished metal calling to mind a high-security jail to boot. Below stretched the extraction site the size of a football field, bustling with gleaming white machinery styled as the remainder of this town. Intrigued by the building's heptagon shape, Craig noted the glass-encased office secured at the pointed far opposite end. He let his fingers run over the ice-cold railing that separated the corridor from the area below. His fingerprints evaporated within a split second, his breath dissipated without crystallizing, and he stopped exhaling lest he appear lurid to invite the aura to invade his presence. He remembered how Cherido had ravished to bestow sweet small kisses onto thin air. Maybe this is where out of necessity he had learned such tact as the sole means to leave any trace or imprint? Gliding ahead on featherlight steps, Craig stayed close to the railing where, gradually enticed, he began to feel the presence of a kindred soul. He had not researched any chemistry for this trip, and what was broiling in frigid air below exuded such a melting invigorating sense of peace, the sheer sensation slinking on his skin convinced him of erudition and safety sufficient to proceed without faltering into the sanctuary. The last hundred meters he took in stride, swallowing his disgust at the sight of the crude callous machine-inspired living statues of the Whitewater Security guards in battle gear patrolling the area around the right bend of the corridor. The guards fired contemptuous glances in his direction. A god sent from heaven, the CEO prided himself on an open-door policy just like any democratically elected official, which the guards had to rigidly enforce.

Knock-knock. "Door is open!" 'Open' inaccurately described the tone — cold, somewhat irate and not at all interested in vying with the frosty entryway which was waning a distant grey. Craig pushed with the tip of his fingernail lest his skin would stick to the handle as if to ice. In terms of contradictory elements, the large office inside defied all description. The back wall was covered with a custom-made panel depicting an Art-Deco-styled jungle and beach scape in pink, yellow, green and blue pastel tones. The slab of burnished iron in monochromatic grey elegantly serving as desk in front of the picture enlivened the jungle and beach scape with energetic flair. The front panel of light azure glass boasted bright red metal casing vesting the structure with an aura of bolting out, over and above the extraction site, were it not for the figure clad in a white linen suit with a matching pastel blue tie in control behind the desk. Sticking in his head through the open door, beaming curiosity and his own sleek brand of shyness, Craig caught a glimpse of a graph depicting a long horizontal line on a computer screen that the white-suited figure did not attempt to keep secret. Donning a preoccupied angsty mien intended to beseech the CEO to maintain balance and command, Craig proceeded to enter slowly. He placed his feet in white leather loafers onto the plush white carpet with more reverence than he would in church while clutching his laptop and file, betraying apprehension they would fly away from him.

"Hey, I know you!" Patrick Chataway sounded rude in line with the postures of the guards outside while behind silver-rimmed spectacles he warmed to some curiosity. "You tried to squeeze in front of me at the border to this territory a couple of days ago! What made you drive a 1970s Ford pickup into a war zone?" Craig decided not only was the tone loud and crude, but the string of words also clipped like a pair of precision electric scissors. Craig called to mind Mauricio's warning outside that 'they' pay great attention to the precise nature of speech. Harsh notes emphasized the need for the gray slab of the desk and white carpet to lend elegance and a sense of flow.

"You wanted to speak to me, didn't you?" Now the tone echoed, pompously overbearing. Craig glanced at him, indicating incredulity at the poor fit of the manner of speech with the stylish suit and accomplished Art Deco backdrop. He couldn't suppress the thought that Patrick sounded boorish quasi on purpose, because Patrick did not wish any contact or affiliation with Moura to cloud his tone, which astutely he kept so aloof. Craig proceeded with tiny bird's steps towards the silvery leather cushioned chair facing the desk. "But now you seem mute," Patrick proceeded clear eyed. "What's the matter, were the guards outside unfriendly? I know they can be unpleasant at times!" Patrick

Chataway manifested guffawing under his breath rather than any desire to apologize, gloating over his inquiry how this frail five feet two inches tall one could be caused pain.

Craig dropped himself onto the seat delicately as if he were made of satin and silk. He thought it best to show intrigue and appreciation at the challenging innovation exuded by this place. He pulled one ankle over his knee, burying the tip of the other shoe into the carpet, an athlete ready to jump and pirouette. All the while, he maintained a studious and courtly mien.

"I certainly understand," Patrick Chataway grumbled sonorously, gearing himself up into full battle mode. "Whitewater doesn't employ the most affable types. The most recent hire has a criminal record longer than my resume, topped with a stint at the military meant as rehabilitation, from where he was fired as he couldn't manage to be on time. Then he came here, and I *had* to hire him. Each and every month I receive files of criminal convicts from the US government that I *have* to hire." His settled features attempted to feign consternation as he managed a squint which made Craig wince internally. The pained resignation Patrick implied reminded Craig of the spirit in which Moura several times had responded to questions she had not wanted to answer.

"The US government isn't the most affable type either." Craig acted that he sought to pacify him.

"You must know, since the General in command of this region is your friend and hell no, he isn't mine!" Craig winced anew, now making mental note that Patrick aimed to finish his thoughts and sentences as Stefan had at the meeting in the basement. They weren't both trying to dissect him hoping he had internalized Moura as his client, and they could gain access to her by means of rummaging his brain?

"Have you come here with the General?" Patrick queried. His attempt to convey demure attentiveness instead again resulted in lack of patience as if to punch the air. Craig resolved to play the charade of the genteel professional gay lawyer outshining his colleagues at a corporate board meeting.

"Oh no, I am here on business. I would like to speak to you man to man, as they say. I am not representing any particular party, not at the present moment. I have a story, and I need to weave its threads."

175

"I am ready," Patrick shouted, veering back to his favorite rude unfeeling tone that made him feel very much at home in the personable pastel surroundings.

"You studied theology, sir, at Cambridge University?"

"I was a double major in chemistry, only top marks, graduated far ahead in my class, the one after me was still in the twilight zone while I was handing in final papers. But they were racist and hateful and made my life a living hell."

"Racist?" Craig quizzed.

"Yes, racist!" he bellowed not understanding the question. He basked in reminiscing hateful incidents towards him as other people enjoy basking in the sun. "And I don't mind telling you why. It is one of my favorite tales, quite incredible and ingenious to the bone you will admit: Because my father was German and a POW. Had I been in Germany, they would have been Nazi racist because my mother was British, and in France they would have been hell-bound racist because my parents were British and German. I guess I wasn't all that badly off, but they made it much worse instead. You must have a lot of experience with racism from your human rights clients," he suddenly added after a brief pause. "I have seen your picture in the paper. What would you have counseled me? I already know what: Not to answer their communications and certainly not to enter into any contact. Instead, I went to them directly, uncoerced and voluntary, I handed myself in without having done anything wrong, I know, I know..." Craig shook his head so as to cut off this slew of vituperating self-pity.

"That's done and over, sir. It happened a long time ago, now you've got your successful company."

"Yeaahhh..." Patrick pinpointed him over the brim of his glasses, blue eyes very bright. "Why are you asking me about studying theology and chemistry at Cambridge?"

"Because it is fascinating, Patrick, if I may call you so. One is the humanities and history, the other strictly contemporary science..."

"You can call me Patrick." He nodded, shifting in his chair where he suddenly felt uncomfortable. "Even though I don't know if calling me Patrick will get you what you came here for. And I hope you came here for something substantive and not because you like the make and color

176

of my suit. There are other suits in Ara Pacis, fascinating black Armani ones. And the one in Parliament not far from here wears charcoal black because he has heard somewhere that is the attire preferred by bankers…"

Craig acted the sleaze, baring his teeth in a soundless laugh, making sure his pearly white sharp canines set the tone.

"To be honest, Patrick, I have nothing to do with any of those."

"The self-made genius type, out on a quest for justice, independent bold and adventurous, just like me! We should play on our commonality instead of acting… the apes in Parliament. Or are you suggesting it is the apes in Parliament we also have in common?"

Craig bared all, lifting the corners of his lips as high as he could in a dazzling smile.

"As far as I am concerned, there are no apes in Parliament, and neither are there reptiles, or actual human beings… Parliament, dear Patrick, is an entirely empty shell."

"Okay, so you are neither racist nor out for political power, and clearly you have a good job, so you are not here for money either." Patrick turned to gaze at the graph on his computer screen in silent contemplation with folded hands.

"Does that graph, your deity, fuse the allure of theology as well as of chemistry? I'd just like to note that the curve going back up will not solve your problems, even if the end result were vertical as the cliff and piercing the skies."

"I know it won't," Patrick snapped. Evidently, he enjoyed the blunt directness since he fell back into his cruel pain-causing mode.

"Then let's return to your theological fascination as a young man," Craig goaded his vanity, "and I won't dwell on it more than I have to, since I am not the type that causes embarrassment or puts anyone on the spot… Since it was theology that came first, and you were training as a minister before you came to this part of the world."

"You're not trying to embarrass me? Then why don't you leave, and we'll pretend we never met?" His posture, baring his neck, chin lifted high in anticipation of the final blow, struck Craig as the correct demeanor for expecting him to unleash his own venomous tirade.

Craig bent forward, attentive with laser focus and eyes wide open, as he clearly had learned his lesson by heart and passed the exam.

"Because, Patrick, I am an NYC attorney with thirty years of experience and all my interns and colleagues work the NYC courts. I hear from the woodworks things you couldn't imagine even if your company had truly been imperialist and your administrations would govern territories of entire countries which clearly was never on your mind. It was a horrible miscarriage of justice that happened to you. The latest I have been hearing, and it is awful and terrible that's why I came here in person to tell you, is your wife is filing for divorce from you. And it is not primarily that. Just last week she was seen walking in broad daylight on 42nd Street towards Times Square with a gash bleeding on the left side of her head." Craig just hoped he had copied her signature from the check correctly to append onto the court petition, should he have to file it.

"What a story you have told," Patrick voiced levelheaded. His pointy features turned a pale crimson, then a faint greyish green, reverting to the pallid tinge at the sight of the graph on his computer screen. "And a story is all it will stay. You know I don't believe in stories, since if I would I wouldn't guard myself with my own security."

"You are welcome not to believe. I agree it is a horrible, horrible thing. I just don't want it to happen, as has happened before with many others, that you return home, this war being over, and you find your Fifth Avenue mansion wiped empty and clean. Are you going to call me to ask for a mattress to sleep on? Here, you've got my number!" Trembling with agitation cum indignation at the terror he was accounting, Craig handed him his business card, clutched between fore- and middle finger. "Apologies I can't stretch that far; I have a sciatic nerve and a developmental disability from when I was a child even though I am much better now." Patrick snatched the card with the Times Square address and slammed it onto his desk, hoping that would pulverize the case.

"Why don't you tell me about theology?" Craig proffered, throwing him a life saver.

"The bitch interfered with it, that's why. She raped a teenager a year younger than she under my eyes or almost so, because when I saw her enter that hut with him, I fainted out of the decency of my heart."

178

"Raped?" Craig exclaimed. "But Mr Chataway, that occurred one year after it had become evident that your wife wasn't happy with certain treatment by you!"

"Yes, raped, that is what I said!" Patrick flared. "Her entering that hut, she did not have to do that, her rebelliousness and bad taste in insulting me had nothing to do with anything that came before or after... She thought it would finally get her pregnant, since what she had been accomplishing up to that point in her life had been ending in miscarriages or abortions, I don't even know what she was attempting, since as you rightly pointed out, I was studying theology and double majoring in chemistry amongst hateful racists. She forced herself on him, an unsuspecting naïve sixteen-year-old, an unemployed illiterate living in seclusion in a hut on an island growing up without parents or any family. She was convinced that would finally solve her many problems. That's the vile bitch she already was at the age of seventeen, whereas I was working twenty-four-seven on this company that you see here today now! It ruined the poor man's life. He has been living in darkness ever since, going out at night in the mud and filth. No one ever sees him in daylight. If someone does, he cries like a baby pointing fingers, they are all persecuting him. That is how hurt and broken he has stayed ever since. The problem is I fainted and couldn't snap my picture. I am a human being; I have feelings, some noble ones too, and I deeply care for my fellows. But the sight of her arrogant, snotty, proud and superior act to all was just too much to bear."

Craig acting the complete innocent let himself be carried along by the charade, on edge to enunciate concern with Stefan's innocence and brokenness. At that time Stefan was cavorting with vagabonds and small-town criminals, stealing books from libraries. Craig's train of thought was cut off as the door through which he had come in abruptly tore open and banged shut. George burst in, brazen and disoriented, holding a thin file. An arrow quivering in full flight, George suddenly halted fazed and demoralized, then turned to immediately depart again.

"Not now, son, I am not done with the attorney," Patrick called out. The remark struck Craig as surprisingly considerate and kind, yet the alluding inflection hit George like a raised shield thwacking him in return.

179

"Never mind, it is all wrong anyhow. This is not the right place…"
George darted out promptly, leaving Patrick to exhort Craig to "Do me a
favor and stay away from him. That is my son, he acts like that from time
to time."

"Has he also been raped?"

"Listen, Mr Malcault, I won't say Craig since I also am the snotty
formalist. We can debate our respective innocence's and highly
attenuated culpabilities. In the end we might have even scales. But that
is not the point! The point is the bitch betrayed my theological aspirations
and for her to obtain any divorce, she will have to be barred from this
territory, which is my company forever, which won't work because then
the ape will lose access to his information on the ground which he needs
for this whole garbage to function, which won't work once in a million
years… So we will have to draw up the paperwork you and I, you as my
attorney obviously, then we will draw the line, with underneath it what
she will get: Jail time for many years since only before traveling to jail
will she have to return her information to both me and the ape."

Craig shook his head resolutely and uncompromising, leaning
askance in his chair.

"My dear Patrick, I am afraid you didn't understand: She already has
drawn up her paperwork and she is ready to file a petition in court any
minute. There is no time to draw up any additional paperwork. That is
why I came here to inform you, passing through a war zone at my
expense and risking my life and safety. I don't want you to return home
to an empty two floors on Fifth Avenue! As I said, I have more interns
and colleagues than sand on the beach, including friends high up in the
US government. Some of these may just be your friends as well… I have
no reason to lie to you!"

"Where is she now, the bitch?"

"You would know that, since she is your wife." Pallid crimson
creeping up his neck anew, Patrick shifted his posture to Craig's inner
gloating — he was finally looking up his calendar!

"Oh yes I do know where she is, every minute of every day, she is
inside me in front of my mind's eye a cancer, an ulcer, a hideous sore, a
bag of filth so impossible to get rid of and discard…" The higher
George's pitch of rage had been in his rapid emergency appearance and

disappearance, the more settled Patrick now became, the more content and gratified. The crimson failed to stand a chance against brisk complacency and calm resolve. Craig grasped that befriending mania and rage constituted regular daily habits and Patrick's real as opposed to second feigned skin.

"So sorry you won't divulge more on your studies of theology," he interjected casually. "I also was an avid student once, even though I then decided on law."

Patrick's head shot up from behind the computer, entirely transformed. Craig grinned back sheepishly at the smiling features now blending effortlessly into the breezy pastel. '*I just hope he is smiling at me!*' Craig pondered inside.

"Vengeance is Mine, I shall repay, Says the Lord. She can't take away what He gave, and then act arrogant, superior, always knowing better to boot. Being a cunt is not how you fit a camel through the eye of a needle. Pause for a second, will you and duck in your head? The atmosphere is moving in places where it is not supposed to. I see drops! Don't budge or try to look. You only see these things if you've been staring at them for decades as I have."

Before Craig could congratulate himself to his significant victory, he endured another round of searing accusations, this time grave disappointment at Global Resources employees. Hired homeless off the streets and trained at company expenses, some employees then fell asleep on the job, unable to follow basic posted instructions. "They have bargaining rights, which include the right to incompetence and breaks every other hour since the environment is challenging and they have to stand in the ice cold."

Craig nodded, forced to agree that at least some Global Resource employees were ingrates with no sense of ownership in their labor and hence scant interest to do it right given the biting cold and ice in which they were moored. Craig had the rare opportunity to make the point to one a couple of billion dollars wealthier than he and bent on murder now dashing with a toolbox from behind the desk to the door.

"I can't use my phone because we are in a war zone and my escort won't pick me up before another half an hour."

"Don't go outside, wait here, my friends the security personnel can be terribly harsh at times." With that, Craig was left back in the freezing pastel-toned office, discarded without further notice. Not even the slab of iron desk deigned him a stare, having shut itself down and closed like the owner presently jumping down resounding metal staircasing.

'*So, the study of theology convinced him she is a vainglorious, proud, gluttonous, self-interested, arrogant bitch who he's had to spend his life exterminating, for which purpose he devised the company as inquisition punishment... So the bare act of speaking out in front of him about things as mundane as the weather or what to have for lunch amounts to the tone of her voice inciting insubordinate rebellion against his heavenly kingdom, mortal offense and unforgivable insult against his sacred person for which she is to be beheaded without further...*' Craig decided to sneak out and past the guards to the mouth of the crater downstairs. The clammy and breezy airport-terminal-type cavity provided the more welcoming, intimate and comforting surrounding to spend twenty minutes waiting, even with the silent armed personnel breathing down his neck.

***

"How was it?" Back in the vehicle, Mauricio stared ahead alert, the perfect chauffeur greeting him in a dignified way which gave Craig a sense of being below contempt and just released from jail.

"He is chewing his victims all right." Climbing in, Craig slammed the door shut to protect against the mounting heat.

"Alora andiamo." Mauricio shrugged his shoulders. Chewing victims or chauffeuring the released from jail to yet another reformatory just so fitted the type that governed many parts in Ara Pacis to his knowledge at least. Mauricio prided himself on having outgrown that attitude.

A speedy left turn away from the ocean leaving behind sedimented surveilled pathways, they found themselves accelerating along the same borderline George and his cargo had pursued, only now the road curved land inwards eschewing the islands. Having switched his phone back on,

Craig opened the message, sender unknown: "Pls. bill me for thirty minutes of negotiating, M" next to a smiley face.

"This is the one event the Americans fought to outlaw," Mauricio notified him, referring to their destination. "They found it on satellite, recruiting children into prostitution."

"And you are not uncomfortable," Craig mused.

"I'm not." The road proceeded easier now underneath opening treetops. The blue arrow that delineated the sky ahead invited the conversation despite the gloomy fatalistic bent of some dawdling straying tree clumps. "Once, several years ago we went on one of Stefan's missions to Washington D.C. to meet with a higher level Middle Eastern official they had been inducting into their 'Hall of Fame.' It turns out the man was a womanizer afraid in general and repressed by his traditionalist home culture in particular. The Americans needing him for on the ground operations, they lavished him with attentions, favors and opportunities which he wasted in bawdy hotel rooms. At one point, he left behind used condoms and sex toys to hurry back to his family with the promise he will be back 'later', so the hotel doesn't think he checks in and out 'just for this.' You will note the trail of incoherencies and inconsistencies: The seconds it takes to flush condoms down the toilet and pick up evidences of paraphilia carelessly disregarded by a person panicky to be found out, however leaving the 'crime scene' unattended, 'to come back later' after rushing away, defying the purpose of not being labeled as using hotel rooms 'just for this'? Craig, you will understand they needed him so sorely for their on the ground operations, he was getting away with murder of basic security precautions... That is when I stopped believing in American judgments of what is proper and not. Stefan, of course, who is something of a saint in comparison, they give the stiff upper lip."

"The DOD's judgment of what is proper and not," Craig corrected him. "I have some great friends at NYPD who would strike you as very different." Mauricio turned to him, laughing.

"Amigo, your American DOD is what we get to see of your country!" Craig breathed a sigh of relief that Patrick Chataway's corporate irresponsibility and presumptuous fusion of personal rage with corporate expansion apparently hadn't struck Mauricio as American, or if it had, he had gifted it another less politically incendiary name.

***

The ride terminated after a few short hours and a drive up a rocky highway through a vast plateau defined in the distance by craggy mountains. Lamentably, Stefan couldn't grant use of a helicopter as that would have been interpreted as an act of aggression in the theater of war, hence Craig had resigned himself to long rough rides behind black-tinted windows. The scene unfolding initially elated him with its exotifying setup of a large stage beneath a heavy tasseled green and red ribboned gold canopy erected at the front of a small field filled with folding chairs. The vehicle parked in orderly arrangement with about thirty other similar vehicles. Craig, disembarking, felt like walking onto an airfield in the breezy, cooling mountainous air, yet any casual nonchalance immediately dampened at the sight of the event about to begin.

The open-air house in front of the tasseled ribboned canopy was packed at over one hundred youths clad in black uniforms, however without masks. Their faces and hair were exposed to the at-times strong wind.

"These are the new recruits," Mauricio the presumptive supervisor and circus-master whispered secretively to Craig. He pulled him along to the front rows of folding chairs, a light blue orangey dot in the sea of black. Craig estimated their ages to range from ten to sixteen. He halted with Mauricio next to a gawky, dark-complected adolescent with curly black hair flowing down to his shoulders. The youth exceeded Mauricio's height and couldn't be older than fifteen.

"Meet Romualdo, secretary of the event." Craig deduced from the youth's spirit of impenetrable aka polite distance that this equally secretive boy-toy just christened 'Romualdo' was volunteering as secretary to spare himself a darker fate in the esprit of altruism. When Craig attempted to approach him for a proper, full and formal introduction, Mauricio cut him off at the pass, grimacing concerned at Craig with Romualdo — and instead told Craig, "Wait and I'll get you a seat." He told a grimly focused youth not older than twelve that he was

184

the Director of the show and had his seat reserved for his guest of honor, pointing at Craig. Mauricio raised his leg in preparation of a hard kick at which the youth accepted his lot, hurrying to take his place on the lap of a fifteen-year-old, ostensibly his lover whom he proceeded to hold in a tight and defensive embrace.

"Take this seat NOW," Mauricio whistled, attracting Craig's attention for him to sit down. While Craig mouthed "Gracias", Romualdo wouldn't countenance a glance at him for reasons Craig had yet to comprehend.

Romualdo, the event's secretary, took his place center-stage, amplifying his voice through a battery-operated megaphone: "Damas y caballeros — ladies and gentlemen — we're now ready to get started with the show, silence now but your laughter, tears and participation are welcome throughout the show." Was he really the Master of Ceremonies? The secretary? Shouldn't it have been Mauricio? He had already exited to the side of the stage however, having ensured that the megaphone was operational.

For the intro, they had the stereo blaring to some macabre Spanish Gothic rock. Romualdo then re-emerged center-stage with his battery-operated microphone. He had changed in a black and white costume of sorts reminiscent of Halloween — his torso and legs visible on black metallic fabric depicting his glowing white skeletal bones, his face adorned with a black mask revealing his facial and skull bones à la Grim Reaper. "Are you alive and ready for the mysteries of life and death?" He indeed sounded haunted.

The crowd shouted back, "Yes, alive and ready!"

"Let me introduce you to my wife Guillermina," cueing a youth Craig remembered to have been introduced to as Alejandro at Headquarters to emerge center-stage to place his derriere on a fold-up chair, dangling a damp handkerchief from his hand.

"Now why would he use the more plebian stage name of Guillermina when he could have had Alejandra with a husky 'J' as a more unique pseudonym?" crossed Craig's mind.

"And who am I?" Mauricio asked the crowd, shaking his head to those who erroneously guessed "a clown", "Bat man", "Jesus" until one very young one guessed right: "You're La Muerte — Death!"

185

"Right, my name was Romualdo while alive but now I am your death... But why is my wife crying?" he queried the audience.

"Because you're dead, buried beneath the earth and left him with neither inheritance nor any money?" The very young one's guess caused others, mostly very young as well, to nod and snigger in agreement — since most of them didn't benefit from any inheritance if 'married' to older ones who spent their money on younger rivals.

"Dona, you're so right but how and why did I die?" Romualdo asked to which the youth blushed in ignorance. "Well, why don't we listen to Guillermina tell you about my downfall into death."

"People, I'm too ashamed — I don't want to talk about my maldito — damn — husband's death," Guillermina intoned angrily into the microphone, standing up and smudging his mascara intentionally, while he wailed with his handkerchief.

Romualdo prompted the audience to cheer him on, "Que nos lo diga, Guillermina sin pena — Tell us Guillermina, without shame!" which the audience echoed several times in unison.

"Agreed — between us, my dear husband died of a heart attack at the young age of sixteen," Guillermina claimed, continuing to wail and smudge his mascara.

"Guillermina... Don't you remember that your padres — parents — taught you never to lie..." Mauricio as the specter of death interjected. "Why won't you tell the truth? The truth will set you free. Otherwise, you know God won't ever forget you for your sin and won't let you up into Heaven but send you down to Hell where I am now..." Mauricio pointed to the sky and earth below to depict Heaven and Hell for the audience.

"But how can I be judged on Earth by all these total strangers?" Guillermina looked at his deceased husband plaintively.

"They are not your strangers but your close friends, family, Doctor or Priest," Romualdo had Guillermina imagine.

Whipping out and about his rosary beads with the crucifix of Jesus, Guillermina proceeded, "Dear friends, family, Doctor and Priest — I have to tell you my secret truth... My husband didn't die from a heart attack. Instead, he died from SIDA (AIDS). How you dare ask me as a widow? Well, it shames me to tell you that he contracted SIDA from one

186

of the many prostitutas he cheated on me with since he was soldier just like any one of you. I only learned that he had SIDA when he was in the hospital on his death bed… And to make matters worse, he left me infected with SIDA and I am scared that I will soon die like him!" Guillermina bellowed, mocking tears with his hanker chief.

Romualdo interjected on the megaphone. "How mean and stupid of his husband, what do you think?"

The audience, particularly the very young ones, agreed with many comments including "Si," "He deserved to die," "How could he do this to his wife?"

"Yes," Romualdo continued, "But what could Romualdo have done in reality to prevent this tragedy?" His question prompted many in the audience to shoot up their arms suggesting a range of answers such as "He should have been faithful from his wife if he was married to her," "He should have avoided the prostitutes,"— "He could have told his wife before he started dying," "He could have worn a condom both with the prostitutes and his wife."

"How intelligent — you are all correct!" Romualdo cheered the audience, emphasizing in slow speech the key lesson to this morality tale. "'IF A MAN HAS RELATIONS WITH SOMEONE ELSE BESIDES THEIR PARTNER, HE MUST WEAR A CONDOM TO PROTECT HIMSELF AND HIS PARTNER."

Guillermina jumped in with another lesson, "AND DON'T FORGET, COMPANEROS — WE MEN HAVE THE DUTY AND RIGHT TO INSIST THAT OUR PARTNER TELL US THE TRUTH AND USE CONDOMS IF WE SUSPECT THAT THEY ARE UNFAITHFUL!"

Mauricio took to the megaphone again, "But what could Romualdo have done when he was with the prostitutes over such a long period of time besides wear a condom with them?"

Audience participants had vivacious, astute answers such as "Go to the Doctor,"— "Get tested for SIDA,"— "Confess his infidelity to his wife".

"I can't believe this audience." Mauricio looked at Romualdo and Guillermina. "Why are they so intelligent and wise?" Mauricio, Romualdo and Guillermina gave them a round of applause.

"So is the lesson clear to all the public?" Mauricio asked. "IF YOU HAVE RELATIONS WITH SOMEONE WITHOUT A CONDOM, FIRST, THE MAN NEEDS TO GET TESTED FOR SIDA EVERY SIX MONTHS, THAT'S EVERY SIX MONTHS SINCE IT TAKES UP TO SIX MONTHS FOR SIDA TO SHOW UP IN THE BODY AND TEST. SECOND, THE MAN HAS TO AVOID RELATIONS WITHOUT USING A CONDOM DURING THE SIX MONTHS UNTIL HE GETS HIS RESULTS. THIRD, THE TEST IS STRICTLY CONFIDENTIAL AND NOT REPORTED TO THE GOVERNMENT OF ARA PACIS BY NAME AND CANNOT BE USED AGAINST THE MAN OR HIS PARTNER. DO WE UNDERSTAND NOW?"

Mauricio goaded the audience which shouted back, "Yes, yes, and yes!"

Romualdo segued to treacherous terrain asking "And what about taboos? Like men who have relations with many men or other partners or even with women while on travel for money or not? What should they do?" Romualdo scratched his head at the audience.

The dead silence was deafening — until a sixteen-year-old wearing sunglasses conveying life experience jeered: "If you mean those damned prostitutes-lesbians, THEY WILL ALL BURN IN HELL FOR THEIR SINS AGAINST NATURE AND GOD — LIKE ROASTED CHICKEN!" Unfortunately for Romualdo, the roasted chicken metaphor elicited the audience's callous and raucous laughter- even though Romualdo noticed the bevy of youths familiar with prostitutes-lesbians in the audience redden in sheer anger.

As Romualdo needed to turn this rage off, he intoned gently and genteelly, "Well, companeros the same can be said for men who cheat on anyone whether husbands or wives and the husbands and wives who cheat. These are sins in the eyes of God, right? BUT WE ARE TALKING ABOUT HUMAN BEINGS HERE WITH FUNDAMENTAL DIGNITY AND RIGHTS WHILE ALIVE ON PLANET EARTH TO PROTECT THEMSELVES AND OTHERS FROM DEATH FROM SIDA."

"Hear, hear!" some audience participants shouted in agreement, much to Romualdo's relief.

"I don't care. IT'S AGAINST THE LAW TO BE A PROSTITUTE-LESBIAN IN THIS TERRITORY - THEY HAVE AND DESERVE NO RIGHTS TO EVEN EXIST," the sun-glassed contrarian pushed back, his face and tone fiery in ire, making Craig classify him as a higher-level plant at best.

Having to high-jack back the discourse, Romualdo gingerly rebuked, "Thank you, we understand your perspective loud and clear but that's not my lesson- so I'll tell you the right answer. ANYONE WHO HAS RELATIONS OUTSIDE OF A FAITHFUL RELATIONSHIP MUST USE A CONDOM. IT DOESN'T MATTER WHETHER IT'S WITH A MAN OR A WOMAN TO PROTECT THEMSELVES AND OTHERS FROM SIDA, RIGHT?"

Romualdo goaded the crowd to cheer in unison, "'CONDOM, YES! DEATH, NO!" All cheered, including the most shy and youngest.

Guillermina turned the megaphone again to Romualdo. "Can you tell us about your illness and death from SIDA so that the audience will know what it's like?"

Romualdo acquiesced, "Yes, but it is far from a source of pride." He narrated in graphic, grotesque detail the symptoms of fever, diarrhea, night sweats leading up to his SIDA, whereupon he wasted away with painful crustations of Karposi Sarcoma (KS) lesions devouring his body. To make his point, he withered to the ground gasping, "MY RELATIONS WEREN'T WORTH ALL THE PAIN AND SUFFERING I WENT THROUGH WITH SIDA WHICH MADE MY DEATH A RELIEF."

Guillermina, the aggrieved widow, intervened, stroking Romualdo's corpse. "I'VE NEVER SEEN MY HUSBAND IN SUCH PAIN — AND I NOW WORRY THAT WILL BE MY FATE TOOO SINCE I CAN'T AFFORD MEDICINE IT BEING SO EXPENSIVE IN THIS TERRITORY."

"But wouldn't the government give free medicine against SIDA to everyone afflicted?" Mauricio quasi-rhetorically asked the provocative question through his megaphone, alluding that the higher levels of the mid-twenty-year--olds and above referred to as the government equally had sexual relations with anyone who could be afflicted.

Shaking his head, Guillermina explained, "I'm sorry, Romualdo. Sadly, you can only get the best medicine in private clinics for the ricos — or else leave this country to another where they give the medicine for free to the entire population."

Surprisingly, the audience spontaneously booed at the government, triggering the sun-glassed heckler to spout, "BUT WHY SHOULD THE GOVERNMENT CARE SINCE THEY DESERVE THEIR FATE IN HELL AS SINNERS AGAINST GOD?"

Fatigued by the heckler, Mauricio sought to drown him out, asking, "OKAY DEAR PUBLIC, YOU'VE HEARD OUR COMRADE'S OBJECTION. SO HOW MANY OF YOU THINK ROMUALDO AND GUILLERMINA DESERVE TO DIE WITHOUT PROPER MEDICINE SINCE THEY DESERVE THEIR FATE?"

The audience became even more animated and opinionated shouting comments like "Not if they didn't know about condoms,"— "Not if he lied to his wife about his infidelity," "Not if his wife didn't give him enough relations to begin with,"— "Not if he was sent on missions separated from his wife for long periods- what could his wife expect?"— "Not if the prostitutes seduced him while drunk or lied to him about their own SIDA if he asked them."

Relieved by their engagement, Mauricio egged the audience on, "Yet again, you are all correct. No one deserves SIDA. And remember that the all-powerful God forgives the sinner for his or her sins."

Romualdo rose from the dead, adding, "But I was too ashamed to confess to the Priest before I died from SIDA, so that's why I am in Hell now..." He fell back down, playing dead.

Romualdo's comment led Mauricio to riff, "So how many of our dear audience think one should confess to their Priest or Church about SIDA? AS YOU KNOW, JUST LIKE THE TEST FOR SIDA, CONFESSION IN CHURCH IS STRICTLY CONFIDENTIAL."

Alas, the sun-glassed heckler was inexorable, hurling like acid, "But the Catholics get away with murder. All you have to do as a Catholic is to sin over and over, confess and get forgiveness from the Priest and a free trip to Heaven. Other Churches instead expel the sinners and condemn them to Hell," obviously referring to some of the strict evangelical congregations.

"Thanks, but let's get back to my question." Mauricio was composed. "SO HOW MANY HERE THINK CONFESSION TO THE CHURCH ABOUT SIDA IS A GOOD PRACTICE?"

"Yes!" The majority of the audience, apparently Catholic, thankfully cheered.

"Okay people, you're all so intelligent about the risks of SIDA and how it is transmitted by relations outside a relationship."

***

The audience participants departed in orderly lines incongruent with the lively crowd they had intimated during the presentation, leaving Craig to ponder the distinctions and relationships between life basking underneath the haloed Jesus fresco on the one hand and consumed by costumes of glowing white skeletal bones on the other. Thankfully, Mauricio remained feet apart. Contorted in his favorite corkscrew pose, Craig inwardly compressed his chortles at the setup of the tasseled ribboned canopy swaying majestically in the wind coupled with Mauricio's distant demeanor. The artifact called to mind a scene of one hundred congregants now exiting mass at a cathedral to the deafening dirge of organ pipes, its bells chiming in solemnity. While envisioning the congregants making the sign of the Cross to pray for the damned, they were leaving behind, they couldn't even countenance the remainders of the blasphemy which had occurred and hurried home. With the bells and whistles welcoming their exodus, the cathedral glinted with an incendiary hue of hell.

Craig couldn't contain it any longer and let out a loud guffaw.

"Amigo," he called out to Mauricio, shaking with laughter, "you shouldn't have lied to me, man, that you liked or wanted to supervise this type of an event, you also witnessed the angels while not appreciating their fall… Who are you protecting, your Honorable Burrito?"

Mauricio thankfully did not have ready a witty response. Instead he proposed that Craig remain seated until he had calmed himself, and his attack over truisms in support of efficient operations was over.

Now that the crowd had finally dispersed, the music turned off and the vehicles were leaving in formation, the area was virtually empty besides the volunteers tasked to take down the spectacular canopy and fold the chairs. Mauricio asked Craig for his real reaction. "First, tell me why you didn't bring Cherido the expert to add to your presentation and where he is now?" Craig baited Mauricio.

"He's seen this presentation too many times — he got bored by it today — he preferred to stay home — next time, I'll involve him, promise, it is not a bad idea," Mauricio dissimulated, segueing back to "So what did you really think?"

Craig acted enthused, his belly still aching with laughter. "It was marvelous — highly participatory, interactive, entertaining and educational. I'm just surprised that you were not the Master of Ceremonies, that's to say 'MC'?"

"I used to be the one and only MC when we first started but now it's all about empowerment of the team members, volunteers and recruits. Our government requires alertness and preparedness by each one of us, including those you noticed staring at the sky. What constructive criticism would you have for us for our future presentations?" Mauricio actually was eliciting his opinion.

"Well, you didn't distinguish between HIV and AIDS, but I can understand why given the limited education of your audience." Craig hoped he would manage coherence. "Additionally, I can now understand why you are so skeptical of the U.S. DOD labeling these events as soliciting prostitution, since none of the youths here, whether very young or old, appear to have or want to have any choice and starting it off with death from relations is a fitting venue to introduce the subject. Additionally, you balanced it with humor, love, tenderness and care — which is obviously completely apposite to prostitution. I also wonder why you didn't do a pre- and post-evaluation of audience members to gauge the knowledge, skills and empowerment that they acquired through the presentation. Having them all leave a faceless crowd tends to beg the question.'" Craig poured his unadulterated commentary out, lightening himself of the ache in his belly.

"I understand your points, but HIV versus AIDS is too sophisticated an emphasis on medical terminology for the community feeling I seek to convey. If you have HIV, take it that you will also have AIDS, since the point is prevention rather than testing. Your point on love, tenderness and care meanwhile is well taken.

"Your idea about before and after evaluations makes me think of some of our subsidizing government's endless demands. You should understand that with a crowd this big full of recent recruits, the purpose is to give expression to what the majority already knows and practices in any event, since this is the only world at their disposal. The damned in hell don't have all that many words, my dear, while they have plenty of ears, eyes and noses for their senses... I am certainly not implying that everyone here was damned or even remotely so. However, once you will get closer to the theater of war this afternoon, you will know what I mean. The main purpose is to make everyone see each other's faces, since otherwise we are all alike and even identical if you will... This is a one hundred thousand strong community, for God's sake!" Mauricio paused, noting that Craig had regained his senses.

"Well, Mauricio, let me say that I really appreciated the aphoristic references to religion and the government which added hot sauce to the presentation, making it culturally and politically relevant for the audience," Craig tempered his litany of criticism. "But I really didn't welcome the distasteful participation of the sun-glassed critic and of the very young wisecracking — even though the majority of the audience appeared to side against them."

"It goes without saying that we will always have a critic or two in larger audiences — but you saw how Romualdo was able to shut him down and off through diplomacy." Craig nodded in agreement to Mauricio's assertion. "You are not happy for other reasons. I have X-ray vision into your soul. Quo Vadis with witnessing the angels while not appreciating their fall?" Mauricio, by training never to be the gawker, suddenly displayed maturity beyond his years.

"Thanks for commiserating, my friend." Craig persevered in his barrage of words since they had the remaining few hours of the afternoon free, and he wished to make use of Moura's case to elucidate the absurdities of living on the edge in constant warfare which he hoped would be useful to Mauricio planning his own, even though not necessarily Burrito's relations. "I have a client whose husband has been beating her since she was sixteen and a half to be precise. They met a year before in a bar, even though she also references meetings at a church where he was seeking to become minister which then didn't work out because of his busy schedule, including a nefarious court case and the company they were building. The point being, amigo that in the husband's mind, his wife's pregnancies and him beating her in response became even more entwined than Burrito and Cherido last night. The falling angels not even falling forever and certainly never even angels, since the moment she raises her voice, he perceives that as a mortal sin against his person, consistently pelting off the grounds like bullets with salvos on constant re-loads… After three miscarriages she finally found someone else and got pregnant again. Obviously, she left before he could cause another miscarriage. Then she had to return because of the work she had put into the company which she had been continuing even while gone even though her returning was a big mistake, however a justifiable one. Clearly the first husband continued to beat her since that was now the modus operandi of their relationship without which they could neither face one another nor could their relationship exist. And here the added hammer: Over time, the first husband became immensely popular and very successful in the business. Some people even thought he could become President of the United States… And such a loving father to a child that is not his, even though he has made himself even madder than he is by convincing himself that it IS his son… Obviously one can't move children on a chess board and change their parentage at will, that has nothing to do with forgiveness…" "Snorting and huffing in contempt and ire, Craig took a break pulling out a handkerchief to wipe the spittle from his mouth. "See why I tend to laugh at musings over anything that is not witnessing the angels full frontal center with never, ever any fall…Falling angels make me collapse in guffaws, my friend!"

Now it was Mauricio's turn to poke his fun at Craig. "How many acting classes has this husband taken, I wonder? Can't you find better clients, less gullible ones?" and "That couldn't happen here, our boys know how to defend themselves."

"No acting classes." Craig shook his head resolutely. "He believes everything he does and says as if written in cold stone. In his own eyes he is infallible, you get it…" Mauricio derogatively shook his shoulder.

"That's what you have to put up with, I guess, since you really want to stand in the middle of the desert conversing in a custom-made light blue suit with orange daisies and be chauffeured through the rainforest in official vehicle at no cost to you!"

Craig poked him in the rib with his elbow. "You instead were supposed to be astounded at the husband's psychology and be derogatory of the hypocritical and cruel elements that made him. Let's not forget that what I do here inures to the benefit of Ara Pacis exclusively for which I charge you naught. Keeping me safe from the reptiles and jaguars is the least you can do for me."

"Well..." Mauricio forced his grin to ascend to his cheek bones. "Then let's get back to work you and I. Tonight we sleep in the barracks next to the war zone to continue the immeasurable benefit you bestow on Ara Pacis, and so you can witness the lady's plotting."

"Barracks?" Doubtful Craig raised an eyebrow. "I was here summer of last year with your maker Dr Juan Carlos Delfin, and at that time you resided in luxurious glossy black tents made of genuine leather."

"Agreed, the living standards one gets if one doesn't let anyone beat one around and about are superior to what *you* would expect my friend but not quite meeting our expectations at Headquarters."

They giggled and teased one another, enjoying the sight of the ochre-colored rocky plateau strewn with sand undulating like desert waves in the breezy sun until Craig queried impromptu, "So we aren't breaching security measures to dive deep into the war zone?" Mauricio pinched his forearm to ensure Craig wasn't dreaming.

"What war zone are you talking about, the one in your head? Don't tell me you were on the front lines in Iraq in plenty of the desert under the pretty sun! The theater here is urban warfare. Remember the icy constructs we witnessed this morning at Resource Global? The territory is full of constructs such as these, they form tiny villages in places. In other places, two or three of them together still have different levels, interwoven rooms and winding in-and-out roads to make for insurmountable labyrinths for anyone. Then around is the jungle and you know what trees can hide… Hasn't His Eminence told you he won't give you a permit to enter the war zone?"

"Told me what?" Craig retorted, the mention of Stefan feeling bitter gall in his innards as he had just vicariously re-lived the client's trauma.

"He told us he ordered you in a recent meeting in Washington D.C. to not enter the war zone."

"Oh, that…" Reeling sideways Craig clutched his forehead. "That's what he meant by me not entering into contact on his behalf with the DODs. I get it. What a way to express himself! Say amigo, does anyone in your royal environs ever state anything straightforwardly or in plain English?"

"Since you're American, your presence in the war zone would immediately put you into contact with you and yours, unless you were to sneak out and about at night as you did in Iraq and elsewhere but won't get the opportunity to here." Leisurely they returned to the vehicle side by side. The rugged mountains ebbed behind as the rainforest foliage surfed around the plateau they had ascended.

"Don't worry about His Eminence, he doesn't need legal representation, neither does he have any case in any court of law in any jurisdiction. Strictly speaking, he is homeless since he lives at Parliament which is his place of work rather than a residence, and a job, he really has none since his government, which he has spent his life instituting consists in harmony amongst disparate parts and can't be found on anyone's map… The one legal entity rather is his mother, and you'll be glad to live to thank the gods for never having to meet her. She roams the war zone and can't be let out." Mauricio returned Craig's intrigued perceptive wink with the same fervor.

"You'd meet her if you'd as much as set foot where the action is. A jaunty sixty-year-old, she makes the scene unsafe in flowery hoopskirts, worn gym tops and faded oversized I Love NY T-shirts knotted on the side, red and blue Adidas sneakers with pink laces, and her chest, throat and arms are heavier with gold jewelry than the iron bolting on her floor hiding her treasure. Not to speak of her white hair touching her arse, braided through with red and orange stones. You'd love to shake her like a Christmas tree. Of course, she hasn't spoken to His Eminence in thirty years, neither does she have to since he can hear her yell, and now that the theater is overboiling, she's been throwing stones and rocks at American forces with gusto. It is frightening and I speak like a man. She is convinced of His Eminence's incompetence, as she declares at every twist and turn and that she must do his job. It is hard to watch and impossible to control." Nodding, Craig measured the escarpment, quiet and absorbed by the desolation of the barren weathered rock.

VII
DAWN

"I don't know if they make powdery blue flak jackets, neither would I want you to strain your baby blues too far through binoculars while crawling on your belly through the underwood. So we'll stay inside Ara Pacis closer to where we are heading and a distance from the war zone, in what you from your hysterical client-infested perspective folksily refer to as 'a tent,' which is the same structure in which all of us sleep..."

"I am a boy in BLUE!" Craig contended with emphasis, hinting at the pink-hued coloring predominant in the frescos at Headquarters as well as in Cherido's homemaker's robes. The backdoor of the vehicle wide open, he rummaged through his Pineapple and Kiwi box for his notepads and other essentials.

The hexagon shape melting into the dark rugged tree trunks defied the description of a tent with its gold-plated fixtures in the adjoining portable bathroom and the thick sheepskin and woolen carpets, pillows and bedsheets adorning the interior.

"Might as well die in style, since dying is your salvation," Craig commented. He acted morose, glancing at Mauricio out of the corner of his eye, at which Mauricio whisked himself some distance away to point at the glass green-spiked leaves of a cactus flowering with bright pink ribbon-shaped buds.

"Kalanchoe Pink Butterflies, native to this region. Undemanding and reproducing by virtue of plantlets that just fall from the mother plant and start rooting effortlessly..."

Climbing onto the Land Rover's sidestep, Craig folded his arms on top of the door, examining the scene with a pen sticking out from behind his ear.

"I like your reproduction euphemism even though I am not convinced by your use of the term 'undemanding.' When are the models arriving?"

"Soon, and there are twelve. Cherido wouldn't mind serving as the thirteenth man at the table."

"I am glad you agree to the appellation of models, since elsewhere in the world they would pass as prostitutes."

Mauricio waved away what he perceived as puritanical American judgmentalism. "Referring to them as soldiers at this point would be overstating the obvious."

"Sure, and you do want your boys to be respected and not to be looked at as fodder to the animals." No matter how hard he tried, Craig couldn't get used to the mores in this region, clothing what always risked to degenerate into exploitative self-serving disrepute, in picturesque poetic allusions.

"I must have told you they know how to defend themselves?" Sincerely bewildered, Mauricio pulled out his phone to check on the arrival of said models.

"*They* will turn green in their faces and walk backwards out of Parliament and out of the territory," Craig commented. Wrapped in his black plush bathrobe, he was enjoying a simple dinner of homemade chili enchiladas while seated cross legged on the hood of the Land Rover, which he had wiped clean with one of the expensive woolen towels inside the 'tent.'

"Your apple has already been green for a very long time. The bees will never even stick to it. He lacks honey and is sour." Mauricio was dozing on a flat rock in the evening sun, which Craig understood as a sign of frustration since Mauricio hadn't been briefed on the entirety of the operation. Or was there something else in his tone, a languorous timidity that betrayed some fear?

"Do you really think that Cherido will be the thirteenth man at the table?" Craig called out loudly.

"It doesn't really matter since according to your scriptures, Satan entered into Judas as soon as Jesus gave him some bread, and Satan at present already is inside this friend of ours Cherido..."

"Means he might as well skip the meal." As much as he hated to keep secrets from friends, Craig had to admit to himself that nothing topped a top-secret mission through a jungle, up sky-breaking cliffs, in exhilarating experience, punctilious planning and meticulous execution.

"You are welcome to hand me anything to eat Craig, I will take it gladly, including your enchilada if there is any left..."

Craig was slurping the insides of his enchilada, delighting in the mixture of molten cheese, chilies and the ravishing, sweet goat meat indigenous to this region.

"Do we have anything new to report?" Mauricio added.

"Not really, only that the sun will rise again tomorrow morning and again in the mornings thereafter, many and innumerable..."

"Then I'd suggest you go to sleep now so you can get up at three a.m. far ahead of that sun of yours."

"You are invited to New York, together with Cherido," Craig concluded. "Meals at my expense, and my partner Juan and I have a beautiful living area where there is enough space for a thick fluffy mattress underneath some poetic picturesque Bonsai trees."

"Cherido and I may have to travel on separate planes, but I am happy to accept your invitation."

"No worries that he will sleep with you on the mattress either. He'll find someone to fund his stay at the Lowell, the Pierre Hotel, the Four Seasons on the Upper East Side, you name it, before he has even embarked from this place."

'*And he may already have found someone...*' Craig preferred to triumph in silence. Too many abused and neglected gay young men had been his clients for him to be envious of the glitz and glam of what life truly had to offer. Yet he kept his thoughts to himself, not wanting to offend or alert someone who, even though with heart in the right place, still had to witness a few more angels fall before he could arrive whole and untouched at the sanctum inside heaven.

***

The night, cold at three a.m., Craig in the buff waded into the shallow water of the riverbank next to which he had slumbered on sheep skin in nature, protected by genuine leather. He applied a few drops of his favorite coconut, almond and apricot scented L'Occitane shower oil, pondering at the dark effluvium curling downstream. Craig relished the sensation of taking a bath at about the same coordinates where according to Moura twenty-seven years ago Patrick would vanish at night. Returning enraged, he had been left bereft, unable to perceive even the stirrings of faith. Instead, he resorted, stranded and ravaged, to the icy enclosing of his corporate machine. For his own part, Craig, who had never prided himself of being strong either in faith or in will, clearly discerned the dreary vegetation of the opposite bank cutting jaded into the darkness. His feet, firmly planted in sediment, pebbles and sand, alerted him to hurry and be quick since this was not his home or living place.

Craig ensured he ascended squeaky clean, leaving behind a residue vapor from his body heat. Wrapped in a woolen towel, he spritzed and powdered his coiffure at a golden lit mirror inside the tent. He greeted Mauricio who was waiting near him in battle gear, assuring him that he too was slowly befriending the many reptiles and snakes, even though "were they to return the sentiment and bite me, my kindness towards them would not have mattered, and I would not have had the time to fully express it to them in any event."

Mauricio measured him from head to toe while the tent filled with the odors of the L'Occitane shower oil, powders and tuberose-scented cologne. He silently handed Craig a small-sized black Armani costume to which Craig retorted, "And I am slowly starting to befriend this attire too, even though at night all cats are grey, and I am not really attracted to anyone in this region..."

"You won't need a helmet since we won't encounter any flying bullets. We will however get to see a lot of pitch-black night." Appreciating the hint, Craig made sure the uniform fit together with a pair of combat boots before thanking Mauricio and boarding the Land Rover next to him.

"Now we will drive for about fifteen minutes and the remaining half an hour has to be on foot. Climbing your way through foliage is well worth what is at the other end. And here is your pair of binoculars, for you to precision-dissect the night."

"My favorite pastime." Craig sighed.

The depth of the night indeed was blinding and Mauricio a master driver who in the dim drizzle of the headlights neither rustled a leave nor trod on a flower. Craig marveled at the array of flowers that were blooming in the darkness. Gathered in clumps, their colors glided by, hazily multiplied like living cells, leaving behind a twinkling trail exuding sober but indefatigable life. Driving at night differed radically from driving during the day. In daytime the sky and openings between the trees could serve as their guide, whereas now at night the vehicle plowed ahead as if a bullet, its trajectory set.

Before long, they arrived at their determined location, disembarked on tiptoes and dove into the foliage so thick and lush their texture would have lulled Craig to sleep would it not have been for his burning desire to find out what hid at the other end. Night butterflies and other nocturnal insects waved by. Tiny feathers and fuzz tickled as Craig passed briskly through clammy drafts.

***

Finally, they arrived at a stony edge beneath which a long narrow valley divided by a slithering brook effervescent with dew stretched into the edges of the cliffs. The craters of the cliffs were completely obfuscated by climbing tree branches so that the valley appeared a self-contained microorganism. Mauricio motioned to the far end of the stony edge where they could sit on some boulders underneath heavy overhanging foliage. He pointed to an area about two hundred and fifty feet into the valley where a sandy precipice diverted the brook into a pronounced S shape.

"What bugs me, amigo," he whispered, refreshed and wide awake at the favorite time of the day of the defenders of Ara Pacis, "is that this is where Resource Global first started several decades ago. They thought they could build on the precipice in the back protected by the cliffs. What a place to hold her meetings now!"

"The lady is entitled to her opinion," Craig murmured, raising the night vision binoculars. Not before long their watches pointing to four a.m. sharp, a small, armored SUV pulled up from the jungle behind the sand. Moura got out at the same time that Cherido emerged from the opposite side of the brook with exceedingly nimble gait, wearing the uniform of Ara Pacis.

"He was in the war zone last night and must have been walking for the last few hours… I loved doing the same when I was his age. There is something about… spreading your wings, so to speak from tree to tree… that is unsurpassed by anything you might experience on the ground."

"*You* aren't feeling old, amigo, are you?" Craig looked up from his binoculars in some alarm. Relieved at Mauricio shaking his head he continued "Where is the plotting?"

"Just look at her," Mauricio hissed. "She does meetings here with arrays of individuals in darkness, each one of which to my knowledge possesses contradictory and irreconcilable information."

"That is not what I call plotting! Plotting means subterfuges, backstabbing, and trying to bring about things behind the backs of others who have been trusting you to do something else instead."

Mauricio numbly returned his critical stare. Craig gazed attentively through the binoculars at Moura holding out to Cherido a pile of papers with earmarked edges. Cherido stood there motionless like a statute. At her persistence, he raised his right hand in the gesture of a Buddha enunciating an unambiguous sign of Peace together with an irrefragable NO. A sporadic wind carried over fragments of her loud voice.

"Cherido, it is forgiven and forgotten, Stefan bears no one a grudge, and not in these circumstances."

"Now it is up to *you,* your Eminence to forgive *me*, because *I* am going to tell *you* that you seem somewhat mad and your plans so crazy, they make ours look like genius." Walled behind a commando exterior, Cherido stood on order with his feet apart firmly planted on the ground.

"What is crazier than to do *this* to someone you love?" She waved the papers in front of his face. Even through the binoculars, Cherido's bared demeanor transformed into a mask.

"You can throw those out, Your Eminence. Burrito knows them by heart."

Evidently getting nowhere, she spun around to kick the vehicle and then she threw herself on her belly onto the hood, clutching her head and hitting the tire with her fists.

"That doesn't strike me as the right path to immortality," Cherido called out. "You need my help to get off that car?" Now she curled into embryo position, defenseless and iron willed even though entirely lost. She lifted her chin to look at him over her shoulder.

"I am expressing frustration."

Cherido giggled in a hollow tone, sounding satanic indeed to both Craig and Mauricio. Craig now noticed what Mauricio had known all along that the effeminate coy tone Cherido had been adopting with Craig and other foreigners was just a snare he used to prevent them from probing deeper. Throwing her long hair over her shoulder, Moura lounged provocatively. In the waning moonlight her mien froze over like a porcelain doll's while her lower lip pointed in the vein of her desiring to shoot Cherido a snake's forked tongue.

"Have I heard anyone say that the devil's mother is worse than the devil himself?" Mauricio whispered barely audible. "Why doesn't she just give him an order to end it all? Why is she prolonging the situation? Amazing, the distance of at least ten feet at which she keeps him, don't you think? Is she inviting him to go off on her destitute hot mama image?"

"Obviously, she has no clue as to what to say next," Craig whispered back at what he perceived to be inane questions. "And she isn't Cherido's mother, either."

"I am not sure you understand the consequences of your actions," she finally blurted hopping off the hood shaking disheveled hair. The night vision binoculars enrobed her in ravishing air. The fluorescent slickness of her appearance, set off by a pair of neon yellow eyes, fixated in the saintly resignation of a Madonna. She raised her combat boot to take aim at Cherido but then changed her mind, her eye lids bristling bright.

"'Well...'" "Cherido yawned brusquely and pulled out his face mask to denote that the meeting was now over. "Neither did you when you went down for one year inside that hut on the island, even though back then you were smarter."

Craig zeroed in on Cherido's features as he applied the mask to himself. The shadows of long lashes hid eyes that suddenly glinted, then extinguished at the easy smile that flourished on full childlike lips. The brief bliss vanished behind the black material.

"Anything else?" Cherido stood on attention.

"You have sort of ended it all, what else would there be?"

"Life eternal, Your Eminence."

She jumped on one foot, the other leg angled, kicking the car behind her, apparently denoting her last split-second agreement with Cherido's implied plan. Her features, still frozen fluorescent, were simultaneously so gravely concerned that Craig began to doubt, even resent his own assertion, even though undoubtedly true, that she wasn't Cherido's mother. Cherido the silent whisperer had disappeared back towards the war zone, leaving behind a breezy wind untangling the sand just as if he had never even been there. Bending over the place where he had stood and left a trail in the sand, Maura made sure his traces were erased. She kicked the dust, sand, pebbles, small rocks, all in the bull's eye of one single determined fury.

"No plotting anywhere, and not even to my attorney's eyes only."

"We — ee — ll, well," Mauricio imitated Cherido slightly. "She should have ordered him to take back the paperwork instead of stowing it into her car. Had she any compassion, she should have ordered them to terminate this mission of theirs, otherwise she should have decapitated him instantaneously and impaled his head here, on this original headquarters of Resource Global, for high treason. Instead, she is now washing the dust off herself at the brook and combing her hair!"

Now it was up to Craig to examine Mauricio with grave concern.

"Don't you know, my very dear, that those who love with the Gods *live-with-them-in-their-own-space*?" Mauricio's manifest ignorance of the Gods galled him. "Who knows," Craig added with a chuckle, "Burrito might alight to see *her here* with the force of all angels, not to speak of the thunderbolts of the Gods, had she as much as expressed doubt at their idea!" He laughed without a sound, feeling warm in his belly.

"I just wanted to protect her opinion." Mauricio tried to sound matter of fact as he mimicked Craig's manner of thinking.

"We'll worry about freedom of expression once we get down to the mundane nitty-gritty... In particular since you don't really get the higher-level point. Psst, someone's coming."

"The husband who has been wearing horns as outdated fashion statement."

"Stop it!" Craig motioned to pierce Mauricio's toes with the heel of his boot at which Mauricio recoiled apologetically. The commotion thankfully evaded the valley below where Stefan now pulled up as the first rays of the sun cast very long shadows spreading through a faint golden gold.

"If these two start to make out, we turn away and leave, since this is private," Craig instructed Mauricio in a biting whisper. They both glared cautiously and intensely at the two figures standing side by side at the brook speaking in hushed tones.

Mauricio suggested, "He should just show her the ledger in his car with all the corpses he has been counting these past few hours. Then they should do more plotting on how to exterminate the bees on the apple and his pest."

"I don't think they care about him at all. I don't think he even exists for them. I think their problem is with maintaining the harmony on which the territory rests."

Glowing and animated, Moura in a tank top used her shirt to dry off the water from the brook while Stefan grabbed her to shake sense into her.

"Let go of me," she laughed. "I will climb those cliffs all by myself, you will see!" Sharp as a tack in the rising sun, her features ignited blossoming pink. Evidently, she aimed to paint herself in the nude onto the rocks rising towards the cliffs where she yearned to enchant, resplendent in blazing colors and languorous pleasant mien.

Nodding, Craig and Mauricio threw each other tell-tale looks, turned their backs and stomped back the same path they had treated.

"What was that about?" Mauricio inquired when they were at a safe distance.

"She doesn't want Stefan involved in Burrito's and Cherido's idea, that's why," Craig responded with priestly mien.

"Are we going back now so you can do your meditating and thinking before we proceed to Parliament?"

"That is what we should do, I guess," Craig quipped gamely. He pulled out his phone to confirm with sources that Kevin Applebee indeed had taken off in the wee hours and would alight in the area beyond the islands to proceed to Parliament where he hoped to arrive today at dusk. Then Craig checked in with the models to double confirm.

"Where did Cherido go, do you know?" he called back to Mauricio, in stealthy gait obediently behind him.

"How would I know? Didn't you say yourself that those who love with the Gods *live-with-them-in-their- own space?*"

"Maybe you'd like to give Burrito a buzz to try to find out?"

"I already did, and he didn't pick up."

"Burrito is not the cold-hearted one to ignore his friends!"

"He isn't, and that is not what I said. I said that he did not pick up."

"Oh God, where do we go from here?" Craig wheezed, his joints slowly starting to ache at the brisk walk, through heavy foliage. "Jesus, please show the way!"

"You sound like your client in the valley right now, even though by Jesus she does not mean the Christian son of God." Mauricio attempted to crack a joke in the face of imminent disaster. "Seriously Craig, take my advice which you already know, since you gave it to me yourself. Let the Gods be. No matter how brilliant an attorney, how compelling and complete your reasoning, neither Burrito nor Cherido will ever listen to you. I have witnessed it myself, including yesterday morning when you also were present. They don't hear, and they don't listen. All you accomplish is grow yourself more gray hairs. *Mi hai sentito?*"

"Grazie, si."

"Quindi tutto bene."

Craig scratched the back of his head puzzled by Mauricio's assertion, "all is well." Craig decided to give him the benefit of a doubt and not to continue to analyze and probe, to hack to pieces hearts, minds and events sealed off impermeably and even already discarded from this world.

***

Energized by the dawn now pouring its rays through bright green foliage, Craig had ambled ahead when Mauricio's hand suddenly descended on his shoulder. "I hear noises, let me go and see." Another fifty yards in,

Craig indeed detected a cacophony of sounds, angry voices interspersed with the rumbling of vehicles.

"I tuoi amici, from the press," Mauricio informed him when he returned. Craig immediately assured him that he had few friends in the American press, which could be "like Berlusconi's."

"Amici by necessity then. His Eminence terminated their passes at four a.m. today, and they were picked up in the war zone and brought straight here. You have an interview scheduled with them today?" Craig retorted no, he had no interview scheduled, neither was he expecting any interlopers. Without a word, Mauricio unfastened and removed from the upper arms of Craig's uniform the territory's insignia consisting of a red sun cut into two halves by a golden thunderbolt. At first Craig was dismayed because the insignia to his mind was identical to the memory of seventeen-year-old Burrito composing the icon in early dawn in the tranquil shadow of a tree. But Craig came to terms when through the gate of parted foliage what he considered as one of the loudest and most obnoxious journalists at a leading American media outlet greeted him with upheld hand from a distance away. The man couldn't move, fenced in by a tank and two masked guards, which he didn't mind. Craig remembered he held something like a Pulitzer Prize for war reporting and was used to such treatment. Next to him a blond female crouched on the ground fiddling with a microphone, her eyes cast down in sadness.

"You can't use this equipment here," Mauricio informed her while the journalist was announcing loudly that he was in charge: "The pass was for the war zone only, here anyone has freedom of the press!" Craig was well familiar with the many articles elucidating to his erudite readers excruciating details of on-the-ground operations. The reporter brought home the war by means of the particulars he recounted from observations of what occurred within the space of a few square meters. Craig recalled one especially. Centered on the front page of the leading news outlet depicting an American Apache helicopter engulfed by smoke with title referencing Iraq, the picture startled, since at that time the invasion of Iraq was still in the future. Even hearings on the subject in Congress were yet to be conducted! Nevertheless, to this man's mind, a war had to be already presumptuously conducted or announced, which amounted to the same.

"Just don't take a picture of me against these lovely trees with flowers and the sun shining. Your readers may falsely believe I am on vacation!" Only half in jest, Craig pulled a menacing sneer, propping his combat-booted foot on top of a sallow rock. "More to your liking?"

"You are doing your fellow citizens a disfavor by opposing the freedom of the press." The journalist sauntered towards him intoning the cultivation of a history professor at Harvard University. He flung back the front cover of a notepad to a fresh page at which Craig instinctively lowered his sunglasses.

"You lied, man; we have nothing scheduled."

The journalist pointed to the guards over his shoulder. "*They* lied when they claimed the war zone extends to the entire territory and a pass is needed everywhere." Craig showed his canines.

"Amigos," he shouted. "Did you tell him that the war zone extends to the entire territory?"

A confused shaking of heads responded. "He was asked to leave at four a.m. and there was no sign of him leaving. Instead, he proceeded into the war zone…"

"Why does it matter if the war zone extends to the entire territory? His opinions are too obnoxious, and he was causing war by interrogating several of us."

"By law which he knows, the territory is divided into military leases and he has no right to walk onto those without anything further even if there were no war."

"He should just leave, since no one invited him."

"Hey man," Craig exclaimed, opening his arms. "It looks like no one wants you here, which places the burden on me to provide entertainment until you deign to request your free ride out!"

"How cordial you are by comparison when schmoozing with the rich and famous in your law firm perched atop Times Square!"

"All right, how can I be of service?" Craig acted beguiled, glancing at the notepad.

"I am not sure if I want to talk to you at all now, since you seem to be with these evil forces or at least their emissary. But let me ask you this."

Concerned shouting interrupted from the back. "No one here is evil, apart from who refuses to obey our laws."

"We are very polite and friendly, just now the situation is not right."

"If he really wanted to befriend us, he would have made an appointment ahead of time instead of barging in at the worst possible time."

"How disgusting, to speak like that about people you don't even know!"

"You are outnumbered." Craig raised his shoulders. "They must have caught you in a pretty outrageous act. These are good-natured, laidback folk who wouldn't just pick up anyone like a prisoner of war."

"Let me ask you, Malcault: Are you even faintly aware that there is a real war going on just a few miles from here, a fight over power and resources, at the time that we are expecting the head of security operations to arrive in Parliament by tonight?"

"Pheewww... You want me to meet and greet with the head of security operations? I have more pressing issues on my mind."

"I don't care about your issues; I am a war correspondent! There is a full-blown war going on, I was trying to get close to count the dead bodies since your side or whoever side they or you are on tends to misrepresent. How many representatives sit in Parliament, Malcault?"

"There are twelve seats," Craig responded evasively, feigning boredom.

"It might interest you that two of these were assassinated in the past two days and no one is allowed to report on it. They keep on saying they know nothing. They keep on saying Parliament has been dissolved a week ago and there are no empty seats which amounts to the same."

Renewed shouting came from the back.

"No clue who he is referring to as having been assassinated, soldiers die in wars all of the time."

"He would have been dead by now himself, would he truly not have been allowed to report."

"He is overly anxious to stick his nose into other people's business."

"The Parliamentarians are meant to be anonymous for everyone anyhow."

"Why do we even need a Parliament? I have never seen one here! Doesn't he know we govern by strength, power and integrity?"

"Man, it makes sense to assassinate those, since they set the prices for the resources, goddamn you, stop taking me for a fool. What kind of a war correspondent are you?" Craig spewed his contempt at the war correspondent like poison.

"What if I were to report then that two Parliamentarians setting the prices for resources were assassinated at the same time that our friend Applebee is set to make a visit to Parliament."

"I'd ask you to clarify, among other things, the connection between our hunting people we refer to as terrorists, who in reality may just be defending their own resources, and resources disappearing and being sold at below market value…"

"You know there are no terrorists defending resources." The man's sense of righteousness nauseated Craig.

"I may know there are no terrorists FULL STOP. At least none that grow like flowers out of the ground, of which you seem to believe there are plenty. And I just stopped reading the article you referred to as you being in the process of reporting for. Not only that, but I also left you a nasty reader's comment, calling you… names including coward and sycophant…" Feeling awkward, Craig waived his arms about, clapping his hands, at a loss of what else to say. It was not in him to belittle or speak disparagingly of other professionals.

Noting irreconcilable differences there to stay, the journalist sheepishly retreated. "I am just trying to warn you, Malcault. This is not the right time and place to travel around with a convoy of masked men."

"Time's up," Mauricio announced. "Sir, as sorry as I am to let you believe we have somehow manhandled you, which we did not, to which Craig is a witness, we now have to escort you to hand over to border control that will check your papers and immediately let you pass to the other side."

Knowing that Craig was resolute more than anything to arrive at the cliffs and would stultify anyone opposing his path, Mauricio offered the journalist the easy way out, particularly since a convoy of ten additional armored vehicles was arriving, pushing its way easily through the foliage. Before the journalist could make a comeback, he was unceremoniously shoved into one of the armored vehicles together with his microphone-toting colleague. Behind their backs, Craig pointed at the mirage-like approaching black mass. Metal and glass gleamed forbiddingly delineating visages blurred of expression, the occupants a cloud of giant hornets swarming to cloud foliage and trees. Next to Mauricio, Craig swung into the front seat, rapidly pulling the door shut to drown out the choir of humming engines.

"Let's go," he demanded in the cool interior, flinching as his tone might resonate cavernously like Cherido's Buddha figure in the valley, a prospect he then suspected as neither unwelcome nor unpleasant.

VIII
QUEEN OF THE NIGHT

The narrow walkway that spun around the upper level of Parliament housing Stefan's office was exposed to the elements. At almost seventeen thousand feet, the whistling of the air, paired with the hollow tumbling of the wind against the cliffs and metal below, orchestrated a scientific serenity. Speckles of rainforest green interspersed with rocks the color of deep mahogany extended vaulted towards the horizon. To the far left, the capital of the adjoining country punctuated the sight with white buildings adorned by several skyscrapers. Their grey towers needled the sky, fighting against desolation by pushing like sail boats into the ocean. Fields of lush tropical vegetation undulated from the far right, steaming in the burning midday sun. In the stillness, very tall clumps bowed their wind-tussled crowns, surging in waves from the earth. The encompassing sky accentuated the vast galaxy of the sun, lighting up brightly in diamond-hued translucent blue. Straining his eyes, Craig detected grayish puffs of smoke indicating the war zone amidst the green and the rocks. The smoke dissipated rapidly, both because of the wind as well as due to the ill match of their claustrophobic column shapes with the panoramic scenery.

"Venus is the closest planet to earth. What is down there doesn't come remotely close." Stefan had guessed his thoughts. His emaciated furrowed mien spoke volumes of what he had gone through in the past few days. Ocular stateliness clawed at bypassing images, ripping their umbilical cord, attaching them to coherence and order. Stefan likely visualized by means of fangs churning his mind, his lips cracked dry from all night trips and the diatribes in which he had to involve various subordinates. "Step closer to the handrail if you will, you're too small to fall. See those parapets along the jagged rocks forming these cliffs? A couple of years ago, they were the locus of United Nations personnel piling up. They were looking for children. They had come here in reality and truth expecting children as young as toddlers waddling all over the cliff and adjoining garden. When they couldn't find any, they turned around and left."

"Are they looking for children this time also?" Peering down the dizzying height of the steep precipitous incline, Craig caught sight of the stony slivers alongside. The stepping stones dissolved into the thin mist that separated the lower layers of air from the upper.

"That's a pathway. If you want and have the stamina, you can scale the entire height of the cliff up to the entrance to parliament." Stefan radiated enthusiasm which made Craig fear he would bound to descend the entire seventeen thousand feet just to demonstrate how to master the ascent. "Children? They have been looking for children for a long time by now, unable to find any. How should I say… You do your part, and I do mine. Then we meet to compare notes. Why don't we leave it at that, agreed?"

The powerful machine used in this war bent over Craig, blocking the ethereal backdrop with its shadow dripping the exhaust of vehicles, dust and other chemical odors onto Craig's L'Occitane and tuberose-scented powdered and puffed demeanor. Craig perceived the stony visage erupting into a broad grin as a coup de grace, releasing him from the network of abstract orders so Craig could do his thing and fight his own demons.

"Today at sundown at the black lotuses upstream from JC's tomb across the narrow river bend?" The bulletproof jacket pleated neatly as Stefan pulled out a dust-coated phone device. The vestment folded about elbows and collar, surprisingly left intact by many scuffles and unwanted contacts. The nameless exotifying location Craig subconsciously had clearly guessed as imbued with meaning by recent events was now a time and place with precision identified and saved in Stefan's calendar — dark and alive, it beckoned as the borderline guarded by Cerberus to prevent the deceased from escaping his tomb.

***

George arrived brusquely to plunk into one of the flat leather fauteuils the same style as where he had bumped into W and M two days ago, but located down the hallway, away from Stefan's sanctum in a large open space serving as antechamber to the labyrinth of offices. Today empty, the area containing the offices was a veritable maze of shapes, sizes and arrangements. The arrangement in places was as extreme and disorienting as a triangle inserted into a rhombus. The corridor could also be shaped like a broken thunderbolt to connect spaces that were devoid of any indication if the next office opened at the broken area or at the end of the next sharp corner. The idea, as Craig readily surmised, was to facilitate the stop or arrest of uninitiated persons wandering or sneaking astray in the labyrinth.

"I'd rather have Hermes breeze me through this place than Cerberus devour me each time I seek the company of the living," Craig jested, glancing at the leather loafers that appeared to glide on wings, which surprised George, judging from the impromptu raise of his brows. *Or is he signifying vanity?* Craig mused.

"Cerberus can be trained, whereas Hermes steals." Even in jeans and a white T-shirt imprinted with DKNY in white crystals across the chest, George exuded an imposing grace accentuated by the uncanny natural fairness of his skin and the wetness of freshly washed tangled tresses. "But what he steals, he sacrifices to the Gods, which can serve as solace. Plus, I am not Ariadne and would cut straight through the labyrinth." Moura, aka Ariadne, flung a comb of black stone from the hiatus of office spaces which George caught in flight, reminded he was to comb his hair. Craig examined the strange creature so aloof in fluid professional hair styling and yet so personable as drops of water continued to spritz on Craig. George apologized several times without ceasing his activity.

"I shouldn't go it alone, you mean?" George interjected, shaking his head at Craig's last-minute query that he meet with him, here on the eve of disaster. His surprised dampened as his combing proceeded even though something about this attorney bugged him.

"Not alone, but I don't know yet with whom. With me? I am not yet sure."

"George, there is water pouring all over the leather," Moura exclaimed in exasperation from the back. Nimbly in stilettos with hair perfumed and dried, she approached. Eyes averted and half closed as if still recovering from an unslept night, she wiped the drizzle off the fauteuil with a towel.

"So, what happened that night when you were a 1L at Fordham Law School?"

Bent forward, elbows on his knees to let his mother dry the leather, George stared at Craig. He responded to the question regarding the incident with Patrick Chataway graven and with a sullen maturity. "I kidnapped him with a bunch of friends and drove him to a secluded area up in the Catskill Mountains where we were about to wring his neck when he broke down and confessed." Sporting the joyous mien of one who has never felt the burden of reprimanding her son, Moura plopped onto the fauteuil's arm rest. She hugged George's shoulders and planting a kiss on top of his head. "But he did not confess to what I had expected." Reciprocating, George squeezed her in return. Craig's chin dropped, baffled by the extraordinary resemblance of mother and son. Her articulate head resting on top of his radiated nothing less than the sharp dreaminess of Constantin Brancusi's Sleeping Muse sculpture. George's sudden refined upright sense of himself couldn't have better expressed the idea that his mother was his main platonic squeeze.

"Instead, he whined he had never meant to beat me up. Strange because he had never beaten me up, at least not physically even though apparently, he had been dying to. Or he was too panicked to know what he was saying, convinced he would die. I had lost any interest in harming him before we even arrived in the Catskills."

"Why is that?" Craig queried.

"There was no reason why I would, apart from that he was getting on my nerves, which is not a reason... I still remember him sitting there handcuffed and babbling... there just wasn't any connection between him and me. I felt nothing, we had nothing in common. He could have been on the moon and I on earth and it wouldn't have been any different. I concluded there is no reason to harm someone with whom you have nothing in common, no relationship, no bond, nothing whatsoever..."

"But when you took him, at that time you did want to harm him?"

"Oh yes." The memory was crystal clear to George. "I wanted to have my buddies beat him to a pulp so I wouldn't get my own hands dirty, and then we wanted to force him to provide his bank account

216

information and wire ourselves his one billion dollars, which by now has doubled… I was in a hot rage and not in control of my thinking since something of that magnitude obviously would have been caught right away!"

"Then why did you want to do it? Why didn't you think of a smarter way?"

"I lost it in a rage, Mr Malcault. He was so annoying! You have no clue how horrible he can get. Constant criticizing, analyzing, screaming at me, everything I do was wrong, and he had to redo it all of the time, I better watch and do after him, so I know how to do even the most basic tasks. I had to follow him around like a shadow, and if I was late even thirty seconds, he would come screaming, 'George, where are you, you little shit. You are garbage in my house George, and you better get that clean.' Constantly! He would literally have me clean the live-in attendants' quarters with bleach and to scrub the floors and bathrooms on all fours, so I would know what it means TO BE CLEAN. Plus, I was taking drugs at the time and he was depriving me of the little identity I had. I was twenty-two, and he had pushed me through college in three years. Every time I wanted to sit by myself and just think and reflect, he would appear out of nowhere. He was watching me night and day and berate me that what I was doing was idiotic and I was stupid, and I should go and live with the animals on an island, and if I end up there, he doesn't want it to be his fault, he doesn't want to waste another human life, all this noble grand rant injected at times. Mr Malcault, what can I say? He forced me to do homework and all kinds of special projects. He never waited to see that maybe I wanted to do the homework by myself! Instead, he would pour iced water on my face while I slept at five a.m. because he took that I slept at all as an indication of me wanting to be disobedient. He feared I hid things from him in my sleep. And I could think of projects more captivating than his… founding of corporations, even though maybe not of as many constant big projects. He hid my drugs and when I had withdrawal syndromes, that is when I lost it in one big hot rage."

"At the time that you took him, did you tell anyone what you wanted to do?" His mother had returned to the labyrinth, and George was now

217

repositioned in his normal professional state. The poised mixture between caring and polished affected Craig like a thorn in his side.

'*Is this tender feeling towards this George because I don't have any children of my own?* ' Craig asked himself. '*Or is this evidence sufficient that the DOD is screwing around behind the back of the American people, using taxpayers' money in support of agencies the framers of the Constitution had not envisioned?* ' '*More likely the not having any children,*' Craig concluded, since he had mulled over the taxpayers for too many years. The sight of little downy babies could make him giddy. Those tiny balls of joy smelled so much better than grown humans, poop and pee included! Craig absolutely loved babies, and he now gave to himself as reason for not having adopted that he loved them so much, he felt he already had a baby inside him all along. At his end, George was perturbed as to how this attorney could believe him as stupid as to announce ahead planning and preparations for first-degree murder.

"I didn't tell anyone, not even my buddies. There were three that came along. I thought it would need three to hold him down while I could administer the final fatal blows. I thought I would get him really angry first, and when he attacked me, I would tell them to hold him down. But ahead of time, I only told them my father was driving me mad, and I would commit suicide, which was true, unless we took him out into nature for a ride so we could talk, he and I. It can be easier to convince wealthy kids that your parent is abusive than poor kids. That is at least my thinking. If you are wealthy, he can find you anywhere. He controls your job and your finances. We live in a defined home with closed doors where I have to face him day in and day out. I can't just run away into the forest."

"You're sure you told no one?"

"I told no one, and two of the buddies went overseas. The third was arrested in connection with a murder shortly thereafter but no one arrested or interrogated me. Why do you ask if I am sure? Did he tell *you* about that ride?"

"Oh no, he wouldn't tell me or anyone else about such things." Craig emphatically shook his head. "I want to make sure he is never able to say that it was your mother who influenced you to hate him, with you being on drugs and he is sacrificing his own mental health to get you off them.

218

Remember he took you from the territory after the encounter with the CIA and put you through college, because she was such a horrible bad person that living with her had endangered your life. And before that, when he had put you in a high school in the UK, claiming she then took you from there because she needed you with her to feed her vanity and sick self-esteem."

"I never harmed him." George's smile was exceedingly thin lipped while he brushed now drying hair. "I know other kids who have bad relationships with their overly strict and overly ambitious hateful fathers."

"Yeah... I am sure you don't know anyone else whose father has been trying to kill his mother since at least the nine months before his birth. Tell me about the times when he put you in high school and in college. How did that make you feel?"

"Cold and distant," George responded promptly. "He was cold and distant, not at all human, not a single feeling. He would simply walk by me without even looking. He only cared about the money he was spending on my schools. That he had calculated carefully. Mom told me to make sure I only get top grades and don't spend more time there than I have to, otherwise he will kill her because I am too expensive. You know what I think? Deep down I am convinced he believed I am too young to really notice what is going on, so he can just do as he pleases. And what pleased him most was to ignore me. Other than that, we had a cold cash-exchange relationship. The abuse only really started head-on when he noticed I was doing well in college, and when I got into law school it went over the brink. He was afraid I would develop a successful life of my own, which he couldn't let happen, because then it would be evidence that Mom had done something well. That made him decide that he owns me, in keeping with the treatment of me as one party in a cold cash exchange. So he had to own me, my personality, identity, my heart and soul." George matter-of-factly recounted the story of Patrick Chataway having lived his life at breakneck speed with the emergency brakes on. Clearly, he had successfully rationalized his trauma, looking at it as a third-party observer. "How does that align with him alleging she made me hate him?"

219

"As you said yourself, he thought you were too young to notice what was really going on. As soon as you were able to notice, he changed the tale, making himself into the victim." Craig had to laugh at the depths to which the wealthy, powerful and famous can fall, governed by the lowest passions, but suddenly George's eyes darted to him punitively.

"Why did he save me from the CIA at his own risk, if he really is the self-interested jerk, you make him out to be? He stepped forward in front of the agency and took the risk to spin another tale. This time it was all his fault I had ended up there, he had neglected me, had failed to protect me from nefarious evil, I am his son, and he doesn't want a paternity test so as not to humiliate the mother, he is a saint, he will give his life to rectify all wrongs…"

"I am your mother's attorney, and you will notice the humiliating your mother slant you have just portrayed to me." Craig remained adamant. "Plus, in this society a powerful person has to take sides, and big money does not like big government. Just imagine what would have happened otherwise, had he not stepped forward to assume responsibility? He would have given US intelligence agencies the upper hand in his own private dealings. No, George, his behavior in saving you as you like to see it, is perfectly in keeping with the hard cold cash exchange."

George's eyes were glinting now as if he was making fun of this eager attorney, yet he said nothing so as not to endanger his mother.

"I know what you are thinking!" Craig preempted him from feeling guilty. "There must be something else there to motivate someone to go to such lengths to make someone into his son who is not his son, neither does anyone involved really grasp how you could ever be his son. As you said, you two have less than nothing in common. What should I call it? Excessive pride, vainglory without boundaries, lust for ever greater power over people as well as nature, including the fates of things to which you are the best means, precisely because you are the least likely successful choice. I know, I know, George, don't interrupt! Why would he go to the length of facilitating healthy relationships with females for you? Wouldn't he want you to be just a well-oiled, maximum-efficiency, alienated cog in his machinery at his disposal?" Craig was grinning and snorting in delight that George would finally get the point, which was his most earnest desire. "Because having a top model in his family is the pinnacle of his putridly arrogant aspirations! He knew you would find a model, since your mother is precisely the type. And his father was the Nazi mold into which he beat you, the model having some German roots... Don't worry George, children get caught up in the divorces of their parents all of the time, just like you were just now. You're old enough and terribly smart, you'll get over it before dawn tomorrow."

"It must be me then who wants to look at him in a more delicate light. As you said, I am my mother's type."

"Don't get me wrong, George, you can think about him in whichever light you please, and the more delicate the better for her case. I just don't want to tell you any lies. I don't want to confuse, entangle or befuddle United States security policy by making those involved in it of unsound mind, which having to live with constant lies can do to a person. So, this crazy attorney is more than your mother's attorney, he is also an advocate in favor of United States security policy, and the two conflict, you must now think? Well, there is no conflict because if you are clear headed you are a better son to your mother, and it is better for United States security to have clear-headed professionals who are good sons to their mothers. That is my personal opinion to which I am entitled as you are to yours, noting there are some nefarious higher-ups at the DOD who disagree with me... Let's return to the equally nefarious Mr Chataway. What happened after you were recruited by military intelligence when a 2L student? How did he change yet again? What monster did he metamorphose into next?"

"They approached me because they liked my methodological, hard-hitting, thinking potential, as honed by the nefarious Mr Chataway." Smirking while stretching himself, George put forth a version of himself amused at the attorney's mental acrobatics geared to save his mother from further abuse, his Latino machismo way of saying thanks. "He didn't want me to end up some pervert who would be used and discarded by the DOD like toilet paper, to die on some dangerous suicidal mission in distant lands. Don't worry, Mr Malcault, I got your point! Me dying like that, a pervert, would obviously have obliterated his unsurpassable conviction in himself. So he became so courteously concerned about my private life. Obviously, he knows exactly what a healthy relationship is, yet he has fought all his life to ruin the relationships of others, including his own, which buttresses your point. And he hired me for a good job at Resource Global, so he could control everything and make sure it is all done to his advantage. Now he wants to make sure I become well established in life, so the DOD holds no influence as they really tried to use me as if I were an eternal pre-pubescent, which deviates completely from Mr Chataway's modus operandi as a marvelous, mature, magnanimous person. But according to this spiel, shouldn't he then let go of me soon also, as soon as I have served the purpose of having been chewed up, regurgitated, rechewed and discarded thoroughly. Haven't I served his ultimate aim of establishing forever his own interest and glory in his saintly, immaculate ever-perfect self?"

"Right, and precisely at the point where eventually he is finally able to kill her and do away with her for good, so he remains the only shining star, even though that still may be some way off as I have known some very fit sixty-year-old females." Craig couldn't spare a machismo quip himself to lighten the brooding weight of insights and realizations. "Seriously, you may have heard the theory that a person who lives his life at breakneck speed with the emergency brakes on never gets very far, then why did this one? He has engraved you into his own cells and neurons with his hate. Whichever way he proceeds is the right one for him because it is conducive to his survival. He is the very opposite of someone who has no executive functioning because the pathways in his brain supporting such are erased in the person's victim mentality. Instead, his pathways of survival became well-trodden by hate, then and there only where that made him survive. He has perfect knowledge of himself and is a great strategist. Why does a good soldier kill before being killed by the enemy? A good soldier knows the enemy, even though being a good soldier doesn't make you or require you to be a good person. The two, however, do not exclude one another. See, I am giving praise where praise is due. I am not shy. So no, he won't let go of you, convinced as he is that he has beaten you into being his one and only true eternal son. The other reason why he got this far is because the time is ripe for a person such as him, but that is an entirely different story bearing no relation necessarily to the present case…"

Craig paused to ruminate on the magnitude of the case. He caressed the rings gleaming and glittering on the fingers of his right hand. The dark gold Inka skull with rubies for eyes on the forefinger he had bought for himself at a bazaar in Peru, hoping it could bring him closer and help him save Rico; the fairytale princess diamantine filigree on the middle finger inherited from his adoptive mother; and the white gold Cartier love ring with three diamonds on the ring finger, gifted to him by Juan. Just like the three main protagonists, Moura, Stefan and Patrick in this case, none of the rings in character and appearance fit well with the others. The filigree was joyful and bold, the Inka skull brooding and cautiously painstaking, the Cartier a harsh slab of dominant ice. Yet each was an integral part of the larger whole, balancing opposites and uniting disparate sides. Craig did not dare imagine how his own life would have proceeded would he not have been firmly anchored in the realism of on-the-ground horrors, had he not trifled in the face of repressive authority, or had he failed to persist to pursue the threads to the end despite all wisdom suggesting otherwise.

"Has my story greatly saddened you, counselor? I am afraid I might seem morose!" With an angular smile, Craig half agreed, half disagreed to this Latino innuendo. George hoped to be right in the end but felt too self-effacing and considerate to press the point. The big FUCK-OFFS, on the other hand, for which he could be feared at the DOD as well as at the unrelated Resource Global, George reserved for the American side of the game.

"I have seen it all, my dear. Don't forget I work in an immigration system that is the worst in human history." Vitalized by his love for babies and renewed thinking how he could adopt two, since one would be too lonely, Craig embarked on dishing out his favorite story he reserved for people of at least some sense and morals, of which he considered George to be one. He couldn't dispel the thought that George had given him the cold shower. George had insisted to transition to Chataway Senior, whom George clearly identified as despicable, in a favorable light. He had suddenly referenced Chataway Senior as having saved him from the C.I.A. That effusion had been pampered by the dictum, impressing Craig as flaunting George as solitary, that as his mother's "more delicate" type, he wanted to look favorably at the

223

monster. George's expressed doubt segueing into this conversation, that he shouldn't go it, his life's path ahead, alone, presaged Craig's present thought: Why would George, who had gone it alone against such formidable bulwarks as the U.S. DOD, not to speak of the feat, extraordinary in Craig's eyes, of having kept his sanity in the face of Chataway Senior's habitual abuses, now be concerned with not being able to go the path ahead alone? Why would George feel delicate in the face of what should appear to him a piece of cake? Craig had to admit to himself that he had barely scratched the surface of George Chataway's existence. He resolved to deflect and buy more time in George's presence. "Let me tell you a story. At times I tend to live or set up my tent at 2 Federal Plaza in downtown Manhattan, home of the feared but in places super-liberal local U.S. immigration court. It depends on the judge. One, a good acquaintance actually, is so liberal he sleeps through the hearings and has to use his left hand to lift his right hand to sign whatever paperwork is presented. On this occasion, surprisingly, he was not sleeping. The client of the attorney in front of me and customer of the United States Citizenship and Immigration Service was a pretty eighteen-year-old girl with large gold hoop earrings and beautifully combed hair rudely. She rebuked my colleague and proceeded to present her case herself. She had filed for hardship waivers sufficient to feed a village in the adjoining country here, the point being she was an unwed mother with a two-year-old U.S. citizen child. (Between you and me, the father, who briefly sought my advice, however, could not focus on a resolution, is in jail or released from jail and again walking back and forth across the Mexican border.) 'Oh, a mother!' this judge exclaimed, picturesque and enthroned, beaming respect, signing off on the girl's paperwork. The morale of the tale being, when she had the child while living illegally in the United States, she knew she would get that reaction from an immigration judge, and she had the child with the first dimwit she could find. No way of knowing if she would be a good mother or not, or if she could even try, since if you try to find out, boy do these clients or customers get angry, you might be violating their rights. The same lady, if instead of basking in her seedy sleazy accomplishments, she would have walked in with at least a B.A. degree to defend an H1-B or work visa, she would have risked the judge to investigate and berate her as somewhat egotistical, somewhat not entirely right, unless she made $10 an hour, or the company was bankrupt or barely functional, in which case she might have received compassion and gotten away with a gentle patting on the wrist. I had a client with an accounting degree drag her feet to court with ashen features and a greasy ponytail in baggy clothing pushing a beat-up bike that had broken down to successfully make precisely that point. So dear George," he concluded the lecture. "They don't even attempt to fake marriage, while they punish the well-intentioned, and I have seen it just one time too many. When I was much younger, I used to think it must be the super-liberal Democrats who want to breed a new generation that will vote for them, but at that time there were less than five thousand immigrants in immigration detention whereas at the present there are as many as five hundred thousand, and breeding your vote by any means is… well… I don't want to continue on this route." Craig stopped, fearing he might begin to sound bitter or foolish, keeping his United States citizenship while protesting the fundamentals of his country. Other countries meanwhile praised him a hero! Maintaining freedom meant constantly building bulwarks of freedom, which Craig doubted the immigrant generation eking out a living in the mass service industry of the last few decades, such as McDonald's, FedEx, Wendy's or Hilton Hotels, had any clue of. Neither did the rich, whether immigrants or natives jetting in private planes to dull and monopolizing professional conferences and arrays of meetings, have any interest in the philosophical intricacies of freedom.

George hesitated at a loss of what to say. He did not seem to mind that Craig wanted to probe him. Given his mastery over strings of crises and contingencies, emergencies constituting the entirety of his job, George greatly relished peering at Craig with his mother's austere out-of-the-tank stare. Craig's tale of motherhood gravely wronged had rung a bell and shifted gears to Moura's valence. The emotional value associated with her stimulus now was one of war and distance. Craig pressed on.

"And that is not all." he savored his presently belittled status, providing George with a vantage point into the dark matter that he referred to as his job. Craig knew that dark matter also constituted the stuff that galaxies are made of, while he preferred the light of the sun and the might of Jupiter, whereas George appeared aligned to the marble opaque of the moon. "Engaging with the immigration judges and immigration officials at all federal levels or even with any federal official entails idolatry. How else would applicants, including myself, receive a benefit unless we imbued these judges and officials with supernatural powers granting what can otherwise not be obtained by the powers of mere mortals? It is a deadly affair! People in my country have to be so liberal, excessively and grotesquely, as to take abuse as granted and as a form of gifting grace. Hence all the fake liberals..."

"That is not a good way to build a country." George waved the accurate denunciation away as if swatting at the nuisance of a fly. He bent over to Craig. "Psst, come closer, I have to tell you something... I burned the DOD file with all the details on Parliament." Craig required himself to accept this blatant admission that George had no interest at all in the functions of the United States. An entirely different route indeed had to be taken. Idolatry could not lead to salvation, not even to the resolution of basic problems.

Craig lamented he had no opportunity to string George along to greater length and clarify what George had done with the top-secret file before he had burned it. They were interrupted by Marco, secretly initiated as the new Chief of Staff today, sporting a cascading crown of dreadlocks. Marco barged in with studious mien to prevent himself from being rude.

"Your Eminence, Patrick Chataway has arrived, he says he is here to meet with Kevin Applebee. With him are fifty Whitewater Security personnel. They have surrounded our Plaza downstairs. He says he is here to protect the company?"

"Seat him at the other side of the cubicles closer to the elevators. I don't want him to bother this attorney." George patted Craig's knee with his fingertips, whispering, "I have to go. My father is in one of those offices." Craig made himself comfy, propping his elbow onto the armrest to rest his cheek in his palm, the perfect demeanor of the expectant winged cherub observing from up there in the clouds.

***

"Steff, you are a living nuisance, a rat from hell." Soon enough Patrick's invectives boomed through the open space, clanging metallic veneered with roguish lighthearted spite. "What is wrong with you, are you feeling unwell? I see you have taken a shower; you are all scrubbed clean and now you are typing, working hard today. There is a way out of this and a war out there but Steff here is posing philosophically while down the street throats are being cut. That is what I am used to from you, Steff. I am hardly surprised. Let's get down to the meat of things, which today is my good news as well as some bad news. You want the good news first, right? You are all elegant and smooth, typing an armistice I am now led to suppose... Right, for that one needs the basic ABCs, you know high school literacy, you know what that is all right since until sixteen you were lucid, to fill up a page with what one's demands are in this fucked up place. Oh, I am seeing you are typing more than one page, an entire treatise! Well, I did that too in high school, writing treatises, but mine ended up founding a company, whereas yours, well, *hahaha*! You made my day, Steff, sitting there with that prep boy mien, but why the hell are you wearing slacks and a sweater? Are you advertising your next vacation in a two-star bed and breakfast in a mountainous location where no one can see you, which would be sensible of you? I certainly do not want to see you, neither do you want to see yourself.

"Now to your good news, which is that your mother was a prostitute. That's right, a prostitute, she banged your father for the buck, since being a complete idiot like yourself, Dad was new to this region and how would he know what was required unless it was demanded of him? I have investigated and researched it thoroughly because you know, I have a mother myself and I am deeply concerned. My mother still lives in her own house in Delaware, thank you for asking, I bought her that house with the first money I earned which was a long time ago, as I also paid for my son, for high school and for college, then for some reason my wife started paying for his law school, don't ask me why... Not so you, you were just here somewhere, somehow banging for no buck, as was expected of you, it was expected... Why, that is good news? Steff, count me among the geniuses. It explains your behavior and entire fucked-up existence up to the present time! Including the whoremongering that's been going on inside your head for over twenty-seven years by now.

After your mother discarded you, her little cheap fuck, on an island hidden from view, she went to live in her own hut a distance away, and since then she has refused to see you. How old were you, Steff, when you first found out that water is wet and earth looks different, dry and brown? I'd surmise around twelve, which is when your mother left. Which didn't matter much to you, she had been feeding you snakes primarily of which there are plenty. You see, Steff, having all this knowledge, which is phenomenal and enlightening to me at least, if they ever catch you at it, at this... playing the leader of yours... acting like... at times I'd say you are aspiring to rule a territory consisting of huts and the homeless, isn't that so, Steff? People who would never know you when you walk past, then what is the big deal you must ask yourself, well, there is no big deal that is the answer. The problem is all this whoremongering leadership stuff carousing inside your head, all is low-life prostitution. You are a prostitute, Steff, that is why you live in seclusion...! If they ever catch you, they couldn't hate you, because your origins are so humble, oh boy, people will feel bad for you.

"The bad news, Steff? It is burning on your tongue, you know it already, but I will say it for you: None of this will get you anywhere. The British won the American Revolution. It is a done deal closed and sealed like your mother's cunt once she gave birth to you and she turned from whore into a saint, just like that at the snap of a finger. You people have neither substance nor anything else that is real. Horrified by what had come out of her, she vowed to never let a man touch her again... Hold on, Steff, this is my head of security calling me from downstairs. Hello Bob... What? American soldiers in the theater have been assassinated in large numbers just now today... Phew! The Greek and Roman Gods must still be alive, I guess... What? Americans have come up to the Plaza?? Now you know what the orders are for that Bob, take aim and shoot IF THEY COME ANY CLOSER. This is OUR COMPANY we are talking about! I don't even know why you are calling me to ask such an idiotic inane question, it is on page one of your training. What? We are all American citizens? I wouldn't know that Bob, Americans, Navy Seals, United States citizens, I have no clue, and I don't care you went to high school with them, since you went to jail right after... No, I have no clue what country even issued me a citizenship, why are you asking? Yeah, I

228

know I pass by border security when I come in and out, and that is some paper I hand over, not the crown on my head and certainly not any feathers either! You have to learn to follow my logic, Bob... Ahh you did take aim, and they did back off. I knew they would... Picture this, Bob, if you blunder again and call me to ask idiotic questions, all of which are explained in the manual, I will fire you. Does that mean I have revoked your citizenship? Bullshit! I have no such mystical powers. All it means is that you will be walking the streets until some other company picks you up, which may take some time or forever given your criminal record and the fact that I have fired you. Since I hire anyone, Bob, no one has ever claimed I discriminated against them or let them go hungry... Once fired by me, that means always fired... What? THAT MANY Americans have died in the theater?? Well Bob, what can I say, I am a Christian at heart and wouldn't wish that for anyone... That is right, not ANY-one IS what I said. Oh no, Bob, that is quite all right, I am a liberal and a democrat and care for my fellows and don't mind my people arguing with me, as long as they defend THE COMPANY, which apparently you have done. This case, however, is special, it truly is. Because you know Bob, all those American soldiers dying doesn't even matter in the end... We don't deal with those. We don't care if Americans are now going to leave the territory which is what they will be doing now in any event as they have been wasting their time here for all these decades since there is no schmoozing with terrorists, whereas we have grown big and strong and highly adept at defending ourselves... My intent here was to meet and greet with Kevin Applebee, a smart-assed attorney, a genius just like me tipped me off... Right, now you are following my logic, bit by bit and step by step, I know it is hard to learn... The attorney forced me to come to Parliament, a smart idea since it is ME the General has to see when he arrives, so he knows who is here and who is not... I am not one of the many perverse low-life's Applebee supports because I might be doing the dirty work on the ground on his behalf, and neither are you... No meddling with the files of Ara Pacis. Yeah, that is why I left in a suit in the middle of a war, to meet and greet with a General... But just now I was telling the ape here that the British won the Civil War. Right there you called, and I found out I was right...! You know the ABCs now, Bob: It doesn't even matter! We won and are not dependent on anyone... Hold on, the ape's fax is buzzing... Wait... He is handing me a paper, I just hope it is not so that I read it to him... Oh, he has read it already, he can be quick and fast if he has to, including his crazy typing today and his computer work. Okay. At first, I thought oh my, this won't look good for the ape, as it never does, but now I realize it is looking so-so-so. Well yes, hm, a very many of those... whatever... Americans have died, it is true. Hm.... Tell you what, Bob, you hold your position until I say otherwise, which might be by midnight today, and that is an order. There is nothing going on here, Bob, nothing whatsoever... Nooooo, it is not the little man in the street that I meant by *the whatever*... I didn't mean the good, civilized Americans. Come on, Bob, you know me! I mean the higher-ups at the DOD, those that use the f*** word, the a** word, the f*** y*** m***** words, those that I am meeting and greeting with, we don't deal with the little man in the street.... Bob, we own A COMPANY... Hey Steff, who is that using your elevator? I must be hearing what you can neither hear, nor feel nor see... Someone is embarking in your elevator, for God's sake, wouldn't you care to show interest in what is going on in your own back yard, on the trip to hell downstairs?" Patrick's venom deteriorated into a spiraling rage, crashing, bursting, blasting into bits and pieces of shards of bullets and glass to hit and maim anyone and anything. Craig had tip-toed around the office area, sneaking into a far corner of the elevator where, instinctively mortified, he raised the collar of his jacket to hide his face. "Hell, up here in Steff's heaven must be worse than anything outside... Hell here is ME!" was the last lunacy he heard Patrick pronounce.

Dexterously, Craig had managed to pull on a glove before pressing his ID against the security light. *"Obviously,"* he thought with a sneer, *"heaven can only be hell for a f*** y*** m***** type who hates the joys of the angels more than he hates enemies in real life. What a pathetic fool..."* Craig's contempt knew no bounds. In this environment, he refused the risk of leaving any fingerprint, not even the tiniest trace of himself. Encased in golden light, the elevator plummeted down the sky-soaring height until, with toes curling to avert the cold, Craig stuck his head circumspectly through the sliding door into the dim exterior to ensure no one else was around.

***

Deep at the base of the Parliament at the side opposite the Plaza, Craig stood aside, shadowed by the hull of a rock at the top of an iron yawning. He watched the narrow-enclosed stairway below for Ricardo, the bodyguard who had led him to Stefan at the art exhibit in Washington D.C. Still a little pale and dismayed, Craig refused anyone besides those necessary to know of his whereabouts and even those only indirectly and from a distance as just now.

Deftly, Craig sidestepped the shadow and mounted a rock guarding the entrance to the stairway, from where he carefully stepped onto higher stone until the obscuring hull and final seconds of the downward plunging stairs came into view. The stone parapet alongside was blanketed with erupting twenty-feet-long stems creeping along crevices and slogging in craggy terrain. The veritable garden of Queen of the Night flowers ruminated in wait to blossom at night. In the silence of the isolated spot, Craig detected Ricardo's approach, stamping heavily on unhewn steps, his joints and bones the mechanical hardware of the onwards thrusting merciless machine.

***

Dusk was breaking as the motor of the small speed boat emitted a high swooshing sound reminiscent of launching torpedoes. Out onto the water, Craig's and Ricardo's figures cut stark geometric shapes. Their reflections flittered on the still expanse, the depths of their forms hidden and unseen, oscillating, pushing against the visible, creating shadows where they blocked the setting sun. The steely gray of the water shooting onwards appeared inviting to Craig. He and Ricardo were both silent, Craig still burrowing his lower face behind the collar hiding in shame from the bare memory of the monologue altercation he had witnessed.

The river separated Parliament on the cliff from the landmass of the territory. From close by, the river swept broader than Craig remembered, but that was because they were traversing a bend formed by a narrow opening. At its other end, the bend flowed onto a small gulf harboring JC's tomb. The entire riverbank, including JC's tomb, was the dark

231

orange color of large flat rocks hued blood red by the setting sun. The tomb itself was a modest but majestic creation, a miniature reproduction of the Parthenon on the Athenian Acropolis. Three rows of Doric columns provided depth from the outside to the inside holding up a flat marble roof. Night and day, two masked guards watched the entrance, from the distance motionless statutes blending into the columns in a show of victory over death.

Ricardo, elusive and bound to the cause, halted at the edge of the gulf to rapidly survey the scenery. Pulling the boat around, cutting back into the river bend at high speed, he advised Craig, he would drop him off at the other side of JC's tomb, since the area towards Parliament could not be safe. Bracing himself against the brief gust of lacerating wind, Craig responded, "That is fine with me," whereupon the boat drifted back towards the bank. The water, still like a mirror, speckled ashore with a crowd of flamingos pecking glamorously on stilted legs.

Craig bounced off the boat to a torrent of sundown emptying wave after wave of coral blushing rays. The flamingos pranced gallantly. Dahlia-hued feathered bodices rustled involved with the swirling of water, neither interested in Craig nor shunning him. Craig treaded circumspectly on the rocks on which traces of scattered sand drew the shapes of footprints, of a body being dragged. His feet accelerated on cotton balls, placing down metatarsals first to avoid pounding the rock with his heels. Across the gulf, the coast of jagged cliffs thrust into the sky dreary, its upper regions obscured by swaths fog. Alongside the riverbank some five feet land inwards and up a sandy hill ahead, the jungle fanned out untwisting its cavernous turns.

The tomb surfaced in front of Craig, silent and sedated like a bottomless pond inscrutable at night. Craig's attention was focused on the pin-like golden lights from the sun resting onto the horizon that flickered throughout the crevices of the Dorian columns, flashing across a crimson sheen. The guards like the flamingos paid no heed to the small black-clad figure approaching, as motionless and blended into the stone from up close as they had been from the distance on the water. Craig had reverently mounted the five polished steps when raising his gaze to the casket eased on a low rectangular elevation, his mind began to churn and spit out image after rapid garish image. The back of the structure lifting into gray light shadow screened the colorful carousel.

Molded onto the casket, the masterful stone and iron rendering of the shield of Achilles enveloped its four sides in exquisite grey interspersed by pastel depictions. Blue, yellow, golden and pink figurines glinted from underneath rivulets of blood. Small puddles graced the stone floor incompletely absorbed, reminding Craig of the outer rays of a monstrance. Someone had clearly been skinned if not butchered on top of the shield, its center embellished with the earth, sky, sea, sun, moon, and constellations. Warmed by the last floods of the setting sun, remnants of flesh and organs indiscernible from the distance swam in liquid crimson. Craig staggered, staring into the void while reeling off in his mind the ancient myth of Achilles. Returned bereaved to the same battle in which his lover Patroclus had been killed, Achilles' shield now forged by the God Hephaestus, Craig feared to sense Achilles' presence as victorious in front of him, invisibly occupying the space that separated him from the casket. Craig could have sworn to discern the torn arteries of the heart like the stalks of blooming red flowers, tulips and azaleas together with dahlias and poppies maybe, at the top facing him where he knew JC's head to rest underneath the lush heart. Controlling himself and filling his lungs with deep gasps of air, Craig would not come closer out of respect for both the dead as well as the invisible living.

***

The straight path over the flat rock undulated in sandy dunes along the shore where the water blossomed with an ample supply of black lilies. About twenty feet ahead on top of the next sun and wind bleached dune, Cherido stood naked, hypnotically staring at Craig over his shoulder, turning towards him uncertainly. The wind tore at his hair, casting his features, drenched in blood as was his entire body, the oozing patterns of carnelians, in a spellbound alienated glow. The interlaced studded diamond jewelry adorning his wrists and ankles, dripping from his neck to his navel, glittered as if to dispel all worries. His left hand with the three-carat ring brushed forgetfully against his heavy black hair as if he sought to cover his nakedness. He condescended to Craig's presence with

233

an offhand gesture and piercing gaze, breathing a loud cramped sigh, as if to hallucinatorily signal that they both had successfully bought themselves some more time, here on the threshold between life and death. Craig noted from the graven silence in which Cherido stood enveloped the persistence of a shock so deep it led to unfathomable abyss. Cherido's hand had brushed against his hair too quickly. Entirely unaware of his own self, he had been intent on establishing a barrier of forgetfulness.

"Where did you put the body, Cherido?" Craig shouted, lumbering onward now, planting his feet so firmly on the sand he seemed to have grown out of the ground. Nothing could change his mind that there are no winners in war, including himself, and no matter Cherido's psychotic state he had to prevent that further harm befell him. "Where did you put Burrito's body?"

Cherido cringed with a scream, lurching towards the shore. Strung on a high wire, he elegantly braced the elements, turning and twisting his body to join with the currents of air. Bursts of wind tore his hair off his shoulders. His skin turned raw and translucent as the still hot wind dispelled and dried the blood, hurling him suddenly frail and whimpering the slight presence of a child a few steps further towards the river. The sudden force simultaneously attracted him like a magnet.

Cherido remained deeply rooted in the flesh. Closing in, Craig noted he must have washed and wallowed in blood since now drying miniscule coal-like sparks glittered in a mad dance from within the crevices and pores on his skin. Seeing Craig so close made Cherido stop before an invisible threshold, beaming recognition of a friend. Ever the indefatigable athlete, he bent over backwards to pull out of the sand behind him a large double-edged combat knife reflecting the last sparse golden sun rays on a sharply clear blade. High leaden clouds tumbled rapidly over the gulf, transiently threatening to obfuscate the glittering descending light.

His hair grasped by his brother's fist, Cherida's features looked languid and peaceful, eyes closed, drenched with the water from where he had been pulled. Craig watched in sadness as Cherido dexterously twisted the corpse around. The knife pierced the back of his skull, collapsing the brain and reducing Cherida to a sluggish shell.

"I will fry you on the penitent's bench!" Cherido screeched, his voice escaping the screams of scattering sea gulls. The knife's handle with the insignia of his Ara Pacis emitted a golden spark as it pinned Cherida's head to the ground, remaining upright in the shape of a cross. "Don't think badly of me, Craig," Cherido screeched with outstretched hand as if in self-defense, "he was crude and uncouth, including to you several times, and I am a man of integrity. I couldn't stand having a double, a copy, there is only one single one of me."

"Where did you put Burrito's body, Cherido?" Craig persisted, advancing mercilessly. Burrito's name edged Cherido back towards reality. He batted his eye lashes, battling an exterior force twisting his neck to the right to Parliament, then back to the left to Cherida's corpse. "I want to know where you put Burrito's body!" Craig repeated anew, gullible this time, throwing his palms upwards, naïve, encountering Cherido like his bosom buddy. Cherido grimaced as if struck across the face. His memory was jolted and he now knew with complete clarity what he had done.

Sudden violent tremors electrocuted his body, his skin faded into a ghastly pallor, his presence as if liquefying turned into a specter howling in pain grasping for the coolness of the waves.

"I love him, I love him madly, forever," he screamed in desolation. "Madder than any heat of hell. Tell me, Craig, what is greater love than to kill the one you love most, then when he loves you most... We killed most of them! What greater joy and what greater pleasure than in death itself?" Belatedly thrown back in surprise by Craig's query about the body, Cherido paused to straighten himself. He turned neatly set features upwards and exuded a blindly determined righteousness. His gaze hallowed by truth and ardently devout, he listened in ravaging patience to an inner voice. "We killed most of them," he repeated, folding his hands, entreating Craig's vicarious respect and adoration for the prodigious deed but then he dropped to the ground at the whispering water clutching his head, his shoulders trembling. "Satan and the devil," he groaned. The coming night pushed the remaining sun rays across the beach, casting and shredding them into the deep immaculate disk of the water.

"Are *we* any better?" Craig dared to comment.

"Stay away from him!" Moura called from the edge of the jungle behind, reminding him a ruthless murderer hid inside the whimpering child, a predator licking his lips inside the dissipating specter. Limp and losing sense, Cherido's body rolled into the shallow water, blood foaming on the waves, washing him clean. In the last minutes before darkness the sky burned invisible with nefarious energy, the river exuded a welcoming coolness, making Cherido whole. The low tide drizzled on his hunched body, his head resting on his outer thigh as if in sleep. Behind lowered lids the blackness in his gaze pierced with fury greater than necessary to kill one hundred thousand men, riveted in his brain a door slammed shut, jammed there by a bullet, cut in by a crown of thorns, incised by the rusted nail intended to split his skull. Cherido ravaged the borderline between life and death and hence persisted in the shape of a frail, hurt, moaning teenager in distress.

Before Craig could come any closer, Moura ran up barefoot from the dunes and into the water. Rushing to kneel at the huddled figure, her long hair consumed her black-clad physique in vertiginous torrent. She cuddled him in her arms, caressing his hair, pressing her face intently into Cherido's resting on her shoulder, frozen, fervid. His quivering mien agonized at the separation between him and Moura of a few inches of space. The water streamed about them in pearly vapor, dissipating in dark glinting circles, pulling close the cloak of the night.

"Here, we've now got another one who loves madder than any heat of hell," Craig remarked blandly at Moura. In the descending coolness on the riverbank, he began to feel frigid, immature, an outcast from the real joys of life mysterious to him while blatantly clear to the fervent couple. Moura looked up cradling her treasure, her face radiant since devotion to this child appeared to have erased all traces of suffering from her life. A high wind pulled at her hair, whistling on and away electrifying with the tune of a hummingbird.

"They killed almost all of them." She smiled, beaming with closed lips so as not to reveal too much of herself, emphasizing the *almost all* since the specific numbers in such defeat would never be reported by the media. Watching her pick Cherido up in her arms effortlessly, just as she would her own baby, the vapors barely left a trace at her sudden indomitable strength. Craig mused that the way up the jagged stone

236

panned out very short for her indeed. He felt inclined to measure her setting one parchment-white foot after the other on mellifluous shadows stretching languorously without form. She pushed downward rapidly onwards with the desire to release herself permanently out of the embryo shape in which they had both crouched. The last Craig saw of them were the diamonds dripping off Cherido's wrist as he clutched her around her shoulder, mimicking an ornament clasping her wind-swept hair. 'A detail for Bridal Guides Magazine...' Craig couldn't rummage his overheated brain for a better comparison.

***

The flamingos foraged and pecked in widening circles buoying the black water lilies. Night life rebounded on the riverbank while the hovering mass of the jungle chirped, hissed and roared with the thrill. Half a mile to the left around the bend, fog streamed down the opposing cliffs, threatening to pelt the river with mighty plumes.

"I bet you don't want to go back to Parliament," Stefan called out from the top stair to the tomb, toting a zipper bag with the remains, his features ensconced in darkness, yet Craig sensed his keen smile. "Nature is ravishing in this part of the world." There was no point to berate Stefan anew about his lifestyle and penchant to work in hiding or at night. Stefan's inexorable, albeit covert strategy had unfurled with the clarity of bright noon at dusk, clashing dissonant with the insignia of the sun halved by the bolt of lightning.

Standing sentry at the water with hands buried in his pockets, light-footed, curling his toes inside white socks imprinted with blue anchors on the ankles, Craig breathed in harmony with the sounds of nature while he surreptitiously inhaled the whiffs of a powerful disinfectant. The expanse of the river weighted leaden, gathering them in silent bond. Shivering, Craig buried his chin inside his collar, nodding in agreement.

***

He envisioned the incidents presently occurring at Parliament, which Stefan had counseled he should avoid, at the time that Kevin Applebee was expected. The prospect of the general's humiliation struck Craig as trite compared to George's novice disclosures weighting thorns and nails on Craig's soul, cocooned in the client's beatings and lacerations. A cool wind swept the narrow steep staircase Craig had descended with Ricardo earlier in the day. The gulf far below lay motionless and holed up, stretched taut in places as if with the protruding features of a black mask. Craig thought of Stefan standing at that spot on many nights, critical of the surveillance apparatus emanating from seventeen thousand feet above sea level. Barely perceptive beams of light flittered dimly against the depths, diagonally descending from the high cliffs. He knew Stefan to flinch instinctively at the sight of the fading light, fearing it would emit intense heat, the sign of failure. Instead, today George's tall slim figure at the top of the staircase caught the attention of Craig's mind's eye. George stood cast in a pale sheen by the full moon that shone in through crevices from high above drizzling into the hull of the rock.

In the impenetrable depth of the shore below, the indigenous inhabitants of the area had left raw woolen cloth to dry on stone polished by the waves. Cherido had descended from the speedboat. His traumatized body was regenerating, trembling in the cold, emitting a damp breath where he felt his blood flow anew through his flesh blossoming freshly as if covering bare bones. Adorned in the black uniform, he felt invigorated and very young, as betrayed by the alertness and agility that focused his mien yet strangely matured and more pensive these past few hours. He knelt at the crude pile and pressed against his face the blood-drenched cloth he had brought with him from the other shore, initially intended to carry Burrito's heart before Cherido had changed his mind to leave it with his maker's head. The familiar embalming odor not unlike the scents he had delved in on many raw and sweaty nights cut into Cherido's skin. He decided to not leave the cloth behind and carry it with him always. Jumping up, he welcomed the rapid trickling of blood down his erect spine, denoting the return of rejuvenating life. He smiled at himself, his lungs bursting with the fragrance of the vegetation circling the lower sides of the cliff. Shaking his long black hair with the assuredness of a queen, Cherido conquered the steep ascent. He accelerated with lightness the further the heinous waters fell behind.

In his mind's eye, Craig followed the domed stone railing of the balustrade that circled the awning, curving from the hulled rock into the bottomless pit below. Cold night air billowed out of the pitch-black darkness, speaking of a real presence far down in the depths below. The falling of a pin would have resonated with celestial clarity.

Craig's inner gaze alighted on George's strong hands feeling the cold material with a controlled vehemence, as if he were measuring his ability to rip it out of the rock. Cherido slid from behind him, a perfumed angelic cloud, examining George's determined brow, the narrow scholarly features so much like Moura's. Cherido evidently could not forego a critical pass. He wiped the knife he had recovered from the corpse against the bloodied cloth.

"Why don't we finish him off now and forever?" he queried, the hollow disembodied tone dominating him anew as it had in the valley today at dawn. Then George's thoughtful and distant demeanor kept him quiet. George motioned to focus on the spreading crystal light mounting the stairs instead. Seeming within arm's reach, an invisible demarcation line separated the light from the infernal billowing depths.

Well acquainted with Kevin Applebee's manner of ascent, Craig held his breath, tracing the measured steps of steel since the General tonight walked alone. He felt the inaudible sudden scuffle as George grabbed Cherido by the chest, hauling him back into the hull. Yet Craig grinned, knowing perfectly well Kevin sensed someone hiding in the depth of the stone. Not to his surprise, the General halted leaving barely ten feet of a distance. His figure vivid in moonlight stooped into the shadow of the burgeoning sprawling stems of the Queen of the Night flower. Overflowing from the rock above, the blossoming white of the delicate petals sighed twinkling swaths of veil.

"I know you are there, George." Craig could hear the General's voice wheezing feigning wit to save face. '*Ha-ha*,' Craig laughed, since he had been defeated on all fronts. Breathing in sync with events, he listened closely to the fainting harsh tone, intimating to Craig Kevin's surprise that George was alone, or as good as alone. "At least you get to listen to the cicadas, I have heard they are abundant in this region."

"Can't *you* hear them now?" George retorted from within the darkness, Cherido's knife flashing at his side.

"If you kill me here, George, you know no one will find out, and if you don't, I will just continue to be a pest."

Cascading from the top of the rock the Queen of the Night unfurled diaphanous wings, the discerning sweet scent captivating pollinators. Sweet humming smooched with the air on nimble butterfly wings.

"Find another country to play your sick games in." George's candid suggestion was intended to pelt the General with bullets. "I know you've already done Iraq. It shows from the mess you've been projecting here, having failed so abysmally in Vietnam. But how about Iran? Wouldn't that be next even though you'll say *Been there, Done that*? How many more countries are there where you can steal, kill and strategize? African countries and maybe Yemen? And there will still be more godforsaken impoverished inhospitable regions for you to try yourself out in, games of no end, all blood and gore included with children at the wheel. Pardon me, Kevin for sounding so rude, but why don't you finally graduate from the school of *Defining Our Interests?*" Inhaling Cherido's flowery bloody scent, George twitched at the wet kiss placed on his cheek, irrational since Cherido wanted nothing more than this General dead, yet he breathed contentedly and nestled his head against George's chest and shoulder. Cherido took George by the arm like an old married couple since Cherido had been taught to never without an order act on any other but his own innate intent of a lover.

"You know there were countries who equally discovered the use of atomic power during World War II but refused to use it..." George added the most unambiguous insult and condemnation. At this, Kevin Applebee simply resorted to stomping onwards and past in lunatic gambol without aim or purpose, head bowed careful on the steps, his mien an empty white plate. The most unsteady and uncertain smile smirched his pallor. To an outside observer, he would look the old crackpot, Craig concluded.

"What did you get in return for selling your soul?" the General muttered a jab at a weak defense.

"Well," George propped his elbow against the rock with Cherido cooing his remaining distress, rubbing against George's shoulder. "Like every last one of humanity, we've got stomachs and we all gotta eat. You seem to monopolize the food industry at your whims and wishes, Kevin!" *Mommy will feed you no worries*, George whispered in soul to Cherido.

240

"Ah." The figure had sighed itself into the impermeable façade of Parliament, a sad and provocative sight.

***

The General now inside Parliament and unable to detect Craig's arrival who would enter stealthily on his own whiff of mystery, Craig reluctantly agreed to return with Stefan to spend the night at Parliament. He brushed off attempts at small talk and acted cranky and parsimonious on the ride up. Stefan was neither gay nor a damsel in distress, and Craig at present could not act his personal attorney without much more insights into the territory for which at present he felt he lacked the wit. At this point, every word mattered, since each of the many sides in this high-stake game had innumerable legitimate grievances, and anything Craig said could be used against him. Already pained by George's sweet and vulnerable Latino side, he eschewed further exposure, à la disenfranchised-heterosexual-male-in-severe-systemic-discrimination-mutiny. Deep down in his heart of souls, no matter how hard Craig tried, he just could not sufficiently appreciate Stefan's lackadaisical furtive busybody type. Neither had Craig done too well in the past with straight Latino military types for whom he often slipped from obtaining the basics, such as phone calls to federal officials. Was it that the gay ones, due to talent and conviction, posed the real threats, whereas straight gangbangers stultified actual damage with lampooning machismo? Craig remained evasive, remorseful that his aversion to Stefan in reality signified Craig's own distrust and censure of anything that smacked of aspiration to perfect government.

On the Plaza, past the Whitewater security personnel holding their positions in the pitch-black darkness, Craig resorted to exiting the vehicle terse and cryptic, eyes cast down. The stars flickered chased by rapid high clouds dispelling yet another tropical storm. Craig had to find the way by himself to the room down the corridor from George's where he would sleep tonight. Stefan was examining the sky out of the lowered window while Craig dismounted, clutching his knee since he had refused to stretch or even as much as move on the entire ride fearing Stefan might take genuine human interest in his well-being and deign one of his languorous spellbinding avowals of empathy. Craig left Stefan in apprehension the Whitewater security guards might detect a defect in his sky-bound security apparatus and odiously insinuate negligence and endangerment of Moura. Craig arrived without incident in the leather-padded pewter enclosure, the many corridors and floors resounding eerily empty with dull and distant night sounds, even though Craig knew they were not. Craig opened the window wide. He marveled at the massive expanse of foliage beckoning with velutinous gloss, its perspicacious presence entirely lost on the engulfing waves of darkness. The land inwards area boasted crude unmitigated nature opposite the adjoining country's capital. Perpendicularly below the staggering height, the Queen of the Night garden flourished in expectant bloom.

***

As Craig would soon learn from George, Patrick refused to budge from the upper floor. Caught up in the last-minute jarring and unexpected attenuation of the crisis, he had changed compass and relocated to the anteroom where Craig and George had consulted earlier in the day. The American Special Operations Team swarmed the office labyrinth at ten p.m. in astute, even blissful ignorance of him and his Dior navy-blue virgin wool suit intended to drape like a waterfall. Patrick was exacting revenge, lashed out to annihilate anyone who lacked the interest to approach.

"Hey Kevin," he barked into the invisible barrier between him and the labyrinth, "I was discussing with my head of security here, Bob, earlier in the day. I'd agree it is disgusting for Americans to kill fellow American citizens, it really and truly is, because of ideological and those... those... religious reasons it is important to look proper, I'd agree, but that is what I was going to do. I was going to kill and I would die to kill every minute of every day, because you guys have no right, simply no right, no right to damage the company. And it is not only that, Kevin," he added snidely, the silence persisting, even turning into perceptible snow. "My big problem, my problem of conscience, I'd jump up to tell the minister in church, which means I'd jump up to tell myself, which I am doing right now, and it is highly important: What the heck do you even mean by citizenship, Kevin? I have lambasted my brain and look, Kevin, since we are both sitting here, one of the secretaries in R&D, it's my company I am talking about Kevin, not yours, her name is Adria, a gorgeous name, such a beautiful young lady, for whatever weird reason she went to the naturalization ceremony, the natz ceremony as your agency refers to it. *Natz, natz, natz* sounds like Nazi to me, have you been inducted into fascism yet? See, your own people have no respect, they can't be bothered, she left in this beautiful blue suit with her hair done and when she came back, Kevin help me out here, I really don't know what could have happened to her, all I could do is exclaim 'WHAT-THE-HELL.' The lady looked like she had been caged inside an iron box, inside a claustrophobic machine of sorts, she seemed broader than a whale having gained ten pounds in a couple of hours, and the look on her face was of all life having drained out of her. The lady was dead, Kevin, deader than a door nail, and that is not the only time I have observed such phenomenon. What do you do at those ceremonies, *natz, natz, quack, quack, ducks on the pond,* I'd say you scream; "citizen" and hit them with something on the head repeatedly and many times to watch and observe who stands and who falls. It must be fun for you sickos... Plus the police reports from the different countries they have lived your *natz* applicants must obtain, you are looking to create jails whereas citizenship is created out of love and trust."

Kevin Applebee unexpectedly emerged from the cubicles, the flak jacket exchanged for a Land's End down parka, concerned and dumbfounded and not at all the proud rooster with his red coif of hair.

"You of course have never hit anyone?" A rhetorical question rather than a pronouncement, the General had turned into an icicle. He was dripping sweat as a form of contempt ensconcing fear as long as the temperature stayed low at these seventeen thousand feet.

"No, sir." Patrick Chataway engraved himself into the General's presence. "I have never hit anyone unless that person DAMAGED my company. I have a family, a good job, and a difficult child, and I don't need another citizenship. Now let me tell you something else, since I have you in my eyesight even though you look pale. How old are you Kevin, forty-nine? Five years younger than me and already a big animal in the big zoo? You must have done something right but now you are fading. Look at my head of personal security, Bob here," Patrick demanded, pointing to the six-feet-tall bald man with a bird-like demeanor, propped grinning onto the armrest of a fauteuil. "I told him to kill some Navy Seals, and he revolted even though the British won the Civil War and the United States still speaks English in majority, which is a different matter, an entirely different beast of its own…" He paused, looking a little sad and distracted then proceeded at full gusto. "See, I here own a company, and he here likes me and works for me, and I like him too, not necessarily because he is a good worker, which most people are not, most people in our hallowed capitalist system that feeds us all work because they are threatened to work on the pain of starvation only. They'd never admit that to themselves. I like him because he is a nice guy, I like being around him, I like saying 'Hey Bob,' you get the point. When he and I get together we talk a little, we exchange some thoughts, then I say to him, 'Hey Bob, how'd you like a citizenship? Since Bob, you know, we know one another, we work together, we don't mind each other, then how about a little citizenship? I give you a citizenship, and of course you give me one too since good things always proceed two-ways and in both directions… See, that's how Bob and I go through life, I have two billion dollars, whereas he has none and any money he might have right now been flowing through a hole in his pocket onto the floor which he doesn't even see, but that doesn't matter, Kevin, you're missing the point, what matter is that Bob and I meet, we greet, and we give each other a nice little good old citizenship… What's the matter, Kevin?" The truth having dawned on Patrick that his presence was now strategically redundant. The Ariadne's thread had resolved not unfavorably but irksomely so without his domineering involvement, and Patrick spun out of control.

"Hey Steff," he bellowed, "where are you, has the night gotten too bright for you? Your friends are here, the echelons who support the low lives likes of you in your cavorting and secretive slave mentalities and slave existences. I am too much the common honest man in the street by comparison. Are you embarrassed, Steff? Let go of your charade and offer the General some coffee, or at least a glass of water, but I should know you better than to even remind you of basic courtesy, since I have been sitting here all day doing your job, your dirty legwork as I have done many, many times before, and you haven't even offered me a paper cup... You are an asshole, Steff, a dimwit and lame. Think of it that way," he raged on in the astounded silence, "look at it as practice for your upcoming stint, your part-time gig work at McDonald's in NYC. See, I know the filthy dirt that's been turning in your mind, you're a part-time pornographer who lacks the guts. I must admit you can be good at insinuating, but that is furtive and dissipates with the wind like teeny pop. Right now, you want to be in NYC more than anywhere else, you'd kill not only me but in frustration you'd kill the entire world to just be able to spend one minute in NYC, even though it will be an empty place then but how would you ever know... Your problem which prevents you is you have no job, and you'd look a fool walking the NYC streets in your two-star remote bed and breakfast vacationing attire we discussed earlier today, and I know you were filling out job applications typing earlier today. I saw exactly what you were doing, I just hope you were applying to McDonald's and that's because I wish you well, Steff, no hard feelings on my part. I know McDonald's would hire you, so would the sanitation department in the basement of Hosteling International, I really do, I am saying it because it really IS TRUE. I am providing valuable advice. Insulting a man in your position is the furthest thing on my mind. You should go with the Hosteling place, because being linguistically challenged as you are you'd get intimidated by the French fries, those not talking to you in French, neither is the chicken filet a fried chicken like you are, which you'd have a hard time wrapping your head around, whereas in the basement you don't have to speak any language, it's dark and comfy, you just work with the dirt, just like here where you never say anything either, and you've been living in the dark since when now, Steff?... A very long time. You work with the dirt, follow the flow, follow the dirt wherever it goes, it is the exact same..."

One of the soldiers returned from the locked door of the sanctum.

"His bodyguard said he retired for the night," he reported, having taken Patrick at least at some face value. "His bodyguard said he has nothing to add."

"He is lying," Patrick contradicted loudly. "He did not retire. He never retires, always working, working himself into the dirt, working with the dirt... Right now he is standing on that balcony of his, of course he thinks he is at the top of the Statute of Liberty, which he is not, and he is grasping at straws in the thin air, you know, where only could he find more dirt. The likes of him would like to see the Statute of Liberty disappear beneath a pile of dirt. And maybe I want that also, who knows, who knows. There is no knowing by anyone of what goes on inside my mind. Anyway, changing the subject, I got your fax towards five p.m. today, Kevin. I was here working."

"I didn't fax you!" Applebee interrupted briskly. "I faxed his Eminence. He deserves the Nobel Prize for Peace in my opinion..."

"However, that may be," Patrick grumbled, a dark cloud descending on his illustrious mien. "I don't know what has been going on between the two of you, I am a regular guy not familiar with the many back and forths you've been hiding from the entirety of the world that you're alluding to. All I know is I received a fax..."

"Mr Chataway, you should go home and get a good night of sleep."

"I cannot sleep. You see, you, the United States of America, those assholes I'd rather say in the United States whose names you Google, and you can't get a picture to put on those names no matter how hard you tried, unless they got married, but even then, you'd find more like just a name, you caused me big financial losses, you messed with my business, you messed with me, Kevin. You killed my men and then you said I lied and in reality, you had killed other men who were not mine. You stole my resources... And that fax said..."

"Mr Chataway, everyone will go home." Marco jumped in from the sidelines, a hot arrow on his feet. "No one besides Ara Pacis is holding this place. You stand, or rather sit, on *my* ground."

"Sure." Patrick nodded sheepish assent, staring at his polished designer shoes. "I can see why Kevin here would be afraid of me. I can also see why he would go around trying to influence other parties."

"When I sent that fax," Kevin explained with derisive undertone, "I hadn't yet been here. The fax only said that Ara Pacis was violating the status of forces agreement, and that we should meet about that, even though I understand you would have been so angry, all you could read is 'forces.' Which doesn't matter any longer because since then Ara Pacis as a government has ceased..."

"Did Ara Pacis ever have a government?" "Patrick interrupted, grumbling while fixating on the General with a glare as nasty as plumbing inconsolable. "What?" he erupted. "No government? How come, Kevin, are you admitting your own incompetence? Besides, could Ara Pacis ever even function with or if it had a government?" Hating Land's End jackets, the holy entity the United States military as a whole, and anything that smacked of pretty prep boy image, Patrick's dearest desire to as much as admit his suspicions showed in dismissive conceited pronouncements. He pricked his ears at Kevin's explanation.

This afternoon His Eminence irretrievably deleted from Ara Pacis' computer systems any and all files. Ara Pacis' systems of government, in other words, consisted of one single clean slate. Kevin pointed to the complete and glaring absence of any information or data from which to deduce the existence of a government of Ara Pacis. Parliament was a cliff of impenetrability withstanding any and all elements, whether from this world or from the beyond.

"You are a coward with a desk job, Kevin," Patrick concluded dryly, chafing over his own wasted time. "I came here to meet and greet, I gave you a citizenship... well, sort of, a citizenship... I'm not really sure... No data... No government... All's been deleted..." His tone ebbed as if in a wave of nausea. He thrust his eyes skywards addressing Bob. "Get me out of here, please!"

The creaseless Dior suit and the pinched bird's face ambled towards the elevators, passing Kevin Applebee where Patrick balked to point his forefinger at his opponent's petrified demeanor. The tremulous fierce claw on the verge of inflicting harm, the pinched bird's face gripped him by the arm to pull him towards the elevator. Patrick's screeches punctured the labyrinth until they vanished in echoes. "You are a mass murderer Kevin, you really are. Look at your feet, you are treading on corpses. A liar to boot, since whenever you open your mouth... calling the most miserable of men worthy of a Nobel Prize, making fun of poor foolish Steff pressing the crown of thorns into his lambasted brains. I am wondering how you can breathe, Kevin, or maybe your nasal passages and your larynx are not connected. You steal, look at your jacket, worth $10 in materials and selling at over ten times more... You have stolen my resources tenfold, Kevin, TEN-FOLD! I don't need your militarized society, your spies stinking of animal fodder like the homeless who never yet sees a penny of MY TEN-FOLD which didn't go to any heaven either, Kevin, as much as I'd die to give it to them…"

***

In the dim golden light of the elevator Bob enunciated that the conference room referred to as Parliament this evening boasted an array of gay models prohibited from using the term American as such was discriminatory, instead instructed to refer to outside forces. Bob was repulsed by the wall of silence in cascading blue leaning in laissez-faire attitude against the mirrored wall.

"He's got his strong points too, Steff really does, only no one will ever see them, they will forever remain hidden."

"I heard the fashions are spectacular!"

"Neither do I care, I don't care at all… Kevin & Co couldn't move into Parliament at all, you mean?" Patrick's interest suddenly sparked.

"It's not that they couldn't," Bob chuckled. "They wouldn't have anything to do there and neither could they take it, there being nothing to take as this country's files and computers are emptier than your stare right now. Beyond that, the territory, it is all held by their military."

"I get it! The fauna and the flora, right? The more nature, the more nature flows back, who would cut anything down, he might trip and fall over… I do get it! Grown men cutting down flowers is the most idiotic occupation in the history of mankind, and probably also the oldest, even the caves had gardens."

"Something along those lines."

"Imagine the idiocy of shooting at a Cavalli costume."

"I couldn't even imagine such."

"My dear Bob, that is why I asked!" Patrick guffawed. "I know you couldn't even imagine such. Do I strike you as one who would listen to their pornographical accounts of shootings flowering on their battlefields?"

Exiting onto the Plaza, they were met by Moura leaning against the closest Whitewater Security vehicle, arms crossed over her chest which in Patrick's opinion gave her too brazen an image.

248

"The day of showers has come and gone," he called out to her, referring to her freshly washed and brushed hair. "How many times did you have to shower today for God's sake?"

"The river's bed down below needed a shroud to cover remains," she responded, still too impudent in his view. "And it's not blooming only with blood!"

"Really? You mean you've actually been up to some real-life important things?" As she began to walk towards him, a move he judged necessary to reach the front portal, he noted her self-possession now a sign of a dazed, barely-there state, which disquieted him. The last time he had witnessed the same cagey perturbation located her in the tent at that time functioning as Headquarters of Resource Global, having recently given birth to George, which might as well have occurred on her death bed, as since then he had been counting her among the living dead.

Passing him at a few inches, he noticed to his consternation the tip of a switchblade pointing at his ribs ready to pierce his heart. She stealthily withdrew the weapon as her hair brushed his shoulder with the faint smell of blood and Queen of the Night flower.

"You are not one of the angels," she stated bluntly before disappearing into the portal indistinguishable in its hushed majesty from the enveloping night.

"I'd ask this chick to marry me, would I not know better," Patrick mused. Now it was Bob's turn to look back perplexed. "At the least sign of her distress I would melt into her, if I were an angel is what she meant," Patrick explained. "But as things stand nowadays, she has to wait for a better day."

"Isn't today your wedding anniversary?" Bob grumbled.

"Who cares? That is why she was standing there just now waiting for me, and she did not care either."

"I know we have to stay here until the masked military of Ara Pacis also leaves, that too is in the manual," Bob interjected, exceedingly uncomfortable with discussing his boss' private life.

"You got the last word right, which is good for you. Just make sure we don't sit here like fools uncertain whether our last vehicle should leave first or the masked ones' last vehicle should leave first over our last vehicle. That would be idiotic, Bob, you understand."

Rolling back into the jungle on the front seat, Patrick deliberated with himself, calling to mind his ludicrous pretending to be the spelling bee to impress the silly fifteen-and-a-half-year-old who contended she couldn't sleep at night since nothing felt right. In the bedroom upstairs in his mother's house, she had begged him from uncreative doll's eyes to accept responsibility. "'Why did I persist with the nut case, knowing from the start how it would end, since what I needed was someone who shared my passion for the Kingdom? Because I loved her, that's why!" Patrick addressed the pitch-black night, welcoming the leaves and branches pelting against the windshield, popping and breaking at the speed of the flight. He had instructed the driver to cut through the shortcuts not only in order to evade the coming storm. Knowing exactly how to balance the books with last night's losses which he desired to complete before the break of dawn, they dashed ahead, not considering any delay in getting back to headquarters.

***

Dazed in half sleep Craig lifted his head from the velvet pillow, asking himself if he had fallen asleep as his eyes fell on the lit dials of the bedside alarm: 12:05 a.m. The forest green gleamed diabolically, prompting him to cover the numbers with his fingers lest the digits proceed to shiver and jump, denoting satanic grinning poking fun at him when he noticed he had left the window open. Cold night air was gushing in, causing him to shiver at the midnight hour. Craig fumbled for the switch of the bedside lamp.

"You are sleeping covered in $1,500 bills: Yves Saint Laurent T-shirt and black floral jacquard shorts!" Stunned, Craig discovered Cherido seated in ballerina grace next to the open window. Draped in a pewter night gown adorned with heavy ruffles rustling in the breeze, Cherido swished with the allure of a being of feathery wings. "What's that red dot in the middle of your chest?"

"You came here dressed up the Queen of Night flower!" Craig praised him in bonne homie. "The red dot is printed in between Saint and Laurent, see?" He twisted his upper body for Cherido to have a better view. "I figured if I died tonight, at least I'd die in my favorite fashion."

The presence of Patrick Chataway intertwined in his mind with ballistics and explosions, and Craig sincerely had planned for an early but not bitter, instead for a forward-looking death.

"I came in through the window. I'd better close it." Cherido's slim frame rose, a maiden greeting the starry light before the sliver of a moon. He alighted back into his seat, the window now closed. "I was taught how to scale the cliff and walls outside," he added apologetically. "But now I have something to ask you about." Craig nodded at the rapid sweet voice.

"As an attorney, please tell me: How much do I get as a widow?"

"You're planning to retire form the military?" Craig queried.

"I've always sort of been retired already, because I am the best and too good," Cherido chirped. "But now I want to travel the world, and that costs some money. I also want a stable with horses."

"That's smart of you, to think of a stable together with the horses, since you'd want them to have a place to call home." Cherido giggled, blushing at the compliment. Evidently, he felt shy at being courted by someone he held in high esteem and struggled to keep his composure.

"Burrito has a secret Swiss bank account, and I am the only one who knows about it. If you want, I'll give you a list of his concubines. There are seven sheets in a binder in my bedroom at headquarters, and you can interrogate each of them to ascertain the truth of my statement, which is that he told no one else about that bank account."

"Did your husband have a will?"

"No, but he told me he wants me to have that bank account, and he told no one else about it. Does that mean I get everything that is in it?"

"That is what it would mean, according to our civilized understanding of inheritance, since Burrito left no other heirs."

Cherido swayed in his seat uncertain, hair gushing sideways conjuring the image of a nymph pouring growing feathers over his shoulder before he straightened himself strictly. He breathed with sighs as his married life had been marred by much hardship.

"I am not so sure," he lamented. "First, I thought it is too much money, but then I remembered all those nights I slept on his door mat with the concubines stepping over me, and I couldn't leave since I had to provide security. That was tiring and hard."

"You get all of it." Craig desired to cut off any ugly thoughts but Cherido had already digested as evidenced by him blurting the next question:

"Her Eminence obtained a passport for me with a visa so I can go to New York with her in two days. She did that because such is her wish."

"See, now you even get to see the world for free!"

"Right," Cherido responded as if obeying an order, which is not what Craig had meant.

"Did you get a chance to see the models?" Craig feigned intrigue at the gimmick, worn and faded to his mind yet necessary to hammer home the point that none but the Gods lived beyond the clouds. Everyone else were untoward intruders into the sacred space they perceived as counterfeited simulacra since they couldn't measure themselves against such appearances to boot.

"I didn't." Cherido sighed anew, shaking his head in extreme distress. "I am in mourning, since my husband died."

Craig could have guessed as much from the Queen of Night attire. Appreciative of Cherido's silence allowing him to rest and ponder the mysteries birthed by the night, Craig switched off the bedside lamp, resting his head onto the pillow. In Cherido's presence, he believed he could shape his thoughts with greater clarity than the light emitted by heavenly constellations.

***

Moura had discarded the blood-stained uniform. The harsh narrow confine peeled off and thrust onto the cold stone floor of the bathroom, it could have been the shed skin of a snake, or the withering remains of a cocoon that had burst to let forth new life. She opted for a white latticed gown she had purchased in a bridal store on Lexington Avenue in Manhattan on a shopping spree with George in spring of last year. Having run out of ideas, she had decided to show him how pretty mommy had managed to make herself look when he had been barely born, had not been present in person and in any event too young to remember. She ended up buying the gown to pacify the saleswoman, since she had been trying it on for over fifteen minutes.

The storm-ravaged sky was a vault churning into infinity at seventeen thousand feet. On the pathway circling the uppermost region facing the ocean, Moura's body gleamed like the interior of an oyster shell, hair glistening as if covered in a myriad of diamonds. The water ahead still raged from a recent storm. An American battleship had slowly drifted into view earlier in the day with caution and deliberation.

Moura stretched out her hand to pull Stefan closer, her heart jumping with joy. "Look, they are leaving." She pointed at the battleship.

"What a wasted day," he responded, referring to the forlorn ship. "Open any history book and you'll find in any period of humanity the exact same: Battleships coming to pick up the remains and the wounded."

"This one has a flight deck too," Moura protested, coy and giddy at having him so close. "Some people they want to ferret out faster, I guess."

"Back then they had the gods who immortalized some to better positions than others. Are we still in the periods of the Greeks and the Romans?" Turning to look at her he indicated her presence by tapping her chest with his forefinger.

"I forgot the diamond collier because George was in a hurry and felt awkward in the bridal store."

"It is the same in any period," Stefan persisted. "All war pictures have battleships in them!"

"Well, none celebrate the resurrected Christ, if that is what you mean." She sounded sardonic.

"The Greeks and Romans had no Christ, but they celebrated..." he continued, apparently morose.

"What a day for such morbid ruminations!" she exclaimed, inflamed with interest, examining his features, puzzled as if she had just encountered him for the first time.

Mentally, she placed herself into the moment when George, two years old and not having seen his father for several months, she had waited for Stefan at the edge of the same river now meandering in the infinite depth below them, there where it curved towards the ocean to empty itself in the area of the two islands. The war machinery had been conducting tests nearby, but the night had been silent. Today Stefan held her strongly from behind her battle-ready body pressed against the railing in front, as if to prevent her flying away in joy at the sight of that soon departing ship. Moura still felt the intense curiosity of Stefan's gaze on the heavy golden jewelry she had worn that night, Patrick's gift to her on their second anniversary the day prior.

Resting on a flat stone not far from the current that circled the island, for she loved to swim, she had bent over to touch her naked toes below the hem of her red silk dress. She had not known what to make of his arrival at that place against all odds, or of his profound gaze. She attempting to wrap her head around him even having agreed to this meeting. He had not seen her for several months, and for all intents and purposes she had kidnapped his child to have it raised by another man. Patrick's menacing omnipotence over her she had not bothered to explain, because diverting into such thicket would have been tedious and self-serving. '*I am meeting someone tonight whom by now I have bored to death,*' she remembered having thought to herself. Yet she herself also had arrived at the meeting place to cover the void gaping in her interior.

Tonight, she felt her soul separate from herself to scream inside her, ripping her heart apart. She felt her soul detaching from within an ethereal liquid, repulsed again and again by the iron earthliness of her veins. This thought of denying life had sickened her and forced her to come to this place so that she would not just sit by herself and freeze like a leaf withering in the fall. The moist earth that stuck to her skin glittered with the sequins that had fallen lose from the appliqué on the silk. She had not even noticed that while seated she had trodden on the rim of her gown, struggling to get away from herself. Hearing Stefan approach, she had thought to tear off her dress but at the last moment had decided differently. Her head heavy from the strong scent of her Jasmine and Agarwood perfume that she had anxiously overapplied, her thoughts roamed feverishly and palpitating, shutting out her true emotions until finally an idea hit home.

"How many do you want?" she blurted, taking off the collier dripping with tiny diamonds around her neck and twirling it around her fingertips as if it were a lasso. Her features shone rosily from a forced and greatly contrived smile. The wide-eyed consternation he lunged back at her convinced her he understood her to have said that she wanted to return to live with him on the island, however preferred to pay him rent instead, having brought cash for her expenses.

"One," Stefan finally responded in a flaccid tone that convinced her he did not know the value of money, habituated as he was to the paucity of his habitat. Heat rising in her chest, she jumped up with great velocity to slip into the river and cool her burning skin, not to speak of the bruises from the many beatings.

"I will give you all," she called out to him, "if you stay with me, I will give you all and much more." The red silk tore around her in the current accelerating towards the island, threatening to be ripped off like the petals of a used and aging flower. On the edge of the shore, the sky-high towering cliff had cast a stark shadow on Stefan's eighteen-year-old self, arms crossed over his chest with a quizzical demeanor. Prompted to action in this godforsaken land, he preferred inactivity and silence, having abrogated any thought of any wife and child and lived now perfectly fine by himself, all alone with his newly found peaceful life. Moura had hurried out of the water as if speeding on angels' wings, regret, loss, and a blinding hope washing over her. She could not bear the sight of him standing forlorn without the slightest sense of things of value.

"These diamonds are worth over ten thousand dollars," she cried in dismay at the barrier he had erected. She had lost her composed polished demeanor in a flush of comforting hysteria. Stefan nodded sideways and raised his eyebrows in an effort to demonstrate faint intrepid involvement.

"Maybe then we could talk," he wryly concluded the wretched impossible scene.

Helicopters flickered faintly over the battleship while Moura was in a state of wakeful sleep. Her back leaned firmly into Stefan as she faced the seventeen-thousand-feet height, discerning and not at all perturbed. Her beady dark eyes dissected from behind closed eye lids thin as parchment, shining golden, deeply absorbed in his thoughts. She contemplated the many things she could tell him on how to come to a resolution with the continued presences of these ships in all of his historical periods.

"If only you could hate them the same as I do," she finally resolved to mutter deep inside, in regret that her plan to strike the final fatal blow at Applebee now would take time. This time would plummet precariously into the depths of hell by the drudgery of heavy work. "It would be of such help."

Stefan's hand caressed her hair that felt like liquid rays as if he were sculpting her thoughts, giving measure to the expansiveness of her spirit. "Look up," he demanded since up to now she had been staring either at him, at the battleship, or at the hate inside herself. "What do you see?"

The light of the moon turned vivid as the heavy billowing storm clouds lifted. Far ahead into the narrow strait, the lit edges of towering clouds surged effortlessly gliding over smooth black waters. Flashes of lightning faded immediately into darkness. Still quivering from the storm, the night ahead receded into the vault of the galaxy, a vortex inside a broad tunnel, leaving back a point of light Moura detected into which she resolved to fix herself, to see herself as entirely submerged and cloistered. She stood face to face with her perfected inner image. The dizzying starry nucleus now tore into two by a lightning flash, then closed into itself again in ever repeating infinite cycles. Stefan held her still imperceptibly. His hands covering the soft arch of her womb, she suddenly straightened herself as if awakened, her eyes wide open to look at him with her quick full smile, thunderstruck by an unexpected thought.

"I've got the new insignia for Ara Pacis!" she exclaimed, the current decades-old operations now over as of tonight. "An iron arrow tip touched by the lower half of an angel's wing or caressed. One might want to allude the wing dipping into the iron even though for most, if touched or caressed, it will not be as easy and straightforward to determine."

256

IX
SACRIFICE

"I swear to God, George, I DID NOT call the CIA!" Last night's calculations panned out neatly, and on the tarmac, Patrick, vigorous and refreshed, took George's accusations in stride. "Not when you were sixteen, not now and not since, NEVER. I am not that kind of a guy! I swear on my mother's grave even though she is still alive." He confronted the twenty-six-year-old hovering over him sporting travel attire, a T-shirt glittering purple with the Manhattan skyline, and jeans. George's flat mien betrayed hesitancy as he considered pitying this older man due to incipient age-related frailty.

"You are being arrogant and brazen, George, and what is that towel and toiletry kit you are carrying? You couldn't pack a suitcase and now you want to board my plane berating me?"

The clear sunny day was at odds with the charged tempers. The private plane waiting for take-off flashed the shape of a dove's wing steering into the azure blue. The short tarmac emptied into the ocean, edging narrowly through dense entangled jungle.

"Dad," George jeered, averting his gaze with a grimace so as not to look at the dignified features savoring righteousness, "they knew the precise locations not only of me but also of some people, one of whom was a few inches in front of me. He was their most wanted. Had they not known that location very precisely, they would have killed me instead…"

"Hello!" Craning his neck to look him in the face, Patrick taunted and challenged, hopping back and forth on his toes while pointing to the plane. "I am extremely busy and don't have the time to calculate distances between people. Neither would it ever occur to me to walk into that place on foot to see who is where and what, and at the time I didn't use drones. You aren't trying to change the world, George, are you?"

"What happened wasn't right, and you were the only one who knew…"

"Cut the nonsense, son!" Scowling, he motioned to proceed to the plane. "The agency obtains its own information, and while I'd agree the information is mistaken and defective in majority, in some rare instances, they happen to be right. You had bad luck and I am sincerely sorry for the ills that befell you. Sincerely, George, really, I am sorry! Engrave this into your mind: I did NOT CALL the CIA." He continued to growl, steps clicking like needles on the meshy metal of the boarding stairs with George in tow. "How could I? I am not that kind of a person, I am a liberal, a good man at heart. I even took care of your mother when her life collapsed, which it did for a very long time, still counting." Continuing to vent inside the cream-leathered cabin while George plopped enervated into the far-right seat to blend his gaze with the sun-beaming foliage, Patrick picked up speed, pontificating about his innocence while trumping the sound of the engine with erudite asseverations.

"I am astonished, George. You of all people should know so much better. Not only the CIA, but the entire United States government is also operated by fools. I wouldn't say each person is debilitated by far. Some are very smart bad apples, of which some that are good are thrown into the lot, but overall, the nature of their jobs is what makes them dumber by the day. The garbage they produce nowadays, executive agencies, regulations, everything full of some stuff, miscommunications, no one seems to know what it is made of. None of that was in the original Constitution, since if it were, the country would have collapsed within minutes after inception, no space to kill the Indians, whereas today the killings drown in regulations, miscommunications and ever more killings... To drain parts of the swamp, they even had to hire a gay lawyer, because he is nice, and he listens! Look, I am a combative guy, but I don't want to tell my problems to an ice block who hits me in the face with a law book, and certainly not to one whose credo is we all should be ice blocks. It is better to be an ice block to prevent robberies, thefts, any damage that might accrue to one while navigating the many orders, regulations, killings, departments... Of those there are and remain plenty! That is not my style. I am a good, kind, outgoing man who wants to help others..."

"Hey George, look at me!" When the plane was at cruising altitude, its interior awash in liquid gold shades burnished by the sun, Patrick regained good spirits, chortling, "You're refusing to look at me makes you look immature. Ah, there you go, ha-ha, thank God, George, you are pale. Any more darkness like your eyes and hair would be a death sentence considering the circumstances of me having to pay for it all, including flying you in my plane to your job, commute not being included in your job description, while you carry a towel and toiletry kit with a bad attitude, making all of this so unbecoming. I always meant flying as an aesthetic experience... Oh, I am your father, as we should say?" Shiny white teeth in the anticipatory grin gloated with finality while George twisted beady eyes over his averted shoulder, listening attentively.

"My name was on the birth certificate she sent me, it is true... Even though I don't remember how many she had sent before the one I actually received, or how many after, or if she also sent that birth certificate to others with different names on it that were not mine, none of that I know. But I was the deepest pocket, which I know meant I had to pay since she couldn't get the ape to pay with coconuts. Plus, you are a likeable chap, George, it is not hard to like you. Maybe you think there is nothing likeable about you. Your job has made you obnoxious and aloof and it is me, I just have a weak spot. I have a weak spot for justice. I'd agree, at least in general terms since the particulars of each case only God can know. Can you believe that, George? We ourselves don't know the particulars of our own cases, only God does?"

"Yeah, right sure," George intoned. "The particulars including targeting the clueless innocent with drones and beating them up, not even those particulars we know?"

"Listen closely, son, for what I now say is true: It would be highly displeasing to God if we humans refused to act for our own self-preservation. Martyrdom does not enter my picture, since with the right tricks and rhetoric anyone could be compelled to martyrdom. You're still too young to know what one can get out of people if only one knows how. Pulling the right triggers is a science we have perfected in modern times. But God wants us to preserve ourselves..."

"Preserve ourselves by killing the innocent and beating them up? I am not sure I grasp the fine points!" Knitting his brows, George repressed a nasty retort, having taught himself to keep his cool and vent from the bird's eye perspective.

"A war of all against all would be futile, of course!" Patrick laughed heartily. "There is one thing called reason, another called reality. These two don't connect in today's world. We beat up the victims instead of making them into gods, but martyrdom doesn't count. It never has, not in my world, not in the world of any smart person ever alive. The fine points? There are no fine points." His tone grew menacing. "Are you referring to attacking a country because what they are doing at some point could tend to detract from the self-preservation of the United States? I have heard people in the region tend to hire those who had the smarts to leave Iraq at the time when who was a middle class one day became homeless the next. What a marvelous accomplishment, can you imagine doing that? I couldn't, not for the heck of me. I wouldn't know how to make the middle classes homeless from one day to the next, not even over the long term, not necessarily. What I do is build companies. You and I, we are more like the foolish United States government employees rather than the hawks. We are each one a cog in our respective machines where, unlike those employees, we are not foolish, not foolish at all. We don't lash out at people. Period. What we do is act in self-preservation, which we have to since we don't believe in martyrdom. Martyrdom doesn't exist for us. It is an empty misnomer, the void without which the cosmos could exist. Remember that for the remainder of your existence, whether in this world or beyond, unless you don't want to count like any type of man or woman, whether gay or straight or whatever. What we do is preserve ourselves so we can act for justice, in order to maintain justice. The problem with your views on justice is you're still immature, or not childish enough yet. That will come once you have seen more people and in more environments. I hate to talk that way; I hate to preach."

"Then why not stop talking?" George stated flatly, still clasping him with piercing beady eyes as if with pincers.

"Oh right, I got ahead of myself a little. You are meant to be my security, here in this place."

Having refused to as much as budge for the entirety of the charade, George in wonder watched the pair of blue eyes swimming underneath thin ice haloed from a ghoulish distance.

"You really didn't call the CIA." George meant that to sound pacifying, fully aware his tone didn't sound inviting.

"George, for God's sake! What did I say?" The blue eyes floated, still now scanning the depths. Fierce laser focus gambled at perfect variance with the angry revolted cry.

George threw himself back into his seat exhaling in exasperation, prompting Patrick to whistle, "Don't try to bring my plane down just because you are angry, son!" Steeling himself, George ruminating about the last time he had trained with Burrito a year ago, scaling the height of an extremely high and extremely thin tree. The lower part of the tree unfolded into fleshy leaves resplendent with rock-hard thorns the size of a grown man's palm.

"Your problem," Burrito had called back at George's constant complaints that he was cheating. George's vituperations implied that Burrito's rapid advances were not due to superior strength but to Burrito's enigmatic threats, intimidating George. Burrito had alleged that George's mother as teenager had evidenced better control of such trees than George after many years of training. Implicit in Burrito's furtive ascent, slithering like a lizard, was that he would kick George hard so he would end up impaled on the same thorns that his mother had known to master. "Your problem," Burrito asserted, "is not me. Your problem is you look back too often. How many times have you seen me look back since we started?" George had intended to retort he didn't want to crawl in solitude and pain. He tried to gauge if he could bring someone with him on this dizzying flight, his soon-to-be fiancée maybe, or much better Moura herself. But before he could make any humane inroads, garlands of light blinded his upward glint. The upper soaring of the foliage parted and closed rapidly to engulf Burrito in the searing luminescence of the regions of the Gods.

***

Gamboling through airport security at John F. Kennedy International Airport in New York, Craig toted formless carry-on luggage hanging from his left shoulder, with the Pineapple and Kiwi box balanced on his right shoulder. His present state of exhaustion represented the least of his fun pastimes. Not since the CBP officer almost mistook the Pineapple and Kiwi for a second and third head and Craig himself for an overnight specter requiring the assistance of such marionettes. Prompted by his three decades' long collaboration with the immigration agency during which he had grown well acquainted with the stressful and unpleasant work conditions of CBP officers at airports entitling them to respect by their customers, Craig aimed to neaten up underneath the weight when the officer began to berate him.

"Are you returning from war, Malcault? Is your head screwed on straight?" His passport cast into his free hand, the officer waved him on to "get the hell outta here," propelling Craig out of the cavernous twilight zone of the passports and visas section. He eschewed the crowded luggage belts and explained to customs that the Pineapple and Kiwi were not real, and he had nothing to declare.

"What's with the box, Craig? You're unrecognizable. Couldn't you have purchased a made-in-China plastic leather bag as needed?" Juan, in his characteristic indigenous bluntness, waved in the bustling arrival hall, decked in a bright blue puffer jacket. Today a rare early March snow had transformed New York into a winter wonderland, and traces of slush on the floor risked ridiculing the sunny box. "The cardboard is already crumbling and with the snow it will turn into mush." Then ceremoniously they both stood still a few feet apart and caught each other in iron stares before exclaiming simultaneously "Amigo! And here I *a-a-a-a-m!*" Juan enthused with arms wide open and Craig twisted his neck like an ostrich to divest himself of the hindrance of his cargo and be able to return the hug.

Arm-in-arm, they ambled the short distance to the parking lot, depositing the box with care on the back seat of the Dodge Challenger The Demon while the asphalt greyed with the white profusion.

"The flakes are too small and won't last for long, plus the temperature is too warm and it will likely rain, but we'll be home long before that freezes, then spring will arrive and before long it will already be summer, your favorite season!" Suspecting Craig had returned sour and dour as alluded to by the news report on horrific slaughter and dreadful warlords he had watched on CNN last night, Juan dished commiseration charismatic style and unobtrusive.

"The warlords were rather... corporate." Craig snickered, guessing his thoughts. His baby blues twinkled as Juan geared up, the parking spaces around and in front of them thankfully empty.

"Why'd you think I got you this beast, Craig? You know how to ride the Demon to church? That means you know how to ride the Demon basta, with church or without. You are *the* corporate warrior!"

"You exude civilization, *ami,* where without you there would be none."

Craig luxuriated in the Manhattan-bound ride on Queen's Boulevard on a Sunday evening, breezing through in less than half the time than the bumper-to-bumper stagnation on weekdays at rush hour. The stern trees lining the broad thoroughfare drizzled grey shadows, lending them a primordial sturdy air, dogged and indefatigable against arrays of brownstone buildings hulking in different sizes. All now retreated in the dimming snow scape.

"A sick journalist on CNN described the territory as engulfed in flames... Did you see JC's tomb, did you pay your respects...? Is it as nice as they told you...? How did you get up the cliffs...? Is the island a real place...? Is your client, okay?"

Grateful that Juan had kicked his habit of news aficionado and only deigned to hone the essentials on internet and television, hence at present Juan did not regurgitate the media's stale definitions, Craig cherished his realism and maturity. He missed to confirm the caller ID when the reactivated iPhone buzzed the dunes and waves breeze.

"Didn't you tell your journalist friends you aren't working here any longer and haven't for ten years? I'd appreciate them not coming to look for you in Washington D.C." Craig dropped the phone into his lap to tune out Bubba's enervating tone. His former boss could compile racy Washingtonian experiences in a coffee-table book to earn his lecher's royalties but ferrying seditious messages from the DOD using veiled threat language filled Craig with sincere regret he had ever battled in the trenches for that law firm's reputation.

"Tell you what my friend," he retorted, his most affable cordial self. "No, I couldn't refer you to a divorce attorney now that your wife has finally taken off with all your money… Your mistress won the sexual harassment case against you because the jury already decided before they were empaneled while the judge was celebrating? I can't lend you one million dollars to get you out of that mess! Hm… so she really didn't want to work at the firm any longer…" Aware his tone conveyed real human emotion, Craig rapidly pushed the End Call button. On one like Bubba, even a kick in the derriere was a waste, and so was suave jeering on money and sex as the only things he held dear.

"I hope we never hear from that one again," Juan advised wisely. "Who was that dirty stray dog barking itself hoarse?"

***

Early in bed at nine p.m., curling his toes in white flannel PJs with the Ralph Lauren logo stitched in blue on the lapel, Craig decided to play himself a trick. He would work himself up into the worst anger and hate he could manage, just so to see if he could identify with Patrick in whose antechamber he was to wait tomorrow while Moura would sign the divorce paperwork, or so it was planned. So seeking to raise himself to the feared heights of rage and hate, Craig fanned the fires at Juan for all wrongs real and imagined since they had met, at his biological as well as adoptive mothers because they had died, at Bubba for damaging the legal profession which Craig held like to sacred, at the DOD for not adhering to the United States constitution as well as for stealing, at nonpaying clients, at war correspondents whoremongering with the DOD or with any intelligence agency, at the likes of Patrick for failing to become minister, but not at Patrick himself, who for Craig was a non-entity, at Moura for not leaving her husband, at Stefan for making mysteries into real successes and turning everyone off, at George for being Latino and at times too much so, at his NYC attorney colleagues who still thought that gay clients meant either pro bono charity work or some form of financial corruption. There he stopped since those he held dear the most could also offend him the worst. He now had about enough.

Expecting the worst, Craig braced himself for a heart attack or at least for a fainting spell. Blood accelerated inside his arteries, his rib cage throbbed, his tongue had an acrid taste, his ears crackled and rang, and his diaphragm ossified as if screwed together with real screws. The entire sensation lasted barely one minute before he deflated a punctured balloon. Aghast, Craig noted neither screams escaping him nor foul language fingering his larynx nor ghastly visions alighting of the most-beloved-hated butchered, assassinated, cut into pieces. He opened and closed his fists, feeling his pulse returning to normal. Craig was baffled by the tranquility as his mind amidst the eye of the storm surged to contemplation and he now witnessed himself from the outside.

"Turns out I am not nearly good enough to give meaning to the phrase 'too much hot air,'" Craig mused. Blushing, he encountered Juan bent over him utterly perplexed, his mouth bent into M shape. The tune of the Peruvian flute wafted from the living room.

"You want me to call 911?" Juan proffered for lack of a better idea at the sight of Craig curled on the floor next to the bed. "There are diseases in those countries you visit."

"Thank you for the piña colada and the pollo a la brasa," Craig responded, grasping for the wall and the edge of the bed. "I know those exquisite dishes took you long to make, and you also picked me up at the airport where you were kind and polite. You have been patiently waiting for your Italianate townhouse promised and overdue, not complaining once, for which I thank you dearly. You don't hate my clients even when they call collect and repeatedly from detention at eleven p.m. Thank you for the steadying hand, each time I was unwell, irritated, out to cause mayhem. It is your blessings that closed all deals. I never could reciprocate."

"You're veering into hallucinations, Craig. You're sure you don't want the paramedics? Come, let me help you up from the floor." Craig leaned on Juan's steady shoulder. He looked down to see the blue veins on his feet and proceeded into the living room, where the misty dew from the Bonsai trees Juan had freshly watered exuded the calm and quiet of a rose garden at dusk. His throat parched, Craig sipped a Peruvian avocado limonada in the kitchen while Juan's voice boomed from the beyond. Sounding disembodied and immaterial, Juan elucidated his

265

understanding of the law of karma: "In your prior incarnation you must have been a dog, a Labrador providing disability assistance, which is why I think you came back this time to finally leave behind all of the people whom you have been helping aka who have been exploiting you. Do me a favor and never get yourself into that state again. It looked scary and unreal!"

Nodding numbly, Craig was uncertain his reincarnation had resulted in any real world. The veil slowly lifted from his still-dazed vision to reveal Moura standing in a white latticed gown, her back separated from the Bonsai trees by a sliver of the moon. The girlish candor on her face alluded to an earlier period in her life. The long-lashed gaze she languorously caressed him with pinned him to his spot.

"Is this where you put my check?" she queried, pointing to the right foot of the furthest right Giacometti figure. "The check I gave you where you thought to copy my signature?"

"To append onto your divorce petition," Craig elegantly finished her sentence.

"How did you have that idea?" She could have descended from a cloud; her face wouldn't have been more powdery and lucid.

"If angels were to govern men, neither external nor internal controls of government were necessary." Craig quoted the Federalist No. 51, startling her since at first sight the quote brought Cherido to her mind. Then she approached, pristine on dainty steps. The Giacometti statutes alternated black to white with the passing of her body against the sliver of the moon. Bowing to him, her white latticed body intimated an inverted S curve as she held out her arms and opened cupped palms.

"It has been decided you see…" Bending forwards, Craig verged on dwelling on the small fleshy heart pierced by a tangle of thorns she held in her palms when the vision dissolved, the heart vanished invisible — absorbed by her hands into her bloodstream, or enveloped by wings melting into her pearly skin? Craig wondered. Looking up for her answer, the vision disappeared or completely transformed. Moura, now in a black combat suit, returned his gaze pithily Cherido-style, her long hair thick and wavy, gathering the black and the white in her background into a shield or a halo. The statuesque warrior then promptly shattered by her own force breaking from within her body and was gone.

266

Juan now knelt, grabbing both of Craig's hands. "You are doing much better now and it won't happen again."

"How do you know that?"

"Didn't you hear what you just said, Craig, or have you gone completely loony talking to yourself?"

"What did I say?" Craig muttered confidentially, returning Juan's squeeze.

"You said I forgive it all, it is all done and over with and we will never hate no more."

"But of course, Juan, of course that's what I said!" Craig ruminated. Biting his lips Juan nodded decisively, firmly convinced himself.

***

"Do all gay men in Latin America wear dated FREE WILLIE THE WHALE T-shirts aspiring to American immigration?" The heckler sauntered to intercept Craig, passing to cross Times Square at 7th Avenue at 47th Street. Craig's face was obscured by a white fedora hat matching the color of his trench coat. "And acrylic rainbow sunglasses framed by the Statue of Liberty torch?" Sensing Craig was vulnerable as he was waiting at the traffic light to cross 7th Avenue, the heckler nudged closer. The whiff of hot dogs and beer enshrouded Craig's nostrils from behind his left ear. "Hear, hear," the nauseating insinuating tone proceeded. "You must know this much better than me since poking around is your favorite occupation: Wasn't your fellow kid-show-host Pee Wee Herman right here in a porn theater on Times Square when he chose to indecently expose himself? You standing there in a trench coat brooding so eloquently reminds me of that incident… But then again, the repressed homosexuals governing your favorite territory would have exhausted your appetite with their harsh and compulsive military styles." The heckler spewed venom dripping with the stench of beer and hotdogs to mingle with the nondescript cleaning liquid frothing dirt particles and an oozing greasy mass on the pavement. The scene bore the imprint of Bubba and his friendly homophobic elements raging jealousy at either Craig or the DOD, which one they in their debilitating rage were unable to decide. Even the kinky intonation had been scripted by his former Washington D.C. higher-ups.

"The locus of your favorite memory is Sarasota, Florida," Craig corrected mildly the mistaken Pee Wee Herman reference, his chin pointing at the red TKTS Times Square rectangular ticket seller booth diagonally across 7th Avenue. The metallic gleaming handrail ensconced the swelling five p.m. crowd three hours after opening time. "Why don't you stand in line there where you'd have an array of entertainment to choose from instead of just me, your favorite compulsion? How about *Moulin Rouge the Musical*, no doubt appealing and liberating to your inhibited white middle-class balding male identity, with its sugary, inane, morally deviant, lovesick heterosexuals imitating what should or could have been with gaudy theatrical props? I think it even ends with a fake gun if I remember correctly." Tipping his hat, Craig left the heckler in the dust steaming rancor, but not before seizing the heckler up ostentatiously from behind lowered shades as he swung to cross 7th Avenue.

The pedestrian light having turned green, Craig basked in the flashy Broadway advertisements and multi-colored neons, while traversing the street. He couldn't have cared less about the myriads of items on sale all around or the house-sized animated billboards high above, efflorescing the wintry sky with lambent shadows. Working on Times Square had even further dulled his already sluggish interest in anything related to American pop culture the precise meaning of which he simply failed to comprehend. "Maybe *Entertainment is mine, I shall repay, said the Lord?*" he grumbled replacing the jaded D.C.ish "Vengeance" in Romans 12:19 among other biblical passages with the nicer hued splashy term "Entertainment." As Craig swerving onto 47th Street, the sordid heckler fell behind a boorish figure in a black cap and sad woolen coat soiled with a mixture of snow and cat hair.

When Craig glanced back one last time *to ascertain*, he caught a glimpse of the heckler's back disappearing into the Hershey's flagship store. Craig guffawed, his visage shadowed by the hat. The ludicrous scene boasted a cadaver of Washington's tyrannical powers gorging itself on a relic of American chocolate bar capitalism. Craig could envision the heckler metamorphosed into a bloated dead WILLIE THE

WHALE, molten chocolate streams disgorging from its fleshy mouth twisted into a blessed addicted grin. Or wait, why did the vertical red neon lighting spelling Hershey's towering on the building's corner flash a distinctive tinge of Chinese characters style, the crowning Hershey's Kiss reminiscent of a nurse's bonnet? The scenery could not be more apposite since directly in front of Craig the grey and black domino of Morgan Stanley's Headquarters beckoned with intriguing cerulean corner rotundas and geometric side and upper floor paneling. The structure distorted the canyon scape of skyscrapers with the immersing sensation of an oasis. At five p.m. sharp, Craig glimpsed his law school buddy, turned same sex (as well as heterosexual) domestic relations attorney, Tim's tall lanky figure in the grey suit stroll out of the main entrance. Tim's angular pock-marked features also surveyed the Hershey's and Reese's emblems, repulsed as if stung by a bed bug. Not wasting a second and blessing the fortuity of circumstances that had made today's assignment much less of a drudge and into something of a blessing instead, Craig purposefully directed his step into the gleaming lobby from where he effortlessly meandered through the light crowd to the elevators.

***

The elevator door opened onto the familiar local Legal Aid sign advertising today's national Symposium on domestic violence, including protections for same sex couples in bold Thanksgiving colors. Many years ago, Craig had served as keynote speaker on this topic sponsored by his former Washington firm. Giddy and fidgety by the decorum kicking off the novel and ambitious topic, Craig had pranced to the stage in a neon blue suit, stunning with a bright orange red Salvador Dali hallucinogenic tie. Today he detected nuances in the ambiance as the feather on his hat felt whispers of air. Craig was appalled that, while decades ago, his gay clients fled to Canada to escape at-times abusive wealthy lovers, the 2015 Supreme Court case striking down prohibitions on gay marriage in the United States inaugurated a refreshing period in domestic relations, whereas today his heterosexual client still had to live in hiding lest she be beaten, tortured, if not torched. Sidestepping the few attendees ambling between the late afternoon breakout sessions, Craig signed himself in at the polished model-thin Native American receptionist as covering for his colleague Tim Hull who had to step out for a client meeting. He grabbed his name tag and neat glossy white folder antiseptically imprinted in Arial Black with the program name and sponsor incidentally befitting his pragmatic dulce outfit. Then he took the bull by the horns, adrift in the maze of corridors, pretending to study the program brochure containing the floor plan and layouts for individual conference sessions.

The décor was his favorite blend of art deco and renaissance. Craig fancied himself cherished by the ornaments of pink golden rosettes dazzling on august deep orange wall paneling, humoring his vanity and fantasy that the walls would take mercy should any evil befall. He stopped in front of several electronic screens announcing the program titles and speakers for the respective rooms, breathing relieved that today was his lucky day, and no one was following. One announcement in particular caught his eye — a panel addressing the asylum concept that a person who is forced to witness persecution is thereby subjected to persecution, which he had spearheaded over a decade ago, today as applied to the group nowadays referred to as LGBTQ asylum applicants. Craig lingered on the steely grey lettering, reminiscing how he and a colleague at a Washington D.C.-based children's asylum clinic had crafted the concept one early spring night at 11:10 p.m. —while pursuing the intersection between the gangs MS-13 and Los Zetas particularly the reach of Los Zetas from Mexico into El Salvador and the role of minors, including gay minor clients, in the gangs' executions. He whisked himself off, preoccupied checking his iPhone for messages, shy he might be recognized and mobbed by admirers.

Soon enough, he found himself at the end of a robust hallway girding several conference rooms. The hallway opened around a rotund bent on an elegant oval area. Intimate arrangements of plush pink gold settees displayed stately against damask velvet burgundy curtains heavy with waterfall valances. In a state of perspicacity, Craig tiptoed against the left wall to a settee facing 47th Street through the window. From there he could glance through the thick folds of the settee's padding at the hinges of the door to a conference room, behind him to the right ensconced around the rotund bent.

The sudden loud knock on the door foreshadowed George busting it open, triggering Craig to make himself thin into the folding chenille. After Patrick berated George that the door was open and there was no need to knock, he proceeded to give him what sounded like either an authentic or pseudo- paternal-like embrace, perhaps as penance for his guilt, Craig surmised, clinging to a faint hope in Patrick's decency, as was his habit with any human being.

"You're a little late, son, or they were early. However that may be, you missed the best part." Patrick basked in success as if sunning himself at the beach. "To make matters brief," he began mimicking the intonation of the DOD General Counsel he had just been on the phone with, "*the territory like any other country is a financial institution operated according to applicable financial and economic laws. We therefore don't pay for damages that tangible third-party people like yourself claim to have suffered, and that is not, and I repeat not, just because you can't sue for damages you claim we caused you in pursuit of terrorists and other perfectly legitimate conducts of war Mr Chataway, okay? In addition, the instances of destruction you claim to have suffered are also just simple operations of our anti-fraud, anti-money laundering, anti you name it laws, laws intended to protect the innocent and apply to businesses that do something else than what they claim to do including causing damage to Ara Pacis... right, Steff? Uuhhmm... Hey Steff, where are 'ya...? Steeefffff?'* You dig son?" After a pregnant pause, Patrick proceeded, his tone dripping honeyed defiance. "The asshole called me thinking His mystifying Eminence would stay on the phone to accuse *me, me* of having defrauded, robbed from *him* while holy America was liberating him, the mystified and mystifying one, from many evils... The asshole," he raised his voice to a pitch, singing his aria, the sole survivor on a now empty stage, "thought he could outsmart me, but it didn't work! Because Stefan is a fool and an ape, but he is the best in the animal kingdom!"

"That last line you said to yourself," George uttered, blandly feigning sympathy.

"However that may be, son, sometimes we do speak to ourselves, at other times we clearly don't... Your request to pay you the fare to Afghanistan has been denied. It wasn't me who denied it. The board didn't vote in favor, considering the expense of a commute. Come on, who is paid the subway token from Queens to Times Square? You must be kidding. I was the only one in favor as always. I stood up for you which made me look foolish, but I didn't mind. Then what else, son... oh yes, if you don't go to Afghanistan, then you won't be back on time to get married, and I know how hard that can be. I also was dying to get married once even though that woman then unfortunately turned out to be your mother and she has been a pain in the ass ever since..."

Pressing his ear into the settee, Craig drowned out the violent vituperation strangely matching the mood of the art deco renaissance décor incarnating the succulent sweet drizzles of the equally warmly hued, orange-labelled New Amsterdam Peach Vodka. Thankfully, he soon discerned George's hurried steps thundering away. The men's room door down the corridor banged shut. Craig glanced at his watch since these people had talent for punctuality to the usual hateful truculent and scurrilous banter that had kept them busy and savagely involved with each other for decades, if not, as in George's case, since birth.

His iPhone flashed six p.m. at the tumbling clicking of Moura in stiletto boots traipsing and trampling down the marbled hallway. Craig promptly surmised the gait of someone wounded and still persisting, propelled onwards by the force of irate rage. He propped the feathered fedora on his knees, legs crossed, indicating he desired to avert further damage to her with a knowing "I told you" stare. At the sight of her body clad in a long black leather coat skidding into the open-door, Craig flinched involuntarily. He thought of the climax of a Jack London book he had devoured in teenage years —a man starving in Alaskan wilderness saved himself by drinking the blood of a living wolf too sick to escape. *What similarities between people and animals and between that story and the present time?* he judged, cunning, glimpsing from between the thick folds of the settee her long hair cascading in curls.

Listening to the volley of acidic non-dialogue was like an outer-body experience for Craig. He preferred to absorb attentively while interpreting, dubbing the tape through his own forensic lenses, tuning out Patrick's oblique commentary.

"Okay, only for you I'll endure it," she reluctantly consented. As the scene rolled on and on, she began tearing at her curly black hair and scratching her hands, clasping the sides of her body with her sharp nails. Her peculiar custom of self-mutilation used to contend with today's travails, Craig summarized.

"But Patrick, this is like a nightmare." She started to wail, looking for compassion, rigidly standing in the doorway from where she did not budge. "Good heavens how can this be?" she bemoaned. "I don't know if I can stomach reading more of the b.s. I am being served." She was evidently reviewing the file left for her at the head of the table.

"Some attorney by the name of Tim Hull alleging to represent you had me review this and stated you agree and so should I." Patrick's cruel tone affected suave pretentious sun rays through ice, feigning non-existent but inflexibly assumed empathy.

"Oh, so this is what it has amounted to," Moura hissed. "Now you are lying that someone else prepared what you did instead..."

"Well, I prepared it, but I needed an attorney to review it before you did..."

"So now you are alleging you prepared what you initially just a second ago said my attorney put together." Breathing laboriously, she evidently managed a lot of pain. "Come on, Patrick, who told you to write up this straight division, straight down the middle, with all of these details of every single cent..."

"I did, I got together with an individual who stated he is your attorney, representing you, who then reviewed it. Then this attorney did his own calculations from his side and came out with the same result, so we both did. I don't really remember." Patrick's insouciance amounted to obnoxious defiance of her clearly maimed faltering state.

After the adrenaline high of rushing down the hallway, Moura neared collapse and steadied herself, grasping for the doorframe. "After all the decades spent toiling in the trenches, my earth and my blood and my sweat, all I get in compensation is a paper with numbers imprinted on it... one billion dollars and... and sixty-eight cents?" The "and sixty-eight cents" strung on a highwire, wheezing and moaning. Her body trembled cut into with the shards of the horrible realization. "All I get is this paper… for my earth and my blood and my sweat… and sixty-eight cents?"

"The attorney said it has to be equally divided. Wow, doll, do you look pale and what is that bandage showing at the waist of your risqué camisole? Your mother failed to teach you decency, showing up in a board room with your nipples peeking through lace so abhorrently rude… Look, Moura." At the fatherly tone, Craig pinched his left ear shut with his forefinger, while muffling the lurid speech with the chenille of the upholstery to let only the essentials through. "… upset at and sixty-eight cents? After all, you have fucked yourself through in life but now, she faints at the sight of and sixty-eight cents… Maybe you'd like some flowers to go with that file, will that make you feel better?"

Ducking in his head, Craig witnessed Patrick gush past her, flaunting himself as the most eligible bachelor at the prom. He grabbed her around the waist to kiss her furtively on her forehead before snatching a pink square art deco vase with deep purple orchids off the low gleaming table just outside. Craig averted his gaze as Patrick emptied the contents on her head then smashed the vase to pieces against the doorframe where she had leaned.

"There you go doll, now it is all just perfect. You look the perfect bride, as you always wanted to. It was that compulsive childhood dream you could never reach, but now you have it. You can stop self-mutilating yourself, cutting yourself to enable yourself to face me and go through with the charade. After thirty years, I would agree it is a lot to bear, even though for me that time never really passed. I am as fresh, as gallant as of yore, forever yours. Look at me, doll… Doll, be careful, leave that file where it is, there are metal clasps around its edges…! *Ouch!*"

Agog, Craig grimaced and balked at the travesty. Moura staggered backwards until she stumbled on the back of a settee, leaving Patrick hulking in the doorway where he pressed a lavender kerchief to stop the bleeding at his right brow. She had hit him with the file now dangling listlessly from her hand. Craig observed it plummet onto the chenille seating, a monstrosity in unfinished crocodile and calf leather embossed with what from a distance appeared to be golden metal spikes. Craig sniffed curiously, anxious at which scent he would detect first, the virulent crocodile's still snapping its teeth or the guileless victim's, the calf? Yet any entertainment dulled in the face of the cruel inferno spinning its pitiless tail.

"I don't want to have anything to do with it," Moura hissed, callow and peevish fueling the infinite energy from which they both drew their eternal rancor and spite as life force. "No 'and sixty-eight cents,' no. No paper for a lifetime of labor, no paper for my tears and sweat, my blood and my land all trampled on, no, I don't want any such divorce…"

"Honestly, what and how could I have done better?" Patrick pushed, regaining his composure.

"Nada — nothing — you did your best — you were forceful — persuasive — convincing — putting together an entire perfect division in just a few days, even though overall in this life you were played a bad hand or deck as the saying goes." Moura's rambling commendation appealed to his vanity as a husband, if not as a human being, too.

"Thanks, doll, that makes my heart ache somewhat less — about my skill-set and myself." Dazed, Patrick shook his head since he couldn't believe what he currently faced. "I needed you to review and know it in advance of your upcoming meetings with the hatchet men." He articulated his ulterior protective motive and the blanched truth.

"Patrick, but Patrick, they misled you-and-me," Moura started to bawl louder. "They contacted-me-late-this-morning-and-offered-me-a-role-on-a-top-secret-committee-on-relations-with-the-region-offering-me-an-actual-job." Her pronunciation was slurred and staccato. "While-insinuating-to-you-on-the-call-with-their-General-Counsel-that-you-caused-the-territory-damages-and-them-too—" she confessed.

"Those fuckers," Patrick decried, reddening with indignation. "You of all people of course deserve any position but we can both see through the fog of this war that they sought to accomplish your promotion through my elimination as your protector in order to play their foul pro-women hand while in reality they disguise a display of corpses and scarecrows as runway models. Thank God we have both seen through their farce." Patrick blotted the remaining blood off his brow. His body sparked with fury while Moura sobbed in leaps and bounds, her forehead pointing defiantly to the ceiling.

275

Patrick then inhaled profoundly to regain perspective, batting his eyelashes to clear his sight of any blood and sweat. "But Moura, frankly, I don't give a damn. This is a blessing in disguise for both of us. I got what I deserved as a rogue Rambo renegade corporation and you got what you deserved as a dutiful soldier." He suddenly nodded convinced. "And for me now, I can have my life back except for all those trips back and forth I'm stuck with. And in any event, I'll rack up production — at their paying lackeys' expense." He cackled disdainfully.

"Patrick, are you certain that you're not hurt — or even mad at me?" Moura tilted her head, looking at Patrick earnestly through her teary eyes.

"Moura, never in any language — jamais — jamas — nunca — I promise." Still foggy, he appeared to veer into a distinct reality, taking to speaking with a slight slur insinuating compassion from behind iced blinders whose beastliness wouldn't let a fly scan through. "My worry is how you'll endure what this world has become — i.e., a sterile, antiseptic, valueless, amoral abyss except for the work you generously do, and dare I say, prostitute yourself for individuals to keep you intellectually engaged and motivated — coupled with the compensation in this dire sharks' place. They never really valued my work, anyway. Only the free marketplace does, ever has and ever will. Honestly, I needed and need out of their inferno, back to Ara Pacis," Patrick explicated, surprisingly now channeling inner peace, holding his arms wide open.

With furrowed brow and nodding in silence holding his breath, Craig observed him and Moura entwined in a numb breathless embrace. Patrick's fine white hands cupped on her back with a flowing gesture Craig would have ascribed to a sculptor and to his muse. "Why do you duck so small, forlorn and lost?" Patrick queried, dismayed, trailing tone leaving it unclear if he meant himself or Moura. Two frontline war buddies who haven't seen each other in over thirty years maybe, Craig mused. Or two teenagers on their first date. The scene could not surpass the absurd in ardent affection and devotion and a revolting loss of self and place Craig would associate with the handicapped and deluded.

"Maybe, if anyone asks," he finally heard Patrick murmur, "we can say the three were lost to abortions… And we never beat each other up, I was just teaching you combat skills. There is a way around everything…" Craig gasped astounded when Moura bent over backwards to fling the file with gusto into the conference room, where it shattered the chandelier since the light went black.

"The lady's got aim," Craig whispered, wondering at how simultaneously she had extricated herself from Patrick's artful embrace.

"I don't want any such silly divorce," she rasped, trembling feverishly. Craig watched speechlessly as she held Patrick's palm pressed against her exposed side, averting her face, fighting off surrender and disgust at this man who held her toiling in an iron grip. Finally, she resolved to grasp his hand and place it by his side. Craig noted from the glaze spreading on his conscientious mien that Patrick as the masked one had reigned supreme rather than the one hundred thousand men band. Now Patrick smoldered pinched hollow and cramped in evident solitude.

Craig concluded that the short visit had rested and enlivened Moura, since she now rambunctiously barged down the way she had come from with the speed of an arrow. Determined pallor, was the last he saw of her face at the pain caused when she belted her black coat at the waist. For a second, Craig could careen his head for a better glimpse since Patrick, left in the dark, was kicking the door frame in ire and indignation. Today, despite the many truths that had been pronounced, clearly it still was not his day and he was not the one who would get laid. Craig giggled at Patrick's enervation, realizing his kicking was damaging the expensive door frame.

Shifting out of sight to the opposite edge of the settee, Craig bent to the window to an unobstructed view of 47th Street, a dimly lit strip beyond Times Square. Darkness had fallen after seven p.m. and a whirlwind lifted up light clouds of snow. Craig followed Moura attentively with his sight as she walked the short distance, traversing 8th Avenue to the car parked down on 47th Street. The gleaming billboards and resplendent neon signs were too far up to touch the depths of the pavement. Only some tremulous blue and red shadows propagated dim NASDAQ figures interspersed by furtive flavored advertisements of eateries. "Go, child, go," Craig breathed, barely audible in a sacred space, his forefinger quivering briefly on the cold window where it left behind a crystalline imprint. He envisioned snowflakes settling on Moura in rivulets that froze between thawing on her body's warmth and the icy air.

Craig reckoned her mind, so tortured by the occurrences of the past few weeks, began to spin a web of pleasures she feverishly longed to cast. He fancied to detect a bounce in her step at the sight of Stefan detaching himself from the shadow where he had been waiting in the freezing cold. As Stefan was about to unlock the car, Craig envisaged a strange sensation, a devilish urge to take possession of Moura, to dominate the fire that began anew to rage in her soul, as evidenced by her throwing back her coat to throw it over to roof of the car and raise her camisole in the bitter cold.

"I'll rip this off," Craig fashioned her whispering, staring at Stefan looking down at her with dread. She pulled off a strip of bandage just below her rib cage to reveal a gash that had barely begun to heal. "Look, open your eyes wide, since this is what has happened!" Through the dreary light snowfall, Craig glimpsed fresh blood oozing, instantaneously washed sallow and cadaverous by the precipitation. Craig pondered Stefan rushing to cover her, refastening the bandage and forcing a sweater over her head with so much alacrity and astute appraisal of emergency Craig honestly wondered how any ill could ever have befallen Moura.

"Now, why would you want to be slapped again, and on a cold winter night?" he felt Stefan muse.

"Despair," she responded, "longing. A need to be somewhere." Craig heard her scream in pain as he grabbed her wrist to prevent her lunging at him, blinded by the cold and the snow, or was it the whistling of the wind that hurtled along the myriad glass facades?

"You won't be anywhere today, I guess," Stefan stated. He pinned her down so firmly that she winced, close to fainting. "Maybe another time, if ever." Craig observed him pulling the door open and pushing her inside where she fell back against the front seat and darkness must have slipped away from her, her breath trembling, eyes closed. Craig reflected how strongly the fire in her soul raged against the enclosing night, instructing her pain upwards into the bleak torn sky with an indomitable will to master her existence, her passions, her entire inconsolable, rampaging pure self.

"Put me on speaker phone once you arrive." Craig called her on her cell, stretching his legs, huddled in the warm comfy settee, "and we'll complete Cherido's immigration application."

"But that will be late, maybe 8:00," she chirped. "Is that okay?"

"No problem, Juan is working late tonight." *And I am watching the monster repair his chandelier and embark on meetings until the wee hours, not that that he would spin out of control last minute and ruin everything by dispatching an army of spies and armed personnel,* Craig concluded to himself. In his opinion, Patrick Chataway's fake forgiveness rant had served to maneuver him into the position of the Damocles Sword and major threat par excellence. His unfathomable exterior hid the great unpredictability boiling within.

***

"One more stitch," she whispered a couple of minutes after 8:00, "and we are done."

"I don't mind calling the paramedics, if you need help," Craig enunciated matter-of-factly into the phone.

"No, Malcault, by one more stitch I mean precisely that," she peeped. "One more little twinge."

In the marbled mirrored bathroom of a penthouse suite at the Four Seasons Hotel far above Central Park and Fifty-Seventh Street, Craig by phone witnessed Moura applying emergency band-aids. She fingered sterile steel medical equipment gingerly as if the glimmering metal represented jewelry, enthralling her.

"Could you pick up the other line?" Stefan called out to her, knocking on the locked door. "George needs to talk to you about apartments to move into with Jacqueline. He doesn't know which apartment, and I don't know NYC."

"George, listen sweetie," she purred into the crackling static, masking Craig's presence, "where are you, first of all?" Craig marveled at their rehearsed dialogue, knowing as they did that, they were both bugged and watched, and not by him Craig Malcault.

"Flying to Kabul, Mom, and I can't get anyone off the phone, neither Jacqui nor Patrick, which is worst. First, he called me together with her on the line, then they began to both call, each one from his and her separate phone... They are getting along, which is about the only star in this dreary prolonged mess... Patrick allowed me to go to fucking Kabul, and I don't want to ever come back to Fifth Avenue, aware however I will have to go there to work but not to live." George sounded strained even though with greater alertness and control than the majority of DOD personnel Craig had accompanied into war zone.

"Just tell him off, will you?" she consoled loudly and clearly. Craig chuckled inwardly at how the last thread must be dangling between her fingers, a glistening diamond string. "Tell Patrick you are doing your job and he should cease interfering, and if he has questions, he can refer to the manual. You always do your job, and he knows that. I'll take care of an apartment, don't worry, I'll tell you where to go."

"'K, Mom," George responded, resonant through hollow thunder.

"I apologize, Mr Malcault, Patrick is such a pest, such a pestering pest." A clip and a cringe and she hopped off the bathtub edge into the shower for a couple of brisk minutes. The last drops of blood washed down together with the disinfectant liquid, and the water splashed and gurgled into the tub, a seamless clean white.

Craig could sense her thoughts through the phone, droning onwards where George had left off and now proceeding incognito. Her mind spun in endless circles confounded in places, yet with the elegance of a coil of pearls neither vulgar nor crude, befitting a lady. Of course, that's how it had been, desolate, cold and alone in a bath at her first and second miscarriages, while the third lamentably had been almost public. Only then the bruises had been worse than a gash, hammering into her fate more pronounced, and it had taken decades to unfurl, to even itself out. But the blood was the same, and so was the deafening pain making her head turn and the poignant smell of antiseptics and disinfectants while her hands, at those times, shaking and trembling, now mastered any ordeal steadily. Craig followed each evolution of her breath as he had accompanied scores of torture victims and domestic violence survivors — which to his mind amounted to the same — to countless emergency rooms both internationally as well as in the United States. Moura over the decades had compiled an encyclopedic knowledge of emergency room MDs. The puffiness of the stale air as she inhaled and exhaled, ensuring she could budge a body traumatized and numb, was also much the same as almost three decades ago. The laws of biology and chemistry never changed. Neither did the sweat that accumulated on her pores as she regained warmth from having been submerged into the anesthetic cold. *But my sight is different,* she punned remarkably simple. *Since now I can see...*

"Come out, please." Stefan pleaded, knocking louder. "You've got mail." Wrapped in a silk dressing gown, today a virgin white instead of her favorite black, Moura brushed past him. He was holding up a sheet of paper on which the ink barely seemed dry with gloves so as not to leave any fingerprints. "Take this so I can remove my gloves. What is this?"

Through the large square window, the lights around Central Park flickered amidst a renewed snowfall now subsiding, overpowered by the sweeping night. The tree clumps loomed ominously guiding the gaze along the vaporous night to an invisible point fixed far ahead in the infinite.

"What is that?" Craig queried with foreboding into the phone on speaker. Resting leisurely on the galena-encased and plum-cushioned daybed, still mentally detached by the many visions, Moura proceeded to brush her hair. She leaned back her head, her profile a curl-entranced nymph blending into the starry seascape, distracted smile arching ethereal cheekbones. "Moura?"

"You can touch this, it was delivered for you at Fifth Avenue, I picked it up just now before picking *you* up." Stefan sounded knowing.

"I don't want to touch it. Hold it in front of me.... Oh, from *them*! That same invitation only now put in writing. An invitation to serve on a committee investigating terrorism in the region, 'which is of such extraordinary importance in the service of our nation'?" She gushed the last line as Stefan put the letter aside, understanding that she ceased to listen. He forced himself into the habit to never seem perfunctory, even though the absorbed attention he bestowed on her was a matter of daily routine.

He looked down at her silent small figure and informed her in earnest, "In the service of which nation? Do they know which nation *I* serve?" Her eyes sprung open, blinking curiously in twilight.

"Stefan," she exclaimed, "that letter is addressed to me. They don't know about your existence! Besides, we both serve the same nation!"

"What will you respond?" he inquired. The darkness in his eyes widened with a predatory instinct to protect her.

"We invite them to a lunch and ask them to explain themselves?" Moura responded with a hint of amusement at the intensity of his preoccupation with her and his allegiance. "No, seriously, we have Counselor Malcault on the phone here as witness: First they have to break a person into pieces so as to then remodel her into a puppet in their service..."

"Right," Craig interrupted.

Moura proceeded dully, "And for this they'll never get me, since I didn't like his stupid divorce."

"Hmm," Craig said. "Do you like the prospect of being decapitated by the age of fifty?"

"No, because I'll never see him again..."

"Then how are you not divorced?" Craig interjected.

"Oh well, Cherido will come with me always."

"Oh, you need an assassin to check out the scene..."

"Listen, Malcault, Patrick was in shock today. He said things that are very true and that I never heard him say or as much as indicate for thirty years. He understands many things much better than what you would be led to deduce from just listening to him yell and scream."

"*Your* Patrick," Craig continued unperturbed through the speaker phone, sounding as lucid at 8:10 p.m. as he would in court in the morning, "has tried to kill you once too many times. Most times it has been just over his corporation with no real rational premise besides threats blinded by his own grandeur. He is severely erratic and violent and can't be trusted. And he there in front of you," Craig's smile came through clearer than it would in person in the room together with them, "would rather break his head on a rock in Saudi Arabia than betray the least human emotion, which would be protesting the nonsense you just said."

Now it was up to Moura to snicker, swinging her head back and forth, enthralled by an inner rhythm that shone a blush on her features.

"Mr Malcault," she erupted authoritatively, "I appreciate all you have done for George and for me, and it is true, without you I would not have been as alive as I am now, and neither would Ara Pacis be as much of one piece, so we owe you a lot, Craig! But I must pose you the blunt question: When you were much younger and getting all those accolades from working with indigenous people, did any government come along to tell you that instead, you were endangering the human population and had to be exterminated promptly yourself?"

"No," Craig responded rapidly. "Later when I came out as gay, some people were insanely jealous because I did so much better than them and yet I was entirely different, and they couldn't stomach that. That was because their natures were lowly and frustrated and living in their own hateful closets. That's how I taught myself to think. I realized it wasn't really as much about me. But not when I started out working for indigenous people."

"Mr Malcault," she now beamed into the phone, "Patrick was robbed of his means of subsistence, his identity, even his citizenship by people in great authority. And we are speaking about a very small-town society. There were no indigenous there for him to work with. He had only me," she added, her undertone at the last split-second modulating into a bon mot flair, cutting into Craig's heart.

"Hmm," he huffed, well familiar with Patrick's tragic early twenties story. "You are one resolute iron cookie, Moura!"

"Not really all that iron." She humored him, agreeing she did not wish to be decapitated by the age of fifty. "All I am asking is you give him some freedom. As you did for me, so do for him. Don't suffocate him with sixty-eight cents. Let him breathe, then drop by his office in a few years to say Hi and you'll see him playing with at least one grandchild and his daughter-in-law bringing him chamomile tea, I promise at my own expense!" Exasperated, she flung herself on her back onto the daybed, cringing in pain then breathing hard. She closed her eyes, stretching herself, her visage growing dimmer and fainter, retreating into herself. Or was it that Stefan had resolved to dim the light and waved a blanket to cover her with? Now threading the thin line between perfunctory and punctilious, he eschewed offending with insensibility and placed a warm kiss on her forehead.

"Let's say a prayer," Craig intoned at the sound of Stefan opening the sliding door to the small terrace ajar to step outside where he could cogitate in the cold and mist as was his habit. "A non-denominational international prayer. One between you and me, as only we know how to."

Her mind enlivened by the short breeze fragrant with dewy snow the door immediately shut, Moura nodded agreement. She tilted her head back, anticipatory genuine smile contending with the twilight.

"We'll sound silly and childish and even idiotic for God's sake, since what we'll have to say won't be all that smart, but thus is life and here we go: Dear God, we seek in spirit a totality of conditions, a unifying force, to provide guidance in the matters of the heart. We are not bothered by Stefan inflicting self-punishment freezing outside, nor by George and Jacqueline who possess what we really should have possessed, and certainly not by Patrick Chataway and all of the issues that he has caused. In the oblivion in which we let memories of him sink, we are telling the truth, for it is expedient that he went away to make room for the spirit of truth who reproved him of righteousness and judgment. At the thought of the spirit, our hearts lift up in blessings, because only the spirit is guidance into all truth for us. The spirit never spoke of himself but received from an inspiration of compassion to show us through George of things to come. So, we see Patrick again in our inner eye, after a lament for irrecuperable loss, a tender voice of great intelligence counseling us that still and nevertheless whatsoever we will ask for in the spirit's name, it will be given to us, as happened these past few weeks. And much still remains to be given, for as we well know by now the world so far could not even remotely fully receive the spirit of truth. We follow our minds far beyond the edge of the abyss that grounds the outer boundaries of human existence until the dark shadow of a looming cliff counsels us, reminiscent of human finitude."

In the brief silence, a pin could be heard falling on the snow outside until Cherido queried, puzzled, from the gold lamé-plated table at the far right where he had been brooding in near darkness over paperwork, "What does prostitution mean? It says here 'Have you ever engaged in prostitution'?"

"Thank you, counselor, for the bright introspection," Moura called into the phone, raising herself to stretch her shadow a fluttering bird's wing motioning to the far right of the room. "I owe you much. And you, over there, are too young for college and shouldn't be asking such questions..." In a burlesque red costume pinched at his already slim waist, flaunting tight ruffles around the shoulders with a feathered cape flowing down his hips, Cherido held up his passport between pointed burgundy fingernails, noting his age as eighteen. His eyes, meanwhile, glittered sparkling coals in flinty disapproval.

"So, what does it mean?" he pressed.

"It means sex in exchange for tangibles, for the purpose of your application." Craig handled the topic ruefully.

"Oh," Cherido was thinking hard. "So, they don't mean to prohibit *me* life? They don't mean to tell me I shouldn't be alive, for it is life I love!"

Laughing, Moura cavorted massaging Cherido's shoulders so he should relax. "Just tick no," she advised.

Cherido leaned the back of his head into her abdomen at Stefan returning clicking the door shut behind him. Cherido examined him with longing, the fire inside him leaping in delirium as Moura's warmth enveloped him.

"You are so good to me," he purred.

"Go to your room, dear," Stefan commented. "It is after eight p.m. We appreciate you offering to sleep on the door mat, but thank you, we won't need that from you."

"No one knows you as well *here*, heh?" Cherido bantered, titillating. "No real difference between the outside and the inside in this place, not with all of their praying, and it's somewhat cold and dark while we are filling out applications..."

"You're astute and perceptive, amigo!" Craig erupted in laughter. "Why not start a career in journalism, penning a piece on the bottlenecked straitjacket rationalism of some American bureaucracies strangulating and suffocating with iron slabs as the very wrong definition of what it means to be rational..."

"I'm female so I wouldn't know," Moura commented, "since all I am according to that definition is a whiff of perfumed air to be cajoled around, courted, flattered, married and divorced to be taken out again and dated until they sap the last life out of me and I dissipate, an empty soul without form to be kicked to or more elegantly and appropriately dropped forgotten onto the curb, but of course that was just oversight and we won't let *that* happen again, whereupon I guess they'd name a late night TV show in my honor or some sitcom…"

"Better to spend your life incognito with your cash buried deep underground," Stefan infused. "Thus, you meet likeminded people who haven't fallen among the cogs of this capitalist strangulation since most money in this country isn't honestly earned. Some has been but the smallest parts of this humongous evil whole. Regretfully and unfortunately, the man on Fifth Avenue in this regard is one of the few honest ones, minimally so, as well one of the rare ones with luck, and I make that assessment with very heavy heart, Moura, you know me. I want to apologize for my idiotic response at the island — when was that, twenty-five years ago? And it still seems like yesterday — where I said we can talk since now we have a cash exchange which makes me less lonely… And that changes nothing about how I interact with him or *them,* nor do I mean to change." Flaunting the crystalline white of her attire against Cherido's blood red, Moura hadn't budged and now brushed his hair while biting the tip of her tongue between her teeth. Her sight suddenly dropped in space, marooning her in the quizzical position of refusing to advance against marvels and wonder.

"You are staring into a void where there really isn't one," Stefan interjected, motioning she'd rather want to draw the curtains on the freezing snow hovering over the expanse of Fifth Avenue at Central Park. "I have never been the type, Moura, to ask anyone for any money, and I very sincerely want to apologize." She immediately pulled in her tongue, coiffing Cherido's hair into straight glossy strands parted in the middle which donned him her style at the time Stefan referenced, twenty-five years ago. Now wasn't the moment to act the snake, whereas back then she had been neither acting nor pretending at all in any event. Her and Stefan's eyes met, ricocheted off each other, then entangled in a wrestling marathon to last for ages and at least until they returned to Ara Pacis a few days from now.

Before he could witness more highly intimate details not relevant to her case, Craig expeditiously seconded Stefan, instructing Cherido to go to his room where he will call him tomorrow at 9:30 a.m. sharp from his office to complete one of those accursed ever-present immigration applications. Craig assured Cherido he will neither be outlawed by the immigration agency nor will applying for immigration benefits cause him to dry out like the ink on that paper. Glancing over the back of the settee, Craig revolted against the mental notes Moura's impressions would now prompt him to make. Patrick was receiving appointments tranquilly in a boardroom, heroically trying to come to peace with the horrible injustice he had suffered in his youth, or so Craig liked to convince himself. The first visitor after Moura left, at the sight of Patrick deserted shriveling and grumbling in a corner felt compelled by the misery to exuberantly congratulate him. "Of course, how beautifully your wife has rearranged the chandelier, too bad she had to leave so fast..." Wasn't Moura the same person who, just very recently having been slammed with her head against a computer, bitterly lamented that women in her family had already been too compassionate? Now she had barged onto the scene with loads of more compassion. Rubbing the back of his neck, Craig mentally surveyed the landscape of absurdities he had encountered in his career spanning several continents, from the Iraqis made home- and jobless for one generation by the American invasion then penning internationally published eulogies about their "liberators" — their brains probably fogged by imminent starvation, so Craig concluded — to the myriad of minority survivors of various ethnic and other clannish conflicts who then didn't mind to bow in secondary role to the power that had caused their revolution. *Of course, total separation is never the solution*, Craig surmised as the last visitor, an enthusiastic Japanese businessman, sailed into the conference room, *but neither is the pretentiousness of forgiveness*. Craig mentally latched onto a German Jewish cardiologist who had lost his entire family in various concentration camps before arriving in the United States as a refugee child. Astonished at the man's complete ignorance of hate and bitterness towards Germans, Craig had asked him how he felt growing up an orphan in a foreign country, his entire family having lived in Germany for centuries now lost. He had received the bewildered response of "Why? I am German also," which Craig first took as an admission, over which he pondered for nights, that being German he knew exactly what the Germans had in effect done to themselves, then metamorphosing into the insight concerning how learned innocence of that very insight granted an enlightened status of being German infinitely superior to the spiritually

287

dead, miserly in soul, currently European Germans. Craig didn't know Germans all that well, however, inclined to be right with his final assessment.

Working on work messages, his fingers flitted on his iPhone since he wouldn't leave until two hours had passed with the monster quiet and appeased in his liar. Craig knew Moura and Stefan were seated tête-à-tête on the zestful daybed, deciding what to do about the brazen and inopportune intelligence insinuation before cuddling. She fell asleep, carried into Yahweh's highest heaven, into the seventh heaven of the eastern traditions or the Christian third heaven, whichever was the same to Craig for whom heaven could primarily be located and dissected in the hell here on earth. He appreciated her falling asleep cuddling Stefan in particular since according to the white supremacist trade experts who drowned out the other floor at his law firm, Stefan was the main squeeze of terrorism facilitators and fit the bill of living hell on earth…

Nine p.m. finally arrived and the last guests of the symposium departed. Craig texted Juan, "come and get me on the Demon @ 47th and 8th" before tiptoeing with his back against the wall out of sight of the debates, calculations, and strategies directed by His Majesty enthroned underneath his brand-new repaired glorious, adored, divine chandelier. Returned to the corner inhabited by the droll marriage between the Chinese bonnet and the capitalist deluge of all sweet cravings, edible and more, Craig turned up the collar of his trench coat against the gusts of wind. The fedora hat partially drenched dribbled askance over one ear. Hearing the familiar growl of the Challenger from two blocks away, he stepped onto the skiddy street, waving into the two round light beams approaching to a halt, shining two suns at night. The snowy slush sloshed into rain a welcoming starry sheet, warmed by the aurora of the two golden flares.

**

At dusk, the fusion of garish neon lights blazing on the amalgam of theaters, shops and the mandatory office buildings cast a synthetic spell on 42nd Street between Times Square and 6th Avenue. Dilapidating brownstone alternated with dated classic exteriors, carousel movie theater awnings and edgy floorings of skyscrapers to cofound any but the most discerning eye. Breathless hurry and quizzical alterations of times and places were finally trumped by a sense of loss and waste of time.

Still flustered by the recent call with Moura two days ago and pressing for truth, on Friday evening, Craig, comfy in jeans, worn leather boots and a thick woolen sweater bearing the orange and green colors of the Irish flag underneath a jacquard blue blazer, strolled along with the seemingly endless rush of pedestrians. Retro-style small round shades darkened his sight for a black and colored view of the compendium of humanity flowing by on the two laned pavement: Tasteless dull businessmen, agitable high-maintenance females, loitering pretentious artist types, drab and fading gig workers and the arrays of grim huddling shapes in dire need of his legal services presented the effluvium in which here, as maybe the only place on earth, he would never get caught, entangled or even recognized.

Craig's heart jumped when suddenly Moura, on time at six p.m., flounced into the pink dusk out of a bawdy-tinged shop catering to tourists, jaunty in stiletto heels hand-in-hand with Cherido. Her black-clad silhouette was a cryptic slant to the Bank of America Tower's whimsical vertical concrete and slag shape. Streaked with façades of rectangular glass panels, the structure was coming up half a block ahead. Craig paced his step to intercept them drifting side by side. Cherido, shaking his straightened gleaming hair to reveal pendant diamond earrings, grabbed her around the shoulder breathing a kiss on her forehead, his hawk's eye peering backwards.

"We saw you," Moura exclaimed, Craig still caching up until he tickled the stuffed plush pink panther. She cradled its head resting on her shoulder, a pink diamond piercing its ear.

"I thought I'd meet you one day carrying a Lady of Guadalupe-styled Madonna and humming 'The Girl from Ipanema'," Craig commented wryly as they proceeded in step, all three side by side. "Until very recently I didn't know of your penchant for self-mutilation."

"My spouse is not the Girl from Ipanema," Moura reprimanded him adamantly, "and I need something soft, fleecy, and fluffy to cover myself with. Open wounds and raw flesh get you only that far." At the sight of

Cherido pulling her close while she cooed gayly, Craig decided to let be with their definitions of marital relations. Too much of the same amounted to more thereof, at least to his rational mind. He should focus on the law instead, even though the two were so intimately related… "By the way, I don't self-mutilate. Do you want to walk with us up 6th Avenue and snap a picture at the Time Life building?" Craig nodded assent, their jazzy threesome attire obviously one of the best means to find out if they were still — or yet again — being followed.

"So your attempt to cut into your uterus was more cultural, like the Chinese women binding their feet, a practice no longer in vogue, yet once the institution. I heard hobbling makes for an alluring swaying gait attractive to the male gender and steels your thighs for better sex while your partner doesn't have to do anything at his end…"

Moura let him vituperate. They crossed 42nd Street to meander up on 6th Avenue, their features a rosy sheen dissipating swiftly to merge into the pearly grey shadow of the Bank of America tower. Craig in particular relished the brisk evening breeze after a full day of work at the office. The spring snow shower had cleared for the balmier clarion sounds of spring. He swore he could hear birds chirp from Bryant Park falling diagonally behind. The jungle of glass paneling bedecking the office buildings now rose untamable on the left and on the right of 6th, sparkling unmistakably lucid.

"Your comparison, Craig, of cutting into the uterus to men wanting to have sex with a woman is… Nah." Cherido eloquently suppressed a disparaging guffaw, greatly pleased by the soft and fluffy body he was leading at his side one inch of a step ahead, as evident from the bareness of his face without makeup. He shone possessed of immutable resolve.

"It was meant metaphorically," Craig interjected, cringing internally at the unmistakable resemblance of barefaced Cherido to Burrito embarking on his trip, his destiny on the broad white highway out of MS-13 hell ten years ago with Craig on the backseat. "It makes the men feel bad and give in to you while here we are with a pink panther as sole solace."

"Counselor, stop it!" Moura cried out, stomping her foot. "Patrick can come to his own conclusions and Stefan doesn't feel anything for anyone, believe me, he is on the battlefield twenty-four hours a day even when he is not there at all. And there are two very different kinds of battlefields," she continued before Craig could rebuke her for being inconsistent. "One is personal, the other belongs to Ara Pacis. They don't need *me* to make them cry!"

"Yeah," Craig snarled feigning a drastic drop in mood, "besides that, the personal battle also was for an altar of peace, and the reason they dropped their weapons *is* because you made them cry," adding "and I nudged them and only a tiny little. I really never wanted to do this with you, Moura, discussing their personal issues while all you have for solace is a pink panther even if it is a panther with a diamond earring. Besides," tears welled up in Craig. His face turned blotchy red while a few drops rolled down his quivering cheeks, "you remind me of Burrito, Cherido, without the make-up, of how bold and brave and singularly astute he embarked on this journey called life, and yet no one will ever know... You have no clue how he faced the monsters alone."

"You're ruining our evening with emotional melodrama," Cherido spat out harshly to Craig's eminent approval. "Yes, you have to be the perfect bodyguard, otherwise you'll be fired before you know it."

"Hey," Moura turned to Craig solemnly, poking him in the rib with her elbow, "no false humility and no aggrandizing of others at your expense! I turn to you for advice, not to Stefan or Patrick. What do we do about... these?" She pulled out of her breast pocket the intelligence missive with the job offer to hand it to him with an unsympathetic scornful look. The letter instantaneously disappeared in Craig's breast pocket. "Take it, I don't want it on me. Put it in my file and never mention it to me."

"Ignore them," Craig opined casually while his tears dried in the breeze. "Think of it as something they sent to one hundred others, waiting to see which dumb spy would bite, again and mind you, without them doing anything at their end whatsoever, just waiting for the dumb to do the leg work on their behalf."

"Counselor," Moura protested, "there aren't one hundred ones of me, and I was singled out for this. I am sure you will see, given the timeliness in light of what has occurred. They can't keep a trace of me otherwise, but I agree with the dumb part. If I disappear entirely, they will take that as ominous innuendo of things to come. If I stay and ignore it, they will find some other way to track me since I have much of what they want." Startled, she drew back as Craig cut off her path, the tips of their toes almost touching. He reminded her of the dusk advancing and a deepening purple sheen coolly shading tired eyes. There was a reason why he did not have a thorn in his flesh, at least as far as *they* were concerned.

"I mean that is what you should do in your mind, ignore them. Not in reality, where you should do nothing. I'll pen a response and send to them."

"Oh, and that's all you have to tell me about that?"

"Yes, because not only the walls but also the thin air has ears, and by thin air I don't mean Cherido who instead has quite some mass. So dear," Craig drastically changed the subject attempting a trifling tone so as to continue their walk, "what have you decided on your mercurial disappearances and re-appearances vis-à-vis the ice man whom you have engaged for twenty-seven years now ongoing and counting?"

"I told you counselor," she drawled, "two nights ago in Stefan's presence where I wouldn't lie: I'll only see him again with Cherido present as bodyguard."

"And that's precisely the point." Craig smirked sugary sweet, glancing at her slickly. "Of course you wouldn't do anything to lie, since you *are* the accomplished liar." He whistled pointing sideways, indicating he was ready to evade any blow or other harsh treatment threatening to erupt from her side. Instead Cherido shot him a snake's flare. Moura reared her gait, her gaze surprisingly clear, calm and ever so dark out of a tank's belly. Craig *pheew-ed*, erupting sighs while mulling over his thoughts and rummaging in his pants' pocket for a chewing gum.

"I am Stefan's soldier, his bodyguard, Cherido is my bodyguard, while George will live a fancy life," she explained patiently, convinced she had to teach Craig in grade school.

"I could see you are his bodyguard from that tape which I duly returned to you." Having located the gum, Craig flipped it far out onto his left with a snap of thumb and forefinger. Anything sugary suddenly tasted bitter to him. "Regretfully, Moura I'll have to hold you to what you just pronounced when you will call me from hospital intensive care unit."

"Look, Malcault," she entreated, "that was me back then on that tape jumping off a tower. Now I am walking alongside you on Avenue of the Americas in New York City holding my head quite high. The same me," she laughed, "you lover of the angels! While the snake by my side is still for real, too." Cherido beamed. Pride tickling her now healing wound, she returned his hug with such flamboyant thrust of her upper body, Craig almost believed her even though deep down he knew better.

"All I am asking of you counselor," Moura persisted, "is to please let Patrick breathe and pay him a visit when his grandchild is around in a year or two." Craig looked out over the greenery now speckling alongside the broad pavement, flashing his sharp jaw into a razor grin. Indeed she had calculated what would happen to Patrick in the coming year or two! Craig needed more quiet than he could have on this busy Avenue to reflect on what to her mind was represented by the term "grandchild."

"You've got that part of the deal," he grumbled.

Approaching the infinity-edged Lilholts Pooley Pool on the left, Craig again abruptly changed the now sealed topic and gushed: "Look Moura, when I went to law school there was an entire row of such pools here between 49th and 50th Streets with benches and trees to sit in the shade in summer, an entire resort atmosphere in the middle of the city. Dragonflies and birds at times felt at home here too. Now it's all overgrown with the weeds of office buildings starting with Chase Manhattan Bank. Just guess at the reason for such demolition!"

As Moura and Cherido expectantly watched the waves cascading off the infinity edges into the pool below now dimly sparkling in the descending dusk, Craig pontificated, elucidating the real reason for the destruction of nature. "Security, or the likes of them, claimed to have observed in the shaded places a welcoming hiding place or congregational spot for unsavory characters, criminal minds, plotters, you name it in the middle of this neighborhood that is one of the biggest money-making machines on planet earth, hence infinity edges now present a finite view. And here is the hammer, be prepared." They cocked their ears. "Recently I found posted online pictures of Pakistani, Asian

and Arab-looking young men —— the former shady characters ——
posing in touristy fun around this pond. At the time of the demolition,
they would have been too young indeed. You get the public relations
point, folks, of course you do since you've come with me thus far. No
one has or is discriminating obviously, this is the young generation, the
bad old one simply an unfortunate coincidence at this time and place,
their spirit long stomped out underneath the concrete."

"What one doesn't have to put up with as an American!" Moura
marveled at Craig casting her a long stare. "Acquiescing in such security
failure…"

"Of course, I know," Craig enunciated. "I respected and represented
some of the old folk. There is a veritable mass of people buried right
here, silenced forever underneath the concrete besides in the back
drawers of the files entombed in my mind. On to our Time Life Building
hither across 50th Street replete with purplish pink magnolia shrubs as
befits the tone of your pink panther."

***

They traipsed onto the black and white interwoven concrete free of
crowds at this evening hour. The opalescent glass and frosted beams of
the abutting Time Life Building carved into the sky a seamless veneer.
At street level the glass paneling served as reflecting pools capturing the
environs burnished in translucent silver.

"As you can see, here all is light and squeaky clean, much like the
World Trade Center redone a starry-eyed sparkle, all's been washed
sterile, disinfected, and chaste and put up into heaven! Now I wouldn't
want my panicky peeing in my pants at my own commentary to freeze
into an icicle piercing the skies for the entire world to see. But that is my
personal opinion. I hope I am not unnerving you with my culturally
insensitive tour guide speech. Now give me the animal or plop him down
there at the far end since you want the purplish pink bushes rather than
him as background. A single shot is all you get so make it a good one!"
Moura obediently discarded the pink panther. Both nodded assent,
comforting Craig no, they had not been unnerved, particularly since